Prologue

From the moment the cupboard door was slammed shut, trapping them both inside, she knew something was different. It should have seemed just like every other day, but somehow it didn't. She felt the familiar pain and discomfort—the same as always. So what was it?

The girl soundlessly inched her feet across the confined space, searching for her sister's toes with her own, both to seek and to give comfort. She had to try to make her sister feel safe. It would soon be over. But the fingers of an undefined dread were crawling up her spine.

Then her sister made a strange gurgling sound. She'd never made that sound before. It was as if something was stuck deep in her throat and she was trying to force it out. The girl silently willed her sister to stop.

Shh. Be still. Be quiet.

She rested her chin on her bony raised knees and repeated the words over and over in her head, praying that her little sister would hear her thoughts and understand. If either of them made a noise, The Mother would be angry, and it would all be so much worse. Worse than suffering in silence.

She had tried to say that they would be good. They didn't need to be put in here. But The Mother always said the same thing.

'I am The Mother. You are The Daughter. You do what I say. *Don't* argue. I've told you what happens to bad children. The Bogeyman gets them, and eats them for his dinner.' And then she laughed. The girl was scared of The Bogeyman. Perhaps he would be even worse than The Mother.

She lifted her head slightly. A narrow crack in the wooden door let in a dusty sliver of light, illuminating a slender fragment of her sister's face. It was white and shiny—a bit like a boiled egg when the shell was peeled away. She had never seen a face look like that before. Her sister lurched forward and bent over. Her hair was sticking to her forehead in damp curls, and she was making a noise in her throat. An awful noise. And there was a horrid smell too.

They had to be as silent as baby mice or they would get a beating. Luckily, at that moment the strange sounds coming from her sister wouldn't be heard. It sounded like The Grunter was here today. He made noises all the time—like a pig she'd once seen on the television. She hated the noise, but it was better than The Shouter. He always cried out, using words that sounded mean. She didn't know what they meant, but he sounded nasty when he shouted them. Then there was The Moaner. She had once tried to peep through the crack in the door because The Moaner sounded as if he was in pain, but she didn't like what she saw, so she never looked again. It didn't stop her mind from working, though, and every time she heard The Moaner, all she could see in her head was an ugly white bottom, rising and falling.

The Grunter never lasted long. Her sister was going to have to stop making that sound very soon.

The pig noises from the room outside the cupboard were much stronger and coming closer together now, and that meant The Grunter had nearly finished—he always got very loud just before the end. She didn't have much time. She needed to soothe her sister before it was too late. She hated to see her punished. The girl tried to shuffle across the confined space, but the bindings on her wrists and ankles were rubbing on the bruises and sores and she had to stifle a gasp of pain. As she got closer, her sister looked at her through eyes that had the bright shine of unshed tears, and then her little body shook with a huge force.

The girl realised with horror that her sister was being sick—but the wide brown parcel tape across her mouth was preventing the vomit from escaping. Then she watched as the little girl's eyes rolled upwards and out of sight, leaving only the glossy white showing, and she slumped over against a pile of old, dirty shoes.

Somebody had to help her sister. The girl knew she was going to be in trouble and that her punishment would hurt, but she didn't care. She threw herself sideways and rolled onto her back with her legs in the air, kicking out with her bound bare feet against the wooden cupboard door. And she kept kicking. She heard a shout of surprise and a growl of anger from the room beyond, and the door was wrenched open. A man with a huge red face and a fat blue nose leered down into the small opening of the cupboard, his trousers and a pair of dirty white underpants round his ankles.

Finally, she had met The Grunter.

1

Day One: Friday

Ellie Saunders took a couple of onions out of the vegetable rack, and started to peel them. Cooking always soothed her, and tonight she needed to do something to stop her mind from wandering. Not that chicken liver pâté required much concentration; she could probably make it in her sleep. But it was better than staring at the walls and wondering what was happening elsewhere.

'Stop it, Ellie,' she muttered out loud. 'You're being ridiculous.' She chopped the onions with more force than was entirely necessary, and ripped off a piece of kitchen roll to wipe her streaming eyes.

Transferring the chicken livers from their plastic bag to a plate, Ellie jumped as her mobile started to vibrate on the worktop next to her.

Her breath caught, and her arm froze in mid-air. She knew without looking who it would be. Should she answer? Would it be worse to speak to him, or to ignore him? She didn't want to speak to him ever again, but couldn't predict what he would do if she started to avoid him altogether.

Snapping out of her momentary paralysis, she wiped her hands nervously on a tea towel and picked up the phone.

'Hello,' she said softly.

'Why are you crying, Ellie?'

He was here. Ellie nearly dropped the phone as her eyes flew in panic to the huge bi-folding glass doors that lined one wall of the kitchen, leading out to the side of the house. But the combination of the stormy skies and the brightly lit room made it impossible to see into the murky depths of the garden beyond.

The voice continued.

'I'm watching you. I love watching you cook. But don't be sad. It's going to be okay, I promise you.'

Ellie's heart pounded but she tried not to let her voice waver. 'I'm *not* crying, and I'm *not* sad. Where are you? Please—you shouldn't *be* here. There's nothing more to say. I've said it all before.'

There was a sigh of exasperation from the other end of the phone.

'Why don't you let me in, and we can talk? I'm right here.'

The voice was quiet and persuasive, but Ellie shivered in fear. She turned her back on the window so that her expression would be hidden from the watcher in the grounds. He mustn't see that he was getting to her.

'Of course I can't let you in. Max will be home any minute now. Please don't do this. Please.'

A quiet tutting sound told her everything she needed to know, even without him speaking.

'You know he's not going to be home for a long time yet. He's at the party—and he's with *her*. We both know that. I've *seen* him with her, Ellie. It's obvious to a blind man how close they are. But I'm here for you, darling. I would never hurt you like he's doing. So let me in. I just want to touch you and hold you.' He laughed gently and his voice dropped an octave. 'What I'd really like to do is lick your silky skin and cover every inch of your body with my lips. You taste delicious, do you know that? The velvety smooth texture of your flesh reminds me of Italian ice cream. Hazelnut, I think. Cool on the lips, a dark creamy colour, and a slight nutty flavour. Let me in so I can taste you again.'

'*No!*'

Ellie slammed the phone down on the worktop and leaned against her hands, which were the only things stopping her from collapsing. What would she give to be able to crumple to the floor and lie there until this was all over? But he was watching, and she had to stop showing weakness.

She could hear the tinny echo of his voice through the phone, but couldn't make out the words. She had to end this, once and for all.

She picked up the phone again.

'Listen,' she said, in what she hoped was a firm and decisive tone. 'I love my husband. What happened between us was nothing—just a mistake. Please, *please* leave me alone.'

She was hoping for anger or hurt, but all she got back was more of the soothing tones.

'Come on, Ellie. You know it wasn't like that. You were so sad, and I made you feel better. I know I did. And I can make you feel better again.

Remember what it was like? Remember the burning feeling of our flesh as our bodies touched? What are you scared of? Nobody will know—just you and me.'

Ellie's forced calm had dissolved, and terror ripped through her. *What if Max finds out? He will never, ever forgive me.* But she couldn't say that, because then she knew she would have lost. She took a breath, and forced her voice into an even tone.

'I'm not scared. I just want this to stop. I'm going to hang up now, and turn my phone off. Then I'm going to close all the blinds so you can't watch me. I'm sorry. I never meant to hurt you, or lead you on. But don't call again.'

Ellie disconnected, and very deliberately held her phone up so that if he was watching he would see that she was switching it off. With her head down so she didn't risk making eye contact with him wherever he was hiding in the dark garden, she strode briskly towards the windows and closed the blinds.

Immediately, the house phone began to ring. She marched across the kitchen and switched it off. She could still hear it ringing upstairs, so she picked up her iPod remote, selected a Coldplay album, and set the volume so it was loud enough to be heard in the back garden.

Her display of bravado was short-lived, though, and tears of despair were seeping from the corners of her eyes as she grabbed a handful of garlic and crushed the life out of it with the side of a very sharp knife.

2

Indicating left, Leo Harris swung her Audi Cabriolet from the main road onto the high street of Little Melham. Most people thought she was mad having a soft top and living in Manchester, but tonight the Cheshire air was warm and muggy and it was great to have the roof down. The drive from her home had only taken about half an hour, and once out of the city traffic and into the countryside the wind in her hair felt good after the stuffy heat of town. Rain was threatening again, though, and the dark sky belied the fact that it was a summer evening. It had been stormy off and on all day, and it suited her mood. The odd flash of distant lightning against a black and turbulent sky was almost a mirror of her emotions.

As she drove slowly through the village she looked at the pretty shop fronts, noticing the new wine bar with its aluminium tables and chairs outside on the wide pavement, a line of huge planters separating customers from pedestrians. There was even a trendy-looking restaurant squashed between the greengrocer's and the baker's, and she glimpsed high-backed dark red chairs and white tablecloths through the soft light in the window.

A perfect place to live.

Smiling at the irony of her thoughts, she turned off the main street and down the lane towards the house.

As she saw the open gates ahead, her foot jerked off the accelerator. An automatic reflex. Fighting the compulsion to turn the car around and go home, her foot found its way back to the pedal, and the car moved steadily forward. She hoped that the driver of a lone car parked in the lay-by down the lane hadn't noticed this strange behaviour. She turned into the bottom of the drive and stopped.

A chilling thought struck her. The first time she had arrived here by car had been twenty-two years ago. She had been with her father, and they had stopped in almost this exact position. She remembered feeling as if she'd been crying for days, but it had only been a few hours. Her father had tried to talk to her but she had refused to acknowledge what he was saying, and in the end he'd left her out here in the car while he went into the house alone.

She remembered that her weeping had finally subsided into occasional hiccupping sobs. That was when she'd heard the scream. She had never heard anything like it in her young life, but it sounded as if somebody's soul was being ripped from their body. It went on and on.

Leo closed her eyes as the memory stabbed at her gut.

Seven years later she had walked down this drive for the very last time without a backward glance, shunning both the house and everybody in it. For a while that had even included Ellie, but her sister had refused to give up on her and for that—and so much more—Leo owed her. She had never imagined for a minute that after all this time she would be back here, sitting in this exact spot, trying to find the courage to walk through the front door. She'd put the visit off for so long, but tonight, driven by a strange and compelling impulse, she had thrown some clothes into a bag, grabbed her car keys, and set off, not knowing whether she would make it to her final destination or not. Just the thought of Ellie's inevitable astonishment and relief when she opened the door was enough to spur Leo on.

The one good bit of news was that the house was impossible to recognise from the horrors of the early years of her life. Clever concealed lighting provided subtle illumination in the gardens, which were a picture with open lawns and wide beds filled with roses; a far cry from the neglected and unloved garden of her childhood. The cracked tarmac had been lifted and the drive re-laid with old cobbles, and the window frames were painted a pale cream that sat beautifully against the old red brick. But the biggest change of all was an impressive new atrium, linking the long, low house to the adjoining barn. Flooded with light to compensate for the dark and gloomy clouds, it looked warm and inviting even to Leo.

She leaned back heavily against the headrest. She couldn't just sit here, though. She had to get a grip of herself.

She flicked the switch to operate the electric roof. Even if she failed to make it through the front door and had to beat a hasty retreat, rain wasn't far away. And anyway, it wasted a few more moments.

With the roof firmly in place, she completed the journey up the drive and parked in front of the house. Acting more decisively than she felt, she swung her legs out of the car, grabbed her bag from the back seat, and walked determinedly to the front door to ring the bell. She didn't have long to wait.

'Leo! God, *Leo*! What a fantastic surprise. I was beginning to think we would never see you again.'

Leo looked at Ellie, and knew that her decision to come had been the right one. Ellie's long, chocolate-brown hair framed her oval face and fell in waves to her shoulders. Her brown eyes were shining, but not with the pleasure that Leo had been expecting. The remnants of tears hung in slightly red-rimmed eyes, and although her wide and generous mouth was smiling, it was clear to Leo that this was an effort. Usually her smile could light up a room.

'Come in, come in—it's so great to see you. Welcome to the transformed Willow Farm.'

This was the moment Leo had been dreading. She had expected her senses to be bombarded as she stepped over the threshold, but was amazed that—for the moment—she felt nothing. No racing pulse, and none of the once familiar unease.

And then she got it. The house didn't smell the same. Gone were the musty odours of neglect, and the sense that the house was short of air. A cool breeze was blowing through an open window, carrying the light perfume of roses. She looked at her sister, and waited for Ellie's usual hundred-watt smile. But it didn't come.

Leo picked up her small suitcase to avoid the inevitable sisterly hug and leaned forward to peck Ellie on the cheek.

'Oh, before I forget. I found this on the step,' Leo said, holding out a yellow rose.

Ellie stared at it with a look that Leo couldn't interpret. She didn't take the rose, but she seemed mesmerised by it.

'Are you okay, Ellie?' Leo gave her sister a concerned frown.

Ellie waved her hand in front of her eyes, as if fanning away the tears.

'Oh yes—the eyes. Sorry—I've been peeling onions, and they got to me a bit. Chuck that rose on the garden, will you. It's probably one I dropped when I was cutting some for the house earlier. Anyway, I'm fine. And I am so pleased to see you. I can't tell you what it means that you've come, and I hope you're going to stay for a while.'

'I've brought a few things with me, in the hope that you could put up with me for a few days,' Leo said, lifting her case a bit higher as evidence. 'I couldn't keep making excuses—at least not if I wanted to see you and Max more often. Not to mention the twins. Where are they all?'

'I've only just put the twins to bed—but we can pop up in a minute and see if they're still awake. They'll be delighted to see you. Max is at his school's end of term barbecue. Staff only. No partners allowed. It's at the rugby club and it will go on forever, so God knows what state he'll be in when he comes home. For a load of teachers, their behaviour can sometimes be pretty appalling. A good job the students don't see them.'

Leo gazed around her, and was staggered by how beautiful the old house was looking. The wide hallway was no longer full of clutter, and instead of the dreary faded wallpaper that had adorned the walls when she had lived there, they were now painted a pale honey colour, and hung with a couple of large modern landscapes. A tall side table stood against one wall, made from a dark wood that seemed old, but was fashioned with clean, straight lines. And the alcove that had previously housed a battered rolltop desk, piled high with dusty old correspondence and torn envelopes, now had a new floor-to-ceiling window looking out over the garden, with a comfortable armchair and a low table displaying a huge vase of apricot and yellow roses, the source of the delicate fragrance she had noticed.

Leo glanced at Ellie, who was looking at her with a nervous expression. She probably wasn't sure if Leo was going to turn tail and run.

'It's okay, Ellie. I'm all right. Really I am. This is quite stunning, and I would never guess that it was the same house. Relax.'

Ellie smiled with relief. She grabbed Leo's hand and pulled her farther in.

'This is only the start of it—if you like the hallway, wait until you see the dining room and the kitchen. I'm delighted with the whole place. I'm only just getting used to it, and it's sometimes hard to remember that it's our house. We nearly didn't do it, you know. I think Max wanted to sell it, but I couldn't—you know that. It had such huge potential, and we've exorcised the ghosts—and I mean that quite literally. Max danced around, demanding that all spiritual entities be evicted, in the name of a higher power—that higher power, of course, being him. You know what he's like. He even found some Islamic verse that is supposed to repair the damage caused by witchcraft, and given that he always referred to my mother as The Old Witch it seemed very appropriate. I laughed so much I could never again think of there being a single spook left.'

Leo could well imagine this scene. Always the clown, Max could bring a smile to anybody's face.

She dumped her bag at the bottom of the stairs as Ellie dragged her forward past open doorways through which she glimpsed rooms that she barely recognised. There was nothing here to remind her of the past, and although she hadn't been here for such a long time, she could remember every inch of how it used to be.

'It's amazing. You're right. You *have* transformed it.' Never one for going over the top, Leo did her best to reassure her sister that she loved the place. But her words didn't accurately convey her astonishment at the difference.

The room in which they were now standing was completely new in every way. If you could call it a 'room'. They were in the atrium that Leo had noticed from the drive. She remembered the old barn, of course, but she didn't recall it ever being used for much because in her lifetime this had never been a working farm. And now Ellie and Max had created this incredible atrium dining room, complete with old flagged floor, to connect the barn to the main house. Its pitched roof was constructed of aged oak beams, with huge panes of glass between. The dark and sombre clouds gave way to a burst of sunshine, which bounced the warm tones of evening light from the walls for a moment, and Leo could imagine the parties that Ellie and Max would host.

Her sister must have been reading her mind.

'We've invited a few people over for dinner tomorrow to celebrate the fact that the house is now finally finished, and I'm looking forward to christening this room.'

Leo's heart sank. Ellie loved to entertain, but she preferred to deal with people one at a time, and the idea of a big dinner party the following day filled her with dismay.

'Oh, Ellie—I'm sorry. I should have called before just turning up. I can always either go back home tomorrow or stay in my room while your guests are here. I'm good at keeping quiet, as you might remember!'

Ellie smiled and looked as if she were about to try for another hug. Leo took a step backwards, and saw a flicker of disappointment in her sister's eyes.

'Don't be silly, Leo. There's no way that you are going to rush straight off now that we've got you here. Stay as long as you like. There's plenty of food, and we already have an odd man coming. I don't mean that he's odd-odd, just that he's an odd number. He's actually rather nice, but he's on his own and only recently moved into the cottage next door. He's a policeman, so you'd better watch your step,' Ellie said with a smile. 'Come on. The kitchen's through here now, in the old barn. And beyond my dream kitchen is Max's dream media suite. But I'll let him show you that tomorrow.'

Leo could just make out the vague smell of onions, and persuaded herself that they really were the cause of Ellie's tears. She couldn't help but feel slightly disappointed that she wasn't going to have Max, Ellie, and the twins to herself all weekend, but perhaps this was a better reintroduction to her old home. She certainly couldn't remember a single party of any description in the years that she had lived here.

What bloody awful timing, Ellie thought. She had waited so long for Leo to break through the barriers that had prevented her from visiting during the renovation. Now she was here—and Ellie couldn't help wishing she wasn't.

She loved her sister, and Leo's dreadful memories of her life in this house had almost been enough to stop Ellie from moving here. Almost. Max hadn't been madly enthusiastic either, although he had gone along with it. Perhaps he simply didn't care where they lived anymore. In the end, neither of them had fought her. They knew why it was so important to her, even though they thought she was chasing rainbows.

She opened a drawer and pulled out a couple of napkins and grabbed some cutlery to put on a tray. They could take supper through to the sitting room—away from the kitchen and the memory of the earlier phone call—and she would open a decent bottle of wine. For the first time in her adult life, Ellie felt that she didn't need to worry about money, and yet life didn't seem better. It felt infinitely worse.

Their newfound riches were all thanks to her mother. If that hadn't been so sad, it would have been enough to make Ellie laugh. Her mother had pleaded poverty since their father had disappeared all those years ago, but when she died she had left Ellie not only the house but a vast sum of money that she had clearly been squirreling away for God knows how long. But not a penny for Leo.

Ellie mentally shook herself. Leo would be down any moment, and she needed to get her head together. The twins had been overjoyed to see their aunt, and Ellie could only imagine how many stories they had demanded. Leo was totally unlike her cynical and unyielding self with the children, but Ellie couldn't watch tonight. It would have made her emotional, and that would have been hard to explain.

She moved to the fridge and opened the door, hunting out some bits and pieces for supper. They could eat the pâté, even though it was still a bit warm, and she'd made some houmous for the twins' lunch. There was still some of that left.

Her mind drifted.

She stood gazing into the fridge, feeling a cool draught of air on her cheeks and staring blindly at the shelves of food. Nobody could see into the kitchen now, but she could sense *him,* skulking outside in the darkening night. She could feel his eyes penetrating the closed blinds, and was sure that if she drew them back, his face would be pressed hard against the window, his features distorted as they crushed against the glass. She glanced over her shoulder, almost expecting to see him lurking in a dark corner somewhere.

Snap out of it. Her eyes came back into focus, and she surveyed the contents of the fridge. Cheese. They had a ton of it, bought for the dinner party the following night. They could eat some of that too, and she would get some more tomorrow from the deli in the village.

Uncovering dishes and unwrapping cheese, Ellie thought about her predicament. Why wouldn't he accept that it was over? She just wanted him out of her life.

She knew Leo would help her if she asked. But for the last twenty-odd years Leo had been secure in the knowledge that she could rely on Ellie; the one person she believed was beyond reproach. Ellie couldn't be responsible for destroying the last of her sister's illusions.

Putting the final plate of food on a tray, Ellie threw a last nervous glance at the closed blinds as she switched off the lights, painted a smile on her face, and went in search of Leo.

3

It was late by the time they made it to bed, but Leo was glad that she had managed to conquer her anxiety and finally set foot over the threshold. It was so good to see Ellie; she'd stayed away for far too long. It had always seemed better to meet up in Manchester or Chester for the day, or invite the whole family over to her place. But tonight she'd done it. She had fought her demons and won. Now all she had to do was prove that she could sleep here. No doubt the wine would help.

She was sleeping in Ellie's old bedroom, and the tiny box room that used to be hers was now a perfect en suite. Everything had changed in there; the old door from the landing had been plastered over with a new door opening from the bedroom into the shower room. The modern white fittings looked bright and shiny against the dark grey tiles, and twinkling spotlights reflected off the huge mirror that hung behind the sink. No old memories here.

Leo hadn't been allowed in Ellie's room when they were growing up, although both girls had sometimes risked incurring the wrath of Ellie's mother by disobeying. But Leo had never broken the rules when it really mattered—when Ellie had needed her. From the night Ellie realised that their father had gone for good without a word of goodbye, she had grieved alone in the privacy of this bedroom. Leo had lain in her own bed, listening through the wall to the sounds of her sister crying, knowing that she should try to console her. But she didn't know how. Ellie couldn't understand Leo's indifference to his departure, but Leo truly believed that in the last few years of her life in this house she had become devoid of emotion. She had spent so many lonely nights after her arrival here. She had been the one sobbing herself to sleep then, and her father had done nothing to help her. It was contempt for him that had driven Leo to withdraw from others.

Unfortunately, Ellie had this ludicrous notion that once he realised his wife was dead, he would miraculously reappear like the prodigal father. And now that she lived in this house, Ellie believed he would know exactly where to find her.

Leo had to do something about this. She had to find out what had *really* happened to him.

She thought about her sister. Lovely, bubbly Ellie, she'd heard Max call her—and that was exactly right. There were moments tonight, though, when the sparkle had faded slightly and Leo hoped that her arrival hadn't somehow put a damper on anything.

'Are you sure you're okay, Ellie?' she'd asked again. 'You seem a bit preoccupied.'

Ellie had leaned forward with a frown, while studying the contents of her wine glass and fishing something invisible out with her little finger.

'Me? I'm fine. Really I am. It's all been so exciting for the past few months with the renovation and all the changes. Now it's over, perhaps the adrenalin is fading away. I'm probably just tired, but I'm completely fine. Really.'

That was two 'reallys', and two 'fines'. But it made sense that she was tired. With the work on the house to oversee, five-year-old twins, and still working a few days a week, it was more than enough to wear anybody out.

Unusually for Ellie, though, she hadn't even given Leo the customary lecture about 'letting down her barriers' and finding herself 'a good man'. Leo knew that her past had left deep scars and some serious issues, but she had long ago come to terms with her own limitations. They were part of her. But neither Ellie nor Max seemed inclined to accept that.

She grabbed her laptop and balanced it against her raised knees. She needed to write today's blog post before she went to sleep, but for some reason the words wouldn't come. Since becoming a life coach, Leo had tried to use ideas from her own experiences each day to write a brief post for her clients. She might be inspired by an article on the news, a conversation overheard in the supermarket, or simply by observations of people's behaviour. But tonight her mind was blank—or rather it was filled with a nagging concern for Ellie. In the end, she gave up and picked up a magazine that Ellie had thoughtfully left by the side of the bed.

Sleep proved elusive, so it was after midnight before she was able to switch off the light. But only moments later the sound of a telephone ringing roused her from the beginnings of sleep. Leo's room was across the hallway from Ellie's, and she could hear the quiet murmur of her sister's voice, and then a clear note of tension. Ellie sounded as if she was saying 'no', her voice rising in pitch. That was the only word that Leo was able to make out, but Ellie seemed distressed and she wondered if she should check that everything was okay. She had just resigned herself to getting out of bed when she realised that Ellie had stopped speaking. A couple of minutes later, she heard a creak and knew that it was the second step from the top of the staircase. Clearly they had failed to fix that small detail in the renovations. Ellie must be going downstairs. Then there was the distinct sound of the front door closing very quietly, and moments later the low hum of Ellie's brand-new Mercedes four-wheel drive.

What on earth could she be doing going out at that time of night?

Leo felt a momentary disquiet, but brushed it off. That was the house talking to her, casting its evil magic over an event for which there was undoubtedly a perfectly reasonable explanation. Nevertheless, she switched on her lamp and jumped out of bed to open the door slightly. She needed to listen for the twins in her sister's absence, which made it all the more strange that Ellie had said nothing.

Resigning herself to the fact that there would be no sleep for her that night until Ellie was safely home, Leo returned to bed, picked up her laptop, and started to write.

A Single Step: the blog of Leo Harris

Searching for your rainbow

I woke up this morning to the sound of rain beating relentlessly on my window, and I thought of tears and sadness. A rumble of thunder and my mind turned to anger. A flash of sunlight, and I believed in joy all over again.

But what of the icy winds of winter that chill your flesh through to the bone? The snow that looks so beautiful but hides treacherous paths beneath; the stunning stalactites of ice that hang down from gutters and can pierce your heart in a moment?

Which of these is a reflection of your relationship?

What is your reaction when your loved one walks through the door? Has the sun come out, or do you hear distant rumbles of thunder? Does cold ice settle around your heart, knowing that the road ahead is going to be fraught with slippery patches, or can you lean back and enjoy the sunshine?

Think of your heart and your soul as the weather, and listen to what they're telling you. You are entitled to feel the heat of the sun's rays, but getting to that warm place may mean you have to survive some rainy days first.

"When it rains on your parade, look up rather than down. Without the rain, there would be no rainbow." Gilbert K. Chesterton

4

The sky was pitch black and heavy with storm clouds, and the grass that she was crouching on behind the hedge was wet and cold on her bare feet. But the girl knew she mustn't move. She was certain that she was being followed, and the slightest movement could give her position away. She tried to control her breathing, and swallowed a sob. She mustn't make a sound.

Escape had seemed impossible, but she'd done it. With her heart hammering in her chest, she had seized the moment, grabbed the door handle, yanked open the door, and fled into the dark night. All she had to do now was find her way to a road, to a person who could help her. Then everything would be okay. She had to stay strong. If only she could get home, her mum and dad would protect her.

'We won't let anybody ever hurt you again, sweetheart. You're safe with us.' Her parents had been telling her this all her life, and she was sure that they had believed it. But who would have thought . . .

She couldn't think about that now. She needed to concentrate. Which way? She could feel the sweat pouring down her back, and yet her arms and legs were covered in goose bumps. She wrapped her arms around herself for a moment in an attempt to stem the panic that threatened to swamp her. Cowering low behind the hedge and keeping her head down, she looked around. Danger lay back the way she had come, and for now all she could think about was getting as far away as possible. She hadn't thought about where she was going—she had just run as fast as she could. But only the hedgerows and an occasional tree offered anywhere to hide. The fields were empty, and there weren't even any cows to provide cover.

The silence was broken by a sound that chilled her to the bone.

'Abbie, it's okay.' The voice was soft—and very close. 'I'm not going to hurt you. I'm sorry if I surprised you. Abbie—where are you?'

Abbie crept along the spiky hawthorn hedge that separated one field from the next, desperate not to make a sound. Suddenly she felt an excruciating pain in her bare legs and feet, and choked back an instinctive scream of distress. She had walked into a bed of stinging nettles, and the hot, throbbing agony was almost unbearable. She could feel her feet and the bottom of her legs swelling up. She had never reacted well to nettles. She wrapped her arms around herself, as if to hold in the cries of fear and misery that were trying to escape her throat.

She risked moving slightly away from the hedge, wincing in pain, so that there was enough light to see the ground she was walking on. But the moon and stars were obliterated by the black clouds scudding across the sky. Tears were flowing freely down her cheeks, but she daren't so much as sniff. She wiped her face and nose with the back of her hand. She had no idea where she was heading. These fields in Cheshire all looked the same, and she could be taking herself off into the middle of the county and in totally the wrong direction. Away from help and safety.

Stop, Abbie. Think. With her eyes darting from side to side in fear of seeing a shadowy figure emerge from the gloom and her ears interpreting every rustle of the bushes as danger, she forced herself to focus. It would be so easy to give in. But she couldn't. She thought about where the house was—the house she had escaped from. But she didn't really know. She had been blindfolded when she'd arrived.

In the distance she could see streetlights. They had to be the lights from the village. But to get there, she would have to go back the way she came. She couldn't do that. She needed to find a road; find somebody, anybody.

Out of nowhere came a memory, as if her dad were trying to speak to her. The stars. He had told her about Polaris—the North Star, and how to find it. She looked up, and willed the clouds to break for long enough to get her bearings. The moon was still covered, but she could see the Plough—and that was enough. She should be able to work it out, but her brain wouldn't function. She twisted her body round so that she was facing roughly where she thought the North Star should be, and straightaway she knew where she was. She was to the east of the village. *Thanks, Dad.*

By her reckoning, that must mean that there was a road somewhere to her right. The back road, her dad called it. If she could get to that road, she could find somebody. Somebody who would help her.

Abbie knew that she needed to get across the open fields somehow. But she would immediately be visible because of her white T-shirt. Quickly she whipped it over her head, and rubbed it on the grass—even a cow pat would be helpful. She didn't care. She pulled the dank clothing back on, and realised with alarm that she must have made a noise. She heard a rush of footsteps coming towards her across the wet grass.

'Abbie—I know where you are. I'm coming to get you. Stay there. I won't hurt you. I promise.'

This time the voice was much closer, so Abbie took to her heels and ran as fast as she could across the open grassland. It didn't matter if she could be seen now. She had to get away and the road was her best chance. She didn't wait to listen for sounds of pursuit. She was out of options. And she couldn't scream—no one would hear her.

Her legs were aching from the nettle stings and she was panting for breath when she saw a flash of headlights. The road must only be about two hundred metres ahead. She had been right. She forced herself to keep going, covering the distance in under a minute, but it felt like hours. Then Abbie sobbed in dismay. Between her and the road there was another solid hawthorn hedge, and no way through it.

But surely there must be a gate? There was always a gate. She scanned up and down the field, and was horrified to see that the only gate was back towards the house, and she was certain that way would lead to danger.

Abbie turned round slowly, petrified that she might see the terrifying figure of her pursuer racing across the field towards her, but although it was dark she didn't think anybody was there. Perhaps she was safe. But she knew too much, and she would never be allowed to escape. Maybe it would be safer just to sit here until morning. Her parents were bound to be worried silly by now.

And then she remembered. She wasn't supposed to be going home at all tonight. Her parents thought she was staying with Emily. They had been so pleased for her, so they wouldn't be missing her at all. She had been stupid, and so very naive.

Tears of self-pity and fear were streaming down her face. The road was quiet; absolutely nothing had passed since the headlights about ten minutes ago. Abbie felt a sudden glimmer of hope as she looked back along the way that she had come. So intent had she been on checking whether she was being pursued that she had failed to notice there was a small opening in the hedge. If she could get into the next field, perhaps there would be access to the road.

Checking carefully that there was no movement behind her, she crept towards the gap, expecting any minute to see a figure loom up, out of the darkness. Her heart was thumping so loudly that she was sure it could be heard fifty metres away. Keeping her head below the top of the hedge, she inched forward. Then she was through and running again. With a choked cry of relief, she saw a gate at the far end of the field. Finally she would be able to reach the road.

Breathless and desperate, she climbed over the gate and started to walk up the road, away from the village. It seemed safest, somehow. On the other side of the lane were the woods—a place she had visited with her father as a child, to see, but never to pick, the bluebells. It looked so different at night, and she glanced towards it nervously. The relief of hearing a car approaching from the village was enormous, and she turned round and jumped into the middle of the road, waving her arms for it to stop. Only at the very last minute did she recognise it. She had been in that very car only a few hours previously. Her tormentor had gone back for a car—and found her. Screaming at the top of her voice, she leapt out of the way and raced across the lane into the woods. The car screeched to a halt in a narrow lay-by, and a door slammed. She was being chased again—but she knew these woods. Scary as they were, perhaps she had an advantage.

Her energy came from somewhere, and she ran a few metres into the trees. She couldn't be seen from the road, but she was close enough to jump out if she saw a car coming. There was no footpath, and the twigs and stones that covered the ground were cutting into the tender skin on the soles of her feet, adding to the pain of the nettle stings. What little light there had been in the open fields was gone now, and although her eyes had adjusted, the black silhouettes of trees emerged threateningly from the shadows and she was forced to slow her speed. The unlit lane didn't help, although an occasional glimpse of moonlight breaking through the brooding clouds and reflecting on the wet tarmac helped her to keep her bearings, and stay as close as she could to the road.

She knew she was running farther and farther away from the village and civilisation, but she didn't know what else to do. She stopped to catch her breath, and she could hear somebody crashing through the undergrowth behind her. She remembered her dad saying that fear lends you wings, and for the first time she understood what he meant. She needed those wings now. Her breath was coming in deep rasps, so loud that she was unable to hear how close behind her pursuer was.

There was a moment's silence as she held her breath and listened for sounds of pursuit. Nothing. She knew the instant she moved she would give her position away, so she waited, trying to control her breathing and expecting to hear the eerie sound of a voice, softly calling her name. But the next sound she heard was much sweeter. It was the roar of a powerful engine.

She raced to the edge of the wood, ready to throw herself in front of whoever was coming. She leapt out into the road, but she was moments too late. The driver was going so fast, as if they themselves were being chased. She waved her arms in the air behind the retreating car, but the driver never even noticed her. A howl of anguish escaped from her throat. And now she had given away her position. She scrambled her way back up the bank to the edge of the wood, and without glancing behind her she carried on running.

Then against the dark, stormy sky she saw a strange light coming towards her. In an instant, she realised what it was—it was the headlights of a car lighting up the canopy of branches above the road. *Thank God,* she thought. She had to time it right. She would hide in the trees close to the road until the very last moment, but she'd be ready. She didn't want to give away her location in case the car didn't stop.

And then she heard it. 'Abbie, Abbie. Stop running. I won't hurt you. Wait for me.'

Her pursuer was right behind her.

She saw the car as it turned the bend. She waited until the last possible moment, and then she jumped.

5

Day Two: Saturday

Leo was downstairs in the kitchen making the children some breakfast when a bleary-eyed Max made an appearance. His short, dark brown hair was even spikier than normal, and black stubble covered the lower half of his face.

'Morning, Leo. Lovely to see you—I think.'

Leo raised her eyebrows and waited to see if he would dig himself in further.

'I mean it's lovely that you're here, I'm just frightened of opening my eyes properly because it hurts too much.' Max's cheeky grin made a fleeting appearance. 'Ellie said you'd arrived so thanks for sorting out the kids' breakfasts.'

'I didn't know if you would be sufficiently compos mentis last night to take in the fact that I was here,' Leo said. 'I was prepared to be greeted with shock and horror.'

'Never.' Max picked up a tea towel and threw it at Leo. It missed by a mile, which was way off his usual accuracy. 'You should know better than that. I'm delighted that you're here, and it will be one less thing for your big sister to worry about. And I hope it's not just a flying visit. You know you can stay as long as you like. Ellie said she'd woken you and asked you to feed the monsters, for which I will be eternally grateful. She was out for the count when I got home last night, thank God! Good job she didn't see the state I was in.'

Max walked over to his children, who were happily eating their breakfast cereal and muttering away to themselves in a language that nobody else understood, just as they had done since they were tiny. He dropped a kiss onto each of their heads and pinched a piece of toast from the pile in the centre of the table, much to the disgust of Ruby, who had apparently wanted that exact slice.

Leo was glad that Max had his back to her, and by the time he turned round she was sure that she had her surprise under control. What the hell had Ellie been up to in the middle of the night then? She had convinced herself that her sister had gone to pick up Max from his end of term party. But she was wrong.

'I presume you didn't drive home under the influence? Now you're in the money you can afford a taxi, I suppose.'

She couldn't help probing a bit further, but Max gave her a self-deprecating smile.

'Old habits die hard, kiddo,' he responded, between mouthfuls of toast. 'We drew straws last week to decide who was driving, and fortunately—or unfortunately as it feels now—it wasn't me. I'm going to have to get my act together for tonight's dinner, though. Ellie's going to be panicking; she thought she had all day to prepare and now she won't be home until about three.'

'What's the problem? She told me she had to go out, but I was too groggy to ask about it.'

'A crisis at work, apparently. She only does a few shifts a week now, but there was some emergency last night, and the hospital was short of qualified nurses to deal with the situation. Usual summer problems with everybody on holiday, I expect.'

'I can look after the twins if that helps,' Leo offered. 'Just don't ask me to cook.'

Max grunted.

'If either of us interfered with the cooking we'd be in deep trouble. I understand that Little Miss Organised has ordered everything, so I need to go to the greengrocer, the fishmonger, and the butcher. And I gather you scoffed half the cheese last night, so I need to get some more of that too. We've already got the booze, unless you drank that as well. Everything has to be right for the swanky party. I'll be about an hour. Can you cope?'

Leo frowned at his tone, but he didn't notice.

'It'll be a pleasure,' she said. 'I'll probably take the twins for a walk, if that's okay with you. If I'd thought about it in time I would have swapped cars with Ellie so that I would have had the car seats.'

Max raised his eyebrows.

'You think she'd have allowed you to drive her new car, do you? Dream on.'

He ripped off a piece of kitchen roll to wipe his buttery hands.

'I've got to ask, Leo. How are you coping being here? Joking apart, it can't have been easy for you but I'm so glad that you came. Ellie was worried that us moving here would create an insurmountable barrier.'

Leo avoided Max's eyes. She had known this man since she was fourteen years old and he felt like a brother. But she had grown so used to hiding her every emotion that even he wasn't allowed to pierce her carefully constructed defences.

'It's just a house, Max. Bricks and mortar.'

Max laughed, and then held his head because it obviously hurt.

'You don't fool me, kiddo. Brave words, though. And speaking of being brave . . .'

Leo groaned, because she knew what was coming.

'. . . have you been brave enough yet to find yourself a man—as in "relationship" as opposed to one-night stand—or are you still judging every man on earth by one rotten example? We're not all bad, you know. In fact, some of us are pretty impressive beasts,' Max said, pointing with both hands at himself and beaming at Leo.

She shook her head in mock despair. Why did every man consider that a woman was failing in life if she didn't have a husband?

'I'm happy as I am, thanks. You ask me this every time I see you, and I always give you the same answer. And before you start trying to get your vicarious thrills from asking for details of my sporadic sex life, just butt out.'

Leo cast a worried glance towards the children, who thankfully were still busy chattering between themselves and hopefully wouldn't have a clue what she was talking about.

This was usually a cue for Max to give her his 'happy marriage' lecture, but fortunately this time he declined to comment, and Leo took the opportunity to change the subject.

'Speaking of my rotten example of a man, what are we going to do about Ellie and this obsession she has with our father? It's part of the reason I came, to tell you the truth. I tried to talk to her about it last night, but I didn't get very far. He's not going to suddenly appear out of thin air, Max. Why can't she see him for what he was?'

Max looked serious for a moment.

'Whenever I've asked her about him, she hardly seems to know anything. He seems like some sort of ghost figure that drifted in and out of your lives, giving as little of himself as possible.'

'That's pretty accurate,' Leo answered, nodding her head. 'He used to come and go apparently on a whim. Ellie's mother appeared to hate him, but he was impervious to it all. Answerable to nobody. But when he was here, Ellie tried so hard to please him. She would run up and hug him as he walked through the door. He'd ruffle her hair and say something like 'Goodness, you've grown' or 'You're looking very pretty today'. That was it. He handed out compliments as a reward for devotion, and let's face it, Ellie was thirsty for some love and affection. Of her parents he was undoubtedly the lesser of two evils—but he was largely indifferent. It's not surprising I've no time for men, is it?'

Max had tried many times to convince Leo that her father was the exception, rather than the rule, but this time he merely gave her a look which she interpreted as 'you're hopeless' and walked over to the coffee machine, lifting a cup in Leo's direction.

'Want one? This fancy machine makes the best—and most expensive—cup of coffee in the world. Every home should have one, don't you think?'

He pressed a button. Leo heard the beans grinding and the room filled with the delicious smell of fresh coffee as a dark brown flow slowly filled the small espresso cup.

'Does it do cappuccino too?' Leo asked.

'It does, but that requires a small amount of human intervention. Grab me a bottle of milk will you, and I will reveal more of the mysteries of this marvellous and essential piece of kitchen equipment.'

Leo had never considered Max to be strong on sarcasm, but maybe it was the hangover talking. Or maybe she had been wrong about the house. Maybe its malignancy couldn't be obliterated by a few coats of paint.

6

A few hundred yards away in a red-bricked cottage, Tom Douglas relaxed on his comfortable sofa with the Saturday papers spread around him. An old Fleetwood Mac album that he'd bought out of nostalgia was playing in the background. His dad had played *Rumours* nonstop when he was a kid, and when he saw it on iTunes he couldn't resist downloading it.

He was struggling to get used to these lazy days, though, and after a couple of hours of doing nothing, he was getting restless. He'd just decided that he should get up and do something useful when the doorbell rang. He couldn't imagine who on earth had tracked him down here. He knew hardly anybody except the neighbours who had invited him to dinner that evening.

Remembering that one job he still had to do was to take the front door off and plane a bit off the bottom, he opened it with a sharp tug to welcome his unexpected visitor.

'Steve! Hi! What a surprise to see you. What brings you to this neck of the woods? Come on in.'

It was good to see an old friend. Steve had been Tom's sergeant in Manchester a few years previously. He had taken a promotion by moving to the Cheshire force and they had kept in occasional contact but hadn't seen each other since Tom had relocated to London three years ago.

Tom had forgotten how tall Steve was. He was one hell of big guy, in girth as well as in height, and although Tom had checked that the low beams and ceilings of his cottage were sufficient to accommodate his own six-foot height, he hadn't allowed for the extra five inches that Steve could boast. And no hair on top to cushion him either, Tom noticed with surprise. It was obviously longer than he thought since they had seen each other.

Ducking as he made his way through to the sitting room, Steve spoke over his shoulder.

'Sorry it's the first time I've had a chance to call round. I couldn't believe it when I got your e-mail to say you were moving back up north, but I don't blame you.'

Steve looked around the sitting room.

'Wow—this is a bit smart, Tom. I didn't know you were into interior design. New career, is it?' Steve winked at Tom, a habit of his that Tom had completely forgotten. He remembered thinking that Steve had some sort of facial tick when he'd first met him.

Tom glanced at the dark aubergine sofa and stone-coloured armchairs grouped close to an inglenook fireplace, and the fat porcelain lamps on chunky wooden side tables.

'You've got to be kidding,' he said. 'I found a great shop in Chester, and they sorted the lot. After the place I had in London—which was übersmart, but always felt cold and stark to me—it's a pleasure to have somewhere that feels like home.'

'Never could stand London myself. Anyway, it's good to have you back up north. I'd have popped in sooner, but things have been a bit hectic with work. You know how it is.'

Tom grinned. He certainly did.

'Before I sit down, can I get you a drink of anything? Beer, wine, or tea or coffee if you're on duty?'

'I'd love a beer—only a glass, though, as I'm driving. I officially came off duty a couple of hours ago, but I had stuff to do in the neighbourhood.'

'One beer coming up. Have a seat—I'll only be a minute.'

Tom made his way to the kitchen, opened a bottle of beer, and grabbed two glasses.

'Here you go,' Tom said, handing a glass to Steve and filling it slowly.

'Thanks. I'm ready for this.'

They chinked glasses, and Tom sat down.

'You never did say what made you decide to make the break from London, Tom. Just that you were moving back here. Problems?'

'No, nothing like that.' Tom shook his head, while admitting to himself that he wasn't being entirely honest with his friend. 'Lucy's back in Manchester with her mum, and seeing her for the odd weekend wasn't working for either of us. She's only eight, and I felt that I was missing out on so much. So I wanted to be within driving distance. She's coming tomorrow for the day for the first time. Her mum's bringing her—but you know Kate—she'll just want to have a nosey at my new home.'

'So how was life in the big league then?' Steve winked again, and Tom glanced down at his beer to hide a smile.

'If you mean the Met, I had a great boss. But he took early retirement after a health scare, and I couldn't think of a single good reason to stay. So I packed up and moved here. And now I'm job hunting.'

'Bloody hell, Tom—that's a bit of a risk, isn't it? What will you do if nothing comes up?'

'Something else entirely, I expect,' Tom replied with a shrug of his shoulders. He was keen to move the focus of the conversation away from himself. 'More to the point, though, what are you doing in this part of Cheshire on a Saturday afternoon? I don't suppose you were just passing?'

Steve took a long gulp of his beer, and set his glass down on the coffee table. The smile disappeared from his face.

'Pretty horrible case, actually. Some kid got herself knocked over last night on the back road, if you know where that is. It's the local name for the lane that cuts through between the two main roads on either side of the village. Anyway, whoever hit her dragged her to the side of the road and left her there. Left her to die.' Steve shook his large head. 'The bastard. I bloody hope I catch whoever it was, that's all I can say. We've got a team working the area, but I thought I'd take a detour on my way home to see how they're doing.'

Tom leaned back hard against the sofa.

'Oh God, Steve, I'm sorry. I've always hated cases like that. Give me a murder any day, but hit-and-run smacks of cowardice doesn't it? How old was she?'

'She was, or rather is, fourteen. Despite leaving her on the grass verge like roadkill, somebody found her pretty soon after it happened, it seems. She's in a coma—but she's alive. Barely. The doctors don't hold out much hope, I'm sorry to say. The trouble with the back road is that there are no cameras at all, and although we've picked up what we can from the ones in the village, it's going to be hard to prove anything.'

Steve filled Tom in on some of the background and the two men discussed all the usual routes to evidence. As he listened to the details of the investigation and everything that the police had found—or failed to find— Tom had to admit that it didn't sound too promising. It was easy to see that Steve was feeling a sense of hopelessness, and Tom felt bad that he had no words of wisdom to offer.

Steve looked regretfully at his watch.

'I need to make a move, I'm afraid. Sorry it was such a short visit, but I've been working silly hours recently and I was supposed to be home hours ago.'

He pushed himself up from the sofa and made his way to the door, keeping his head bent low as he went.

'If you hear any gossip, Tom—being as how you're so well in with the neighbours—give me a call, would you? You know how it is. The locals in a place like this always know everything that's going on. There's no such thing as a secret in a village.'

Tom smiled. 'I know what you mean. Go into any shop around here, and you can hear them talking—usually about the person who walked out thirty seconds previously, although to be fair it's usually without malice. God knows what they say about me.'

Steve gave Tom a knowing smile, a final wink, and lifted his hand in a farewell gesture.

Tom closed the door and walked through to the kitchen to make a cup of tea. He didn't think there'd be any shortage of alcohol at tonight's dinner with the neighbours, but tomorrow was going to be a special day for him and Lucy, and a hangover wouldn't be ideal.

He was looking forward to the evening ahead. When he'd bought this cottage, he hadn't realised how it would feel to spend long days without speaking to anybody. He'd always been happy with his own company, but nowadays he sometimes felt as if his vocal cords had seized up.

The other problem with spending long hours alone was that it gave Tom too much time to think. He'd always had such a clearly defined concept of right and wrong, but in the last couple of years he'd been forced to question his own values. He had thought that taking a break from the police might sort out his muddled mind, but instead he'd discovered that too much introspection confused him even more.

Now he just wanted to get back to work. Especially when he heard stories like the one Steve had just told him. Tom felt his scalp prickle, a familiar sensation when something about a crime didn't seem quite right, and he wanted to be there, on the front line, working out just what it was that didn't fit.

7

A radio was playing quietly in the kitchen. Nobody was listening—it was there for background noise and to drown out the silence that pervaded the house.

A half-empty glass of warm vodka sat on the table. It didn't matter that it wasn't cold—it was fulfilling its purpose. It was numbing the pain without leaving any trace.

The music stopped, and the six o'clock news began. More of the same, of course. The economy, the Middle East, back to the economy. The same as every other day. Who cared, really?

'And in local news, we have a report on a hit-and-run accident in the quiet village of Little Melham. A young girl was knocked down on the B522 and the driver failed to stop. This road—locally known as the back road—connects the A564 and the A5194 but according to the police is normally only used by locals. The girl, who has not been named yet, is said to be in a critical condition. The accident took place in the early hours of this morning, and the police are asking anybody who was out in the area last night to . . .'

An angry hand reached out and switched the radio off.

Why did she reject me? Why was she scared? Why did she run?

All that planning, months and months of it, blown away by an impulsive action—an opportunity that seemed too good to miss. Abbie was all alone—abandoned—and nobody was missing her. It was so very easy.

Abbie—I just wanted you to love me. Our little secret.

But those eyes—the stark black terror in their depths when she learned the truth. *Why?*

And then she ran.

What if she'd made it back to the village? What if that driver had been paying attention, driving more slowly, and picked her up instead of knocking her down? It didn't bear thinking about.

My life would be over. Everything I've worked so hard for would be destroyed. Again. By Abbie.

But now Abbie couldn't speak. She would probably die.

That was never my intention, Abbie—but you shouldn't have rejected me. I wouldn't have hurt you if you'd been nice to me. You're dead to me anyway, now.

But there was another problem.

The driver saw me, standing in the woods, watching but doing nothing.

And that was a danger. Safe for now, but if the police identified the car, the driver would be sure to tell them.

A cry of frustrated misery pierced the silence, and the now-empty glass was hurled into the sink, where it shattered on impact.

'I need a drink,' a weary Ellie muttered as she plonked herself down on the bed.

What a day! She could have done without going into work, but in view of the circumstances she'd had little choice. There had been no chance to catch up with Leo, and she'd barely seen the twins. And after last night . . .

No. She mustn't think about that. It was too terrible. Too awful. For tonight, at least, she had to push it all to the back of her mind.

She had somehow managed to go through the motions of preparing everything for tonight's dinner—all she had to do was drum up the enthusiasm to get herself ready. The babysitter had arrived—a ridiculous extravagance in Max's mind, given that they weren't actually going out—but at least the twins were occupied and all she had to worry about was the food.

Staring disconsolately at her wardrobe and hoping it would provide some magical solution to what she should wear, she heard the bathroom door opening. She could see Max's reflection in the large mirror that hung over their dressing table, and couldn't resist watching him as he rubbed his thick dark hair on a towel, another one draped around his middle. Not an inch of fat on him, she could see the muscles in his stomach from where she sat, despite the thin covering of dark hair. He's so hot, she thought. Was she really losing him?

She sighed.

'What's up, my lovely Ellie Jelly Belly?'

'Don't call me that—you know I hate it,' Ellie said, scowling at his reflection.

Max laughed.

'I've been calling you that since you were seventeen, and you loved it then.'

'Of course I did—principally because it wasn't true. Now it is, so think of something nice to say or don't say anything.'

A brief tap came on the door, and it was nudged open to reveal Leo, dressed in nothing more than a black T-shirt that just about reached the top of her thighs and clung to her slim hips. Her slender legs were enviably long and lightly tanned.

'Leo—do you *have* to wander in here naked—or as near as, damn it?' Ellie said.

As Leo opened the door fully, Ellie saw her glance sideways at Max.

'Sorry, Max. I didn't know you were here. I thought you were with the twins. And I'm perfectly decent, Ellie. People walk around the centre of Manchester in fewer clothes than this. I came to see if I could borrow your straighteners. I forgot mine, and my hair looks a complete mess if I leave it curly.'

'Max could have been naked himself, but I don't suppose either of you would have been bothered.'

Ellie wasn't surprised to see a look of puzzlement pass between Leo and Max. She knew she was being a grump, but seeing her svelte sister made her feel more frumpy than ever, and she was sure Max couldn't fail to make a comparison. Leo had always been tall and slender; even as a child she had been taller than her older sister. But with her long dark hair and her preference for wearing black—when she was dressed, that is—with her lips painted a bright crimson, she had a vamp-like appearance that was at odds with her personality.

Max had been quiet to this point, but in an obvious attempt to lighten the atmosphere, he started to sing the well-known opening notes of 'The Stripper', throwing the towel that he had been drying his hair with to one side in a flourish. To Ellie's dismay he started to tease open the towel around his waist. She knew what he was going to do, and she had no way of stopping him. He had never had the slightest of inhibitions about his body— and why would he? But she wanted him all to herself. He wasn't to be shared—she couldn't bear it.

Before she could utter a word of protest, Max ripped the towel from round his waist to reveal a pair of tight black shorts which in many ways were even more sexy than if he'd been naked.

Leo gave a slightly derisive snort at Max's antics, pinched the straighteners from the dressing table, and made a swift exit.

❖

Max watched Ellie carefully in the mirror for a few seconds. Her head had dropped back down and she was gazing at the floor as if transfixed by the pile of the pale cream carpet. He could see she wasn't impressed by his little performance. Normally she would have shrugged off his silliness, or laughed with him. But not anymore. A pang of guilt struck him hard in the chest. He knew what he'd been doing to her for the past couple of months, but he couldn't help himself. Every morning he gave himself a good talking to, and every night he acknowledged that he had failed once again to stick to his resolutions.

Max walked over to the bed and sat down beside Ellie. Fully recovered from his earlier hangover he was now looking forward to tonight, and he could see that Ellie was tired and very down. This was so out of character for her, and he had to blame himself. He put his arm around her shoulders and gave her a squeeze.

'What's up, Ellie? Why are you so down tonight? You were looking forward to showing off the new house to everybody. But it doesn't seem to be giving you the pleasure that you expected. What is it, sweetheart?'

Ellie bit her bottom lip.

'Work was pretty awful today. A young kid—it nearly broke my heart.'

'Ellie, your patients nearly break your heart every day of the week. So it has to be more than that. Come on. Tell me.'

'I've got nothing to wear, I haven't got time to straighten my hair, and couldn't now because Leo has pinched the straighteners, and that all sounds so pathetic and self-indulgent in relation to other people's problems.'

Max rubbed her shoulder and gave her another squeeze.

'Sometimes it's the little things that get to you, because you don't want to think about the big things, so let's deal with those points in order, shall we?' he said. 'Why haven't you got anything to wear, hmm? You've spent money on everything else, why not yourself?'

'You know why not.'

'No, I don't know why not.'

Ellie's head dropped even further onto her chest, and she mumbled her response under her breath.

'Because I was waiting until I was thinner to buy new stuff. You know that. I've been waiting for three years and that's why I never buy any clothes.'

Max did, of course, know this. They'd had this conversation so many times, and it never got any easier to convince her. But he would try again. Anything to get that lovely smile back.

'Sweetheart, you know I think you're beautiful just as you are, so why not go with the flow? You are what you are, and to me that's voluptuous and sexy.'

He put his other arm round her and hugged her tight. She pushed his arm away.

'Bollocks, Max. You don't think that, or you wouldn't always be trying to make me exercise. You want me to be thinner.'

He swallowed a sigh, knowing that it wouldn't help.

'No, I don't want you to be thinner, I want you to be fitter, because then you would be healthier. I don't care about your size. And you're not fat. You're not a stick insect, but thank God for that, I say.'

'We all know that nowadays men only find skinny girls attractive—girls like Leo and that PE teacher at your school.'

Max paused. He needed to get this right, and the best bet would probably be to ignore the last part of that comment.

'Now you really are talking rubbish. Look at Nigella Lawson—arse the size of a small bungalow, but men still think she's sexy. And you're about a third of the size.'

'She's lost a load of weight, actually—so obviously even she didn't think it was very attractive.'

Realising that once more he wasn't going to win this argument, Max got up from the bed and made his way to the wardrobe.

'What about this black dress? You look sexy in that.'

'I wear that every single time we go anywhere, and that cow Mimi is bound to comment. What is Pat doing with her, Max? He must be mental, leaving Georgia for her.'

Max couldn't fail to agree, but this was another discussion they'd had several times in the last couple of months, without resolution.

'Look, why don't you go and have a lovely long shower—leave your hair curly, because it suits you better like that, and I'll go downstairs and bring up a bottle of ice-cold bubbly which we can drink while you're getting ready. Wash away the trauma of your day. Nobody will be here for a couple of hours, so there's loads of time.'

Ellie pulled an apologetic face.

'Ah. I forgot to tell you. I asked Fiona and Charles to come early. I wanted somebody else to be here when Pat and Mimi arrive, so we've got about an hour. Sorry.'

Max groaned, not relishing the idea of being landed with bloody Charles for an hour while the women nattered in the kitchen. But he put a brave face on it. Anything to see his wife's beautiful smile.

'Fine—well, we can still have a couple of glasses, courtesy of The Old Witch. What do you say?'

Max was pleased to see a flicker of a smile as he closed the bedroom door.

8

Grabbing a silk dressing gown from the bed, Leo thrust her arms into the sleeves. What on earth was wrong with Ellie? It wasn't like her to be so tetchy. It felt like a bad omen for the evening ahead, and Leo couldn't help thinking that in some way it was her fault. She had been so sure of her welcome here, but maybe it had been wrong to act on impulse.

Plugging the straighteners in to warm up, she walked over to the open window and leant her elbows on the sill. The view calmed her; it hadn't changed in all these years. The flat green fields stretched for miles behind the house but she could just glimpse the dark hills in the distance. Her bedroom hadn't had a window—it was more of a cupboard, really—so whenever she had been able to sneak in here she had always stood gazing at the scenery, thinking about other places, other times, and other lives.

Without warning, her mind was assaulted with a memory so vivid that she gasped. She recalled standing in this very position gazing out of the window, and she remembered the day clearly. She must have been about fourteen, and she'd been sent home from school because of agonising stomach pains. She hadn't wanted anybody to know because there would be no sympathy, so she had sneaked into the house unobserved. She'd never said that she had started her periods, and her stepmother hadn't bothered to ask. Leo had to take everything she needed from Ellie, or sometimes Ellie would hand over some of her pocket money. Leo didn't get pocket money, of course.

She remembered that she had sneaked upstairs and come into Ellie's room to raid her top drawer. It had been a day much like today, and the window had been open. Nobody knew she was there. She had no idea why her father was home that day, but he was unenthusiastically hoeing the flowerbed below the window—probably the last time the garden was touched until Ellie and Max had taken it over. She had moved back, afraid to be seen, but the voices still invaded the room, and their bitterness and hatred seemed to be tainting every surface they touched.

The first voice was her stepmother's.

'You can't hide from me out here. I haven't finished with you yet. I've always known you lack moral fibre, but I thought you'd finally learned your lesson. I suppose that would be too much to ask, wouldn't it?'

'Shut up, Denise. You don't know what you're talking about.'

'Hah! You'd like to believe that, wouldn't you? But I know you. And I know what you're up to when you're not here. I didn't know about your brat, but do you think I didn't know about her mother? Your whore?'

'She wasn't a whore. She was my wife. And she's dead—more's the pity. She at least made me smile.'

'I'm your wife. Me. Maybe I should tell the police, have you done for bigamy. As it is, I can't show my face in the fucking village. Since SHE came, your little bastard, everybody's talking.'

'Your language is a disgrace, Denise. And Sandra was more of a wife to me than you will ever be. If you wonder why I have to look elsewhere, take a good look at yourself.'

'Looking's one thing. Touching's another. I don't care about those sad cows that find you irresistible. But what about those that don't, eh? What about the clever ones who are not taken in by your slimy charms? What do you do to them? As if I didn't know. But you don't like it when they say no, do you? And they're getting progressively younger, aren't they?'

'I'll say it again—you don't know what you're talking about. You're making things up. And for Christ's sake, woman, keep your voice down.'

'Or what? I've told you—I know you. I'm not stupid. The latest one's gone now, poor little bitch, but I know what you did. So who's next, hmm?'

'Just get out of my sight.'

'Oh no. This time I'm not backing down. I want you gone. Do you hear me? Gone. You were lucky this time. But you're not going to shame me again.'

Shaking herself back into the present, Leo pushed herself away from the window. She didn't want to remember any more. It was years ago—maybe she hadn't recalled it correctly. The venom in her stepmother's voice was accurate, as was the contempt in her father's. But the conversation? She couldn't be sure, but it had seemed so clear as the words leapt into her head. She remembered the pain of listening to them discussing her mother, but the rest hadn't meant so much at the time. It was just like every other row. But if her memory was accurate, what did it mean?

Leo had known from the day she arrived in Little Melham that her stepmother despised her, and she had stopped caring about that long ago. But her own mother had been special. So much fun. Hearing her described like this brought back the pain she'd been burying for years. She had been sure that her father had loved her mother, because she made him laugh and he had looked happy when they were together. She'd never seen that expression on his face again after her mother had died. But then she had avoided looking at him after the day he brought her here. He had never comforted her as she cried. Only Ellie had tried—and Leo had shunned her sister's affection.

She bent down to her holdall, pulled out her laptop, and searched for a file marked 'father'. Whether those words had actually been spoken or not, she was going to add them to her notes. Ellie's mother had never told them the truth about their father's disappearance, Leo was positive of that. And Ellie had never been able to accept that he was dead, and still lived in hope that one day soon he would walk back through the front door. Why else would she have chosen to live in a house that brought back so many bleak memories?

For her sister's sake, Leo needed to find out where their father had gone, and more to the point, why he'd never come back.

9

As Fiona Atkinson walked down the wide staircase of her detached Edwardian home, she caught a glimpse of herself in the huge mirror by the door to the dining room. The brilliant blue of her dress with splashes of emerald green looked wonderful against her tan, and the hem of its handkerchief skirt rose from mid-calf to mid-thigh in places to give glimpses of her toned legs. Every inch of her body was honed to perfection, and her short blonde hair was gleaming. Marco had done a wonderful job with her highlights as usual. Her only concern was her shoes. She was sure that Ellie would expect them all to wander round the garden, and there was no way that these heels were leaving the safety of the house.

All eyes would definitely be on her, and that was just what she wanted. One pair especially, if he was there. She hadn't wanted to ask, though. It wouldn't do to seem too keen.

'Right Charles, I'm ready,' Fiona announced as she swept into the room in a cloud of Hermes' 24 Faubourg perfume. 'What do you think?' she asked, posing with one hand on her hip.

Charles was standing by the window, looking out at their immaculately maintained garden with a glass of something colourless in his hand. She knew it wouldn't be water. Dressed in a navy blue pinstriped suit and red tie that were entirely inappropriate to the occasion, Charles turned to look at her. His brown hair was slicked back from a wide forehead, and his dark bushy eyebrows almost met over a pair of small brown eyes, giving him the air of somebody who was constantly perplexed.

He lifted his glass to his lips, then lowered it and spoke in his usual measured tones.

'Is that the Ferragamo you told me about?'

Fiona did a small twirl.

'It is. Divine, isn't it?'

Charles frowned.

'Are you seriously wearing that? To go to Ellie and Max's? A bit OTT, wouldn't you say?'

'Well, clearly I wouldn't say or I wouldn't be wearing it. What's your problem?'

'I would have thought that something a tad less ostentatious would be more appropriate, given the company we'll be keeping.'

Fiona rolled her eyes.

'Stop being such a snob, Charles. Ellie and Max are loaded now—they are among the wealthy, so no need to turn your nose up like that.'

He walked over to the drinks table and put his glass down.

'Well, they might have money now, but who else will be there? Not people who would appreciate Ferragamo, I should imagine.'

Fiona could never admit to Charles that each designer dress, each piece of exquisite jewellery, was a symbol to her of how far she had come and how completely she had left her past behind.

'It might surprise you to learn, Charles, that I don't dress to suit anybody else. I dress to suit myself.' She followed him across the room. 'As far as other people invited tonight, Patrick will be there with his new woman, no doubt, and Ellie said there'd be a few others, but I'm not entirely sure who.'

Fiona glanced down to pluck a non-existent hair off her dress as she spoke, avoiding Charles's eyes. Despite the distance between them, sometimes she was amazed at how well he could read her. He gave a soft snort of disgust.

'Patrick and his new woman just about sum it up. He's an idiot for leaving that rather splendid Georgia—what on earth possessed the man? What's she like anyway, this new woman?'

'I don't know. I haven't met her. She's called Miriam but apparently prefers to be called Mimi.'

'Oh God,' muttered Charles.

'Ellie says she's like a wet blanket, and Pat's as miserable as sin.' Fiona glared at Charles. 'Am I getting a drink tonight, or do I have to get my own?'

'Sorry, darling. What would you like?'

Fiona shook her head in irritation.

'I'll have what I always have, Charles. You ask me that every weekend, and my answer for the past five years has always been the same. A vodka martini no olive, sliver of lemon peel. And did you sort out a taxi?'

Charles busied himself at the drinks table, measuring a precise amount of vodka into a crystal glass as he spoke.

'Well, I sorted out a car. I booked Jessops and asked them to send a Mercedes. They're picking us up early, as you requested—about fifteen minutes from now, and I've ordered them to collect us at eleven.'

'You have *not*. Honestly, sometimes you're unbelievable. *Eleven*? We can't leave at eleven—how old are you really, Charles?' And what do we have to get back to, anyway, she couldn't help thinking.

Fiona took a sip of her drink. Whatever his faults, Charles certainly knew how to mix the perfect martini. Perhaps his ability to reproduce perfection time after time was down to his obsession with precision. He couldn't bear to go anywhere without a plan—how long to get there in order to arrive at the optimum moment; how long for each course; what would be the perfect time to make a dignified exit. He would constantly be checking his watch to make sure things were working to his schedule. But there was no way that she was going to be the first to leave tonight. She was going to milk this evening for all that she could. She was going to be the star, and wanted every man's eyes to be on her. Charles was *not* going to ruin it for her.

Fiona walked across to the mirror over the sideboard, and moved a wonderful display of summer flowers out of the way so that she could see herself better. She was pleased with what she saw.

'Well, darling, you can leave at eleven if you like, but I will be staying. I'll try not to wake you when I get in. I'll call a taxi.'

Fiona contemplated the evening ahead. Perhaps tonight should be decision time. She had nearly relented the night before, but had decided the game could last a little longer. Maybe it was finally time to stop playing.

The gleam of anticipation in her eyes was reflected back at her, and even through the carefully applied makeup she could just make out a hint of a flush to her cheeks.

She sensed movement behind her, and saw Charles watching her in the mirror. She quickly glanced away.

10

To Leo's surprise, the kitchen was empty when she had finally finished straightening her hair. She was relieved. She had no intention of sharing with Ellie the memories that had been flooding her mind, but she wasn't sure how much her face would reveal.

She hadn't brought anything smart with her, but had a figure-hugging black vest and some white jeans that she thought would be fine if she dressed them up with a bit of colourful jewellery. She'd been going to raid Ellie's bedroom to see if she could dig out a dark red, chunky necklace that she had bought her a year or two ago. It would go well with her lipstick. But given the earlier episode, maybe she should ask first.

She looked around the kitchen, which was amazingly well organised considering there were ten of them for dinner. But then it was a vast kitchen and nothing like the poky little hole of a room they'd had when Leo and Ellie were growing up. Now there was the most enormous black Aga that she had ever seen down one side of the room. As if that weren't enough, there were two separate built-in ovens along one stretch of wall, and a six-burner hob with a separate griddle plate in a central island that was in itself probably bigger than the former kitchen.

On the other side of the island was a table to seat six, and over by the folding glass doors to the garden were a couple of comfortable-looking armchairs. As she had discovered the night before, the kitchen took up half of the downstairs of the barn, with Max's playroom—as Ellie liked to call it—next door. She had only poked her nose in there, but the television screen covered most of the wall, and there were twelve recliners for added comfort. Completely over the top, of course, but then Ellie would have wanted to make sure Max had something that made moving here worthwhile. He had been perfectly happy in their modern semi.

From the kitchen, a spiral staircase led to the first floor, where there was a full-sized snooker table and various other boys' toys that Leo wasn't even slightly interested in. With all this, it was strange that both Max and Ellie were the most spiky that Leo had ever seen them in their nine years of marriage.

She wasn't the world's greatest cook herself, but Leo was just beginning to feel a bit of a spare part hanging around the kitchen and doing nothing when Ellie finally made an appearance, looking a bit more chirpy than she had an hour ago. Max had obviously worked his magic, and Leo was glad that her sister seemed more like her usual self. Her long dark hair was waving around her face, and the low-cut neck of her short black dress showed a cleavage that Leo was insanely jealous of. Ellie never overdid the makeup, but tonight she wore a touch of lip-gloss on her generous mouth, and her eyes were emphasised by a subtle hint of grey shadow.

Ellie smiled, as if to atone for her previous grumpiness. 'Leo—you look lovely. As always.'

'I don't—but thank you. I'm sorry I didn't bring anything smart. You look terrific, though. Are your guests likely to be ultra stylish tonight, do you think?'

Ellie was busying herself putting various dips into bowls for the canapés, but she stopped for a moment and looked at Leo apologetically.

'Well, Fiona and Charles are coming—so I guess Fiona will be in some posh frock or other.'

'Oh God help us. She's become such a snooty bugger. Does she still wear polo shirts with the collar artfully turned up at the back as part of her "casual look"?'

Ellie grinned, but declined to comment.

'And I've never worked out why she married that plonker Charles. She didn't exactly choose him because he was sex on legs, did she? I know she was your friend at school, but I can't believe you have a single thing in common with her now.'

Ellie gave her sister a tolerant smile.

'She's not always had it easy, you know. Put your face straight, Leo. There are things about Fiona that you don't know and I can't tell you—but half of her performance is an act. Be a bit more forgiving of people.'

'Ellie, you are the softest touch in the world. Always have been, always will be. I, on the other hand, do not suffer fools gladly—although tonight, as they're your friends, I'll be on my best behaviour. So is there anybody else that I know?'

Leo walked over to the massive fridge as she spoke and found an open bottle of white wine. She waved it in the air, and Ellie nodded as she carried on with her work.

'Well, Pat's coming—you know him.'

Leo pulled some glasses from a cupboard, and with her back to Ellie gave her verdict on the next pair of guests.

'Excellent—that's good news. Not about Pat. He's a nice guy but a bit limp, if you know what I mean. But Georgia's great. Tough cookie and a straight talker. Thank goodness for that. I can resist taking the piss out of Fiona and do some bitching with Georgia.'

She turned round with a big smile on her face, only to be greeted by Ellie's look of dismay. One hand to her mouth, she muttered through her fingers.

'Oh Christ. You don't know, do you? Sorry Leo, I meant to tell you but it kept slipping my mind.'

Leo passed her sister the glass of wine, and watched her take a rather long drink. She said nothing and waited until Ellie was ready to talk.

'Pat's left Georgia. Well—Georgia kicked him out, to be accurate. And she's my best friend so I'm on her side all the way, except that Pat is *Max's* best friend, so it's all a bit difficult.'

Leo said nothing, knowing that her sister would fill the silence without her having to ask the obvious questions.

'It was so awful. It all started because Pat wanted babies. You know what he's been like with Georgia over the years. He idolised her, and as she rose up through the ranks at work he did everything for her. They both put her career first, on the basis that a corporate lawyer makes considerably more than a school teacher. He could have looked anywhere in the country for a promotion, but she wouldn't budge. And when Pat said he wanted to have kids, she said no. He said he would stay at home and look after them; she didn't even have to give up her job. But she still said no.'

Ellie put her wine glass down and glanced at the time, obviously wanting to get this story over before anybody arrived.

'Pat had an affair. There's a pub that they all go to when there's been a late meeting or whatever at school. She was a barmaid there. Max said that he should have seen it coming because he saw Pat spending a lot of time with her, but it never occurred to him. Now he thinks it was desperation on Pat's part. He felt . . . I don't know how to put it; *unnecessary* would be the best description, I think. This girl made him feel important. Anyway, Georgia found out. We don't know exactly what happened, but apparently she received an anonymous text message. She kicked Pat out. I think she thought that he would come round to us and we'd talk some sense into him. But we were away for the weekend, and so he did the daftest thing. He went round to the other woman's house, and that was it as far as Georgia was concerned.'

Leo raised her eyebrows. Ellie frowned at her.

'You don't look very surprised. I would never have thought in a million years that they would split. They were devoted to each other. I thought you'd be astonished.'

'Come on, Ellie,' Leo said. 'This is me you're talking to. When did I ever have expectations of any man? So Pat has gone the way of them all. Shock, gulp, horror.'

Leo held out the hand clasping her wine glass towards Ellie as if she were pointing with it.

'Georgia's better off on her own.'

Ellie shook her head.

'She's not, you know. She's as miserable as sin. Pat is too, but he won't admit it. Max says he's been like death warmed up at school for the last few weeks. At least now it's the summer holidays he might use the break to get a grip, although apparently he disappeared from the rugby club last night part way through the evening. Well, at least that's what Max says, although how the hell he would know given the state he was in when he got home, I don't know.'

Leo couldn't help thinking that Pat wasn't the only one who had disappeared last night—something that she still hadn't got to the bottom of.

Mimi's sitting room had to be one of the most depressing rooms Patrick Keever had ever seen. He didn't mind that it was small. Small could be cosy. But it was devoid of . . . well, anything really. The only thing that lent any colour to the room was the hideous, swirly patterned carpet, and only then if orange was your thing. Other than that, it was a beige-on-beige effect. He longed for the pale sage green of his own sitting room carpet, with the soft, chocolate leather sofas, the open fireplace, and the black-and-white photos that he had taken himself, and spent so long framing and hanging.

Of course, he had nobody else to blame for how things were at the moment, but try as he might he couldn't seem to work out what to do. Georgia said she still loved him, but whenever he offered to leave Mimi and move back—which he would do in a flash—she narrowed her eyes and shook her head, looking at him as if he were mad. He appeared to be missing something, but Georgia wasn't offering any clues.

And now he was going to Max and Ellie's for dinner with the woman who had—to all intents and purposes—replaced Georgia in his life. It was hard for his friends, and he understood that. He and Max had been close since university—chalk and cheese, Georgia had always called them. Max the sporty, fun-loving guy who made everybody laugh, and Pat the serious, studious type who loved the theatre and the arts. But somehow they had clicked.

He looked at his watch. 'Mimi, are you nearly ready? We should be going,' he shouted up the stairs. You didn't have to shout too loudly in this room, though, or the neighbours would be knocking on the thin walls that divided the houses.

Mimi didn't answer, and he wasn't going to call again. He didn't want to go at all, if truth be told. But if they were going, and they ought to, he would rather arrive on time or a little early. He didn't want to walk into a room crowded with people. He always got the sense nowadays that people were talking about him. He'd had enough of that the night before at the end of term party. He had been so glad to escape—although in view of what had happened later perhaps he would have been better staying where he was. He hoped nobody had noticed his disappearing act because if they had, he would have a lot of explaining to do.

Pat was dreading the next few weeks. School holidays. As a teacher, he would normally look forward to this time, loving the sense that he had space in which to think about the following term, and to give some thought to his lesson planning. In previous years he'd had the house to himself for most of the holiday weeks while Georgia was at work, and he could read, make notes, listen to music, and generally prepare himself mentally for the academic year ahead. But this year he would be here, in this dump, with Mimi around far too much of the time for his liking.

His musings came to an abrupt end as he heard Mimi's heels clattering down the open-tread wooden staircase. She stopped at the bottom of the stairs, resting her hand on the newel post, and looked at Pat.

'Will I do?' she asked.

Pat couldn't quite work out the expression on her face, but it seemed to be a mixture of defiance and nerves. He felt a hard lump of guilt in his chest. He had to stop making comparisons, but her black dress was not a good length for her, falling just below her knees. In spite of the fact that it was the middle of summer, she was wearing a fuchsia cardigan with ruffles round the neck that didn't complement her skin tone, but he could see that she had made an effort.

'You look very nice,' he responded. He knew it wasn't enough. She wanted more, but this was all he was capable of. He'd been so attracted to her in the early days, but he had just wanted somebody to listen to him and see things from his perspective. She had stood on the other side of the bar in their local, and agreed with everything he'd said; told him what a catch he was and how Georgia must be mad to do anything to upset him. Mimi had said everything that he had wanted to hear, so when—after a particularly bad row with Georgia—she had invited him back here for a glass of wine and a place to calm down, he had broken down completely. And that had been his undoing. She had knelt on the floor at his feet and tried to kiss away his tears, and he couldn't bring himself to push her away. God, he was such a cliché. As a student of English he had read enough to know the potential impact of grief on desire, and as they had ripped at each other's clothes in a frenzy of lust, he had felt himself drowning in a maelstrom of churning emotions.

And so, here they were.

'Are you ready?' he asked.

'I suppose so. Do we *have* to go, Patrick? Can't we make an excuse? I'd rather be here with you—just the two of us. They wouldn't mind—Ellie doesn't even *like* me.'

Pat suppressed a sigh. 'Yes, we do have to go. Or at least, I do. Stay here, if you prefer.' He stifled the feeling of hope that she would agree.

'Of course not. I know it's been difficult with your friends, but you're with me now, and they're going to have to accept it.'

'Give them time, Mimi—please? Just be nice, and they'll come round, I promise.' He could see that was the wrong thing to say.

'I'm *always* nice to them. But they think they're better than us because they've got lots of money. He's only a teacher, and she's a nurse so I don't get why they think they're special.'

'Just to remind you that I, too, am only a teacher—and they don't think they're special. They're not like that at all. Ellie is the kindest woman I've ever met.'

Mimi walked towards him and grasped his upper arms. 'You're a deputy head, Patrick. That's not *only* a teacher at all. And you *are* special.' She leant towards him and kissed him on the mouth, her lips tasting of toothpaste and mouthwash.

Extracting himself gently, he grasped her hands. 'Come on. We'll be late. It's about a ten-minute walk, so that will be good timing.'

Pat forced a smile on his face, checked his mobile phone was in his pocket, and steered Mimi towards the front door.

11

Since Ellie's surprise announcement about Pat and Georgia, the two woman had said little and just worked side by side to finish the preparations for dinner—Ellie dishing out the orders and Leo trying her best to work to her sister's exacting standards. She had been wondering how to broach the subject of Ellie's mysterious behaviour the previous night, and as Ellie was busily transferring some tiny canapés onto a baking tray to pop in the oven, Leo decided this was probably the best chance she was going to get.

'Ellie—there's something I've been meaning to ask you. It's about last night. I heard you go out just after midnight. I assumed you'd gone to pick Max up, but he says not.'

Ellie spun round with a look of alarm on her face.

'You asked him? You told him I'd been out?'

'Calm down, sis. He mentioned that he'd been brought home by a mate. So I realised that wasn't why you went out. So what was it?'

Ellie had bent her head over the canapés again, her dark hair swinging down to hide her face, but Leo could hear the stress in her voice as she replied.

'Nothing. It was nothing. Just a friend in trouble, that's all. Please—don't mention it to Max, Leo.'

Leo was excused from responding by the ringing of Ellie's mobile. She watched her sister walk over to where she'd left it charging and pick it up. But she took one look at the name on the screen and rejected the call, throwing the mobile back onto the worktop.

Leo was puzzled but said nothing, observing her sister carefully. The phone rang again immediately, and Leo was amazed to see her sister's eyes narrow as she switched her phone off and pushed it as far away from her as the worktop would allow. Ellie's mouth was drawn in a hard, straight line of irritation.

'What's going on? Who was that on the phone? Is there a problem?'

There was no time for Ellie to respond as just then they heard the ringing of the doorbell. To Leo, it was almost as if Ellie sagged with relief as she turned round.

'Forget it, Leo. Just forget it, please? That will be Fiona and Charles. I'd better let them in.'

Wiping her hands on a tea towel, Ellie headed off to welcome the first of her guests, and a puzzled Leo made a hasty exit before she could be trapped into making polite conversation with Fiona.

Ellie was glad to have been saved from further interrogation by Leo, although she suspected it was a temporary reprieve. But Max had come down from reading to the twins and the moment had been avoided. Thank goodness.

Fiona had breezed in on a whiff of very expensive perfume in a dress that Ellie guessed must have cost thousands. It was gorgeous, but for God's sake, she was only coming round for dinner, not attending the Queen's Jubilee garden party. She handed Ellie a tastefully gift-wrapped box.

Ellie was still stressed by the events of the last half hour but forced herself to calm down. Her phone was off so she was safe, and Leo would keep quiet. She took a deep breath and painted a smile on her face as she unwrapped the present.

'It's good to see you both and thanks for the gift. It's very generous of you.'

'I sent Charles for it,' Fiona said, waving the back of her hand rather dismissively. 'He's quite good at that sort of thing.'

Ellie looked at the beautiful glass bottle of Pomegranate Noir bath oil. Much as she loved it, she thought she might put it in Leo's bathroom as an apology for being such a grumpy guts earlier.

'We've got a few minutes before I need to make any progress with the food. Perhaps Max could show Charles round. You've already had the tour, Fee—so do you want to have a drink in here, or go out into the garden?'

Fiona walked over to the window, no doubt to check the garden paths. Clearly finding them wanting, she took a seat on a chair by the window.

'Here's fine, darling. We don't need to go outside yet, do we? If that's fizz in the ice bucket, I wouldn't say no to a glass.'

'Of course. We can toast the house. I know I shouldn't say so myself, but it does look pretty amazing, doesn't it?' Ellie said, pouring two glasses of the delicious sparkling liquid. 'It's taking some getting used to. We've been here three weeks already, but it still all feels very new.'

'Your builder was quite a guy, wasn't he?' Fiona took the drink from Ellie's outstretched hand. 'Not only did he make a great job of the house, he had a hell of a body too. Especially when he was working without his T-shirt. I know you think I came round to offer moral support and ooh and aah over progress, but it was actually primarily to look at him. Don't you just love a man with wide shoulders and narrow hips?'

Ellie's reaction was instinctive.

'God, Fee. I wasn't looking at his body. He was here to do a job, that's all. For somebody who has no time for men, you're pretty observant all of a sudden.'

Fiona studied her glass for a few seconds. She didn't respond to Ellie's tone, and it was clear that she had another agenda entirely.

'Actually, Ellie, I'm not one hundred per cent sworn off men any more.' She looked up and straight into Ellie's eyes, a sly smile playing around her lips. 'I'm thinking of taking a lover.'

Ellie felt a wave of irritation at Fiona's flippant manner.

'*What*? Come on, Fiona, this is me you're talking to. You don't do sex. Not since . . .' Ellie glanced over her shoulder to make sure nobody else was in the room. 'Well, you know when. What's all this about? And if you've decided it's sex that you want, why not Charles?'

'Now who's being ridiculous? I chose Charles precisely because he isn't remotely interested in sex. But I want to know, before it's too late, whether I really am frigid or whether what I have is . . . curable. Look, nobody else knows what happened to me. I haven't even told Charles. He thinks sex isn't my thing, and I've never explained. At least you believed me—which is more than can be said for my marvellously supportive parents,' Fiona said sourly. 'Is it so wrong to want to know for sure?'

Ellie sat down on the chair facing Fiona. She knew she'd been a bit sharp, and it wasn't Fiona's fault that she was so stressed. Leaning forward, she looked at her friend and tried her best to show some sympathy.

'No, it's not wrong. But why now? What's happened to make you change your mind? I think it would be great for you to be having regular sex. There's nothing like a mind-blowing orgasm to make the world seem a better place.' She gave Fiona what she hoped was a supportive smile. 'But don't take a lover. Honestly, Fee, it's so much better when it's with somebody you love. And it could go horribly wrong. Look what happened to Pat and Georgia.'

'First of all, Charles and I are nothing like Pat and Georgia,' Fiona scoffed. 'I don't think he'd be too impressed if he found out that I'd been unfaithful, but as long as nobody discovered at work or at the golf club so that he could be labelled a cuckold, Charles would be fine. And what makes you think that I don't have orgasms?'

Ellie nearly choked on her drink. 'Okay, I get it. Spare me the details, please! I don't want to know. But it's not the same, you know. Not even close.'

'Well, you're right about that,' Fiona said, with a self-satisfied smile. 'It takes less than thirty seconds and it's a good deal less messy.'

In spite of everything, Ellie chuckled. For somebody who tried to be so posh, Fiona was after all just a girl from the village—and from the rough end at that. She might behave as if she was the queen of Cheshire, but her sense of the vaguely ridiculous had never left her. Except for that moment long ago that altered her life forever. Fiona may have alluded to it, but Ellie knew better than to mention it herself.

'So, do you have a candidate for this aberration of yours then?'

'Well, obviously it's nobody you know, but I've been stalking a man for a while. I'm not sure if he's going to deliver the goods yet, but I'm taking it slowly.'

The smile left Ellie's face.

'Don't use the word stalking, Fee. It's not funny, and if that's what you're doing then you need to stop it. Right now.'

She was relieved that at that moment Leo appeared in the doorway. It seemed her sister had been raiding her jewellery box, but frankly Leo deserved a whole lot more than a red necklace.

Fiona gave a small shout of surprise.

'Leo! I had no idea you were here. Ellie didn't tell me. What brings you to Cheshire? I thought you'd never darken this doorstep again.'

'Hi, Fiona. You're looking well—and looking expensive too, if I may say so. It seems your marriage turned out exactly the way you wanted it to.'

Fiona gave her most supercilious smile.

'How very cynical of you. But you are, of course, absolutely correct. Charles and I are perfect for each other.'

Ellie glared at her sister. So much for her being on her best behaviour. Fortunately, Leo appeared to pick up Ellie's thoughts and belatedly managed to force a smile on her face.

'As far as returning to this house goes, it's not recognisable is it? And I don't believe in ghosts,' Leo said, shrugging with a feigned indifference that may have fooled Fiona, but not Ellie.

'I'm not sure that I would want to be haunted by your mother if she was a ghost, Ellie,' Fiona said. 'What does Max call her? The Old Witch? She was such an embittered woman. She spent twenty years of her life hating people. I think that's rather sad.'

'Not when you're the one that's hated, it's not,' said Leo, with feeling.

'Well, she's gone now and left a bucket load of money so that you can all celebrate her passing in style.'

Ellie looked sadly at Leo, knowing how hard any conversation about The Old Witch was for her. So much so that Leo had refused every single penny that Ellie had offered her from the vast sum that her mother had been secretly amassing.

Once more, though, they were saved by the bell. Fifteen minutes early, so now they had to face the joys of bloody Mimi.

Much as Leo had liked Georgia and enjoyed her company, she had to say that she was intrigued to meet Pat's new woman. Max seemed somewhat relieved when he showed them both into the kitchen, no doubt because he wouldn't have to search for yet another topic of conversation with Charles, whose sole interest appeared to be money and all that it could buy.

Leo might not be a fan of parties, but she loved watching people and their reactions to each other, and tonight was one of those occasions when it felt as if people were not entirely comfortable. Bringing this new woman into the equation forced everything out of kilter somehow. Max had coped with Charles for years, and Fiona and Leo tolerated each other for Ellie's sake, while finding every possible opportunity to wind each other up. They both enjoyed it, although Ellie had never appreciated that. But the minute Pat walked through the door with Georgia's usurper, tension rippled through the room.

Pat didn't seem to have changed much, as far as Leo could see. His wheat-coloured hair always came as a bit of a shock because it looked like the colour came from a bottle, although Leo was positive that it didn't. Besides, it was cut so short that you'd see regrowth within a matter of days. He was what she would call Mr Regular. He was about average height, not skinny, but not much in terms of a physique. Insubstantial, she would say. Nice features, and a quiet but friendly voice, she'd always found him a bit bland next to Georgia's vivacious personality and dynamic style. But nice enough. Strange that this inoffensive man could now be causing such a stir.

Ellie tried to ease things, as she always did. She walked over to Pat and gave him a hug.

'It's good to see you, Pat. Have you recovered from last night? Max was decidedly ropey this morning, but he seems to have just about got over it. For a couple of teachers, you're a pair of reprobates if you ask me!' She kissed him on his cheek and gave him a grin, turning to greet his partner with a smile that looked forced to Leo.

'Max told me that Pat left early, though—obviously keen to get home to you, Mimi.'

Mimi? Leo thought. What sort of a bloody name was Mimi? Pat was looking a bit flustered.

'No, I didn't leave early. Not at all. Max has got that wrong, Ellie. He must have seen me pop out for a breath of fresh air. It gets very hot in that rugby club. Then I got lumbered with the serious folk at the other end of the bar. That's what comes of drinking orange juice all night, I suppose. Max probably thought I'd left, but I hadn't.'

'Oh well, I don't think he could see straight anyway. Come on Mimi—come and meet everybody.'

Leo watched as Mimi's eyes flicked around the room, first to Fiona, who was lounging in a comfortable chair, then to Leo, then quickly back to Pat—as if he might come to her rescue. But he had already turned towards Max and Charles, and was deep in conversation.

Ellie guided Mimi across the vast expanse of kitchen towards Fiona.

Mimi was nothing like Leo was expecting. A barmaid who had lured Pat away from Georgia had to be something special, surely? And yet this woman who was probably a couple of years younger than Leo was nothing out of the ordinary. She was taller than average, but stooped slightly as if she wasn't entirely comfortable with her height. Slim and rather flat-chested, with fine blonde hair which hung limply in waves around a face thickly covered in foundation at least two shades too dark as if to hide poor skin, she was pretty in an insipid kind of way. But there was nothing particularly interesting about her, and not a hint of a smile on her face. Perhaps Pat had become tired of living in the shadow of Georgia's radiance.

She could tell from where she was standing leaning against the fridge that Fiona was at her condescending best—or worst. Poor Mimi. It was pretty clear that there was no common ground for conversation, so Ellie steered Mimi back towards Leo.

'And this is my sister, Leo.'

Leo was not a great one for a handshake, so just smiled and said hi. But Mimi had a puzzled frown on her face.

'Half sister, surely?' she said, darting glances from one to the other. 'Have I got that wrong?'

She went pink under the orange makeup, and her neck a blotchy red. It was clear to Leo that she had spoken without thinking.

'We're sisters,' Ellie said.

Mimi turned to Ellie.

'But Patrick told me that's why you got all the money, and she didn't get any.' Mimi was digging herself in deeper and Leo was trying to think of a way of letting her off lightly. But she hadn't allowed for a slightly sozzled Fiona, who had come for yet another refill.

She leaned across in front of Leo and spoke to Mimi. 'I rather think the details of this family's finances and fortunes are their business, and theirs alone, don't you?'

Oh God, thought Leo. Now the poor girl's going to feel even more stupid.

'I'm sorry, but Patrick tells me everything. I didn't realise it was a sensitive subject.'

'It's okay,' Leo said. 'Take no notice of Fiona—she's pissed.'

Ellie obviously decided that this had to be nipped in the bud before it got out of hand.

'Well, right now I have some canapés to finish off. Everybody else will be here soon, so can I have some volunteers to help? Not you, Fee. You might splash something on that dress.'

12

The red Porsche pulled up on the cobbled drive outside Max and Ellie's front door, and Gary turned to his wife.

'Stop blubbering, Penny. For fuck's sake. You're going to make a complete fool out of me if you don't shut up. Stop it now, or I'll really give you something to cry about.'

'I'm sorry, Gary,' Penny said through her sobs. 'It's been a horrible day, and you seem so angry. I've only seen you for five minutes all day.'

'I *am* fucking angry. I don't just *seem* it. You whinge all the time about your day, your life. And I can't cope with you on top of everything else that I have to deal with.'

Gary glanced in the rearview mirror, and saw an unfamiliar figure walking up the long drive.

'Jesus. Now we're going to have a bleeding audience.'

Gary leaned across and grabbed Penny by her upper arms and gave her a sharp shake. She gave a small yelp of pain.

'Christ, woman—I'm not hurting you. Now, for the last time, sort yourself out. Blow your nose, put your sunglasses on, and behave like the lady you're not. For once in your life.'

Gary threw open his car door, and jumped out, a big smile plastered on his face as the newcomer got closer. Walking round the back of the Porsche, he approached the man with his hand outstretched.

'Hi. I'm Gary Bateman. I presume you're here for dinner with Max and Ellie. Good to meet you.'

The two men shook hands.

'Hello. Tom Douglas, the new neighbour. I only moved in myself recently, and Max was kind enough to come round and invite me tonight so I could meet some other people.'

'Well, they're very hospitable, and great neighbours. I should know. They lived next door to us for years before moving here.'

Gary started to fidget as he saw Tom glance towards Penny. When would she get out of the sodding car?

Just then, an old black Discovery swept into the drive, usefully distracting the attention from the passenger in the Porsche.

The familiar form of Sean Summers jumped out.

'Hey, Gary. What are you doing here, mate? Is something going on?'

Gary laughed with relief. A small diversion to prevent Penny showing him up even more.

'We're all here for a party. Max and Ellie are having a bit of a housewarming, which means Ellie's cooking—a treat not to be missed. This is their new neighbour, Tom. Tom, this is Sean—the guy who remodelled the whole house from the dismal place it used to be. You come to gate-crash, Sean?'

Sean looked uncomfortable for a moment. 'Oh bugger. It's a bit embarrassing turning up like this if they've got a party on. I'd better go. I brought round a spare set of keys that I'd been hanging on to, since I was passing anyway. Maybe you could give them to Ellie. Just let her know I was here, would you?'

Sean glanced towards the car. 'What's up with Penny—is she planning on staying in the car all night? Not that I blame her in that car. Since when did you have a Porsche, Gary? What's happened to the Beemer?'

Gary's irritation at Penny was growing by the minute. If she didn't get out of that car soon, he was going to have to make some excuse to take her home and come back on his own. He'd bloody kill her.

'I've got the car on trial. She's a beaut, isn't she? I've had her a few days. As for Penny, she had a sneezing fit on the way here. She can't stop, and apparently it's ruined her eye makeup, or something daft like that. I'll go and see how she is.'

Before Gary could move, the front door of the house was flung open, and Max came out to greet them.

'Good evening, gentlemen! What are you all doing hovering on the drive? Come in, and welcome to Willow Farm—unrecognisable, I think you'll find.' Max pointed to Sean. 'And it's all thanks to this man. Have you come to join us, Sean? You'd be very welcome. Do you want to go and get Bella?'

'Sorry, Max. I didn't know you'd got something on tonight. I'll get off, thanks. Bella's not so good tonight, so she wouldn't be able to come anyway.'

Gary was tempted to laugh. Of *course* Bella wouldn't be able to come. She be totally wasted and out of it by now, no doubt.

'Would she worry if you didn't get back, do you think? Or you could phone her and see if she's up for it if you like. Anyway, come on in, Sean, for goodness sake. Ellie will be delighted to see you.'

Sean appeared to hesitate, but not for long.

'If you're sure—that would be great, thanks. The kids are with my parents this weekend, and Bella will be asleep by now. If you're positive it's not going to be a problem?'

Gary was about to lose his cool completely if Penny didn't get out of the car in the next ten seconds. He glanced over his shoulder to see that the neighbour—Tom, was it?—had gone round to the passenger side and had opened the door. He was now crouching down talking to Penny. Jesus, he hoped the silly bitch maintained the sneezing story. What sort of an impression would this guy have of him, with a wife like that?

The kitchen was a hive of activity. As nobody appeared to want to move from the pre-dinner hubbub, Ellie had told Fiona to keep the men amused and Leo was laying out the canapés and preparing the asparagus and leek tarts to be popped under the grill for the glaze to brown. She hoped she was doing it right, but sincerely doubted it. Max had gone rushing off at the sound of the dull throb of an expensive car, and following the earlier hiccup with Mimi, things seem to have settled down.

Fiona had returned for yet more liquid refreshment when Max made his entry into the kitchen, along with not three, but four guests.

'Ellie—one extra guest for dinner! Look who I found lurking on the doorstep bearing gifts.' Max jangled a set of keys in the air, and placed them on the worktop.

As everyone turned to look at the new arrivals, Leo heard a sharp intake of air from somebody behind her. She turned her head quickly, but had no idea where it came from. Someone had received an unwelcome surprise, it would seem. This was getting more interesting by the minute.

Two faces Leo recognised were those of Gary and Penny Bateman, who handed Ellie a beautiful bunch of summer flowers. Penny seemed unable to meet Ellie's eyes, but Gary was grinning with rather excessive heartiness, while unashamedly looking Mimi up and down, no doubt trying to understand what kind of woman could have enticed Pat away from Georgia.

But any discomfort was dispelled by the new neighbour, Tom. He had brought Ellie a Hotel Chocolat summer basket, which looked too good to eat. Almost. He gave Ellie a peck on the cheek and thanked her for her kind invitation, and then passed a bottle of wine to Max.

Unwrapping it slowly, Leo could see Max's eyes open wide as he saw the bottle it contained.

'Tom, this is amazing. We're used to plonk, though, so anything would have done for us.'

'My brother was a collector of fine wines. I inherited them along with everything else of his. So I now have a shed full of bottles like this. Please, just enjoy it.'

Tom gave a modest smile, clearly not wanting Max to make too much of his gift.

'Well, all I can say is, I hope your shed has a good lock on it then!' Max responded. Leo was glad that he'd had the tact not to query the word 'inherited'. There had been enough of that already for one night.

'I'm a policeman. What do you think?' Tom said with a laugh.

Now here was a man who seemed comfortable in his own skin, Leo thought. He appeared confident without being cocky, and she liked his casual style and easy laugh. His blue eyes turned to look around the room without any sign of self-consciousness. Not a pretty man—his nose was too big for that, and his jaw a bit too wide—but there was something reassuringly normal about him.

Introductions were made all round, and gradually Max managed to move most people out into the garden. Fiona had been reluctant to go, until Max told her to take her bloody shoes off and feel the grass between her toes. She appeared to think that was very funny, and had gone along with the idea, her usual aloofness giving way to an uncharacteristic giddiness. Mimi had become even quieter since the rest of the guests had arrived, and had retreated further into her shell, clinging to Patrick as if her life depended on it with her eyes downcast. It was almost as if she wanted everybody to forget that she was there. Leo could only assume that it was the champagne that was making everybody slightly unhinged.

She had stayed in the kitchen to help Ellie, who was gathering together extra cutlery and glasses, banging each item down on the worktop as she collected what she needed from the various cupboards.

'I'm going to have to move everybody round a bit, to make space for one extra person. Can you put the last of the canapés onto plates when the oven pings and take them outside, please? It's a good job I made a couple of extra tarts in case one fell apart. I'll bloody kill Max. Why didn't he just take the keys that Sean brought round and let him go home?' Ellie stomped out of the room.

Leo frowned. Ellie had always been delighted to feed anybody at the drop of a hat. She hoped that having this smart new house wasn't going to change her kind and generous sister into a Fiona clone.

As she waited for the oven to do its work, she walked over to the window to look out into the garden where Ellie's guests were gathered. She could see that the builder guy looked a bit uncomfortable, but Max was doing his best to make him feel at home and Fiona was all over him like a rash.

Sean had what Leo would describe as a crumpled face, as if he was always either laughing or screwing his eyes up to look into the sun, and he had the strong physique of somebody used to carrying heavy weights, emphasised by his white T-shirt and black jeans. With his longish mid-brown hair and designer stubble, she could see that he might appeal to a lot of women.

Mimi was still clinging to Pat's arm, but in spite of that Leo couldn't help noticing that she seemed to be surreptitiously watching Gary's every move. Totally unaware of her scrutiny, Gary had wandered away from the crowd to examine with great interest Ellie's flower beds, but Mimi's eyes barely left him. What was *that* all about? Gary was one of those people who might have the right arrangement of features, but somehow he failed to be in any way attractive in Leo's view.

The oven timer sounded, forcing Leo to leave her contemplation of the strange behaviour of Ellie's guests to do as she had been asked with the canapés. She was in the process of transferring them to plates when she sensed somebody behind her. Turning round, she saw Gary appear in the doorway, standing watching her, apparently holding something behind his back.

'Sorry,' he said. 'I thought Ellie would be here.'

'She's in the dining room—she'll be back in a minute. Do you want me to go and find her?'

'No, it's okay. I'll go. I know where it is,' he said, with a slightly arrogant laugh. 'I should do. I approved the bloody plans.'

Leo hoped Gary wasn't going to start griping about his ill-fated career in the planning department, as usual. At least the canapés provided her with an excuse to escape.

'Okay. Tell Ellie to give me a shout if there's anything else I can do, would you?'

Gary sidled around Leo, keeping his hands behind his back. *Odder and odder*, she thought as she picked up the tray of food and made her way to the door.

13

The starters had gone down well, and there was plenty of buzz around the table, but Ellie had refused all offers of help to serve up the second course. She'd needed to escape. She was trying. God knows, she was doing her best. But her throat was almost closed with tension, and her jaw ached from maintaining a fixed grin. She had a feeling that her life was out of control. When she'd planned this dinner, she had expected it to be a joyful occasion, but it wasn't.

Working on autopilot, she took the plates for the next course from the cupboard, and walked over to the fridge to take out the sea bass, already prepared for cooking. Opening the door, she stopped dead and stared into the fridge.

Sitting next to the plate of fish was a single yellow rose.

She could feel her body start to shake. *He's been in here—alone.* She spun round, her eyes exploring every corner of the kitchen in case he was still there, hovering in the shadows. When had he done this? And why had she ever told him how much she loved yellow roses?

He wants me to know he's watching me, she thought. But I already know that—he never lets me forget. How *can* I forget?

With one swift movement, she grasped the rose by its thorny stem and threw it in the waste bin. She placed both hands on the worktop and leant hard against them, trying to calm her shaking. Noticing blood pulsing from her thumb, she grabbed a piece of kitchen roll, and wrapped it tightly round the wound.

Then she saw her mobile sitting there. She needed some support, and there was only one person she could talk to. Grabbing the phone, she switched it on.

Six missed calls. All from the same person earlier this evening. She shouldn't have ignored him. But what was he *thinking*, calling her here when

Max was around. She should have answered and told him again to leave her alone. She'd thought he would get the message if she ignored him.

Stabbing her finger hard on the screen, she deleted the calls, and quickly started to write a text. Hearing a slight sound behind her, she turned round with a guilty start.

'Ellie, are you okay? I came to see if I could help at all.' She wondered how long Mimi had been standing there, and felt uncomfortable as she met her inscrutable gaze. She put her phone down quickly. The text could wait.

'Sorry, Mimi. I caught my finger on something and wanted it to stop bleeding. It wouldn't do to drip blood on the fish and I didn't think it would matter much if the next course was delayed.'

'I'm sure everybody will be fine for a while,' Mimi said. 'Thanks for introducing me to your friends. It's good to meet more of Patrick's circle. Maybe when we get a bigger place after his divorce we can invite everybody round to us.'

Ellie nearly choked at the word 'divorce' and wondered if Pat knew that he was getting one. She was damn sure Georgia didn't.

'Do you mind if I ask you about your friends? It's just that you all seem to know each other so well, and I feel a bit out of it if you know what I mean.'

'I'm sorry,' Ellie said. 'That's not intentional. What do you want to know?'

Ellie knew she sounded abrupt, but she couldn't help it. She had to try harder, though—for Pat's sake.

'Fiona and Charles—they seem a bit different to the rest of you.'

Ellie nearly smiled at that.

'Charles is a very wealthy investment banker. He works in London and he met Fiona when she was living there. She used to go to school with me, and then she left the village and we lost touch. She's only been back a few years. Don't worry about not knowing anybody, though. Tom knows nobody at all, and at least you've met me and Max before. You're not the only newcomer.'

'What about the other couple—Gary and Penny I think you said they were called.'

'Gary's head of planning for the local council—they used to be our neighbours before we moved here. You may have seen him in the pub, actually—although I'm not sure which one he goes to these days.'

'I don't remember him, but I get to meet a lot of people that way. My future husband for one,' Mimi said with a tinkling laugh that Ellie couldn't echo. 'And of course, people come in from the school all the time. Max has been in a few times recently with that PE teacher he seems so fond of.'

You little cow, Ellie thought. And I was trying to be nice to you.

She'd only met Mimi three times, and this was the second time she'd mentioned the gorgeous Alannah, and Max's relationship with her.

Well, whatever was going on, Ellie wasn't going to rise to the bait now.

'Yes, Max has mentioned that they've been in. Now look, Mimi, I need to get on with the next course, so if you don't mind spreading the plates out, I'll have the fish done in a few minutes. Do you think you could take the cling film off the chillies and ginger, and all those other bits, please? I'm going to grab my wine glass from the table.'

And I might just throw it in your face, she couldn't help thinking.

As Ellie went out, Mimi started to do as she had been asked. There was no way she was giving them any more reasons to think she was a waste of space. They already thought Patrick was mental, and they didn't try very hard to hide it. She knew she was a good actress, although occasionally she couldn't stop the odd flush to her skin and neck. But these people were all so self-satisfied in their perfect little worlds, and she was struggling to keep a smile on her face.

She was going to keep Patrick, though, whatever they thought. Maybe causing a bit of disruption in the Ellie and Max household might distract them for long enough to forget about her and stop interfering. They may have invited her tonight, but she knew they were wishing Georgia was here instead. How did they think that made her feel?

She savagely tore the cling film off the highly organised individual dishes that Ellie had laid out with the ingredients to accompany the fish, screwing it up into a tight ball.

She despised them all—but one more than the rest.

Lifting the lid of the bin, she was about to hurl the ball of cling film in when she saw something that caused her frustration to be replaced by curiosity. A perfect single yellow rose lay on top of the rubbish. Strange. Why would Ellie have thrown it away?

As she turned back to the worktop, she caught sight of a mobile phone, and remembered that Ellie had been typing a text message when she'd interrupted her.

Mimi peeped around the opening into the dining room, and could see that Ellie was talking to Charles. She couldn't help noticing that Patrick had left the room too. Her mouth tightened into a thin line.

Turning her back to the door, she picked up Ellie's phone and touched the screen. And there was the message—incomplete, but complete enough. She narrowed her eyes at its content. So *that's* why the rose was in the bin. An unwanted gift. And she knew exactly where it had come from.

Mimi's skin prickled with the heat of anger when she saw who Ellie had been texting. She quickly typed a text of her own, pressed send, then erased the evidence.

At that moment she heard the message tone of her own phone, buried in her handbag on the kitchen table. She hadn't thought she would be needing it tonight. She walked over and checked the screen, already knowing what it would say.

14

The mood around the table was strange. To Leo it seemed as if everyone was acting a part that was different from any version of themselves she had ever seen. As an observer of this intriguing phenomenon she had the best seat in the house, between a slightly manic Max, who appeared determined to be jolly, and a very subdued Pat. She was opposite the new neighbour, who appeared remarkably sane in comparison to everybody else, and looked casually trendy tonight in a white linen short-sleeved shirt over dark blue chinos. She was keen to learn his story, but perhaps now wasn't the right time.

Mimi was like a limpet around Pat—whom she insisted on calling Patrick because apparently Pat was a girl's name. Max, being Max, had tried to oblige for about two minutes, but had quickly forgotten and reverted to the name he had been using since they met at university nearly eighteen years ago. Pat, on the other hand, seemed almost uncomfortable. There was no evidence of his occasional moments of dry humour tonight.

She felt a bit sorry for Ellie and Max's builder. He had been seated between Mimi and Gary, and was definitely ill at ease. Mind you, that wasn't surprising, as Mimi wouldn't speak to him in case she missed something that Pat was saying, and Gary, as usual, was only interested in talking about himself and in an even louder voice than normal. Leo hadn't seen Gary for some time, and had forgotten what an idiot he could be—especially in the way he spoke to his wife. Penny had hair the colour of butter shortbread, and she'd grown it long so that when she leaned forward a shiny curtain of pale gold hid her face from view. With a sixties-style fringe, there wasn't much of her left to see. She had barely lifted her head all evening, apparently intent on focusing on the food, but on the occasions that she did look up, Leo noticed that the skin under her eyes was tinged with purple, as if she wasn't getting enough sleep. Penny had been a kind and thoughtful neighbour for

Ellie, especially after the twins were born, and Leo was sure that Max only put up with Gary because he was Penny's husband.

Gary had the sort of haircut that required constant brushing back with the fingers, or even—God help us—the occasional flick of the head like a shy girl on her first date. There was no doubt that he was technically a handsome guy, with piercing blue eyes, a broad forehead, and sensuous lips, which opened to reveal the brightest teeth that Leo had ever seen. Somebody had been a little excessive with the whitening treatments, it would seem. But he wore the look of a person who believes himself to be superior, as if he were looking down his nose at everybody around him. Leo couldn't help enjoying the fact that she could see the back of Gary's head in the mirror on the wall behind him, and there was undoubtedly a sign of thinning there. He wasn't going to like that one little bit.

As Mimi was whispering in Pat's ear, Leo took the opportunity to lean across them and talk to Sean.

'You've made a wonderful job of renovating the house, Sean. It's superb.'

Tom chipped in too, obviously realising that Leo was trying to bring Sean into the conversation.

'Yes, it's beautiful. I've recently done my own place. Not a patch on this, of course. Are you working on any more projects?' Tom asked.

'I've got something on the go, but it's still a bit hush-hush. We're hoping to get everything signed in the next week or so,' Sean answered. 'And then we need to get the plans approved, which my friend on my right here tells me shouldn't be a problem.'

He nudged Gary as he spoke.

'What do you do then, Gary?' Tom asked

'I'm head of planning for the council,' Gary answered. 'Crap job, but somebody's got to do it!'

Leo knew all about Gary's thwarted ambitions. His favourite line was that he was originally going to be an architect, but Penny buggered all that up for him by falling pregnant. She wasn't going to give him the opportunity to bore everybody with that line again, so Leo turned to Ellie.

'The food is amazing, Ellie. As always.'

'Thanks, Leo.' Ellie turned to the rest of the guests. 'I had to go into work today, so I didn't have as long as I'd wanted to prepare. I hope everything's all right?'

Leo looked at her in disbelief, as everybody passed on the congratulations. How could she think it was anything *other* than okay? Ellie was a wonderful cook, and after the oriental sea bass, they had feasted on a tender fillet of beef in a soy honey glaze. In fact, half the table still hadn't finished and were taking it slowly.

'I seem to remember you saying that you're a nurse, Ellie—is that right?' Tom asked.

'Yes. At the Royal, in the ICU. I only work three shifts a week, and not usually on a Saturday. But we're a bit short-staffed with the holidays, and we got a serious head injury in during the night. We can't leave them unattended.'

Pat put his knife and fork down and leaned towards Ellie across the table.

'It wasn't Abbie Campbell, was it by any chance Ellie?' Pat asked quietly.

'Abbie Campbell? Why, what's happened to her, for God's sake?' Max said. His habitual smile had disappeared in an instant. The whole table fell silent as Max's tone penetrated the buzz of conversation.

'The Head had a call from the police in the middle of the night to say that a young girl had been rushed to hospital, but nobody had been reported missing, and they didn't know who she was. They wanted him to go and see if he could identify her.'

'The Head?' Max raised his eyes to the glass ceiling. 'I don't think he'd recognise more than about five per cent of the kids. What did he do?'

'He called Alannah at about four thirty this morning, apparently. She knows all the girls, of course.'

'I'm amazed that she was sober enough to identify anybody,' Ellie said in a slightly acid tone.

'Oh, she wasn't drinking last night. She was driving, wasn't she Max?' Pat asked. Without waiting for an answer, he continued. 'Anyway, she identified Abbie. I was going to tell you, but I decided to wait until later so as not to spoil the evening.'

'Christ. What happened to the poor kid?' Max asked.

'She was knocked over last night on the back road. A hit-and-run. Left for dead, I'm afraid.'

'God almighty. What sort of a bastard would do that?'

Max looked stunned for a moment, then glanced around the table realising that his guests were a bit excluded from this conversation.

'Sorry, everybody. But this is dreadful news. Abbie's a pupil at our school. She's only fourteen and she's a nice kid, if a bit quiet. I don't have much to do with her personally, being the boys' PE teacher, but Pat's a deputy head, and he knows her quite well. Do you know how she's doing, Ellie?'

Nobody was eating, and everybody's cutlery had been gently laid down as the shock that something like this could happen in their village permeated the room. Turning towards Ellie, Leo couldn't help noticing her sister's expression. She looked close to tears.

'I'm afraid she's in a critical condition. I'm sorry to say that it's not looking very hopeful,' Ellie said.

For once, even Fiona had the sense to be quiet. Tom Douglas broke the silence, looking around the room as he did so. Ever the policeman, Leo thought.

'I heard about the accident, actually. A friend of mine is on the investigation team. Apparently she was found in the early hours of this morning. I don't know much more than that, though.' Leo had to wonder how honest Tom was being. She didn't doubt for a moment that—one policeman to another—his friend would have shared some of the finer details, but Tom wasn't about to reveal more than the basics.

'The early hours? And she wasn't reported missing?' Max said. 'That doesn't sound right to me. She comes from a good family—there's no way they wouldn't know where she was. I can't believe she would have snuck out in the dark on her own. She's not that kind of kid at all.'

Nobody appeared to have any suggestions to explain this, and the table remained quiet. There was a stillness in the room which Leo found hard to place, as if more than one person was holding his or her breath. She was being fanciful.

Max broke the silence.

'Did you see anything on your way home from the barbecue, Pat? I never worked out what time you left the rugby club. One minute you were there, the next you weren't.'

'I didn't go home that way,' Pat said quietly.

'What do you mean? There isn't another . . .'

'Can I top anybody's wine up?' Ellie said in a loud voice, giving Max a glare that only he and Leo could see.

Tom was watching reactions round the table. He'd been asked to see what gossip he could pick up, so maybe this would be as good a place as any to start.

'How well did you know this girl, Pat?' Tom asked. Pat had been pretty quiet all evening, and had seemed a bit bland in comparison to the others. If he'd been interviewing him, though, Tom would have said that Pat was a man with something to hide.

'I know her quite well. I look after the pastoral care side of things at school, and Abbie has a few issues. She's a quiet, well-behaved girl, but she does have problems making friends.'

'Obviously not as quiet as you think, darling,' Mimi said. 'What sort of fourteen-year-old is out on the streets at that time of night?'

Tom saw a brief spark of anger in Leo's eyes. She spoke sharply, her cheeks flushed.

'We don't know what goes on behind closed doors, do we? We don't know what her home life was like, and we shouldn't condemn the girl out of hand.'

'Her parents are good people,' Pat said. 'I doubt she was running away.'

'I'm with Mimi on this,' Gary added, twirling the stem of his wine glass in his fingers and studying its contents. 'There's no way that my kids will be out at that time of night when they're that age. Bloody ridiculous.'

Pat's lips had tightened.

'I think it's probably best to reserve judgement until we know a bit more, don't you?' he said.

Sean leaned forward so that he could speak to Tom across Gary and Penny. 'I've got a fourteen-year-old stepdaughter myself. The parents must be going through hell. What are the chances of catching the person that did this, in your experience?'

Sean's face was a picture of concern. He'd not had much to say up to now, and Tom had noticed a few times that he seemed a bit fidgety.

'It depends,' Tom answered. 'There could be all sorts of forensic evidence; tyre tracks, paint or glass fragments, that kind of thing.' Tom knew perfectly well that there was no evidence found at the scene, but he wasn't about to say so. He expected every word he said would get round the village, and he sincerely hoped that somebody would soon be feeling very guilty, and very scared. 'In this case, it seems that the girl was moved to the side of the road, so that could very well be a source of evidence, and of course there's CCTV and ANPR.'

He noticed a few puzzled frowns.

'I know what that is,' Charles said, looking pleased with himself. 'Automatic number plate recognition. Fancy cameras that can read the characters and store them. That might just catch the scoundrel who did this.' He looked around the table from face to face, his eyes not settling for long on any one person.

'Charles is right,' Tom said. 'I don't know what the coverage is like around here, but I'm sure they'll be checking to find out who was out and about at that time of night, using every resource possible. There'll probably be some cameras on the main trunk roads and in the village—at the petrol station, for example. Anybody who passed through might be questioned. I gather that the back road is mainly used by people from the village, so that might narrow things down a bit. And of course, they'll be hoping that people who were driving in the area at the time will make themselves known to the police and make their job easier. Most people don't realise how often they're caught on camera, so let's hope this bastard is one of them.'

The whole table was hanging onto Tom's every word, as if absorbing the implications. Gary broke the silence.

'Didn't you say it was your end of term party last night, Max?' he said. 'I would have thought the back road would have been unusually busy. It's the most direct route to the village, after all. And I bet half of your mates were bladdered. You should tell your policeman pal that he should start there, Tom. At the school.'

Max sensibly declined to comment but he did look as if he would like to punch Gary in the teeth for suggesting such a thing about his friends. Even Charles gave Gary a dark look, his bushy eyebrows meeting as he frowned. Tom looked at Gary's jutting chin, raised as if he were superior to everybody in the room, with lips curled upwards, although without a hint of a smile in his eyes. Gary hadn't finished.

'And what about all you girls, home alone while the boys were out enjoying themselves. What were you lot up to last night, then? Out on the razz, I bet.'

Ellie was sitting directly opposite Gary, and she appeared to be getting the full benefit of his sly grin. Before anybody could comment, support came from an unexpected source.

'Stop being a tosser, Gaz,' Sean said. 'The poor kid might die, and you're teasing the girls? Bad taste, mate.'

'It was a fucking joke, Sean. Lighten up.' Gary ran his fingers through his slicked-back hair and raised his eyes to heaven, as if Sean were the one behaving like a prat. There was an embarrassed pause as Gary looked round, obviously hoping—and failing—to get smiles of support from the other guests.

Sean's weathered face looked slightly flushed as he turned to Tom.

'I've never noticed any cameras on the back road,' Sean said. 'So if they don't find any forensic evidence, it sounds like it might be a tough nut to crack.'

'Well, I bet there's one person who hopes this child doesn't recover,' said Charles, filling his wine glass from the expensive bottle that Tom had brought.

'Charles, even by your standards that's a pretty crass statement,' Fiona said. 'What on earth do you mean?'

Charles shrugged, casting another glance around the room at those seated at the table.

'If the girl wakes up, she might well remember what type of car hit her. That's all I'm saying. I presume he or she won't want to go to prison.'

Fiona gave her husband a disparaging look.

'Shall we change the subject? This is a bit too depressing for a party, don't you think?' she asked.

Tom couldn't help thinking that it wasn't half as depressing as having a daughter on the critical list in hospital.

Max appeared to drag himself back from thoughts of Abbie and the previous night, as if realising belatedly that he was the host. He jumped to his feet.

'Listen, everybody. It's difficult to forget about Abbie—particularly for those of us who know her, or are in some way connected to her. But I was intending to propose a toast to the new house. Let's have a toast first to Abbie, wishing her a safe recovery, and then move on. There's nothing we can do to help at the moment, other than to wish her well.'

After the round of toasts, conversation returned to normal if slightly more subdued levels.

Tom was sitting next to Penny, who had been very quiet all evening despite his attempts to make conversation. So he was surprised when she turned towards him and spoke in a quiet voice.

'I know we're not supposed to be talking about this, Tom—but what happens next? Will the police want to speak to everybody who was out last night?'

Tom felt, rather than saw, Gary's arm go round Penny. At last he's showing her some affection, he thought. He wasn't sure what had been going on when this couple had arrived, but he had been around long enough to know that although a fit of sneezing could make your eyes stream, it rarely made your chin wobble. And he was well aware that Gary had barely spoken two words to his wife all night, although he'd been the life and soul of the party in all other ways.

He sensed that a few people round the room had picked up on Penny's question and were waiting to hear his response, and he certainly had Leo's full attention. Penny's arm suddenly jerked slightly, splashing red wine on the tablecloth. She grabbed her napkin and furiously started to dab at the stain, as Gary tutted and removed his arm.

Without waiting to hear Tom's answer to Penny's question, Leo smiled across the table.

'Don't worry about that, Penny,' she said. 'It's only a drop. We'll get it out later. And we've not had chance for a catch-up tonight, so do you fancy helping me to clear the table to give Ellie a bit of a break?'

Leo jumped up and started busying herself with the plates, but not before Tom had intercepted the look she cast at Gary.

'I tell you what,' Max said. 'Why don't you all go and have a look round the house? After all, it's what you came to see. Or wander in the garden— let's have a break from Ellie's scrumptious food and stretch our legs for ten minutes. Is that okay with you Ellie?'

Ellie's attention seemed to be dragged back from a million miles away. She gave a brave attempt at a beaming smile and nodded as if entirely in agreement.

'Well, I for one can't move,' Mimi said. 'I sometimes think it's a good thing that I only cook simple food, although I do envy people who just eat what they like and don't give a damn about their waistlines.'

Tom didn't miss the way Ellie's mouth tightened. Without a word she picked up the remainder of the serving dishes and made her way out of the dining room.

15

Leo and Penny had followed Ellie into the kitchen to find her standing by the open window to the garden, with her arms tightly folded.

'Come on, Ellie. I know you think it was a pointed remark, but you're being over-sensitive. She probably thought she was being friendly by praising your cooking.'

'Like hell she did. Did you see her face? I suppose she also intended it to be a compliment when she said that I *always* look nice in this dress, even though she's only seen me in it twice. Max doesn't get it that there is one extra word in that sentence that changes its meaning. He thinks I'm paranoid about Mimi. If only he knew.'

Leo had the sense to realise that arguing wasn't going to achieve anything.

'Leave it, Ellie. Go and enjoy your friends. Penny and I have got this.'

Ellie's arms dropped to her side and the stiffness melted as if all the energy had been sapped from her body.

'Thanks, you two. But I think I'll take a few minutes on my own, if that's okay. I'm going to go upstairs, but I don't want to go through the dining room. I'll go round by the garden and let myself in through the side door.'

Without turning round she headed out, melting into the dark shadows of the night.

Leo turned to Penny with a smile. She knew Penny would wonder what had just happened, but would be too polite to ask.

'Sorry about that—it's nothing to worry about. Let's get these plates sorted.'

Leo had met Gary and Penny years ago when they lived next door to Ellie and Max, and she'd always felt theirs was an unbalanced relationship, but until tonight there was nothing she could put her finger on. She decided to try to draw Penny out of herself a little and move away from the tricky subject of Ellie's incongruous behaviour by asking about another of their guests.

'Did I hear Sean say that he has a daughter? Where's his wife tonight?'

Penny turned round and leaned on the Aga rail.

'Ah, well. There's a bit of history there. Sean was known for years as the village stud. Everybody's idea of the perfect bit of rough—always smiling, twinkly eyes, but hard, calloused hands and muscles to die for. He was single and he loved it. Then Bella arrived out of nowhere about five years ago. She was so glamorous, all the men were agog. She's got a daughter—about fourteen or fifteen, I think—and Sean fell for Bella. Hook, line, and sinker.'

Leo waited. Penny went quiet.

'And . . . ?'

'I hate gossips, Leo. There but for the grace of God, I always think when I hear bad things about people. At least if I tell you, it will be fact and not the embroidered version you'll probably hear in the village.'

Penny paused. She picked up a tea towel, as if to dry hands that weren't even wet.

'They had a child—a boy. Bella started to drink after he was born. Now, it seems, she's become an alcoholic. Nobody knows much about her before she came here, but maybe she was already ill and disguised it well. Or maybe it was kicked off by postnatal depression. Whatever it was, everybody slags her off because of the way she is now. It's true that she does look terrible. A bit like a blown-up version of what she was, if that makes sense. Everything that was once big and seductive, like her lips, hair, and figure, are now twice the size. She apparently lies on the sofa all day watching the television, from what Gary says. He knows Sean quite well. And then she gets smashed and Sean puts her to bed. He's great with the kids, though.'

Oh goodness, poor Sean, thought Leo. It wasn't appropriate to ask more, and the two women were silent for a moment.

'Awful news about the accident, wasn't it,' Penny said, changing the subject. 'My girls knew about it. One of their friends has a sister in Abbie's class, and she says they all went out for an end of term celebration last night to the burger place in town. Abbie was with them—but nobody knows what happened after that. The worst of it is that she was knocked down on the back road. Other than people from the village, nobody else uses it. It might well be somebody we know. Imagine how awful that would be.'

'It must be difficult having daughters of your own when you hear stories like that. A fourteen-year-old being out that late and in the middle of nowhere. I don't know how you sleep!'

'Hah—that's easy an easy one to answer. Badly! I have a prescription for sleeping tablets, but I don't always take them. It depends whether Gary's home or not.'

The conversation was interrupted by a worried-looking Max.

'Have you seen Ellie, Leo?' he asked. 'I wanted to check that she's okay.'

'She was here a minute ago. She wasn't very happy with Mimi, though.'

'I'm sure it was just a throwaway remark, but Pat's given her hell for being insensitive, and she's stormed off somewhere saying that he's never on her side. Now it seems everybody's disappeared, so I think I'll go and look for Ellie.'

For some reason, Leo had the feeling that this wouldn't be a great idea.

'She said she needed a couple of minutes, Max. She's probably feeling stressed about that poor kid she's been looking after at the hospital, and the talk about the accident tonight just reminded her. I think that if any of us tries to speak to her, she might crumble. I'm sure she'll be back in a few minutes to finish off the dessert, when she's got herself together.'

Ellie knew she was behaving badly. But she felt wretched. The phone calls, the rose, the constant, nagging doubts about Max. How she was going to survive the rest of the evening she didn't know. She felt as if a scream were building up inside her chest, just waiting to be released.

She walked around the back of the house, away from the kitchen, away from people. She was glad of the dark now. All she could hear were her own footsteps on the gravel path and the occasional rustle of leaves as a light breeze brushed them. After all she'd learned tonight, she needed time to think.

She had known about Abbie's accident, of course, but she hadn't been given any of the specifics and she'd had no idea where the accident had happened.

The back road. What if . . .

No. She mustn't think like that. She had to be wrong.

Tom said the police were going to want to know who was out and where they were going. How was she going to keep this to herself? She hadn't been through the village or on any of the main roads, so her car was unlikely to have been picked up on camera. She had kept to the lanes all the way. But it wasn't only *her* car that she had to worry about. What about *his*?

She should have refused to meet him last night, but somehow he had known that Leo was there—of course he had. He was always there, watching. So the children were no excuse for her to stay home. Besides, she had sincerely hoped it would be a chance to put an end to it all. It hadn't worked. Each day it seemed as if he wanted more from her.

If his car had been spotted, he would have to say where he'd been—and possibly who with. She had no idea of how far she might have to go to prevent Max from discovering the truth. How would she ever be able to explain it to him?

She should go to the police and admit that she was out. She knew that. But she hadn't seen anything, and the impact on her family if the reason were made public would be catastrophic. If it hadn't been for the accident, none of this would have had to come out. She knew what she *should* do, but . . .

She turned towards the far side of the house, past the gravel parking area that they had created but never used. Without lights from inside the house, the night was black and it settled around her like a dense fog.

But Ellie's mind was elsewhere. There was one thing that nobody had mentioned tonight. She had been the one looking after Abbie today, so she'd seen the terrible state of her feet and her legs. What had happened? She couldn't say anything, of course, but it was so strange. How had she got that way?

Ellie was abruptly jolted out of her reverie.

What was that?

She'd heard the soft crunch of gravel, as if somebody had taken a step, and stopped. She stood still for a second and glanced over her shoulder, her gaze trying to bore a hole through the inky night.

Oh no. Not tonight. Please.

She turned back, and started to move more quickly. The sound of her footsteps drowned out any other noise, but just as she made it to the side door, she was sure she heard somebody whisper her name.

Ellie.

Fiona had made her way into the room that Ellie now called the library. It was quite a small room in relation to the others in the house, but it was cosy with an open fireplace and book-lined walls. Two wingback chairs were placed on either side of the fire, and there was a deep and comfortable-looking window seat. She could imagine Ellie spending hours in here when she wasn't run ragged by the twins.

She left the door slightly ajar, knowing perfectly well that she would be followed. She walked over to the farthest bookshelf from the door and pretended to browse the books. She didn't have long to wait. The door opened slowly, and was quietly closed before either of them spoke.

'I thought I might find you here. An interesting evening, wouldn't you say?'

Fiona smiled. 'A few tricky moments, I agree. I can't help wondering what the sexy new neighbour made of it all. I quite like the look of him.' She knew she was provoking him, but then that was the idea.

'He's not your type, Fiona. Far too straight. You need somebody who's a bit wild, don't you think?'

'Like you, you mean? Maybe. Maybe not.'

He laughed and stroked her arm.

'You look amazing tonight, but then you know that, don't you?'

Fiona randomly pulled a book from the shelves so that she could at least appear to be reading it if somebody came in. She gave her admirer a coquettish smile.

'You said that last night, too.'

The man gripped her arm, and gave her a serious look.

'Speaking of last night, does Charles know that I was round?'

'Of course not. Why on earth would I tell Charles?'

'Well, I do have a perfectly valid reason to call, don't I?' he replied.

'Not if you stay drinking with me until after midnight, you don't. I think that's stretching it a bit. Why do you ask, anyway?'

He turned away from her and walked towards the window.

'I'm going to have to say I was home by eleven. You do realise that, don't you? I don't think I passed any cameras, but if I admit to being out, I'll have to say where I was. So can we keep it to ourselves, do you think?'

'How will you get away with that? Surely you were missed?'

'Trust me, it's not an issue.'

Fiona shrugged. It was best if Charles didn't know. She could do without an inquisition.

'Well, Charles goes back to London on Monday morning, so perhaps I could give you a call sometime. When I feel like some company.'

He swivelled on his heel towards her.

'How long are you going to keep me hanging on, Fiona? We're not kids, are we? What's the game?'

Fiona put the book back on the shelf and walked towards the door.

'The game is called seduction, darling. And you're not there yet.'

She opened the door, and left the room without a backward glance.

Max had taken Leo's advice to leave Ellie in peace, and he had escaped to the garden. His eyes had become accustomed to the low lighting and he saw Fiona come around from the front of the house, her dress briefly illuminated by the lights on the drive. Still without shoes, she looked almost ethereal as she was backlit by the garden lamps.

Max noticed the blond hair and slight form of his friend as he appeared from the darker depths of the garden, cagily pushing his mobile back in his pocket. Pat made his way over to Max and spoke in a quiet voice.

'Listen, Max. Do me a favour, will you? Lay off the talk about last night? You're right, I did disappear. But I don't want anybody to know—least of all Mimi. I've already tried to cover it. Let's leave it at that, shall we?'

Max looked at Pat and frowned.

'It's nothing to do with me, but you need to be a bit more guarded with all that phone activity, you know. You're about as subtle as a flying brick.'

Pat had the grace to look a bit embarrassed.

'I'd better go and talk to Mimi, I guess. Make amends. You and I can have a chat later—I'd love to know what you make of this Abbie business. It stinks, doesn't it? Trouble is, I'm not quite sure what of.'

'Me neither. Has anybody spoken to the parents, do you know?'

'I've got to go and see them tomorrow—boss's orders. We all know that he's useless on these occasions. Mimi's going to be pissed about that too. She had this idea of us going out for lunch, or something. I'd better go and break the news and do something to appease her or I'm dead. I'll speak to you later.'

With shoulders hunched in a pose of true dejection, Pat wandered off in the direction of the fishpond, where Max could just make out Mimi's back. Not for the first time, he questioned what the hell his friend was doing. It was obvious to everybody that he wasn't happy, but Ellie had been right to stop him talking about Pat's route home from the rugby club. She either knew, or guessed, that Pat hadn't gone straight home, which probably meant that Georgia had to figure in this somewhere. What was his friend *doing?* Max almost felt sorry for Mimi.

His thoughts were interrupted as he saw Sean and Gary step out from the glass doors to the atrium dining room, talking quietly to each other. He saw

Gary clap Sean on his shoulder and heard him laugh, and then he disappeared back into the house.

Knowing that Sean couldn't see him easily, he gave a low whistle to attract his attention and Sean made his way across the grass. To Max, Sean had always had the natural swagger of a confident man. Ellie had once said that he strutted like an Italian, and Max knew just what she meant—loose limbed and in no doubt of his charms. Some of his usual self-assurance seemed to be missing tonight, though.

'I'm glad you called round, Sean. It was good to have you here. We should have invited you, but we weren't sure how you would cope with an evening with Charles, and with the Pat and Mimi thing it was already going to be awkward enough. I'm not sure how you'd have felt if we'd asked Bella, either.'

Sean's voice was low.

'I wouldn't have expected an invite, Max. I'm the builder. And Bella wouldn't have come anyway. You know that.'

There was a moment's silence while Max contemplated the difficulties of living with somebody like Bella.

'How are the plans going?' Max asked, wanting to get round to the real reason for talking to Sean. 'I'd love to get all of this sorted and under way before the end of the summer holiday. It's much easier while I'm off school. You know how it is when I'm at work—not much time to do my own thing.'

Sean put his hands in the pockets of his jeans and looked thoughtful for a moment.

'So we've got six weeks to get it all done and dusted, yes? Not that it should take anything like that much time once the money's in place. As soon as it's in the bank, we can move towards completion on the first phase of the deal.'

'I'm off until early September, so I can be wherever you want me to be, whenever you want. I'll need a bit of warning so I can work out an excuse for going out, though.' Max gave a low groan. 'Shit. I'd forgotten. Ellie's booked a holiday for us. I've had nothing to do with it, but she announced it yesterday.'

Sean looked up sharply.

'Really? Where are you going? How long are you going to be away?'

'Hey—it's okay, you know. Nothing to panic about. We can work around it. We're not going for three weeks, and then there's a week after we get back.'

'What brought that on?' Sean asked.

'She thinks the kids need to see the sea, and she wanted us to have some time alone. I think we need it too. It'll be good. She's even searched out some local babysitting service for holidaymakers, checked and triple-checked through some nursing network, so that we can have a couple of romantic meals out. Just what we need. I hate keeping secrets from her.'

'I suppose. I thought, with the house and everything, she might prefer to stay around all summer. Obviously not.'

Max frowned, but at that moment Leo appeared in the doorway and started to make her way across to them. He needed to change the subject, because Leo never missed a thing.

16

Finally everybody had made it back to the dining room. Ellie couldn't think what had got into Fiona tonight. She was practically skipping, and was flirting with every man in the room. Tom Douglas seemed to find it all mildly amusing, but considering the fact that Fiona usually played the role of a condescending upper-class socialite, it was all very strange. The only person getting the rough edge of her tongue tonight was Charles. Poor Charles. He had tried throughout the meal to steer the conversation towards the economic outlook for the UK and Europe, but nobody was interested in any more doom and gloom after all the talk about Abbie's accident.

Ellie didn't believe she would be winning any prizes for being the perfect hostess tonight. On top of everything else, a text had come from Georgia when she was in the kitchen, sorting out the dessert.

'THANKS, FRIEND. THAT WAS JUST WHAT I NEEDED.'

She recognised sarcasm when she saw it, and had wanted to put her head down and cry. Maybe she had been insensitive, telling her about her own problems in view of everything that Georgia was going through, but she had thought her friend would understand. Clearly not. She couldn't even remember what she'd written in that text.

Tom was turning into the saviour of the night. He had an easy way of talking to people—no doubt as a result of countless interviews with people from all walks of life. He was relaxed, although Ellie sensed that life hadn't always been easy for him. Divorce never was. She could hear his gruff Lancashire tones as he tried to draw Penny into conversation, but she couldn't hear what he was saying.

He had been chatting to people about their jobs all evening, normally a fairly safe topic of conversation, and his gaze settled on Leo as Ellie served the last 'trio of chocolate' plates to her guests. Ellie knew how much Leo hated talking about herself, but when Tom asked the inevitable question, she was left in a position from which there was no obvious escape.

'I'm a life coach.' The flat tone in Leo's voice didn't encourage further questioning, but Ellie could have put money on Fiona having something to say on the subject. And she'd have won.

'Good Lord. I didn't really think those people existed. What gives anyone the authority to tell somebody else what they should and shouldn't do with their lives? And I don't want to be picky, Leo, but what sort of role model are you, given your views on relationships and men?'

Ellie looked at her sister, whose chin was firmly raised. She wanted to leap in and defend her, but Leo would hate that.

'I would say that I'm the perfect role model, actually. I have what I want in life. I'm happy. I'm living proof that there's hope for women outside of a relationship.' Leo said, keeping her voice level.

'So is that what you preach, then? The glorious single life?' Fiona asked, followed by a most unbecoming and uncharacteristic snort. Who'd been topping up her glass all night? Ellie wondered.

'I don't preach. That's the whole point. I help my clients to identify what works and what doesn't work in their lives. And then I try to help them find ways of achieving the goals they've set.'

'Hah. That's a joke,' Gary said. 'Goals? Most of us just have to suffer whatever life throws at us and make the best of it.' He took a large gulp of his wine.

Fiona ignored him. She hadn't finished deriding Leo's chosen profession.

'Leo, you hate men. You think they're totally superfluous and out to ruin the lives of all women. You've always been absolutely clear that every woman is better off on her own, and you have so many issues yourself that I'm at a loss to understand how you think you can sort out other people's emotional baggage.'

Ellie was furious, but Leo waved her hand to indicate that she should calm down.

'I'm not a counsellor, Fiona. I don't dredge up people's histories and make them face the horrors of their past. I help them to recognise who they are *now*, and where they want to be in the future.'

'Come on, Leo. Admit it. I bet your sole aim is to destroy the maximum number of relationships so that women are freed from lives of hell with their bastard men, isn't it?'

'Despite what you might think, I don't try to split up happy couples. But I do try to give those that are unhappy the strength to make changes.' Leo paused. 'Of course, there are people that marry for purely materialistic reasons, and while their husbands continue to keep them in the style to which they have become accustomed, life is hunky dory. But I do wonder what happens to these women if things go wrong. We live in turbulent times, Fiona, and the most comfortable of lives are liable to disruption.'

Fiona ignored the jibe. She hadn't finished.

'I bet most people come to you because their marriages are in trouble, and they don't know what to do. Am I right?'

Leo looked as if she didn't want to get dragged any further into this conversation, and didn't answer. But that didn't deter Fiona.

'We all know how many marriages end in divorce—so let's not pretend. And a huge percentage must be because of infidelity. So if somebody tells you their marriage is falling apart because their partner has been unfaithful, what would you say? Would you tell them to get out?'

Leo took a deep breath. 'As I said, I don't tell my clients what to do. They make the decisions. I just ask the questions.'

Charles was looking at Fiona as if he didn't recognise her. His frown had deepened, and he looked even more perplexed than usual, but everybody else was smiling rather benignly at her drunken ramblings.

'Well, Leo,' Fiona continued, 'I do wonder if your judgement isn't somewhat clouded.' She thumped her glass down on the table as if she had made an important decision. 'I know, let's have an honesty session. Given that some enormous percentage of people are unfaithful to their spouses, how many round this table will admit to it? Patrick—we all know about you, so you are exempt. Sean—what about you?'

Ellie wished somebody would butt in and stop this—but half the people seemed to think it was mildly amusing, and somehow she wasn't able to intervene. She looked down at her food, unable to meet anybody's gaze.

'Well, if you listened to the village gossip you'd probably believe that I'd shagged half the women in Cheshire.'

'And indeed, who would blame them, Sean? But the question is—have you?' prodded Fiona.

Ellie looked at her friend, appalled that she would ask such a question. But Fiona was leaning forward across the table, giving Sean what was undoubtedly supposed to be a sexy smile, but came out as a drunken leer. Ellie glanced at Sean.

'I never kiss and tell, Fiona,' he responded, a small smile playing around his lips.

Ellie didn't want Fiona to get to Max. He was a hopeless liar and if there was something to find out, she didn't want it to be like this. But she was saved by the person she least expected. For motives that Ellie couldn't begin to comprehend, Charles spoke up.

'Actually, Fiona, as you appear to find it all so very amusing, perhaps you would be entertained to know that I may have had a small dalliance.'

Fiona burst out laughing.

'Oh, don't be so bloody absurd, Charles. Of course you haven't!'

Seeing Charles's hurt face, Ellie glanced at Leo and her sister clearly read her well.

'Enough. Stop stirring,' Leo said, pointing at Fiona across the table with a chocolate tuile. 'I tell you what, though. I'll give you a free life-coaching session, Fiona. In fact,' she looked around the table, 'I'll give each of the women here a freebie—you'll all make great material for my blog—anonymously, of course. Let's see if that changes your view of what a life coach does. I'll throw in lunch too, if you like. Go home and check me out—see what you think. Google Leonora Harris and you'll find me. Let's see if you've got the guts, Fiona.'

Ellie watched her sister, noticing her defiant gaze as she stared hard at Fiona. She knew that Leo would be embarrassed to have been put in this position, but there was no way she was going to show it.

'That's a very kind offer, Leo.' Ellie was surprised to hear Penny's voice cut through the tension. 'I think I'd like that.'

Just as a furious-looking Gary appeared ready to launch an attack on his wife, Fiona started again.

'Okay, where were we before Leo so rudely interrupted?'

Ellie could sense Leo's irritation with Fiona even before she opened her mouth.

'You know, Fiona, a juvenile truth-or-dare contest at a dinner party isn't helpful to anybody. With the exception of Pat, whose infidelity was unfortunately made very public, I think everybody else is entitled to keep their secrets within their own relationships. So let's change the subject, shall we?'

Mimi put down her spoon with a clatter.

'I'm sorry, but I'm fed up with this talk of Patrick's so-called infidelity, and how "unfortunate" it was. You make it sound like something to be ashamed of. Why can't you accept that he fell in love? With *me*.'

For the first time, Ellie felt a twinge of sympathy for Mimi. She was right. They all talked about Patrick as if he had done something stupid, without ever considering how that must make Mimi feel. However badly she had behaved with her barbed remarks, maybe it was simply her way of getting her own back. But Mimi had more to say.

'You think you're all so superior, don't you? But you're not. I *know* you're not. And although I wasn't going to say anything tonight—not even to Patrick—our love has resulted in the one thing that the *amazing* Georgia wouldn't give him.' She paused for effect, casting a smug smile around the room. 'We're having a baby!'

Ellie couldn't wait for the evening to be over. Everybody was rallying round the new parents-to-be, and Max had thrust a glass of champagne into the hand of a totally stunned and white-faced Patrick. She could see that Max was trying hard to get into the whole swing of the celebration, but even he looked bemused and was making up for his lack of enthusiasm by being far too hearty and effusive. The whole thing had a flat feel to it, with only a self-satisfied Mimi seeming to enjoy it.

Ellie had suggested that they all move to the garden for the champagne—she didn't think she could keep the smile pasted on her face for a moment longer, and the garden would at least provide some cover. She made sure she was either close to Leo or Max the whole time. She didn't want to get drawn into conversations with anybody else tonight. It was all too much.

A few of the men disappeared round the front of the house to check out Gary's Porsche. He'd had it a couple of days and only on loan, but he had already decided that it was the car for him. Charles was waxing lyrical about his Aston Martin, which unfortunately he'd decided to leave at home so nobody had a chance to compare its credentials, but he seemed intent on quizzing Gary on the terms of the trial period with the Porsche. Ellie could hear them all discussing the finer points of the top models, but she had tuned out.

Fiona was slouched on a garden bench, looking decidedly inelegant with her legs splayed out in front of her. Penny was gamely trying to be enthusiastic about Mimi's baby, and Max and Pat were chatting quietly over by the fishpond. Ellie could see that Max kept clapping Pat encouragingly on the back, but it didn't appear to be having the desired effect. Leo was pretending to tidy up the kitchen, but Ellie suspected she was just keeping out of the way, so she positioned herself close to the doorway—keen to appear sociable but within earshot of Leo should she be the subject of any unwanted attention.

Finally, Charles started the exodus. The car he had apparently ordered had arrived, and much to Fiona's disgust he practically scooped her up from the bench and out to where it was waiting. Fortunately, everybody saw that as a cue to leave, and apart from giving Pat a big hug, which somehow felt more like commiseration than acknowledgement of a happy event, Ellie managed to cling onto a rather baffled Max and avoid contact with anybody else. Maybe Leo's approach to personal space had some merit.

It had been a strange night, but now that it was over, the only thing that Ellie wanted was to go to bed, curl up in a tight ball, and lick her wounds in private.

17

With a single touch on the keyboard, the computer monitor sprang to life, its whirling screen saver sending weird, distorted shadows across the walls of the otherwise dark room. A quick movement with the mouse, and the screen cleared. A couple of clicks, and Google appeared, its bright white background illuminating the room as if a lamp had been switched on. The old keyboard clunked as the letters were picked out. LEONORA HARRIS.

A page of references appeared, but only one linked to the official blog. What was the interfering bitch offering?

A Single Step: the blog of Leo Harris

Take control of your life

There are many times in people's lives when they may need help. Sometimes it's obvious: grief at the death of a loved one; the breakup of a relationship; the loss of a job. These problems are easy to recognise.

What if you simply feel dissatisfied with your life? What if you don't know where it's going, and you're not sure you can cope if this is all that life has to offer?

Does any of this sound familiar to you?

My name is Leo (Leonora) Harris, and I'm a life coach. I believe I can work with you, and empower you to **take** control of your life. Together we will set appropriate and attainable goals, and I will guide and motivate you to achieve them. We won't look back and analyse what went wrong. We'll look forward, towards a brighter future.

I specialise in helping people to understand whether their relationships are adding or detracting from their lives. You are a participant in your own life, and sometimes this can blind you to the truth. But step outside of yourself for a moment and become an observer. Have a good look at yourself and the way you and your partner interact. Do you like what you see?

If the answer is no, I can help you to bring about the changes you want and deserve. Together we will analyse what your version of a great relationship is, and identify those needs that are not being met. We will build strategies for change, and a plan to implement them. I will support you and keep you focused on your end goal—a happier, more fulfilled YOU.

So act boldly. Take control of your life and contact me, Leo Harris, by clicking this link.

A journey of a thousand miles begins with a single step. Lao-Tzu

No way. There was absolutely no way that Leo Harris was getting into this house. No way she was going to disrupt their lives. People like her should be taught a lesson for their meddling.

The monitor stayed bright for a few more moments, as if coldly indifferent to the hot fury that swirled within the room.

Then it reverted to its vibrant screen saver, casting blue and green shadows across the furious face of the immobile figure that continued to stare at it.

18

Day Three: Sunday

It was late when Leo finally woke up on Sunday morning, and she instantly felt guilty. They had left the dessert plates and glasses until this morning on the basis that they would all muck in, and by now Ellie was sure to have cleared them all. Leo had a quick shower and pulled on a pair of black jeans and a T-shirt, dragged a brush through her hair, and made her way down to the kitchen.

As she approached the open doorway, she was surprised to hear an argument in full flow. There was no shouting, but the tone of their voices was enough. She was about to turn tail and head back to her room when Max noticed her.

'Come in, Leo. Don't worry about us. I'm irritating my wife, and she in turn isn't listening to me. What would you like for breakfast? Bad temper on toast, or an outraged omelette?'

Ellie and Max were standing facing each other, each leaning back against a worktop with arms folded.

'Err, maybe I'll make myself scarce until you've sorted out whatever it is that's bugging you both,' Leo said.

'Unsortable. No viable solution. So come on in, and join the party.'

Max was obviously trying to make light of it, but Leo could see that Ellie was upset.

'Hey,' Max said. 'Maybe we could add your opinion into the pot, Leo. I have a strange suspicion that you'd be on my side.'

Leo laughed uncomfortably. 'I don't do marriage guidance, guys. Keep me out of this.'

'Nope. Sorry. You're not escaping that easily,' Max said.

Leo looked at Ellie, who still hadn't spoken. Her cheeks were flushed, and her lips were set in an unusually thin line.

'I'll just get myself a cup of coffee and disappear to the sitting room with the papers, if that's okay,' Leo said, making her way to the fancy machine and hoping she didn't have to ask for instructions.

Ellie came across and gently nudged her out of the way with her hip.

'Don't worry. It's just Max being obstinate, and it's getting up my nose. Nothing serious,' Ellie said. 'I merely suggested that we could perhaps go to a few car showrooms today and see if there's a car he would like. Better than driving round in that old rust bucket.'

'I'll have you know that you were delighted when we bought that old rust bucket,' Max said. 'But now it's clearly not good enough.'

Leo realised that her appearance had done nothing to defuse the row, and she really wanted to escape. The coffee was coming through—slowly—but Ellie was obviously set on making Leo one of her favourite cappuccinos, and that was going to take a few minutes.

'So you get the picture,' Ellie went on. 'We've got all this money, and I have a fantastic car, and Max insists on driving round in a six-year-old Peugeot that's way past its best.'

'The difference is, Leo, that I bought and paid for that car myself,' Max said. 'If I can't afford a new car because I don't earn enough, then I'm not having one. End of.'

Why, Leo thought, were all sides of this argument being addressed to her? As if she were going to be the referee. Well, they could think again.

'Listen, guys,' she said. 'Whether you get a new car or you don't is absolutely nothing to do with me at all. I don't know why you think he needs one, Ellie, but on the other hand I don't know why you are so adamant you're not having one, Max. So I am *not* taking sides. Okay?'

'For somebody who refused The Old Witch's money herself, I thought you would be with me on this,' Max muttered, absently pouring more juice into Jake's Moshi Monsters cup.

'Oh, for God's sake, Max,' Ellie said. 'That's different and you know it. We've *got* the money. It's *ours*. Why are you being so unreasonable?' Ellie sounded genuinely distressed, which seemed like an excessive reaction to Leo, who would have let him keep his car if that's what he wanted.

'And, Leo, I didn't see him complaining about the money spent on his media room last night—did you?' Ellie asked.

Oh where was that coffee?

'That's different. I had no say in the matter. You did it as a surprise, and I would be pretty ungrateful if I told you to take it all out again, wouldn't I?'

'Speaking of your media suite, Max—am I allowed to take my coffee in there, because I seem to remember you mentioning that it was soundproofed?' Leo asked in her most innocent tone.

'No—you can forget that. Gulp it down quickly and grab some toast. Max can have the kids. We're going shopping,' Ellie said with a look of irritation. '*We'll* go and spend some of The Old Witch's money.'

Ellie grabbed her keys.

'Oh, and while I think about it, Max, what happened to the keys Sean brought round last night? We could give those to Leo.'

Max looked puzzled.

'I don't know. I left them on the worktop, I think. I presumed you'd put them away.'

Ellie gave an exasperated tut.

'I didn't move them—so you must have put them somewhere else.'

Max was known for losing stuff, and Leo saw a glimmer of a fond smile from her sister as they made their way out of the door.

Ellie was glad to escape the house, and Max was happy looking after the twins. He'd find something fun to do with them—and always something that didn't cost a penny. He would get them making things, or exploring the garden for bugs. They'd have a great time. She smiled as she thought of their chunky little bodies, crouched down and looking in wonder at a worm or a shiny black beetle.

She should have been there with them, but she was struggling so hard not to scream, 'Is it true?' at Max, that it was in everybody's best interests if she disappeared. She didn't seem able to shake off the tension that was gripping her, and was terrified of what Max might answer if she asked him a direct question. It hadn't been a real row earlier, but Ellie got the feeling that Max didn't want anything that was hers. His moral code would never allow him to use any of her inheritance to buy a new car if he was about to leave her.

'Did you get the gist of that, Leo?' she asked as they climbed into her car, knowing her sister would only have seen the superficial problem and not the deeper implications.

'Couldn't help it really. He doesn't want to spend any of that money on himself.'

'The thing is,' she said to Leo, looking over her shoulder as she reversed the car, 'he wants to make sure that we use "our" money, that's the money we both earn, to pay all the bills. We don't have a mortgage now, but the running costs of the house are pretty high so the two things sort of cancel each other out. He reluctantly went along with the move, because he could see it was something that I genuinely wanted to do—although like you he thinks my reasoning is madness. But that's it. We can't change our lifestyle at all, and we have a budget for shopping every week, same as before.'

'So what are you going to do, because you can't carry on arguing about it, can you?' Leo asked, not unreasonably.

Ellie slammed the car into drive, and turned left out of the gates.

'I've transferred the money into his name. I've put him in sole charge of all of our finances. I thought that by doing that, I would make him feel that he was the head of the household, which seems to be his bugbear. But he won't spend it unless he's earned it. He thinks it's *my* money and he won't touch it. And you won't have any of it, so we've got all this money just sitting in the bank! You're the bloody life coach. You tell *me* what to do,' Ellie said in despair.

'It's not like that, Ellie. I don't tell people what to do.'

Ellie glanced sideways at her sister with concern.

'I hope Fiona didn't get to you last night. I thought she was bloody offensive, and I was dying to jump in and give her hell. But I knew you'd hate it.'

'Oh, don't worry about Fiona. I'd have preferred it not to be so public, that's all. I know my job sounds like a bit of a non-profession, but I really do help women, believe it or not. I help them to have the strength to be themselves, rejoice in their individuality, and chase their dreams. We all have issues, Ellie. Every single one of us. But I don't think constantly striving to fix them is necessarily helpful.'

Ellie felt her throat tighten and her eyes burn. She focused hard on the road ahead. How little she sometimes understood her sister. She and Max were always telling Leo it was time to change—to be more tactile, more open to relationships, to put her past behind her. That was so wrong of them. Leo clearly accepted who she was, and lived with the scars of her early life in her own way.

They travelled in silence for a few minutes, then Ellie slowed the car to a crawl and glanced out of the window. They were going down the back road, and they were passing some police incident tape that she assumed marked the spot where Abbie had been knocked over. A few bunches of flowers were lying on the grass verge.

'Do you mind if we stop for a minute?' Ellie asked. 'It's just that having spent all those hours with Abbie yesterday, I would like to sort of pay my respects, if that makes sense.'

Leo seemed happy to get out of the car with her sister. They stood silently by the side of the road for a few minutes, and Ellie wondered what could have driven a young girl to be out here, in the middle of nowhere, at that time of night.

She looked at the woods and she couldn't help remembering the past, when she wasn't much older than Abbie. It wasn't the first time in her life that this had been the scene of a crime, even though the previous one had never been reported. There couldn't be a link, though. It was all so long ago, and such an unhappy time.

Poor Abbie. Whatever she had suffered on Friday night, she didn't deserve it. She was only a child, and Ellie's heart ached for her and her family.

When she finally spoke, her voice was quiet.

'I probably shouldn't tell you this, Leo, but when Abbie was brought into the hospital, her feet and legs were in a shocking state. She was covered in a horrendous nettle rash from her toes to her knees, and her feet were bleeding and bruised. The police don't seem to have made that public, so please don't say anything. She can't feel it now, of course. But it must have hurt like hell at the time. Poor kid.'

It was hard to think how that could have happened, but Ellie would bet on the fact that the police had searched every inch of these woods yesterday.

'How do they think she got here?' Leo asked. 'Has anybody said anything?'

'None of it makes sense—to me at least. She's a good kid, by all accounts. Not the type to be out in the middle of the night, and definitely not a child whose parents wouldn't know where she was. But however she got here, some bastard left her to die, and by the look of her legs, that wasn't the only torture she'd gone through that night.'

The two women were subdued when they got back in the car.

'Would you mind very much if we went via the hospital? I'd like to call in and see how Abbie's getting on. I won't be long, but I can't let you come in because it's only close relatives at a time like this.'

'Of course it's okay. It must be hard to tear yourself away when it's a patient like Abbie.'

Ellie smiled sadly, and put the car into drive. They didn't speak again until they reached the hospital.

❖

Swiping her key card to get through security, Ellie made her way towards the nurses' station. They were a small, tight-knit group on this ward, and nobody had to ask why she was there. She looked towards Abbie's bed and could see that the doctor was there, talking to her mum. Ellie stayed where she was and waited.

Finally he excused himself and headed towards Ellie. Sam Bradshaw was probably her favourite doctor and, like the nurses, he felt no need to query her presence. He got straight to the point.

'Before you ask, Ellie, there's nothing to report, I'm sorry to say. No change with Abbie. Do you want to go and talk to her mum for a while? I'm sure she'll be pleased to see you.'

Ellie couldn't hide her disappointment at the lack of improvement, but adjusted her expression as she made her way towards the bed where Abbie's mum, Kath, was sitting. She seemed slightly more composed today but didn't look as if she'd slept for a week.

'Hi, Kath. I thought I'd pop in and see how you all are,' Ellie said. Giving Kath's shoulder a quick squeeze, she sat down on the other visitor's chair.

'I expect the doctor's told you she's just the same,' Kath muttered. 'Her legs look less sore, though. That awful rash has gone down a bit. What happened to her, Ellie? What happened to my little Abbie?'

The look on Kath's face said it all. She was barely holding it together, and who could blame her? Imagine if it was Ruby lying there. It didn't bear thinking about.

'I wish I could help with that, I really do. Have the police said anything?'

Kath shook her head sadly.

'She was out with friends. She was so *chuffed*, you know. I can't begin to tell you how excited she was. Abbie's always had difficulty making friends. Oh, don't get me wrong; she's a lovely lass. But she finds it hard to get close to people, and we've probably sheltered her a bit. I don't know. It seemed like the right thing at the time. But last night all the girls from her class were going out together for a burger, then to the pictures, and then back to Emily's house for a sleepover. About twelve of them, I think.'

Ellie's eyes opened wide at the idea of that many fourteen-year-old girls in one house for the night.

'I did check it all out, though,' Kath said, as if afraid of being accused of bad parenting. 'I went round personally to see Emily's mum to confirm that she was expecting them. I half thought that they might have been teasing Abbie, and going somewhere completely different. Some of them are a bit like that, I'm sorry to say. But it was genuine. Emily's parents don't live in a big house, and it was all a bit cluttered, you know. Her mum looked as if she didn't care how many turned up, and they could look after themselves. But with so many of them, it didn't seem they could come to any harm.'

Kath went quiet.

'So what happened?' Ellie prompted.

'I've only met Emily a couple of times, but I could see that she could be a little so-and-so. She kind of ruled the roost, if you know what I mean, because she was the one that had the best parties. So nobody ever wanted to fall out with her. The police say they've talked to all the girls that were there, and they're all agreed that Emily said something nasty to Abbie—although they claim not to know what—and they had a row. Abbie told them she wasn't going with them to the cinema; she was going home.'

Kath started to cry quietly.

Ellie patted Kath's arm and turned towards Abbie to give her mum some privacy, holding the child's hand lightly and stroking it with her thumb. She carried on talking softly.

'It sounds to me as if you did everything right. Poor Abbie. Sometimes teenagers can be very hurtful to each other, and I don't think you could have done another thing. Just keep talking to her. We don't know for sure what's happening in her mind, so talk to her about the good times and don't worry about Emily now.'

'Do you think she can hear us?' Kath asked.

'I don't know. Sometimes patients come round from comas and say they had random thoughts and impressions, others that they had lucid dreams. Most say it was a complete void. The brain is such a complex thing. But if I were you I would talk to her, sing to her, touch her. It can't do any harm.'

'Whatever happened after she left the burger place, it must have been a nightmare for the poor love,' Kath said. 'One of the girls saw her using her mobile and texting or something, but even that's missing, and she never went anywhere without it. They left her, the little horrors. How could they have done that? They said they thought she was coming home.'

'Didn't Emily's parents wonder where she was?'

'They asked Emily if everybody was okay, and left them to it. Emily apparently said yes, and didn't think it necessary to say that Abbie had gone home. They didn't bother with a head count or anything. I suppose you wouldn't with that many of them. Still, somebody should have known. I would have phoned her to check she was all right, but I know what she would have said. "Stop fussing, Mum. I'm fourteen," as if that is old enough to take care of yourself.'

'Where do you think she might have gone, Kath?'

'That's just it. I've absolutely no idea. We don't have any other family nearby, and I can't believe she didn't phone me and ask me to come and get her. She *knew* I'd be there in a flash. Well, either me or her dad. Brian didn't even have a beer that night in case something went wrong and he needed to go and collect her. He always says he's "on call" when Abbie's out. Just in case. So none of it makes sense.'

Kath rubbed Abbie's leg gently through the thin sheet and blanket.

'I don't want to touch her legs below her knees. The doctor said she won't feel it, but what if he's wrong and she just can't say? They look so sore.' Kath choked back a sob, wiping the tears that were escaping from the corner of her eyes with the back of her other hand. 'Do you know, when they found her she wasn't wearing any shoes? That's why her feet are so cut up. How could that have happened? The police searched the whole area close to where she was found yesterday, and there's no sign of her shoes. Her feet must have hurt so much—they're cut to pieces.' Kath put her head down and rested it on Abbie's thigh. 'Oh, Abbie love. I'm sorry. I'm so sorry we weren't able to take better care of you.'

Ellie was very quiet when she returned to the car. Apart from saying that Abbie was no better, she hadn't had much to say for the rest of the journey and appeared lost in thought. But by the time they reached John Lewis—Ellie's idea of shopping heaven—Leo was relieved to see that her sister seemed to have recovered a little. The tension had eased in her face, and she was making a concerted effort to be a bit more cheerful.

As it was Sunday the store didn't open until late, so they had a few minutes to wait. Leo saw her sister typing away on her phone, and presumed she was texting Max. She hoped Ellie wasn't having another dig.

'What are you up to, Ellie?'

'I'm texting Georgia. I somehow seem to have offended her, so I'm hoping it was just a mistake,' she replied.

She carried on typing with her thumbs.

'I thought I'd keep it casual, as if whatever I've done to upset her never happened. I've written, "Max being an arse. Gone to John Lewis. Plan to buy lots. Hope to see you soon". Anyway, come on. The doors are opening. Let's see what we can find to spend some money on, and irritate Max even more.'

Leo wasn't a great fan of shopping, and had only agreed to come for Ellie's sake. She didn't see herself buying any clothes from this store and she had no interest in kitchen appliances—Ellie's passion at the moment. After ten minutes of listening to her sister extolling the virtues of a particular set of pans, Leo escaped to the perfume and cosmetics counters to wile away some time trying new fragrances and checking out the latest makeup. Not her favourite pastime, but infinitely better than comparing pans.

Finally, she made her way back to the ground floor. It was forty minutes since they'd arrived, and she had no more than one new shiny red lipstick to show for her trip. Surely by now Ellie would have finished shopping?

Her sister wasn't where she'd expected her to be. The store was busy now, but there was no sign of her. Sod it, Leo thought. I'm going to do one skim of the basement, and if she's not there I'll go and get a cup of coffee. She used the seconds at the top of the escalator to scan the crowds below, and spotted Ellie in the garden department, looking at some imitation flowers. Out of the corner of her eye, Leo glimpsed a figure in the crowd who seemed to be walking purposefully in Ellie's direction. All she could see of him as she looked down into the crowd was the top of his hat. It looked like an Australian leather bush hat, and she had always thought they looked sexy on the right man. He was making a beeline for her sister, but just as he got close, Ellie looked up and spotted Leo, raising her hand to wave. The man veered off to the right towards the greetings cards. Leo shrugged. She must have been wrong.

Ellie was holding a fake bunch of freesias in her hand.

'What do you want with those, Ellie? You've got a garden full of plants.'

Ellie thrust the flowers towards Leo, and held them under her nose.

'I was wondering why *anybody* would buy fake flowers when the fresh ones are so very beautiful. See, there's no smell. Wouldn't you think that by now with all these fake room perfumes they would build something into fake flowers? I was only rooting around while I waited for you.'

Ellie put the flowers back into a huge vase, which was filled with every sort of bloom—from roses to tulips and daffodils.

'Waiting for me? You have to be joking. I thought you would be ages with your pans—and you haven't even bought anything yet.'

'You think?' Ellie laughed. 'Everything has gone to collection, so that I can drive round and pick it up. But I need to pop into the supermarket next door for a few bits and pieces first. Come on. Let's choose some scrummy things for lunch and try to cheer Max up. I won't mention the car again. It's not worth falling out about.'

Ellie linked her arm through Leo's and headed towards the escalator back to the ground floor. Leo gave it a second, and then gently removed her arm. Ellie gave her a sideways glance, but said nothing.

In the event, they were longer than they thought buying the groceries and for once Leo enjoyed shopping for food. Ellie made everything sound so tasty. She could eulogise over some raw prawns, when all Leo could see were grey, slimy-looking things. Somehow Ellie made them sound plump, pink, and mouth-watering.

Ellie glanced at her watch.

'I think we need to do a bit of multitasking here, Leo. I'll walk round to the collection point, but can you take the shopping back to the car and drive round to meet me?'

Leo looked at her sister in surprise.

'Drive your car? To what do I owe this privilege? Max seemed to think that would be out of the question.'

'Hah! That's because I wouldn't let him borrow it.' Ellie giggled. 'It was all part of my cunning plan to get him to buy a new one. But of course you can drive it, and so can Max.'

Ellie threw the keys to her sister, and set off back towards the department store.

Leo pushed the trolley through the car park, and in spite of only having the vaguest idea of where they'd parked, she found Ellie's Mercedes easily and went straight to the rear to unload the shopping. With the trolley returned, she went round to the driver's side, and stopped. There was something on the windscreen.

Strange, she thought. Why would anybody leave a fake flower there? She pulled it out from under the wiper blade, climbed into the car, and threw it on the passenger seat. After giving herself a moment or two to become familiar with the controls, Leo drove round to where her sister was waiting with some large bags. She pulled into a parking bay and jumped out to give Ellie a hand. Everything was quickly stowed in the back of the car, and Ellie surprised Leo.

'You drive. Just to prove that I am not precious about my car.'

Leo shrugged and went back round to the driver's door. As she settled into her seat and adjusted the mirror, she realised that Ellie wasn't in the car. She was standing by the passenger side, holding the fake yellow rose and staring at it intently.

'What's this doing here?' she asked Leo, her voice wobbling slightly.

'Oh yes. I'd forgotten about it. The weirdest thing,' Leo said. 'It was on the windscreen when I got back to the car. It's like those that were on display with the freesias, isn't it?'

Ellie didn't answer. She walked over to the nearest waste bin and threw it in. When she returned to the car, she was quiet. The earlier good humour seemed to have evaporated.

19

Pat had told Mimi that he was going to see Abbie's parents, which was the truth. But he wasn't there for very long. He only stayed for half an hour. Kath Campbell was at the hospital, and her husband, Brian, was in no fit state for visitors, although he had asked if Pat would help the police to talk to the 'little cows' that had been out with Abbie on Friday night to see if they were holding anything back. But then he had given up trying to speak. The poor man had started to weep openly and Pat had found it difficult to know what to say.

He wasn't good at dealing with other people's grief. It affected him deeply, and he needed to share his feelings with somebody. His first thought was Georgia. It was always Georgia. God, what a mess.

He decided to drive his car out into the country. He needed some thinking time, and he needed time without Mimi. He knew he was going to have to deal with his own problems, one way or another. But Mimi was expecting his child now, and whatever mistakes he might have made, it wasn't the baby's fault.

His car seemed to have a mind of its own, though, and within fifteen minutes he found himself outside his home. His *real* home. Georgia's car was in the drive. Without stopping to think, he made his way up the front path and approached the door. He remembered how much they had loved this house from the moment they saw it. A large, late-Victorian semi, it had huge bay windows and high ceilings. With fields to the rear, it had a stunning view over the Cheshire countryside to the hills beyond.

He knocked on the door, realising that using his key wouldn't set the right tone. He needn't have worried. Georgia opened the door, and she was running at full steam. She jabbed her finger at him, as if she would like to jab his chest with a six-inch knife.

'You've got a bloody nerve, Patrick Keever. After the last few hours, I can't believe that you would have the audacity to turn up here.'

Pat looked as his wife in confusion. God, but she was beautiful. Her spiky blonde hair was catching the sunlight, and her huge brown eyes sparkled with fury. Tall and slim, she looked perfect to him. But he had no idea what he'd done. At least, not in the last day or two.

'I don't know what you're talking about, Georgia. Can I come in, or are we going to fight on the doorstep?'

'You can come into the hall so that we can shut the door,' she answered. 'But that's as far as you're getting.'

He walked in and headed towards the kitchen. But Georgia just stood by the door with her arms folded.

'What am I supposed to have done? I've had a shit morning, and I didn't come here for an ear bashing. I came for sympathy.' Even to himself, Pat sounded a bit pathetic.

'What in God's name makes you think I'll give you any sympathy? First you send me a text message, telling me baldly that you are about to become a father. Then when I phone to ask you what the hell you're talking about, you reject my calls. Not once, but three times. And on top of that, I got a message from Ellie last night saying how happy they were for you because—and I quote—"Mimi's a little treasure".'

Georgia's hands fell to sit firmly on her hips, arms bent at the elbow. She was a picture of anger and resentment. But Patrick was totally bewildered.

'I never sent you a text. Why the hell would I do that? I had no idea how I was going to tell you about the baby—I was going to wait a bit to make sure it wasn't a false alarm.'

'Bloody typical of you. Try to avoid the issue and hope it resolves itself without any intervention on your part. It doesn't work like that, Pat. It didn't take you long, though, did it? My God—just because I said I wasn't ready to have babies you have to go and make one with somebody else within about five minutes. You really are unbelievable. And then—yet again—I learn about your behaviour by text. Last time it was with the happy news that you were being unfaithful. This time I get a few words to tell me that you will soon be a proud father.'

'Georgia, we've been through this before. I don't know who could have told you about me and Mimi. Nobody knew. Not even Max! And I wouldn't have told you about the baby this way. Surely you know that?'

'Well, all I can suggest is that your tart must have got hold of your phone and sent it. Because it definitely came from your mobile.'

Pat was astounded. He'd caught Mimi with his phone a few days ago. She said she was looking up the weather forecast, because she didn't have a smartphone. But since then he'd changed the password, and to something that she would never guess in a million years.

'When did you phone me, exactly, because I would never reject a call from you. You know that, or at least you damn well should do.'

'I phoned you three times, between ten and eleven this morning.'

Pat felt confusion and a rising sense of panic. He didn't want to do anything else to upset his wife.

'I promise you, I never got any calls from you. If you got a text, it wasn't from me.'

Georgia shoved past him and stormed down the hallway. He made a move to follow her, but she half turned and held up her hand, palm facing outwards. A definite sign that he should stay where he was. She returned a few seconds later with her mobile clutched in her hand and waved it in his face.

'So explain this, if you're so bloody clever. Here's the text. And look—oh surprise, surprise. It's from your phone.'

Pat stared at the screen in amazement. She was right.

Before they could pursue this any further, his own phone rang. Mimi. Perfect timing. Sometimes he thought she had some sixth sense. He clicked to answer.

'What is it, Mimi?'

'I'm sorry Patrick. Am I disturbing you?' she said in a soft voice. 'Are you still with that girl's parents? I need you at home. I've lost a bit of blood, and I'm scared.'

Pat leaned back against the wall, resting his head there and closing his eyes.

'Okay. I'm about to leave Abbie's now. I'm on my way.'

He hung up and turned to his wife. 'Georgia . . .'

'Piss off, Pat. I won't be calling you again, so you don't need to think about rejecting my calls. I have to say that I'm delighted to see you still don't see the necessity for honesty. I'm glad I'm not the only one who gets lied to.'

She walked away, leaving him to show himself out.

20

The silence in the car wasn't comfortable, and Ellie knew that if she didn't break it soon, Leo was going to start with the questions again. Where did she go on Friday night? Why did she switch her mobile off without answering it? Why had she gone all moody since they got back in the car? And she couldn't answer any of them truthfully. All she could think was that *he* had been there. *He* had followed her that morning and left her the rose so that she'd realise he was watching. He seemed to know her every move, and she felt violated.

Then there was Max. Was he really having an affair? Would he do that to them? She thought she knew him so well, but for the last few months there had been a subtle difference, she couldn't deny it. That's why she'd booked the holiday. Would they still go, or would he want to cancel? And what about the fact that he'd lied to her? Why would he lie about where he'd been if he had nothing to hide? He was such a useless liar too. Using Pat as his cover wasn't his wisest move. How could he think she wouldn't find out?

She could feel Leo glancing at her every few seconds. She needed to think of a topic soon before the inquisition began. But she was too late.

'Ellie,' Leo started. 'Is everything okay? It's just that things don't seem quite normal at the moment, and I'm wondering if I'm getting in the way.'

'What?' Ellie said. She was going to have to play things carefully. 'Of course they're okay. We've all been a bit busy with the house and everything, but that's all done now. Things will start to settle down again. And we *love* having you here.'

'It's just that there were one or two things . . .'

Ellie interrupted.

'Speaking of one or two things, I wanted to talk to you about what Mimi said last night—the stuff about you not getting any of The Old Witch's money. You do know, I hope, that I meant it when I offered you half. You can still have it—honestly. There's more than enough for us.'

Leo laughed, and Ellie was relieved to have steered her sister away from the edge of a very deep precipice.

'I wasn't bothered about that. She was your mother, not mine. She left the money to you.'

'Yes,' Ellie replied, wishing Leo would slow down so that this conversation could be finished before they got home. She didn't want Max adding his two penn'orth. 'She did leave the money to me, but it must have started out as being our father's money—at least a fair chunk of it.'

Leo turned to look at Ellie with a scornful expression. 'Is that supposed to make it somehow more appealing?'

'Oh, Leo. You are hopeless. You loved him once.'

Leo turned her attention back to the road.

'I loved him when I was a small child. That was before I discovered that he had another child living not thirty miles away, and that for the whole of my short life he had been cheating on my mother.'

'Well, for what it's worth, I think you misunderstood him. He made a mistake—people do. Don't be so hard on him, Leo. Perhaps his biggest mistake was marrying my evil mother. You don't know how envious of you I was as a child.'

Leo swivelled round to glance at Ellie, a look of genuine surprise on her face.

'You envied *me*? *Why,* for God's sake? I'd lost my mother and I'd come to live with The Old Witch. What was there to envy?'

Ellie felt heavy-hearted for a moment when she thought of herself and Leo as children.

'I envied the fact that you'd had a mother that loved you. Even if you'd lost her, you knew how it felt to be loved.' Ellie saw the dawning realisation on Leo's face that this might make sense.

'Oh *Ellie*, I'm so sorry. I never knew you felt like that. I'm sure your mother loved you, in her own way.'

Ellie snorted. 'What way was that, Leo? The controlling, emotionless, lying way? She may have made a slave out of you, but everything she made *me* do—the piano, the relentless studying, the extra tutor lessons—they were all designed to show that *her* daughter was better than the cuckoo in her nest. It had nothing to do with love. But I always felt that Dad loved me. I know he wasn't around much, but when he was, he was kind to me. He stopped her from doing her worst, I think. I felt happy when he was there.'

Leo said nothing, and Ellie knew she wasn't convinced.

'I'm sure he would have shown you some affection if you'd only let him in—but you know what you were like. You wouldn't even speak to him.'

'As a parent yourself, Ellie, I thought you would know better than that. You don't give love to your child on the basis that they must reciprocate. He wanted payback for any affection he doled out. He got it from you, but I was too much like hard work and not worth the effort.'

'You mustn't think like that. That's one of the reasons that I hope we can find him now—after all these years. I know she had him declared dead, but that just means she couldn't find him. Perhaps he didn't *want* to be found. He didn't run away from *us*, he ran away from my *mother*. She's dead—so it's safe for him to come back. And you never know, you might see him for what he really is.'

Leo's silence was absolute, and Ellie knew that she was fighting a losing battle. For Ellie, her father had been her saviour—the only person who had the slightest control over his wife's excesses, and the only person—until Max—to show her any affection. For Leo, he was the man that had ruined her life by bringing her to live with a stepmother who despised her.

As she indicated to turn into the gates of Willow Farm, Leo felt quite relieved. She had never thought she would be pleased to see this house in her lifetime, but she didn't want to listen to Ellie raving about their father's finer points. She was going to have to talk to her sister about this obsession with the idea of him suddenly materialising from nowhere, but there hadn't been time. They'd been too close to home when the conversation started. She pulled up and turned off the engine.

With the windows open to let in some of the summer breeze, Leo could hear shouts and laughter coming from the garden to the side of the house and she could see Max playing with the children. They were having a great time, and Leo turned to Ellie with a smile.

'Come on, Ellie. Let's get the car unpacked and go and join in the fun. It looks like they're playing some sort of croquet, of all things.'

Ellie paused for a beat before replying, looking with love at her family cavorting on the lawn. It seemed to Leo that she mentally shook herself and then gave a big smile.

'Good idea.'

Max had seen them arrive, and came bounding over to the car like an eager puppy as they climbed out. He always looked so delighted to see Ellie, and Leo stood still and watched. He put his arms round his wife and gave her a hug, and Leo thought she heard a whispered 'sorry'. Ellie rested her forehead briefly on his shoulder, then looked at him with a sad smile.

'Me too,' Leo heard her say softly.

'Okay girls, you go and play with the twins, and I'll unpack the shopping. I'll bring you out a drink when I've finished and you can tell me what you've been buying.'

At Leo's attempted protest, Max shooed them both away.

Leo and Ellie walked across the lawn to where the twins were indeed playing what could loosely be described as croquet. Max appeared to have constructed some sort of extra-wide hoops out of wire, and they were playing with tennis balls and what looked like an old brush that Max had cut the bristles off, shortened, and fashioned into a croquet mallet.

Having been introduced to the finer points of the game by the twins and been beaten not once but twice each by a beaming Jake, they finally made their way to sit down on a garden bench just as Max appeared with a tray bearing two cups of cappuccino, an espresso, and some orange juice for Jake and Ruby.

'It's been like Piccadilly Circus here this morning,' he said, handing the drinks round. 'Visitors and phone calls from all of our guests—well, most of them anyway.'

Ellie gave him an enquiring glance.

'Fiona called to say how "super" it all was—not that I'm convinced she could remember anything past the canapés. She was in a bit of a strop with Charles, who had disappeared to play golf.'

Ellie shook her head. 'I'm surprised he's speaking to her. I've known her for years, and I've never seen her like that.'

'Tom called round just after you'd gone out too. God knows what he made of Fiona's antics last night.' Max grinned as if he could imagine only too well. 'He brought his daughter round too—Lucy, she's called. A sweet kid, if a bit shy. You only missed him by a couple of minutes. Sean arrived at about the same time. He brought you a gift, Ellie. Said he felt bad about turning up out of the blue last night without anything to offer the hostess, so he called in at the gift shop in the garden centre this morning. I'll go and get it.'

It only took Max a few seconds to pop into the house for the gift, which had been beautifully wrapped—not, Leo suspected, by Sean. He handed it to Ellie, who placed it on the small table by her side. Max sat himself down cross-legged on the grass facing the two women on the bench.

'Well, open it then,' Max said, with an eager smile.

Ellie carefully unwrapped the gift to reveal a scented candle in glass. She placed it back on the side table.

'That was kind of him, but completely unnecessary,' she said.

'He was disappointed that he'd missed you—and he wouldn't stay for a cup of coffee. He said that the present was perhaps something that you might like in the bathroom when you're taking a long, lazy bath.'

Ellie made a 'pff' sound, as if the chances of that were quite remote.

Max turned his attention to Leo, giving her what could only be described as a knowing smile.

'Not sure what you've been up to with our resident policeman, Leo. When I said that Ellie wasn't here and had gone shopping, Tom hung around for a while. I got the feeling that he was hoping to see you, but in the end he had to go because his ex-wife was at his house.'

'If his ex-wife's still on the scene, I think you can stop playing cupid.'

Max shook his head slowly from side to side.

'She brought Lucy, that's all. One of the joys of divorce with kids—you still have to see the ex.'

'Yes, well, keep out of it Max. I might enjoy an hour or so of Tom's company, but I'm not after his body. Or if I was, it would be on a needs basis rather than a happy ever after. Stop interfering.'

As if to take the edge of her words, Leo picked up a stray tennis ball from the path and aimed it Max's chest. He promptly fell backwards on the grass, groaning and shouting for the twins to come and help him. Auntie Leo had tried to kill him.

Ellie watched her husband and children rolling around on the grass and felt that her heart was going to explode with love for them all. Max was wearing an old pair of baggy black shorts and a white running vest that had seen better days, but he still managed to look beyond beautiful to her, even though he would hate that description. He had the kind of skin that easily picked up a tan, and his deep brown eyes were shining with happiness and laughter as he played with the twins. More than anything she just wanted to leap on top of him, and roll around the garden with him and the kids. But the knot of anxiety in her stomach that was tightening by the hour prevented her, and she knew that her laughter sounded forced.

Leo was looking at her, and Ellie couldn't miss the concern in her eyes. Maybe she should tell her. Tell her everything: her worry, her fear, and her dilemma. But that would be so unfair. How many times had Leo told Ellie that her relationship with Max was the one thing that gave her hope? There had to be a better way.

The twins dragged Leo back to their game, and Max did that magic thing that he often did to get up off the floor. One minute he was lying there, and then with some weird leap that appeared to require no effort, he was on his feet. He came and sat down beside her, and rested his arm along the back of the bench. She let her head drop onto his shoulder.

'Thanks for doing such a great job with the kids, Max. You always have such fun, and I feel as if I'm missing out having to work all these extra shifts.'

Max rested his head on hers.

'We miss you too, but it's only this week that you're short-staffed isn't it, and I like being in charge. Selfish as it sounds, I love having their undivided attention.'

Ellie felt a brief flash of happiness before reality struck her and tears flooded her eyes. Max had always said he loved his life—exactly as it was. He had never wanted to do anything but be a PE teacher. He enjoyed his job, and spent hours each week giving extra coaching to kids of all abilities. He had the knack of knowing how to deal with every type of character, from the bullies to the most timid child who hated the whole idea of sport. He somehow managed to get them all to join in and have a good time. From Ellie's perspective, though, having him at home during the long holidays was a huge bonus, and they'd always had a great time together. When she wasn't working, that is.

'I was a bit worried about Penny last night,' Ellie said, hoping her voice showed no trace of her brief emotional moment.

'She phoned earlier, and she seemed fine. Gary had gone out. He's apparently fallen in love with the Porsche, which he can't afford, so unlike some of us his mission for the day is to go round car showrooms to find the next best thing. I'm sorry about the car, Ellie. I know I'm being stubborn. Give me a while and I'll get used to having money.'

Ellie felt a burst of hope as Max appeared to be talking about the future.

'It's not your fault. Let's forget it. Were there any other calls?'

Max shook his head.

'Mimi left her cardigan last night. We need to let Pat know so that he can come and pick it up. Can you give him a call later?' Ellie asked.

'Yeah—no problem. I was thinking, though. I do think it might make things easier on Pat if we tried a bit harder with Mimi. I know you don't like her, but he's going through hell.'

Ellie sighed. What could she say? Perhaps she should tell Max what Mimi had said about him and Alannah—but she couldn't. He might admit that it was true.

She stood up, and picked up the candle.

'I'll go and make lunch,' she said. 'I'll give you a shout when it's ready.'

Max turned his face up to hers with a smile.

'What can I do to help?' he asked.

'Nothing. You sit there. You've done enough this morning. I'm going to put this somewhere—the downstairs loo, I think,' she said, holding up the candle, 'and then I'll start on the prawns.'

She smiled at Max, and walked through into the kitchen and on towards the downstairs bathroom. She eyed the phone as she passed, and thought she might give Penny a quick call back to check if she was okay. She could never remember Penny's number because having lived next door for so long, it had rarely been needed. Typing 1471 and hoping that Penny had called after Fiona, she listened as she heard the automated voice say 'the caller withheld their number'.

At one time, she would just have asked Max who had called, in all innocence. But now the sharp shard of suspicion pierced her fragile trust, leaving an aching void in its place. And to think that just moments ago she had begun to believe that everything was going to be all right, and perhaps her suspicions were unfounded.

On top of all these doubts and misgivings, she didn't know what to do about Friday night. The accident. She had pushed it to the back of her mind since she'd heard when and where it happened. But she couldn't keep ignoring it. She had to do something. She couldn't leave it like this.

She made her way quietly upstairs, through the bedroom and into their bathroom. Leaving the door ajar so she could see if Max or one of the twins came to find her, she picked up her phone and typed in a number—one she knew by heart, but which she had never expected to use again.

It was answered almost immediately.

'Ellie—what a nice surprise,' came the voice she least wanted to hear in the whole world.

'Can you speak?' she asked.

'Always. You know that. Did you enjoy your shopping? I hope you found your present. I saw you looking at them in the store, so I could tell you liked them.' She could hear that he was smiling.

'Don't ever do that again. *Never.* What if Leo had seen you leaving it there? How would I have explained that? Please, please don't make this any more difficult than it already is.'

'It was just a rose, to show you I was thinking of you. Watching you. What are you wearing right now? Tell me, then I can picture you. Have you changed since you got back from shopping, or are you still wearing those black jeans and the red T-shirt?'

'Shut up. Please, just shut up. I'm not ringing about the rose, or about you and me. I need to ask you about Friday night. You must have driven home along the back road. You *must* have. And the timing was right, *and* you were angry. You drove off at such a speed. I need to know if it was you that knocked that girl over. I *have* to know.'

For once, he was silent. Ellie waited. It was difficult to interpret the tone of his voice when he finally replied, but he had lost the teasing note that for some reason he believed she found seductive. Perhaps she might have done at one time. His voice sounded hollow, as if it were coming from a long way off.

'Do you honestly think that I would have left a child on the side of the road to die? Is that what you think of me? God, that hurts. Of *course* it wasn't me. I agree I could only just have missed her, but I swear to you that I could never even leave a *cat* to die on the side of the road, let alone a *child*.'

She knew he was telling the truth. Whatever else he was, and however deluded he was about her, she couldn't imagine him cold-bloodedly dragging a dying child to the side of the road. But that wasn't the only problem.

'I'm sorry. I should never have asked that. But did you pass any cameras? Our neighbour, Tom, says that there will be CCTV at some of the points around the village, and possibly those cameras that recognise number plates. Do you think you would have been seen?'

She could hear him blowing out air in irritation. She knew he had been hoping for so much more when he'd seen her name on his phone.

'I don't know—I've no idea. I wasn't thinking about that at the time, if you remember. I was trying to deal with the conversation we'd just had.' The hurt was there in his voice. 'I know you were lying that night. I know how you feel about me. About us.'

God, what a fool she'd been. This wasn't helping.

'Look, I need to know what you will say if you *were* spotted. The police will want to talk to you. I cut through the lanes, and there won't be any cameras there. But what will you *say*? If the police come to see you. What will you tell them?'

'They're the police. I'll have to tell them the truth. In fact I think we both know that I should go down to the station right now and say that I was out that night. I should go and admit where I was, not wait to be questioned.' His voice had turned serious. She knew he was right, but she couldn't bear it.

'*No*. Please, please don't do that. It won't help Abbie, and if it wasn't you and you didn't see anything, what's the harm? How could I ever explain it to Max? Please, if you care as much about me as you say you do, please don't do anything.'

There was a thoughtful note to his voice when he replied, and at that instant, Ellie knew what he was going to say.

'If I tell the police and they question you, you'll *have* to tell Max, won't you. And we both know that he won't forgive you. So if I admit I was seeing you, you'll be free. Free for me. So tell me, Ellie—why shouldn't I do it?'

At that moment, Ellie saw the bedroom door begin to open, and she quickly hung up and shut the bathroom door.

'Ellie?' It was Max's voice. 'Are you in there? Are you okay? You said you were making lunch, but then you disappeared.'

She took a deep breath, and tried to disguise the nervous tremor of her voice.

'Be out in a minute, Max. Sorry—I felt a bit grubby after the drive.'

Damn this accident, she thought. Damn it to hell.

She knew that was a terrible thought and her suffering was nothing in comparison to Abbie's family's, but if she wasn't careful it was going to bring her whole world crashing down around her ears.

Running some cold water into the sink, and flushing the lavatory for effect, Ellie opened the bathroom cabinet to stash her phone until she could rescue it later. She would struggle to explain why she'd taken it with her into the bathroom.

She looked in the cupboard and paused. She stared for a minute longer.

What was wrong?

Nothing appeared to be missing, but it was as if everything had been moved slightly. Max never opened this cupboard—all his stuff was on the shelf. She kept tablets, antiseptic cream, and some of the necessary but less alluring female bathroom products in here.

She rushed into the bedroom, randomly pulling open drawers.

But she already knew what she was going to find.

❖

Since the children were now happily playing in the kitchen, Leo decided to pop upstairs quickly and get her laptop so she could update her blog. Max had gone in search of Ellie, and she didn't know whether she was supposed to leave the twins on their own or not, but she was sure they would be okay for two minutes. She disconnected the laptop from where it was charging, and headed back down.

Damn, she thought. The lid was fully closed. She must have done it by mistake as she picked it up. She always left the lid open by about a millimetre so that the screen went off, but the catch didn't engage. It had broken a couple of weeks ago, and she had kept meaning to get it mended. Now she was going to have to root around and find a paperclip or something that she could bend to open it. That's what came of being in a rush.

Returning to the kitchen, she fished around in the utensils drawer until she found an old corkscrew. The end of that should do it. She twiddled around and finally managed to open the lid, and the laptop sprang back into life. Vowing to get the catch fixed, she decided to write up some bullet points for her next blog. Her conversations with Ellie today had her thinking about how easy it was for two people who are so close to begin to move in opposite directions, perhaps without even noticing it.

She opened her documents folder, and stopped. She hadn't used her computer since she got up that morning, but three of her files had been accessed. The time stamps showed today's date. Two were only blogs—her client files were all password-protected, thank goodness—but the other one that had been opened was the file on her father.

She looked up as Max returned to the kitchen.

'Ellie will be down to make lunch in a moment, Leo. Can I interest you in a glass of wine? I'm going to get on with the salad so that Ellie only has to worry about the clever bits.'

'No wine, thanks. Water's fine.' She paused. 'Max, have you used my computer for any reason this morning? It's not a problem, of course, but I just wondered.'

Max grabbed a bottle of fizzy water from the fridge.

'Now why on earth would I want to do that when we have a super-duper twenty-seven-inch iMac in the office? Why are you asking? Have you got lots of exciting secrets on there?' Max wiggled his eyebrows suggestively, and turned back to the task of helping with the lunch.

Leo decided to say nothing. Perhaps it was Ellie, although she couldn't think when she would have had the chance.

Max was rummaging around in the fridge and pulling out bags of salad and tomatoes when Ellie came into the kitchen, looking even more harassed than before.

'Max—did you go out at all this morning with the twins?' she demanded in a slightly breathless voice.

'Good grief—what's with the twenty questions today?' Max responded, laughing and shaking his head. 'What's got into you two? Yes, as a matter of fact, I took the twins to the swings. We were out for about forty-five minutes. Why?'

'Did you lock up—properly, I mean?'

Max had clearly begun to realise that Ellie was genuinely concerned about something.

'Yes, of course. It's not like the old place, is it? There was nothing to nick there—but now I'm really careful. Why?'

'Because while we were all out, somebody's been in our house.'

21

A Single Step: the blog of Leo Harris

A game of charades

Definition of 'charade': An absurd pretence intended to create a pleasant or respectable appearance

Definition of 'absurd': wildly unreasonable, illogical, foolish, or inappropriate

How much are you pretending to be something or somebody that you're not? Are you acting out your own charade, and have you thought about how foolish and inappropriate your actions are?

Within our working lives, and perhaps even amongst friends, we see deceptions played out before our eyes: people who pretend to be happy when they are aching with sadness, or to like each other when they feel nothing but contempt. Perhaps these are actions of self-preservation, driven by a will to hide our pain from a wider audience.

Within a relationship, though, pretence is indeed both unreasonable and illogical. Admit to being the person you really are. Never play that deadly game of charades.

"The more definitely his own a man's character is, the better it fits him." Cicero

A hand shot out and the screen went blank. That stupid bitch Leo. What did *she* know about charades?

It was easy to delete her words, but less easy to erase the feeling of rage they had provoked. Well, some relationships had to have secrets. Some things were too difficult to explain, or for other people to understand. So sometimes you had to act the part—pretend to be somebody you're not. Didn't she understand that?

Look what happened when the truth was told, when people showed who they really were. They got hurt. Honesty was rarely the answer. There was safety in lies.

Perhaps it would have been better if Abbie had never known the truth. She would never have guessed.

I only got to touch her once. I stroked her hair and tried to kiss her. I held her hands, and told her what I wanted. I told her we could be close—she only had to keep our secret, and I would let her go. But she screamed and cried, as if I were a monster. She rejected me like I was nothing. Nothing! After everything I'd done to be close to her. I knew how to stop her, though. I knew what would frighten her enough to make her quiet.

Then she got away.

And then the accident.

I thought Abbie was dead, but it wasn't my fault. She shouldn't have rejected me. She shouldn't have run.

It was no good thinking of what might have been. There were things to be done. The evidence that Abbie had been here, in this house, must be disposed of. The shoes and the phone—what could be done with them?

Some pretty pale blue ballet pumps were pulled from the bottom of a supermarket bag, where they lay hidden below a pile of newspapers that were waiting to be recycled. Stuffed inside one was a shocking pink mobile phone. The SIM card had been disposed of in a plant pot full of earth in the back garden. Nobody would look there. But the rest needed a bit more thought.

Tomorrow was rubbish collection day. That's where they could go. *But not in our bin.* Lots of people put their bins out the night before, so a late-night walk on the other side of the village should solve the problem. Perhaps it would be a good idea to smash the phone to pieces first.

That was one problem solved. The other was a much greater one.

The driver looked straight at me, at where I was hiding in the woods. It's a face I'll never forget, bleached white by the headlights, black eyes darting frantically from side to side to check if anybody was watching. And there I was. Perhaps for now we're keeping each other's secret, but for how long?

Abbie can tell nobody.

But the driver knows who I am, and can't be allowed to expose me.

There were plans to be made, and there was one person who was going to help. She wouldn't like it, but she wasn't going to be given any choice.

22

Day Four: Monday

To Leo's disappointment, Sunday had never settled back into the peaceful and harmonious atmosphere of that brief period before lunch. The more Ellie insisted that somebody had been in the house, the more Max had told her that it was her imagination. Not only had she thought that the bathroom cupboard had been tampered with, but she was sure somebody had been through her drawers. Max had joked about the intruder probably being after her knickers, but Ellie had been furious with him for taking it so lightly.

The trouble was, Leo was fairly certain that somebody had been looking at her computer. But nothing had been stolen, and surely they would have taken her laptop if they were so interested in it? If Max *had* left the door open by mistake and some kids had come in—the obvious answer as nothing was missing—he wouldn't be doing it again in a hurry. So it had felt better not to add fuel to the fire.

Now it was a new day, and much as she was dreading it Leo thought it was time she faced up to another of the traumas of her childhood. She was going to walk into the village, and hope and pray that she could replace the old memories that still haunted her with new ones, much as she had done with Willow Farm.

She had driven past the shops on Friday evening for the first time in years. Ellie and Max had always lived on the other side of the village and it had been easy to reach their house by coming down the back road, but to get to Willow Farm she could no longer ignore Little Melham, so it had to be dealt with.

She stopped outside what used to be the sweet shop, and gazed at its old-fashioned facade. It had always looked like a shop out of a fairy story, with its semi-circular bay window made up of over a hundred small panes of glass. She had counted them once. On the outside not much had changed, but Leo could see that now it was a newsagent's too. Sweets alone would be unlikely to sustain a shop in a village these days, particularly as she could bet money on this being the sort of place where health-conscious parents frowned upon their precious offspring eating sugar in any form.

Right Leo, in you go.

She didn't allow herself time to think as she purposefully pushed open the door and walked inside. This shop had the worst memories of all, so it was the best place to start. For most of the other shops, she had merely been a customer as part of her three times weekly grocery trip. The shopping was one of her chores, and the hardest. The only good thing was that it kept her out of the house. If there was too much to carry in one journey, she had to make several. She was known for having the biggest muscles ever seen on an eleven-year-old girl's arms, but if Ellie ever offered to help—which she often did—she was told it wasn't necessary. Ellie had to get on with her piano practice, or her homework. Leo, on the other hand, had to do her homework after dark when everybody was in bed, sitting on the floor of her room with a piece of fabric over her lamp in case anybody was walking the corridors.

But the sweet shop was the scene of her most degrading experience. On the day in question, she had already completed her second trip to the village. There had been potatoes to buy, and onions, carrots, and other heavy vegetables. And then there had been the meat and the bread. Leo thought she'd finished but was sent back one more time to get some aspirin, which she could easily have managed on either of the previous journeys.

And that's when she did something stupid.

Most days as she walked through the village, kids from school would be hanging around the church or the bus shelter. Usually she got jeers and catcalls because she wasn't one of their crowd, but this day was different. When she came out of the chemist, there was a group of about eight of them sitting on the church wall, and for once they spoke to her. Even to be noticed by them was such a rare event that when they called her name, she tentatively went over to join them. She supposed she should have realised that they didn't actually want to talk to her, but they did want something.

'Oy—you—Leonora,' one of the lads called. It always raised a laugh when she was called by her full name, because these were the kids from the rough end of town, and they thought it was a posh name. If only they'd known. She knew this lad—Neil something or other. He was in the year above her, and fancied himself something rotten. She wasn't sure why, because he had floppy, greasy hair and a huge zit on his chin, but it was the first time anybody had paid her any attention.

As she got closer, she could see that some of the girls were sniggering and whispering to each other, but the lads seemed to want to talk to her.

'All right?' Neil asked. She nodded, not quite getting up the confidence to speak.

'Listen, Le-o-nor-ra.' He enunciated each syllable and turned to his friends with a smirk. 'We need you to do something for us. That old bag in the sweet shop has banned us from going in—so get us some chocolate will you?' He pronounced 'you' as 'ya' which Leo thought sounded cool, but she would never get away with it. She'd get cracked around the head at home, and she would sound ridiculous probably.

'Okay,' she answered. 'I don't mind. Give me the money, then.'

They all burst out laughing, as if she'd said something hysterically funny. Or stupid, more likely.

'Tut-tut, Nora. Is it okay if I call you Nora? You don't pay for them, you silly tart. You nick 'em. A couple of Curly Wurlies and a Toffee Crisp will do fine.'

Leo hesitated. She wanted to be accepted, but she had never stolen anything in her life, and had no desire to start now. But if she refused, they would jeer at her even more and it would spread round school like wildfire that Leonora Harris was too chicken to nick a couple of bars of chocolate.

If she'd had money of her own, she would have bought the chocolate and lied, but she didn't. There was enough of her stepmother's money to buy one thing—and she'd have to say she'd lost the change and take the punishment. Perhaps she could pay for the Toffee Crisp and steal the Curly Wurlies. If it meant that the other kids finally accepted her, maybe she could do it.

Leo knew they were watching her as she walked towards the shop, and she tried to look confident. She swallowed hard as she pushed the door open. Mrs Talbot was standing behind the counter, serving some children and their mother. They were choosing from the penny tray, and taking their time about it. The chocolates were on display shelves down the side of the shop, with the big jars of sweets that had to be weighed out on the toffee scale right behind the counter.

Mrs Talbot was a large woman, which everybody joked was from eating too much of her own stock. She always wore one of those crossover aprons with a loud pattern, and her face was set with lines of what looked to Leo like constant irritation. For now, though, Mrs Talbot was being all sweetness and light to the mother of the well-behaved children.

Her face flushing with the fear of what she was about to do, Leo glanced quickly over her shoulder and hurriedly placed the two chocolate bars in her shopping bag. She picked up the Toffee Crisp, and advanced towards the counter, her palms sweating with fear. If this is what it felt like to be a burglar, she thought, she couldn't understand why anybody would want to do it.

Mrs Talbot said nothing and finished serving the family. Leo was relieved. Obviously she hadn't noticed a thing. Mrs Talbot even walked to the door with the customers, opening it to show them out with a smile, and wishing them a good day. But then Leo's fear returned in full force, because Mrs Talbot had closed the door. And locked it.

Without saying a word, she had walked over to her telephone and picked it up. She dialled three numbers, and Leo thought that without a doubt it had to be the police. But she was wrong. Mrs Talbot was calling directory enquiries, and asking for Leo's home number. This was, after all, a village. Everybody knew where she lived, and where she had come from. Now, she wished it *had* been the police that Mrs Talbot was calling.

It hadn't taken long at all for her stepmother to arrive, and what came next didn't bear thinking about. To Mrs Talbot's credit, even she had looked shocked at the hard slap across the face that Leo had received, but Leo knew that was nothing to what she was going to get when they got home. And then, to her eternal shame and degradation, her stepmother grabbed a handful of Leo's hair, twisting it to get a better grip, and dragged her from the shop, past all the sneering kids on the church wall, and took her home. Leo had never set foot inside the shop from that day to this.

But now here she was. A comfortable-looking lady of about sixty stood behind the counter. Dressed in a pink cotton top with short sleeves and some elaborate beading around the neck, she had a pleasant smile, and to Leo's surprise her face lit up when she looked at her customer.

'Leo Harris—well, I'll be blessed,' she said, beaming at a stunned Leo. 'It's good to see you, lass. I'd have recognised you anywhere. Come to visit Ellie, have you? I bet those twins are running you ragged.'

Leo was momentarily lost for words.

'Oh, don't look so worried, love. It's me—Doreen Talbot. I know I've changed a bit. I've been ill, but I'm okay now. I feel twenty years younger, and I've been waiting a long time to apologise to you.'

Leo finally found her voice.

'Mrs Talbot, what can I say? I had no idea that you were still here, but I don't know why you feel you need to apologise to me. I stole from you. I am so ashamed that I did that. I could blame peer pressure, but I should have been strong enough to resist.'

Mrs Talbot leant against the counter on her folded arms.

'Listen, Leo, we all know you had a dreadful time with the old battle-axe. But nothing prepared me for the way she treated you that day. If it had been nowadays, I'd have called child services or whatever they're called. I'm sorry, love. If I'd known and if I hadn't been feeling so ropey myself in those days, I'd have handled things different.'

Leo didn't know what to say. But Mrs Talbot hadn't finished.

'We all knew, you know,' she repeated. 'Not only about you and how you came to be here, but everything else that went on. It's a village. We talk. Your stepmother was evil, there's no doubt. But then she had a lot to put up with, I suppose.'

Not entirely sure that she understood what Mrs Talbot was getting at, it suddenly didn't matter to Leo. Feeling as if her last battle had been fought and won, she was about to thank Mrs Talbot and leave when she spotted the local paper with the headline about the hit-and-run on the back road splashed across the front page. Mrs Talbot followed Leo's gaze and pointed to the image of a happy-looking Abbie.

'And there's another poor young girl. A bit of a solitary soul, or so I'm told. Not many friends. Just like you were at that age, if you don't mind me saying so, lass.'

Not knowing how to respond to this, Leo thanked Mrs Talbot for being so forgiving, and shook her hand.

The lightness that she felt at being exonerated from the shoplifting incident was replaced with sadness for Abbie Campbell. It sounded like she was a loner too, and Leo knew better than most how difficult that could be. Conflicting emotions were fighting for supremacy as she closed the shop door.

'Hello! This is a nice surprise.' She heard the voice before she noticed him, and blinked to bring the day back into focus.

'Tom, hi. It's good to see you.' Leo suppressed her confused thoughts and attempted a smile. 'I'm sorry we missed you yesterday, it would have been good to meet Lucy.'

'I came to say thanks to Max and Ellie, but thought you and I might fix up to have lunch sometime, if you're at a loose end. Because I certainly am,' Tom said, with a sheepish grin.

He indicated the wine bar right behind them.

'It's a bit early for lunch yet, but do you fancy a cup of coffee if you've nothing better to do?'

Tom was genuinely pleased to see Leo. Since Lucy had left the evening before the house had felt empty, so he'd done his usual trick of coming for a walk to the village. Tomorrow he was going to start phoning around because until the right job came up, the least he could do would be to offer his services for training or mentoring, and if that failed he would look up a few charities where he could help out. He wanted to be around people. He was fast realising that solitude didn't suit him.

He admired Leo's casual look, which was perfect for an English summer's day. He had the feeling that she only ever wore black with a splash of white, but with that dark red lipstick and the sunglasses, she instantly stood out from the crowd. Her black cotton skirt finished just above her knees, showing her lightly tanned legs to perfection, and she was wearing a short, loose, black-and-white sleeveless top.

He felt a bit scruffy in his jeans and T-shirt. He hadn't even bothered to shave this morning. He needed to get his act together, or he would become a complete slob if he didn't watch it. Leo didn't seem too worried, though, as they took their seats at a table just inside the wide-open sliding doors. Believe it or not, the sun was too hot to sit outside, which made a change from the incessant rain they had been enjoying this summer.

They ordered their coffee, and Tom turned to Leo.

'You were miles away when I saw you,' he said. 'Are you okay?'

'I've been laying some demons to rest, that's all,' Leo answered, with a satisfied smile.

'Demons? In Little Melham? You've got to be kidding me,' Tom said.

'I wish I was,' Leo said. 'Anyway, never mind me. How did yesterday go with Lucy? Did she love the cottage now that it's finished?'

'She did, although her mother was a bit scathing. But then that's only what I expected. She chose to live in what I would consider to be a modern, charmless box, so I had no expectation of raptures over my choice.'

Leo didn't speak, and just looked at him with her head to one side, as if she were waiting for him to say more.

'We've been divorced for quite a while. We've gone our separate ways but we get on with each other for Lucy's sake.'

Tom didn't want to talk about the breakup of his marriage. Male pride meant he wanted to avoid telling all and sundry that his wife had left him for another man, but on the other hand he didn't want everybody to think that he was the type of bastard who cheated on women. Best to say nothing, on the whole, and let them draw their own conclusions.

'It's a pity you didn't get to meet her. I gather you and Ellie went off on some shopping spree or other.'

'We did. I think Ellie needed to get out of the house. A bit of an escape after the night before. It was a weird party, though. Everybody was behaving as if they were totally deranged, I thought. What did you make of it?' Leo asked.

'I enjoyed it. Of course, I didn't know anybody until that evening, so I didn't know what was normal and what wasn't.'

Leo raised her eyebrows.

'You're being polite Tom. Very diplomatic, I would say. You must have detected some ripples under the smooth surface, though. Come on—you can tell me. They're not my friends particularly, although I've known most of them for ages.'

'There were one or two signs of strain that I noticed, but I've been to dinner parties before now where there have been stand-up arguments or people bursting into tears at the table, so it was fairly mild by comparison.'

Tom wasn't exaggerating, either. Being a policeman had lots of pluses and he loved the job, but he could quite understand that being a policeman's wife was not always that easy. And when you get a load of coppers and their partners together, there was nearly always one couple that was temporarily or even permanently coming to the end of their tether.

'Tell me about you, Leo,' Tom said. 'It was good of you to offer all the ladies your life-coaching services free of charge. Do you think they'll take you up on it?'

He rested his forearms on the table and leaned forward, hoping she would realise that his interest was genuine. He found it quite amusing that they both probably spent their lives trying to get people to admit to the truth, but with entirely different objectives.

Leo appeared to be finding the froth on her rapidly cooling cappuccino fascinating as she stirred it gently with her teaspoon.

'I think that in more than one case there are some problems lying hidden, and I think I can help. Whether any of them will speak to me or not, I don't know. But on the whole, I suspect not. Penny said she was keen, but Gary had a face like thunder.'

Tom couldn't forget how upset Penny had been when he'd arrived on Saturday, and how quiet she was for the whole evening. Gary seemed a cheerful kind of guy, but it was that type of cheap bravado that Tom didn't appreciate in other men.

'I can see that you understand people really well, and that must be a hell of an asset in your job—a bit like mine in that respect.' Tom smiled as he signalled the waitress for another two coffees. 'So tell me more about these demons you're laying to rest. The local sweet shop seems a strange place to start.'

For a second Leo looked cross and Tom thought that he'd gone too far. He didn't mean to pry, and he wondered if he should change the subject. There was an uncomfortable silence.

'Now listen, Tom, you can't play the "say nothing—she's a woman so she's bound to fill the void" ruse on me. I do the same thing with my clients, so I know what you're up to.'

Tom instantly felt embarrassed. He had actually been searching for a safe topic of conversation, but Leo wasn't to know that.

'I'm sorry. It wasn't intentional. Based on your smile, I'd assumed your demons were something trivial—and anyway it's none of my business.'

Leo gave him what could only be described as a calculating look.

'You're right, Tom. It is *absolutely* none of your business—but I'm going to tell you anyway.' Leo sat up straight and looked him firmly in the eye. 'However, as it is now just after midday, the cost of telling you will be lunch and a nice cool bottle of white wine.'

She waited until the wine was poured, and took a large gulp.

'Okay—I'm going to give you the short version. My principle motivation for telling you is that half the village knows most of this, and I would rather you heard the truth from me than some distorted version that has had lots of intriguing—but untrue—embellishments.'

Tom leaned across and chinked his glass with hers, and gave her an encouraging smile. She took a deep breath.

'When I was ten, my mother died. She was epileptic, and she died in the bath. I found her when I got home from school.'

She saw the consternation on Tom's face, and realised that he probably wished he had never encouraged Leo to bare her soul. She mentally gritted her teeth and forced herself to continue.

'We lived in Shrewsbury—me, my mum, and my dad. My dad theoretically had a job that required him to be away from home a lot—three or four nights most weeks. He had a senior position in one of the pottery companies in Stoke on Trent. He told my mum that he was on the sales side, which is why he had to be away so much. But that wasn't true. He was a director, but nothing to do with selling. He was actually the finance director, so in fact he didn't have to be away at all.'

Leo took another sip of her wine. The waitress walked over with the menus, but Tom shook his head, and she took the hint and backed away.

Leo paused for a moment and willed her voice to be level. 'When I found my mum, the police had to track Dad down and ask him to come home. I assumed we'd carry on living in our house and it would just be the two of us, but he took one look at me and went upstairs and started packing a case.' Leo shook her head as a vivid memory hit her. She was sitting silent and speechless downstairs while her dad was banging around upstairs. Neither of them had tried to comfort the other. She had been too distraught to understand what was going on. Her father had bundled her in the car, and that's when she had started to cry. She felt as if she was leaving her—leaving her mum—and that didn't seem right.

'My dad did try to talk to me, but I wasn't listening.' Leo looked at Tom with a smile. 'My mum was great. A real hippy chick, and loads of fun.'

Leo remembered feeling as if she had been broken into tiny pieces. As if bits of her were splintering off. But that was too much to share with Tom. Better to stick to the facts.

'I refused to listen to anything my father was saying. I think I sensed that I wasn't going to want to hear it, and I couldn't understand why he was taking me away. He was bringing me here. To Little Melham, and to Willow Farm.'

Leo swallowed as the memories rose in a huge bubble to the surface, escaping from the black hole where they had been buried for years. She recalled that the journey hadn't been a long one, but her dad had given up trying to speak to her. They had finally pulled up at the very bottom of the drive, and he had forced her to look at him.

'Listen, L,' he'd said. He had always shortened her name from Leonora to 'L'. 'This is going to come as a bit of a surprise, but I need to explain to you that I have another wife. She lives here. She doesn't know about you, but I'm sure you're going to get on fine.'

Leo didn't understand. What did he mean, another wife? And whose was this house? A tiny part of her mind registered her confusion, but the rest was too full of grief to cope with the intrusion of other emotions. Her dad had walked into the house. She hadn't really taken in what he had said. All she could see in her mind was her mother's body.

She had leaned her head against the car window, her sobs having subsided into irregular juddering hiccups, and wiped her eyes on the sleeve of her jumper.

'He asked me to wait in the car while he went to talk to his wife. God knows what he told her, or what excuses he gave. I was still sitting there not knowing what was happening when there was a piercing scream from the house, full of anger and anguish, as if it were coming up through someone's feet and reverberating through every inch of their body. It didn't take me long to realise it was my stepmother's response to having a ten-year-old child that she knew nothing about foisted on her. That, and finding out that her husband was a bigamist.'

Tom was propping his chin up on the clenched fist of one hand, his eyes a picture of concern.

'I'm so sorry I asked, Leo. I had no right to push you to talk about all this stuff.'

Don't give me sympathy, Leo thought. I might not be able to finish and that would somehow be worse than never starting.

'If I hadn't told you, somebody else would. You must know by now what they're like in this village.' Leo mentally gritted her teeth as she continued her story. 'When I eventually went into the house there was this girl, standing by her mum and looking as bewildered as I felt, but that was nothing to the look I got from my stepmother. It was a look of pure malice, as if somehow this was all my fault. From then on, she treated me as a drudge, and had no compunction about slapping me around. But not much more than that. My father took no interest. I think he loved my mum, but was stuck with Ellie's mother—The Old Witch, as Max always called her. But my father was a disgrace. He did nothing to protect me—simply handed me over and lived his own life. I barely spoke to him after that, and he came and went all the time. We never knew where he was or when he'd be back, and nobody ever told us. I left home as soon as I thought I would be able to take care of myself.'

'What about Ellie?' Tom asked.

'Ellie was kind to me. She tried to comfort me, and to look out for me at school. But I withdrew into myself and shut her out most of the time. She tried to please our father and he enjoyed the attention, but as far as I could see she got little reward for her effort.'

Tom shook his head slowly, and reached over to squeeze her hand. Leo fought the urge to whip her hand away quickly. She gave it a moment, and then pulled back to grip the stem of her wine glass.

'The worst of it was the names. Ellie was christened Eleanor, and when I came along my dad gave Mum some cock-and-bull story about why I should be christened Leonora, but it was entirely for his convenience. If he called us both Elle he could never get confused. He wouldn't make a mistake. Anyway, once Ellie and I had realised why we were both called Elle, we told everybody to call us Ellie and Leo. But my dad continued to call us both Elle—out of indifference I think, although Ellie insists it was out of affection—and my stepmother didn't call me anything at all. Having said that, in seven years under her roof, I never called her anything either. She wasn't getting it all her own way. My final memories of my father are of a selfish, uninterested man. God knows where he was and what he was up to when he was away, but he provided plenty of money and all my stepmother cared about by then was vengeance.'

Leo looked at Tom's horrified expression. He didn't need to feel bad. She had told him the bald truth, without overdoing the emotion. They were both silent for a moment, but Tom's eyes never left her face. Leo knew that she had rendered him speechless, and wondered if it wasn't all too much, too soon.

'Look,' he said. 'I do appreciate you sharing all that with me. It must have been very difficult. But now at least I understand why you had some demons to lay to rest. Shall we order some food, and talk about something else?'

He summoned the waitress for the menus, while Leo debated whether to tell him the rest, the undercurrents he'd missed at Saturday's party, and her fears about everything that was *not* being said . . . particularly by Ellie.

23

For the first time that she could ever remember, Ellie hadn't wanted to come to work today, even though it was only to do half a shift. She'd run the usual tests on Abbie soon after she had arrived and those had kept her busy for a while, and she had sent Abbie's mum, Kath, to get herself a cup of coffee and something to eat. The poor woman looked shattered. Ellie sat down on the chair by Abbie's bed, and for a moment allowed her mind to be bombarded by her own doubts and problems. She was praying that the answer would appear in a flash of clarity, but the trouble was, there was no magic solution.

Her doubts about Max were tearing her apart. Just the thought of not being with him was too painful to imagine. And if he found out what she'd done, she would lose him. At any moment, this could all blow up and put an end to everything that mattered. Somebody was bound to have seen either her car or *his* on Friday night, and when the police came knocking she was convinced that he wouldn't keep her out of it. Why should he?

And then there was the phone call. Why would somebody call the house and withhold their number? What was Max hiding?

'Stop fooling yourself,' she muttered out loud. Because hard as it was to admit, she knew exactly what he was hiding.

Leo would say, 'Ask him. Just bloody ask him.' But that would open a door that she wanted to keep firmly shut. As long as Max believed Ellie didn't know about his affair, he would have to find the words to tell her— and she didn't think he'd be able to do it. So he would stay with her. With them. Everybody knew that choosing the right moment to tell your partner that you're leaving is the hard bit. How many marriages had stayed together because nobody had had the guts to admit the truth? And over time, the danger dimmed slowly to become no more than a distant echo. At least, that's what she hoped.

So she *couldn't* ask Max. He might say, 'Oh, thank God you know. I'm so sorry, Ellie, but at least it's not a secret anymore, and we can all move forward.' She had imagined that conversation so many times in the last few weeks.

On top of all this, she wished she had never mentioned that somebody had been in their house. It was *obvious* who it was, and it was equally obvious not only why, but how.

The bastard.

If she was correct, that meant he could get in at any time, even when she was alone, or when they were sleeping. Ellie shuddered. It was one thing trying to manage this horrendous situation by phone and text, but if she found herself alone in the house with him, she didn't like to think about what might happen. Perhaps a masked intruder would be better. She couldn't tell Max what she suspected. He wouldn't believe her, and she could never explain.

Ellie was staring vacantly at Abbie as the turbulent thoughts churned round and round her mind. A flicker of movement caught her eye, and she focused on Abbie's young face. Nothing. But she was sure she'd seen something. Maybe it was the shadow of a cloud moving over the sun, or a flickering light on the other side of the unit. She looked at the smooth, clear skin on the girl's face, the side that hadn't come into contact with the gritty road. She reached out and stroked its peachy surface with the back of her fingers, hoping and praying that she had been right; that there had been some flicker of movement. Suddenly she felt that all her problems were trivial. Imagine if this was your child, she thought. That's what devastation is—not worrying about secret phone calls and foolish mistakes.

Somebody in the village knew what had happened to this child. Why was she out so late, and on her own? Why was she in the middle of nowhere? And who in their right mind could have just left her there, bruised, battered, and practically dead?

Ellie tenderly stroked the girl's hair back from her face. She remembered Kath trying to sing to Abbie on Saturday, but she was so choked she'd had to give up. Ellie had asked her what the song was, and Kath had told her that Abbie had always loved Adele and her dad sometimes played 'Someone Like You' on the piano for her to sing to. So now Ellie hummed it quietly. She didn't remember the words, but hoped that didn't matter.

❖

Ten minutes later, Ellie felt a flicker of hope. She'd seen it again, and this time she was certain.

'Sam,' she said, turning to the doctor who had just arrived at Abbie's bed. 'It might be nothing, but I think there was a small response from Abbie when I was with her a minute ago. Nothing much, but her eyelids fluttered. Only a second, and I know it could have been anything, but I thought I should mention it.'

Sam looked up from the chart he was reading.

'Great news, Ellie. The swelling on her brain has come down, and with the reduced sedatives let's hope we start to see a bit more of a reaction. What was her GCS?'

Ellie pulled a face.

'No change, I'm afraid. But I'll check again in another hour and let you know.'

'Okay. I suggest you don't mention the fluttering eyes to the mother, though. It's a bit early to get her hopes up.'

Ellie nodded. She *had* to get better. She didn't think she could bear it if this child died.

Sadly, there were no further signs of improvement, and although Ellie tried to talk to Kath Campbell, the poor woman was still barely able to speak without crying. All Ellie got out of her was 'it's all our fault' and 'how could we have been so stupid?' She had tried to understand why Abbie's parents were blaming themselves but when asked, Kath just shook her head and cried some more.

So it was with a heavy heart that Ellie made her way from the hospital to her car.

'You okay, Ellie?'

Ellie glanced behind her as Maria, one of the young nurses new to the ICU, caught up with her.

'Not really,' she responded. 'Abbie looks such a sweet kid, and I thought there were signs of improvement, but I guess I was wrong.' Ellie gave a despondent shrug.

'Well, there's something to cheer you up then.' Maria nodded her head towards the car park, and Ellie followed her gaze. A tight knot of panic formed in her throat, but Maria didn't notice her reaction.

'He's a bit tasty, isn't he? I love the sexy hat. Is he waiting for you?' Maria's eyes were open wide as she looked at the figure leaning against Ellie's car, dressed in dark jeans and a navy blue T-shirt, sporting a leather bush hat.

Ellie forced her voice into indifference.

'He's a friend of Max's. I've no idea what he's doing here, but I guess I'm about to find out. See you tomorrow, Maria.'

Ellie walked towards the car, but could feel that Maria's eyes were on her. She tried to be as nonchalant as possible, her smiling face belying her first words.

'What are you doing here? Are you completely mad?' she hissed.

'I wanted to see you. You refuse to come to me, so I've come to you. Let's get in the car, shall we?'

'No!' Ellie realised that she had raised her voice, and Maria was still watching. She was out of earshot, but Ellie had to keep her face calm and her voice down.

'No,' she repeated. 'We are *not* getting in the car. What do you want?'

He smiled.

'Ellie, darling, if you don't get in the car with me, your friend over there is going to wonder if there's a problem. She might come over and ask. Do you *want* her to wonder?'

Knowing he was right, and hating him even more for it, she clicked the remote. He held his hand out.

'Keys, please. Don't look at me like that. If you get in the car first, you'll drive off while I'm walking round to the passenger door. Give me the keys, darling.'

Ellie wanted to look around her, to see if anybody was watching. *Don't call me darling* was the thought echoing round her head. But if she opened her mouth, she would scream.

He opened the driver's door for her, as if he were being polite, and sauntered round to the passenger side. As he sat down, he handed her the keys.

'I suggest you drive somewhere, Ellie. Otherwise you are drawing attention to yourself, and you keep telling me that it's not what you want.'

'Please, can we stop this? I've told you so many times that what happened was a foolish mistake. I love Max. I'm sorry if I hurt you, but that was never my intention.'

He shook his head.

'It was no mistake, darling. You wanted me. I could tell. Every inch of you was craving for me, as I was craving for you. We just need to decide what we're going to do about it. Take me for a drive, Ellie. Let's talk sensibly.'

With shaking hands, Ellie put the keys into the ignition and turned the engine on.

'We can drive, but I'm not going to stop the car. We can drive round and talk—but *only* talk. Do you understand?'

'We'll see,' he responded with a smile.

Ellie knew that he didn't believe her. He thought she was just scared of the upset it would cause if she left Max for him, and she had failed abysmally to persuade him otherwise. The last time she had agreed to meet him—the night of the fateful accident—she had begged, pleaded, shouted, cried. In the end, he had pulled her into his arms and tried to soothe her. For a moment, it had felt good. She was too weak with emotion to resist, and it felt as if he were comforting her. Until he kissed her. She had come back to earth with a crash and screamed at him to get out of her car. She never wanted to see him again. She had thought she'd convinced him—but she was wrong.

Now she drove without speaking. She needed to get away from the hospital; away from where anybody who knew her might see her. But which was worse? If she went down some of the lanes and found a lay-by and they were seen there, that would be far worse than being seen in a public place—something that she could explain away if she had to.

Ellie swung left into the supermarket car park and drove to the most crowded area, pulling in beside a white van and a car she didn't recognise. At least they would be shielded from view from one side.

'What have you stopped here for? I need to be able to touch you, Ellie. I want to hold you. Remember what I said about your skin? I want to taste it again.'

He moved his hand across the car, and started to stroke her thigh. She closed her eyes to disguise her repugnance at his touch, but he immediately misread her signals.

'I know you want me to touch you. I want to take you somewhere and slowly remove your clothes, piece by piece. I want to feel your silky soft skin next to mine, and I want to take hours just loving you. I'll be so gentle with you, Ellie. I want your legs wrapped around me, holding me inside you. We *need* to do this, darling.'

This was all her fault. He had made it plain how he felt about her, and if she hadn't been feeling so vulnerable and unloved that day, certain that Max was betraying her, she would never have let it happen. She'd stopped just in time. But of course now he wanted to finish what they had started.

How could she make him go away? Leave her alone? She had to think very carefully about what to say. She turned to look at him, trying to ignore the gleam of desire in his eyes.

'I'm sorry. I really am terribly sorry. I know this is all my fault. But that day . . . It was a mistake. A stupid, cruel mistake. I thought Max was having an affair, and I was overwhelmed with hurt. Don't look at me like that—I know that I'm probably right about Max, but even so it doesn't excuse my behaviour. He'd lied to me. He said he was with Pat, but he wasn't. I knew he was with *her*. I was so vulnerable, and you made me feel attractive and exciting. For one wild moment I thought that if I could be unfaithful too, it would make it easier to forgive Max. It was such a ridiculous idea.'

'It wasn't ridiculous at all,' he said, gently kneading her thigh. She wanted him to stop, but there was a wildness to his eyes, and she was no longer sure of his reactions. 'Men only lie about where they are if they're somewhere they're not supposed to be. It's all true, Ellie. I've seen them together in the pub. In theory, they're with all the other teachers from the school, but in reality they're always together—talking quietly to each other. Excluding everybody else. I don't want to hurt you, but you need to believe me.'

'Even so, two wrongs don't make a right. I used you, and I am ashamed of that. All I can do is say that I'm sorry. But this business of following me has to stop. And no more roses. Please. I know you don't mean to, but you're scaring me.'

He reached out, as if he was going to touch her face. Ellie instinctively jerked her head away, and he dropped his hand back to her thigh. It made her shudder, but she couldn't push him too far.

'But the roses are symbolic for us, aren't they. Don't you remember?

How could she forget? Why did she ever tell him that her favourite yellow roses were being planted that day? He seemed to believe there was some romantic link between the roses and what had happened between them. It was all in his mind.

'There's nothing *to* remember. Two events, not in any way connected.'

As she spoke, Ellie could see him shaking his head slowly from side to side.

'You're lying to yourself, darling. Look, Max is having an affair. He's probably going to leave you. How much evidence do you need? You know he's been lying to you. So why wait for him? Why not be the one to take control, and tell him that you've found somebody that loves you and wants you, and will never let you down. We belong together, Ellie. Whatever the obstacles.'

Ellie closed her eyes. She didn't want to cry, but she was lost.

'I can't do this. Please, leave me alone. Look—I've just left the hospital where there is a young girl, knocked down and left for dead, who may never recover from her injuries. *That's* a tragedy. Whatever happened to her, she didn't deserve this. We are adults. We have choices, and we should make those that cause the least hurt. And I need you to go.'

She looked at him, and the desire in his eyes had been replaced by something else. Something that scared her more. It was determination.

'It isn't over, darling. This time, I'll go. I can walk back to my car. But I'll be watching, Ellie. Don't get too close to Max or I won't like it. You're mine now.'

She didn't look at him, but she heard him leave. The car door slammed, and he was gone. Ellie sat still for a second. Then her mouth filled with saliva, and she started to shiver.

Oh shit — not here.

But she couldn't stop it. She flung the car door open and leaned down into the gap between her car and the white van as the meagre contents of her stomach deposited themselves on the tarmac.

24

In her mind, Leo always pictured the high street of Little Melham as a black-and-white image, cold and wet with dismal skies and cheerless shop windows. She associated it with heavy bags that made her young arms ache, people laughing at her or pointing and staring. She was 'the bastard'. The child who had appeared from nowhere, and that nobody wanted.

Today, however, she had to admit that it was actually looking quite pretty. The sun was filtering through the branches of the trees that lined either side of the road, creating dappled patterns on the pavement, and the shop fronts looked bright and cheerful.

She knew that Tom had felt uncomfortable with some of her revelations; he had probably expected her problems to be something and nothing, and no doubt wished he had never started the conversation. It had given him an opening to tell his own sad story, though, and Leo was shocked to hear of his brother's death in a speedboat accident. While evidently this had left him considerably wealthier than he might otherwise have been, it made no difference at all to his sense of loss.

After sharing some of their past sorrows they had moved onto safer ground, and Tom had talked about plans for his career here in the north west. He was fairly certain that a chief inspector in the Manchester force was going to be retiring soon, and although it wouldn't be a promotion, he'd be happy with that as long as he was within driving distance of Lucy.

Leo couldn't quite fathom Tom. He seemed confident and comfortable with himself, but there was a slight remoteness about him that suggested something in his life had made him wary. Apart from the story about his brother's death, he had been very quiet about his private life. Although he was happy to talk about Lucy, he didn't say what had caused him and his wife to divorce, and he didn't leave her a suitable opening to ask. She got the feeling that still waters ran very deep. He seemed like a man who laid bare about sixty per cent of his soul, but the remainder would be very hard to penetrate.

At the end of lunch, they said their goodbyes and Leo decided to stroll back through the village on the opposite side of the road from the wine bar. She'd noticed earlier that there was a new delicatessen, and thought she would pop in and pick up a few bits and pieces to nibble before dinner that night. At least that way Ellie might not feel the necessity to cook her heart out yet again.

The shop was busy, but nobody appeared to be buying much. The shopkeeper glanced towards Leo.

'Is it okay if I just have a look around?' Leo asked. 'I've no idea what I want.'

'Be my guest. Let me know if you need any help.'

There was an uncomfortable silence for a few moments and Leo couldn't decide whether to pick something at random and make a hasty exit, or take her time and ignore the atmosphere. The shopkeeper must have recognised Leo's discomfort, and came to her rescue.

'Sorry, love. We didn't mean to be rude. We were just talking about that terrible accident on Friday night. We're all a bit in shock, you see. Are you from round here?'

'No—I'm only staying for a few days. But I did hear about it. The waitress in the wine bar mentioned it too,' Leo responded.

The shopkeeper nodded. 'It's dreadful—and they're saying that the driver has to be from here, because the road doesn't really go anywhere else. The whole village is talking about it. We can't believe it, to tell you the truth.'

One of the other women spoke up.

'Well, they've been checking the cameras—you know—those in the village. There's one at the petrol station, but I don't know if there are any others. Never thought it mattered much. I do know that they've been taking suspects into the station. Two of them are from the high school too. It just goes to show, doesn't it? Teachers? They're no better than the rest of us, are they?'

The shopkeeper leaned her elbows on the counter.

'Do you know which teachers it was, Sally?'

'All I heard is that one is a deputy head—a man. And then they've taken the PE teacher in as well. How awful if it was one of them, and they'd left that girl to die.'

Leo felt a shock at the mention of a PE teacher. She was as certain as she could ever be, though, that Max would never have knocked somebody over and abandoned them on the side of the road. She wondered if the deputy head could be Pat. Surely not?

'It's not only the teachers who've been taken in,' said another of the customers, a large woman with a too-tight perm. 'Our Philip was at the dentist this morning, and he saw that bigwig banker chap—you know, the one that works in London—him who's married to the girl who disappeared overnight from the village all those years ago. I can't remember his name. Well—he was scurrying out of the police station too—looking very shifty according to our Philip. You know what I think? All these sorts from the smart end of the village with their fancy jobs and flash cars to match—they all drink wine like it's going out of fashion. Then they think nothing of driving home. I just bet when they find out who it was, they'll discover that he'd been drinking. It's just criminal is what I think.'

Surely they couldn't be talking about Charles and Fiona? *Disappeared?* Leo remembered that Fiona had left the village, but that didn't mean she'd *disappeared.* And why were they interviewing Charles? He was in London until Saturday.

'Have you heard anything, love?' the shopkeeper asked Leo.

'I'm afraid not,' she answered, shaking her head. She wouldn't bother to mention the connections through Ellie and Max.

'Well, we're all saying that if it *is* somebody from the village, we all need to ask around. Notice if anything isn't quite right, or if somebody was out on Friday night that shouldn't have been. We've got as much chance as finding this villain as the police do—so if you hear of anything, just let us know.'

Leo was relieved to hear the old-fashioned bell on the door tinkle. A memory of Ellie going out on Friday night flashed through her mind, and she desperately wanted to change the subject. However, the new arrival was far from the saviour she had been hoping for.

Fiona.

Even though Leo hadn't taken an active part in the conversation, she could feel herself flush slightly. The woman called Sally turned to study the wide range of goods on the shelves behind her, and everybody was self-consciously trying to look anywhere but at Fiona.

Clearly having no sense of interrupting anything, Fiona looked surprised to see Leo.

'Hello, Leo. What brings you into the village on this sunny afternoon?'

Now Leo felt worse. The women in the shop would think she had intentionally misled them.

'I've come for a few bits for Ellie.'

'Well, I'm glad I've seen you, because I seem to remember at dinner on Saturday night you offered to buy me lunch. I've been thinking about it and that would be very nice. Shall we say the wine bar at twelve thirty tomorrow?'

In the eyes of everybody else in the shop, Fiona had now moved from being nothing more than a casual acquaintance of Leo's to being a very good friend.

The shopkeeper offered to serve them, and Fiona politely indicated the other women in the shop.

'They're browsing, don't worry about them,' was the response. The hard stare was reserved for Leo, who ended up buying rather more than she came for. Fiona only wanted some Parma ham, so they were soon served and left the deli together.

With the exception of the words necessary to complete their purchases, nobody had spoken since Fiona had arrived, but Leo had the strong feeling that she had once again become the person for whom shops fell silent as she walked through the door.

Immediately the village morphed back into its former shades of black, white, and grey. The colour seemed to have drained out of the day as she realised that if the village gossips were to be believed, several of the people closest to Ellie could be implicated in Friday's accident. And she had yet to find out where Ellie had been on the night in question.

25

Since arriving home from work, Ellie hadn't stopped. She'd started by mopping the kitchen floor—which didn't sound like a big deal, but it was an enormous kitchen cum family room, and of course she'd had to put all the twins' toys away first. Max had taken them off to the river to feed the ducks, so she had put her heart and soul into the cleaning. Manual labour was supposed to block out all worries. It wasn't working.

She was so grateful that nobody had witnessed her embarrassing moment in the car park. Fortunately, she'd had a large bottle of mineral water in the boot, so after a quick drink she had managed to flush most of the evidence from the tarmac down a convenient grid. But she hadn't risked so much as a cup of tea since then.

The house was quiet. It had an empty and abandoned feel to it. Ellie realised that it always felt like this to her when Max and the children weren't there. But now it had special significance. Now she was frightened. Was he here? Was he waiting for the right moment to creep up behind her and wrap his arms around her waist? She had to keep busy. Either that, or lock herself in the bathroom until somebody came home.

She was walking dejectedly downstairs with her arms full of the second load of washing when the shrill peal of the doorbell pierced the silence, making her jump out of her skin. Half of the dirty clothes fell to the floor, and she hastily picked them up and dumped them on the hall chair. She stood still, wondering whether she could deal with whoever was on the other side of that door. She didn't want visitors, so perhaps if she kept quiet they would go away.

They didn't. Ellie had no choice but to answer the persistent ringing.

She didn't recognise the two people standing there, both smartly dressed in suits. They weren't smiling, though, so she could tell this was no social call.

'Mrs Saunders? Detective Sergeant Crosby, madam. And this is Detective Constable Lacey. May we come in?'

Ellie was rooted to the spot. This was it, then. Her car must have been seen. Or *his* car, and he had given them her name. Oh Christ. What was she going to do? Thank God Max was out. She mentally shook herself, and held the door wide, indicating that they should come in. She took them into the library, where at least they could close the door and not be heard by Max if he returned.

'How can I help you?' she asked, hoping that her nervousness would not be misconstrued.

'Actually, Mrs Saunders, it's your husband we want to talk to. Is he in, please?'

'Max? You want to talk to Max? Why?'

'I'm sorry, Mrs Saunders—that's something between us and your husband. Is he in?'

Ellie knew that her face must have looked a picture of fear and dismay— not the face of an innocent person wanting to help the police with their enquiries.

'I'm sorry, but my husband's out. He's taken the children to the river. They wanted to feed the ducks, and we had some old bread . . .'

Ellie was rambling. She had to shut up.

'Do you mind if we wait, Mrs Saunders? We do need to speak to him, and it is quite urgent.'

Pulling herself together, Ellie indicated the chairs and both the detectives sat down.

'Would you like a cup of tea or coffee, or anything?' she asked, hoping this was the right thing to do.

'Tea would be good, thanks. We both take it white, no sugar.'

Ellie made a quick escape to the kitchen. She filled the kettle with water and switched it on, getting mugs out of the cupboard on autopilot. But before she had finished, the back door crashed open—the only way that Jake knew how to enter a room—and the twins came trudging in wearing muddy wellingtons. She barely registered that she was now going to have to mop the floor again, and she didn't even ask Max why he'd let them come in without taking their wellies off first.

'The police are here, Max. They want to speak to you.'

Max looked vaguely puzzled, but to her relief he didn't seem at all concerned.

'Okay—where are they?'

'They're in the library. What's it about, Max? I'm making them a cup of tea, do you want one?'

'No thanks. I've no idea what they want, so I'd better go and see. Shall I take the tea?'

'No,' Ellie said. 'It's not ready yet. I'll bring it through in a minute.'

Max disappeared towards the library, and Ellie finished making their drinks, absent-mindedly watching the twins making patterns on the floor with their muddy boots.

She put the two mugs on a small tray with a plate of biscuits, and as she approached the library she heard Max ask the police what he could do to help them. She didn't quite catch the reply, but was very surprised to see Max close the library door. Balancing the tray in one hand, she pushed the door open again, and the room went silent. Max turned a slightly startled face towards her, and then stepped forward to take the tray.

And still nobody spoke.

'Do you mind closing the door on your way out, love?' Max asked. 'Thanks.'

He gave her a weak smile, which Ellie found even more disturbing.

As she pulled the door closed behind her, the front door opened, and Leo walked in with a scowl on her face.

'God, my feet hurt. A daft idea, marching up and down the high street in these sandals.' Leo kicked the offending shoes off and sat down on the stairs. 'I noticed a strange car in the drive. Have you got visitors?'

Ellie was quiet for a moment. She was still unsure what to make of Max's behaviour.

'It's the police. They wanted to talk to Max.'

Sitting on the bottom step and rubbing her feet, Leo barely glanced up.

'Oh, they came here, did they? I got the impression he'd been down to the police station. Ouch—that's a blister.' Leo seemed to suddenly register Ellie's silence. 'What's up, Ellie? You know Max wasn't driving that night. I can't think that you've got anything to worry about.'

'What if whoever *was* driving did it, and Max has been keeping quiet?' Ellie asked.

Leo rested her forearms on her knees and gave Ellie a puzzled look.

'Max wouldn't do that—you know he wouldn't. They probably want to know if he saw anybody when he was coming home. Don't look so frightened.'

Ellie just stood. She felt as if she were frozen to the spot.

'Leo, what did you mean when you said you'd got the impression he'd been down to the police station?'

Leo took her bottom lip in her teeth—a habit that Ellie recognised from when they were children. It always meant that she was going to have to say something that she'd rather not.

'Look, it was just the village gossipmongers. You know how they can make a mountain out of a molehill. I went to get some bits from the deli—there, in that bag by the door. They mentioned that the police had been interviewing a PE teacher, so I presumed it would be Max, but then he wasn't driving, was he? And I thought they said at the police station, but I mustn't have been listening properly. The odd thing was . . . Ellie, are you listening to me?'

Ellie was gazing out of the window and across the lawns. She'd heard everything she needed to, and now she understood why Max had closed the door. He'd been with *her*, and he didn't want Ellie to know. Ignoring Leo completely she made her way slowly back to the kitchen, wondering how she was going to deal with this latest bit of information. Then she felt her phone vibrating in the pocket of her jeans. She kept it permanently on silent now.

She sat down in the corner of the kitchen, as far away from the hallway as possible. A text message. Was it *him?* The number was blocked.

> TUT-TUT, ELLIE. LITTLE MISS PERFECT HAS A SECRET. AND GUESS WHAT? I KNOW WHAT THAT SECRET IS! WHERE WERE YOU ON FRIDAY NIGHT? AND WHO WERE YOU WITH? I'M SURE MAX WOULD BE VERY INTERESTED TO KNOW. BUT I PROMISE NOT TO TELL IF YOU DO ONE LITTLE THING FOR ME. I'M NOT READY YET BUT I WANT YOU TO BE PREPARED AND WAITING. DON'T THINK OF TELLING ANYBODY—BECAUSE I THINK YOU CAN GUESS WHAT I'LL DO.

Ellie stared at the screen for a full minute. She felt the pressure of tears at the back of her eyes, and had to suppress them. Her pulse was pounding, and she felt a tight band of tension gripping her forehead.

Oh God. What is happening to my life?

Who *was* this? Who would want to send her such an evil text? How did they get her number, and what did they mean, a job? How did they know about Friday? What could anybody possibly want from her, apart from money? But it didn't sound like that. It sounded like they wanted her to *do* something. *What?*

Ellie felt a burning anger. It had to be *him*. He was messing with her mind. He was the only person who knew where she'd been that night. He was the only one with something to gain. Why would he *do* this to her?

She felt a scream building in her chest, but a flash of movement caught her eye and she stifled her emotions. Leo had obviously followed her from the hallway and was leaning in the doorway giving her sister a puzzled look.

Quickly Ellie deleted the message and stuffed the phone back into her pocket.

'Ellie?' Leo said, with a baffled expression.

'Sorry, Leo. I'm fine.' She gave a fake laugh that wouldn't fool anybody but she carried on, talking nineteen to the dozen and leaving no gaps for questions. 'It's not every day you get two policeman on the doorstep wanting to talk to your husband is it? I'm okay now. Just being silly. Let's have a cup of tea ourselves, should we? Do you want to put the kettle on, because I'm going to round up the kids and give them wet cloths—see how they like cleaning the floor!'

26

Day Five: Tuesday

After the police had left the previous evening, the atmosphere had been very strained. Leo didn't understand it. There was clearly something that Ellie wanted to say to Max, but for some reason she'd held back, throwing hurt glances at him every time he looked away from her. Max himself seemed confused and uncomfortable, and Leo had never seen them like this. They occasionally argued, but never had she witnessed this obvious holding back of emotion.

Max had told them that the police had only wanted to check his route home from the end of term party on Friday night, and confirm the details of who was driving. That was as much information as he'd offered, and a bemused Leo had realised that Ellie wasn't going to ask any more. At least, not in front of her.

The mood at breakfast hadn't improved either. Ellie could hardly bring herself to look at Max, and he wasn't much better. He looked as if the sword of Damocles was hanging over his head, and yet nobody was even attempting to discuss what the problem was. Leo knew better than to interfere, and she tried to keep the twins amused while the brooding silence between Ellie and Max became ever more strained.

Finally, Max pushed himself up from the table without his usual energy. When he spoke, Leo could hear the tension and uncertainty in his voice.

'Ellie, I think you said you're working again today, so I wondered about taking the kids to that new heated outdoor pool. You know, we talked about it the other week. They can have a splash about, and then do a bit of proper swimming. Is that okay with you?'

Ellie pulled what could only be interpreted as a 'do whatever you like' sort of face.

'Fine. I'm actually only working this afternoon—as you'd know if you'd been listening. But that's okay. I've got plenty to do round here. You go and have fun. I'll get on with some housework, and then go to work.'

Leo looked down at her toast and picked up her knife to spread some jam on it. She didn't like jam much, but felt she needed to be doing *something*.

'I don't mind staying and helping with the housework first, you know. We could go this afternoon? Would that be better? Or come with us this morning—the housework can wait.'

Leo could see that Max was trying, but he wasn't getting anywhere.

'Just go, Max. I'll have gone to work by the time you get back, but I'll be home about eight. Perhaps we can order a takeaway or something, if that's okay with you, Leo?'

Leo glanced up and gave a brief nod. She knew she should probably offer to cook, but she also knew that nobody would thank her for it in the end.

Max looked confused, as if he were about to say something and then thought better of it. He blew out a big puff of air through pursed lips, then turned away.

'Right, you two horrors. Swimming stuff and towels—last one ready and standing by the front door gets no ice cream.'

They set off at a run, Leo knowing full well that Max would fake some fall on the stairs or do some idiotic somersault as if he had tripped—just to make sure he was the last one to the door. And the twins knew it too, but it didn't make it any less fun.

As the kitchen door closed behind them, Leo risked a word.

'Coffee?' she asked gingerly.

Ellie didn't respond for a second, as if she hadn't heard the question. She was staring at the opposite wall, but Leo thought she detected a hint of a nod, so got up from the table. She had now mastered the finer points of this machine, and thought a cappuccino might revive Ellie's flagging spirits. She didn't attempt to break the silence until they heard lots of banging and crashing followed by three voices shouting 'bye' from the hall and the door slamming closed.

Leo put the coffee down in front of Ellie.

'Talk,' she said, taking a seat opposite her sister.

Ellie was staring into space, and for a moment she focused on Leo as if she didn't know what her sister was talking about.

'Less of the puzzled look. Talk to me, Ellie. What the bloody hell's got into you? You're behaving like a witch, and Max actually looks frightened.'

'As well he might,' Ellie responded, picking up her coffee and hissing as the hot drink scalded her mouth.

Leo said nothing, as usual trying the silence trick first. She was fairly sure that Ellie would step right into the trap.

'He was with her—the night of the party. Max was with Alannah. She was driving.'

Ah, thought Leo. So that's what this was about.

'Isn't she the one they were talking about at dinner the other night? The girls' PE teacher? He works with her. He sees her every day. So what if she was driving the car? And anyway, how do you know?'

'I know, because I'm not thick—although it appears that everybody thinks I am. Max couldn't drive that night, he was totally pissed. He said they'd drawn straws and that "a mate" was driving him home. He never said that the "mate" in question was Alannah.'

Leo frowned.

'Did he *need* to? Did it matter whether Alannah was driving, as opposed to some other person he works with?'

Ellie looked up from where she was stirring her coffee.

'Of *course* it matters. If there was nothing to it, he would have told me she was the one giving him a lift home. But he didn't. He let me believe it was one of the guys from school. Then Alannah's car was picked up on CCTV in the village, and Max had to corroborate her story—that they'd never been near the back road. That's why the police came round.'

'Did he actually *lie* to you about Alannah being the driver?' Leo asked, not unreasonably in her opinion.

'He evaded the truth, which is as bad. You have no idea how hard it was to get him to admit to me—finally—that it was *her* car.'

'What made you suspect it in the first place?'

'I thought about it on Saturday night at the dinner. Pat mentioned that Alannah was driving that night. And then you told me the villagers were gossiping about a PE teacher being invited into the police station— presumably because their car was seen in the village. It was enough to make me ask the question—but it was like getting blood out of a stone! You can be one hundred per cent sure Max had no intention of telling me. I had to *force* it out of him last night after you'd gone to bed.'

Ellie slammed her teaspoon down on the table.

'And if it hadn't been for the accident, I probably would never have found out. That's what he was banking on. You can bet your life on that.'

Leo calmly stirred the frothy milk into her coffee and spoke in a measured tone.

'Well, I'm not surprised that he didn't want to tell you if this is your reaction. What are you so agitated about? From what I gathered of Max the next day, he could have been brought back by Angelina Jolie in the nude and it wouldn't have had any impact on him.'

'That wouldn't have worked anyway, because he thinks she's too skinny,' Ellie said petulantly.

Leo laughed.

'It's okay, you laughing. You're not the one whose marriage is falling apart.' Ellie put her head down and started to cry. Leo was shocked.

'Oh God, Ellie. I'm so sorry. I didn't mean to upset you. I wouldn't have joked if I'd known it was so serious.'

Leo leaned across and patted Ellie on her arm a couple of times. She wished she could offer more, but at least she was here.

'Why do you think it's falling apart, Ellie? Just because he came home with this Alannah woman one night?'

Ellie grabbed a napkin to wipe her eyes and nose.

'I'm not quite that pathetic. It's much worse than that.'

'So tell me. Tell me what you know and what you suspect, and let's try and sort this out. I can't believe you're right, though.'

Leo's natural distrust of men didn't quite extend to Max. She might ultimately be persuaded that he was as bad as all the rest, but she would need some pretty strong evidence.

Ellie stood up and shoved her chair back so hard it fell over.

'A great place to start then, if you automatically think that he's so bloody perfect that it can't be true. But this is just the last in a line of things that have happened. And he lied to me. I thought Max would *never* lie to me. That was weeks ago, so this is nothing new, Leo. And as for Friday night, I know there were two other guys in the car that left the rugby club—two other people that Alannah was giving a lift to. He told me about them. But I know where they live, and I know where bloody skinny-arsed Alannah lives.' Ellie bent down and picked up the fallen chair, banging its feet hard on the tiled floor. She turned to Leo and placed her hands on her hips, leaning forward at the waist like a fishwife. 'For Max to be the last one in the car that drove through the village—which it seems was the case—Alannah would have had to drive about three times farther than necessary. Max should have been the *first* one to be dropped off—not the last. But he wasn't. She took the other guys home first, and then came all the way back here with Max. They obviously had to have some time together after they'd got the other two safely home. It makes no sense in terms of a route—it only makes sense if they wanted to be alone.'

Leo didn't know what to say to this. It did sound strange, but surely there could be a reasonable explanation if Ellie would only ask Max.

Ellie had clearly had enough. She walked over to the door and stopped. She turned dramatically towards Leo, with one hand on the doorknob, the other raised high, jabbing her index finger towards Leo.

'You believe what you like, but that's not the only evidence I've got. Max was overheard talking to *her*—his mistress—in the pub. They were talking about some kind of plan that he couldn't tell me about. At least, not until it was too late for me to stop it from happening. But I don't know *what*, Leo. I don't know *what* I would want to stop happening—I can only guess. So how would *you* feel, Leo? Perhaps I should take a leaf out of your book and accept that it's a mistake to ever trust a man.'

The door slammed hard behind her.

Leo decided to keep out of Ellie's way for the rest of the morning. There was no point trying to persuade her sister that she had misunderstood everything when she was in this mood, and she would have to bide her time. But she wondered if Max was aware of the depth of Ellie's suspicions. The trouble was, suspicion was endemic in this village at the moment, with Abbie's accident sitting right at the heart of it. If only the driver of that car could be identified, the rest of the confusion might unravel.

She sat on the bed, leaning back against her outstretched arms. She might be completely helpless when it came to solving a hit-and-run accident, but maybe there was something she could do to reduce the tension in this house.

Her natural instinct was to ask Max what this business with Alannah was all about, but Ellie would be furious if she interfered. Ellie and Max had always been so perfectly in tune with each other, and to see them like this was distressing enough for Leo, so goodness knows how it felt for her sister, who was as taut as a violin string—one extra turn of the peg and she would snap. Max wasn't much better. He was trying to hide it, but his subtle sarcasm on Saturday morning and his obvious discomfort after the police visit the day before were both completely out of character for the normally relaxed and cheerful Max.

Maybe her thoughts about the malignancy of this house hadn't been as whimsical as they'd seemed. Max hadn't wanted to move here. Of that Leo was certain. He'd gone along with it for Ellie's sake, which all came down to this ridiculous fixation of hers. Perhaps that was part of the problem, and if Leo could persuade Ellie that any reunion with their father was a pipe dream it would be one less thing for her to worry about, because Leo was confident that even if he came waltzing through the front door tomorrow, their father would be guaranteed to disappoint.

Fundamentally, Ellie's problem was that she didn't know what had happened to him. Had he actually walked away from them and forgotten about their existence? Did he not even care enough to say goodbye? Or was he taken ill? Ellie couldn't bring herself to believe that her dad could just march out of her life without a backward glance. Leo, on the other hand, found it entirely credible.

And what of The Old Witch? What had she known about it? Something. Of that, Leo was sure.

She tried to drag memories of him from where they were stashed deep inside her subconscious, but practically nothing would come. He had been a shadowy figure in her life, who had not only lied continually to her trusting mother, but who had practically ignored Leo once she had come to live here.

It was different for Ellie, though. She had only seen one aspect of him—the person who was married to her dreadful mother—and she had loved him. He may have been indifferent, but he wasn't unkind to Ellie. Leo, on the other hand, had gone from being the much loved child of her mother to a young girl who was either hated or ignored by the people who were bringing her up.

Leo lay back on the bed and put her hands behind her head, trying to get a picture of the man. She decided to focus on her mother and some of her memories of their time together, in the hope that he would miraculously appear in the scene.

She was in their sitting room—a small room with a dark red two-seater sofa and an armchair. They hadn't had much money—and now she knew why. It was all coming here, of course—to Willow Farm and her father's other family. From their sitting room, a door led off into the kitchen, and she could hear her mother singing. She was always singing. Today it was 'Never Gonna Give You Up'. Who was it by? Rick Astley—that was it. Leo was trying to dance to it, and her mum came in and grabbed her hands so they could both dance together. Her mum was wearing jeans and an Indian smock top—all bright colours and beads, with her long, almost-black hair tied back in a ponytail. She was so young.

Then the door opened, and he was there—laughing at them both. She could see him now, and could appreciate how handsome he'd been. He had a sort of Caesar style of haircut—very short. But he had a full head of dark brown hair and vivid blue eyes. He was quite tall too—or perhaps he had just seemed it to her. She was probably only about eight at the time.

The image faded, and Leo realised that her face was wet with fat teardrops. *Pathetic*. She sat up and brushed the tears away. Maybe she should focus on the years between then and when she left home. That would *really* give her something to cry about.

She grabbed her laptop and pulled it towards her. What *did* she know about him? She'd kept a note of every bit of information—which wasn't much. She opened the file, and started to read.

FULL NAME: EDWARD WILLIAM HARRIS

DATE OF BIRTH: 02/12/1943

PLACE OF BIRTH: STOKE ON TRENT, ENGLAND

EVENTS:

1976—MARRIED DENISE SWINDON (4TH MARCH)

1978—DAUGHTER ELEANOR BORN (29TH SEPTEMBER)

1980—MARRIED (BIGAMOUS) SANDRA COLLIER (8TH JUNE)

1980—DAUGHTER LEONORA SANDRA BORN (24TH OCTOBER)

1979–1995—DIRECTOR, GOODMAN POTTERY LIMITED, STOKE ON TRENT

LAST KNOWN ADDRESS—WILLOW FARM, LITTLE MELHAM, CHESHIRE

LAST SEEN—JULY 1995?

CONVERSATION OVERHEARD (MEMORY!!!): WOMANISER, BEEN REJECTED, 'SHE'S GONE NOW',

GET OUT. OVERHEARD SOME TIME IN SUMMER OF THE YEAR HE WENT MISSING.

2002—DENISE HARRIS (NÉE SWINDON) TELLS DAUGHTER ELLIE THAT SHE HAD HER HUSBAND

DECLARED DEAD AFTER HE HAD BEEN MISSING FOR SEVEN YEARS.

It wasn't much.

The crucial fact was that Ellie's mother said she'd had him declared dead. She told Ellie that she made the declaration in 2002. Armed with these meagre facts, Leo had scoured the records for the year in question. She had searched one year either side too—just to be sure. But there was no death certificate for Edward William Harris within that period. Did that mean The Old Witch had been lying? It would come as no surprise to Leo, but it didn't help either. Her father had disappeared without a trace.

The money had come from somewhere, though. He must either have given Ellie's mother everything when he left, or she had acquired the lot after his death. Leo was no closer to understanding it all.

For a long time, she and Ellie had assumed their father had gone away on one of his usual trips. They often didn't see him for days or even weeks at a time and Leo had paid scant attention, wearing her indifference like armour. She couldn't remember exactly when they had realised that this time he wasn't ever going to come back, but it was December when her father's name was mentioned for the last time. He had already been gone for months, and Ellie had asked her mother if he was going to be back for Christmas.

'I doubt it.'

That was all she had said. Not a word of comfort to a sobbing Ellie. But looking back on that day, Leo couldn't help getting the impression that The Old Witch actually *knew* he wouldn't be back. She must have known something. Ellie was forbidden to ask about him again, but she had never let it go. It was as if Ellie would never be whole until the secrets of the past were exposed.

Leo knew that this was getting her nowhere. She didn't have any answers. She needed a distraction, so she opened a new window on her computer screen and started to type.

A Single Step: the blog of Leo Harris

Living in the present

How easy it is to blame the present on the past, and allow history to shape the future. How many of us justify our current behaviour by reference to events long gone?

Is this true within your relationship? Are you allowing past mistakes to dictate your destiny?

If pain has been inflicted by a loved one, you may search for reasons and explanations that simply can't be found. You pick away at the scar that is trying to heal, and cause the blood to flow again. You seek reassurances that you may never truly believe. The scar becomes ragged and ugly to all who can see it, and you become the walking wounded, waiting to be hurt again.

Accept that your history has changed you. Rejoice in your survival. Let the wounds heal to form a stronger, more resilient you, and remember that forgiveness is not something we do for other people—we do it for ourselves. So forgive *yourself* for being a victim.

Look positively to the here and now. Put the past behind you and think of it as somewhere you once visited, and possibly didn't like very much.

"Do not dwell in the past, do not dream of the future, concentrate the mind on the present moment." Buddha

27

In my dream I'm running. It's dark, and I'm scared. No, it's worse than that. I'm terrified. I can feel the pressure of fear on my chest and in my throat, but I don't know what I'm scared of.

Then I hear it.

'Abbie, Abbie.' It's a loud, hoarse whisper, cutting through the still night. I can hear panic in the voice.

Then I hear another voice saying my name.

'You're a retard, Abbie Campbell. I don't know why I invited you.'

It's not dark now. And the voice is nasty.

How did I get here?

I'm in town. I'm on my own, hiding round a corner. I'm waiting, and watching the burger place to see who arrives. I don't want to be first. I don't want to look like a saddo. But I don't want to be last, because if they're all there they'll stare when I walk in. I shouldn't be nervous—it's only a party. Everybody else does this all the time, right?

I nearly said no—I didn't want to come. But Mum was pleased I'd been asked, so I pretended to be excited. I think Emily's mum must have said I had to be invited, because I'm sure it wasn't Emily's idea.

Just wait until next term. Chloe will be here then, and Emily might think I'm weird, but Chloe doesn't. She's my best friend.

At last some of the others are arriving. Four of them. Perfect. I come out from my hiding place round the side of the post office and arrive at the door just as they go in. They turn and smile. These are the friendly ones—not the sneery ones that hang around Emily all the time.

It's later now. We've all got our burgers, and Emily's showing off, just like she always does. Some boys from year ten have come in, and Emily's being loud and silly. One of the boys winks at me, and I smile back. I know him. His mum's friends with mine—it's not like we fancy each other or anything.

I need to go to the loo, but when I come out of the cubicle, they're waiting for me. Emily and her crew.

They lay into me. Apparently it's supposed to be Emily's night, and I'm ruining it. It seems I smiled at the wrong boy. They call me a skank and a retard, and say I'm not welcome anymore.

I want to cry, but I'm not going to. I bite my lip and say nothing, but I can feel my face getting hotter and hotter. I grab my bag and push past them, out into the street.

Now what? I suppose I'd better call my mum, but I'm dreading it. She always looks guilty when I screw things up—as if she thinks it's her fault that I'm a loser.

I grab my phone out of my bag. One thing I'm definitely going to do is to let the world know what Emily's really like. I open Facebook. I tell everybody—well, a few people anyway—that Emily's a pig and I'm going home.

I'm surprised to get a message straight back. I smile when I see it's from Chloe. I wish she was here.

But that's what she's saying! They've moved in sooner than expected—and she's here! Now!

She's going to come with her mum to pick me up. I've got to wait round the back of the burger place and to look out for her mum's car. And it's a secret. I'm not to tell anyone.

I can't wait to see her. And I won't call Mum. It'll save her some grief.

I'm happy now. I'm going to see Chloe, and I'm so excited. All I have to do is wait for her and her mum. The other girls are leaving now—going to the cinema. Some of them can't look at me, but I don't care anymore.

I've got Chloe.

28

'Go and get in the car, girls. Your mum's car. I'm going to go to say goodbye and then we'll be off. I'll be back in a moment.'

Gary Bateman headed towards the house as his two daughters trudged despondently towards Penny's car. He knew they didn't want to go to his mother's for a week, but he hadn't got any choice, thanks to Penny. He could bloody kill her.

He walked through the open front door, glancing in the mirror as he went. Looking good, he thought, baring his ultra-white teeth and thinking what a brilliant job the dentist had done. He was too good for Penny, that was for sure. He stomped up the stairs, calling his wife's name.

'Penny, I'm off.' He opened the bedroom door, and couldn't fail to hear the muffled sobs coming from the bed where Penny's face was buried in a pillow.

'Oh for Christ's sake, woman, get a fucking grip, will you? If you weren't so pathetic, I wouldn't have had to sort you out. Now I've got to take the girls to my mother's so they don't see your miserable face. Why do you have to be so moronic? Hmm?'

'I didn't *do* anything,' Penny whined. God she irritated him when she used that tone of voice.

'I didn't *do* anything?' he mimicked. 'You only said that you were going to talk to sodding Leo Harris and tell her all about our lives. Are you surprised that I got mad? Huh? It's not fucking rocket science, is it? Have you *read* the stuff she writes on her blog? Somebody needs to sort the silly bitch out, but there's no way you're talking to her. I hope you've got that.'

He advanced on the bed and grabbed a handful of Penny's hair to drag her face out of the pillows. At the look of fear in her face, he gave a grunt of disgust, and abruptly let go.

'You don't tell her *anything*. Are you listening? Now stop snivelling, get yourself up and dressed, and I'll see you later. I'm dropping the girls off and coming straight home for the Porsche. I've got to take it back today—it was supposed to be a three-day loan, but I've already had it for four. Something else to worry about, as if I haven't got enough.'

He stood looking down at his wife, clenched fists hanging at his side. He was sick of her, if truth be told. Three women in the house was at least two too many. Three, if the third one was Penny.

'Remember what I said, Penny. If that bloody Leo comes spooking round . . .'

'Hello? You there, Gary?' The shout was coming from the hallway below. Bugger. He shouldn't have left the front door open. He hoped he hadn't been heard. He gave Penny a last furious glance, and headed out onto the landing, plastering a smile on his face.

'Sean! What brings you here this morning? Got something for me, have you?'

Gary made his way downstairs to where Sean was standing.

'Penny okay, is she? I saw the girls in the car, and they said she's not been too good.'

Gary indicated that they should move outside to talk, out of Penny's earshot.

'She's a bit under the weather. Women's problems, you know how they get. Anyway, I'm taking the girls to my mother's. Told them she's got something infectious.' Gary sneered. 'You'd think it was terminal, they way they bloody go on, wouldn't you. What about you?'

Sean's expression was bleak for a few seconds, in complete contrast to his usual twinkling smile—the one the women in the village drooled over.

'Ah, you know how it is. Life's not great at home. If I had the money, I'd start again. Me and the kids, you know.'

'I keep trying to convince Penny of that. Except in her case, she could keep the kids.' Gary laughed. 'Anyway, you can't become single because part of your attraction to the female population of the village is the fact that you appear as some kind of hero in their eyes. You get the sympathy vote as well as points for the rugged charm, so I'm reliably informed.'

'Penny say that, did she?' Sean asked.

'*Penny?* You must be joking. Penny doesn't recognise anybody's charms but mine, buddy. I wish she would. Let me off the hook a bit, if you know what I mean.'

Gary glanced around him, to make sure that nobody was around.

'Anyway, enough of the idle chitchat—how are we doing with the deal? I could do with the cash, because then I might not have to take this baby back.' He patted the Porsche on its bonnet. 'With a bit of luck and a following wind, I'll be buying one just like it in a month or two.'

'The deal's going to plan. The money's been transferred to me, but it's not cleared yet. Hopefully tomorrow. That's what I came to tell you. I've spoken to the bank, and I can go in for the cash. I had to be interrogated for about an hour, mind you, before they agreed to release it. Anyway, I said I needed it for materials, and they were okay with that in the end. I'll drop it round tomorrow, unless you want to meet somewhere else?'

Gary paused for a moment. It might be better to meet away from the house.

'I'll give you a call on that one. When's it all going to be made public then? When's your private investor going to make himself known?'

'Saturday's the plan. He was getting cold feet, but I worked on him and got things pushed through quickly. He's around all week, though, so he can sign the papers and stuff on Friday or Saturday and then we're off. Technically the money's not ours until the paperwork's complete, but there's only a day or two in it, so as long as you don't spend it we should be fine.'

Gary leaned back against the car with his feet crossed and his arms folded.

'I'm not that stupid, Sean. Penny might be too dense to notice if I bought some nice gear, but good stuff stands out a mile. It's going in my escape fund, if you know what I mean.'

Gary stood up and glanced over at the girls.

'I'd better be going, I suppose. They've been sat there a while, and they were po-faced enough about going to my mother's as it was.'

The two men walked down the drive together.

'When I arrived, I thought I heard you talking about Leo,' Sean said. 'It's the first time I've met her. What do you make of her?'

'I don't have much time for the life coach crap. I've told Penny to steer clear. But Leo? I'd certainly give her one—if only to see that aloof, snotty look wiped off her face. What about you? You're the village stud after all.'

Sean laughed.

'I don't think I'd better comment on that. She's not much like Ellie, though, is she?'

'Ah, Ellie. Now there's a special case. Sees the best in everybody, that woman. Did you see how long she spent talking to that tit Charles the other night? God, I could hardly bear the suspense when he opened his mouth to speak, wondering what pearls of wisdom he was going to bestow on us. But

Ellie looked enthralled. That's the sort of person she is. Anyway, enough of lusting after other women. I'd better go. Talk to you tomorrow, Sean.'

Gary raised his hand to Sean as he walked towards Penny's car, thoughts of women and the idiotic games they insisted on playing running through his head.

But he could handle Penny. She wasn't the problem—it was the other one. He was tired of waiting. He was being played, and he didn't like it. Not one little bit.

Nobody could miss the elegant and flamboyant figure of Fiona Atkinson as she walked up the high street. Leo had decided that as the sun was less fierce today they could risk eating outside, and she could see Fiona was attracting a fair few stares as she headed towards the wine bar. Dressed in a simple but beautifully cut raspberry-red shift dress that on its own would have been enough to draw attention, she had topped this off with a large black straw sunhat and a huge pair of sunglasses. She looked as if she should have been lunching in Paris rather than Little Melham.

'Am I late, Leo?' Fiona asked. 'I decided to have a massage after my session at the gym this morning, and I think we got carried away with the time.'

Leo smiled. Despite Ellie thinking that she was at daggers drawn with Fiona, she actually found her quite amusing, and enjoyed the fact that they could vaguely insult each other without either taking the least offence. She didn't remember much about Fiona from school—only that she was a bit scruffy, and although she'd been Ellie's friend, friends were never welcome at Willow Farm. Since Fiona had moved back to the village, Leo had met her several times at Ellie's old house, and she found her assumed airs and graces mildly entertaining.

While she'd been waiting, Leo had ordered herself a glass of wine, which arrived as Fiona sat down.

'Sorry about this, Fiona. I didn't know how long you'd be. Shall I get a bottle now, or would you like a glass of something different?' Leo asked.

'Just a glass of San Pellegrino for me, please. I make it a rule not to drink during the week. I have to look after myself, you know.' Fiona laughed, as if to suggest that simply by looking at her one could see how her self-discipline was paying off.

'Why do you feel like that, do you think?' Leo asked.

'Like what? Oh don't start all that life coach bull with me, Leo. I know what you're getting at. Why do I think I always have to look at the top of my game? Is that what you're after?'

Leo just smiled and waited for Fiona to talk.

'I want to look my best at all times. I never want Charles to be ashamed of me. I like to keep myself and my home in perfect order, so that we can be happy and comfortable. And you don't hear Charles complaining, do you?'

Charles. The mention of his name brought Leo back to earth with a bump. Here they were, having a bit of light-hearted banter, when dark secrets seemed to be lurking around every corner.

'So you think that the perfect body, wonderful clothes, and a stunning home is the key to marital bliss, do you?' Leo asked, determined to carry on as if nothing had shaken her.

'Look, Leo, could we please order lunch? If this is going to be an inquisition, I need some fuel. And perhaps I will break my own rule and have a glass of something light. A pinot grigio, maybe.'

For the next five minutes, Leo and Fiona studied the menu, although Leo was fairly sure that Fiona would probably eat little more than a lettuce leaf or two. She wanted to know about Charles, and the gossip in the shop had suggested there was more to Fiona's story than Leo was aware of. But a full-blown interrogation was never going to work.

They ordered their meals and settled back to sip the wine.

'Speaking of a stunning home, where are you living now? You're at the far end of the village, aren't you?'

'Yes. About half a mile that way.' Fiona vaguely pointed with her hand over her shoulder. 'The house is a bit large for the two of us, but obviously we do have to entertain from time to time—for Charles's work, of course. We're considering whether to add a conservatory, actually; one that stretches the full length of the house so that we can have dinner parties there. The house backs onto the fields and the views are divine, so a conservatory would be a perfect addition to the property.'

Leo resisted the temptation to poke fun at Fiona. Sometimes there was a smugness about her that just begged for a caustic remark.

'The design we've been working on is a bit more ambitious than an oblong box bolted onto the back of the house,' Fiona continued. 'So we need to get the plans finalised, and then get the relevant permissions. I don't think it will be a problem. I'm rather hoping that deliciously sexy builder of Ellie's will do the work. I've spoken to him about it on a couple of occasions and he's been to check it out. He seems to think that we might be able to achieve what I want. And I'm sure it will all be approved.'

'Do you think Sean's sexy, then? Not my type,' Leo said as her smoked chicken and bacon salad was placed on the table in front of her. Fiona's lips turned up at one corner.

'I didn't think you had a type, Leo. A bit like me, I always thought. Indifferent to the charms of men. Or at least I was. I think it's time for a change. What about you, though? Why haven't you succumbed?' Fiona signalled to the waiter for another glass of wine. It seemed that once she'd decided she was drinking, there was no stopping her. And what was she talking about? Time for a change?

'You know me. I was brought up by a man who showed me quite clearly the way men think,' Leo said. 'Of themselves, principally. That's been my experience, for what it's worth. I don't know if you remember my father, but I'm on a bit of a mission to find out what happened to him. Ellie seems to have made him into some kind of plaster saint, and until we know what happened to him she's not going to let it go.'

Fiona was intent on fishing the most minute piece of shell from her crab salad.

'Some things may be best left alone, you know Leo. Sometimes it's better not to turn over too many stones, because you don't know what might be crawling around under there.' Fiona finally seemed to extract what she was looking for, and removed it to her side plate.

'In my father's case, I'm sure you're right,' Leo responded. 'There must be some good guys out there, but boy do you have to be lucky. Charles seems the steady type, though, in spite of his rather out-of-character confession on Saturday night. Were you all right with that?'

Fiona gave her usual tinkling laugh, although to Leo it sounded ever so slightly hollow.

'I was a bit cross with him. I don't know why he said that, because Charles would no more have an affair than do a bungee jump dressed as a banana.'

Leo nearly choked on her wine as an image of a long and yellow Charles sprang into her mind.

'Good grief, what on earth made you come up with that particular analogy?' Leo asked, laughing openly at Fiona's strangely serious expression.

'I don't know. It was the most ridiculous thing that I could think of; that, and Charles having an affair.'

'Did he give you any excuse for his comment, particularly if it wasn't true?' Leo asked.

'He said that I was behaving like a strumpet. His words, not mine. I thought I was just having a good time, and it was a bit of a gloomy old night, wasn't it? Anyway, he thought that it might shock me into silence; a strategy which unfortunately failed. I know you think he's a boring old fart, Leo, and to some extent you might be right. But he does have some redeeming features, you know.'

'I'm sure he does, and as long as you're happy that's all that counts.'

Leo was watching Fiona's face carefully. She didn't seem to be behaving any differently to normal and didn't give the impression that she was worried about anything, and particularly not Charles.

'Well, you have to admit that it was good of him to agree to move back up here even though he has a hell of a commute, and he's away from home every night except Saturday and Sunday, so I have the house—and my bed—to myself.'

Leo took a mouthful of the delicious salad. She needed to keep an impassive face. She swallowed the food and took a sip of water.

'Does he never come home until Saturday, then? Could he not get back on a Friday night?' she asked, as if it were of no real interest.

'When we first moved up here, he used to come home on Friday, but recently he's said that at the end of a long week it's good to go back to his own flat to relax, and then make the journey on a Saturday morning. I don't mind, if that works best for him.'

Leo said nothing. If Charles hadn't been here on Friday night, what did the police want to talk to him about? Did Fiona know?

'He's not gone back this week, though,' Fiona added, frowning. 'He said he'd decided to take a week off, although God knows why. He's hanging around the house looking bored, as if I'm supposed to provide him with some entertainment. For me, it's life as normal. If that means that I have to go out, he will have to amuse himself. I have a feeling that he thought Saturday night was a bit upsetting all round and that maybe I would be grateful for his support. I have absolutely no idea where he got that notion from.'

'When you came into the shop yesterday, the natives were all a bit over-excited about the accident,' Leo said, thinking carefully about her every word. 'You know what this place is like—without gossip, I think some of the locals would die of boredom.'

'True—and I've been at the sharp end of that gossip more than once, I can tell you. But I've heard nothing about the accident. I thought you might know more—with Ellie looking after the girl, Max and Pat knowing her from school, and you all having the benefit of the dashing policeman next door. I would have thought if anybody was in the know, it would be you.'

Leo shook her head, more convinced than ever that Fiona knew nothing, but surprised that Charles had made a sudden decision to stay in Cheshire this week. Why would he do that? Leo felt a jolt of concern for Fiona, who she realised was watching her, waiting for her response.

'Ellie says Abbie's still in a coma, poor kid. Pat seems to have disappeared off the face of the earth, and the dashing policeman as you call him *isn't* a policeman at the moment, and if he was I doubt he would share anything. I understand they've been interviewing everybody who was caught on camera on Friday night, though.'

Fiona glanced up from her food, and looked at Leo through slightly narrowed eyes. She's assessing what I know, Leo thought. She leaned back in her chair, careful to keep her face blank.

Fiona placed her knife and fork together on the plate.

'Well, I wish I could help with their investigations, but I can't. I was home alone—only the television and a Friday night bottle of wine to keep me company, I'm afraid. Friday is the start of the weekend, before you ask, Leo. So wine is permitted.'

Leo resisted the temptation to ask why Tuesday was being excluded from the alcohol rules, but further conversation was interrupted by the ringing of Fiona's phone.

Glancing at the screen, Fiona said, 'I'm sorry, but I do need to take this.' She pressed to accept the call.

'Hello there,' she said in a silky voice. 'I'm so sorry, but it's not convenient to chat right now. I'm having lunch with a friend.'

There was a pause.

'No I can't, I'm afraid—this week isn't entirely suitable. Charles is staying in Cheshire for the week. Perhaps next week? I'm sorry. I do know that this,' she glanced across at Leo, 'isn't exactly how we had expected things to progress, but it can't be helped.' She paused again, and the silky smooth tones hardened slightly. 'Well, unfortunately there's nothing I can do about it, so perhaps you can hang on until you hear from me.' She hung up. 'Sorry, Leo. Only a friend wanting to get together. It will have to wait.'

Leo didn't think that fitted with Fiona's earlier attitude to Charles's unwelcome stay in Cheshire, but decided to keep quiet. It was an interesting tone of voice, too.

She steered the conversation towards innocuous topics, and while they waited for the coffee they talked about Ellie and Max's restoration of Willow

Farm, and inevitably chatted about Pat, Georgia, and Mimi. It wasn't until the coffee had been served that they got back to the subject of Fiona.

'You know, I don't think you ever said what made you decide to return to Little Melham,' Leo said. 'I know you've been back for a few years now—but why here when there are so many other places in the country that you could choose to go?'

Fiona absently stirred her coffee while she appeared to be thinking of a suitable response.

'You and I are quite similar you know, Leo. I know you don't think so, but we both have things to prove—to ourselves if to nobody else. You probably remember that I came from what was always considered to be the rough end of the village. My father was a layabout, and my mother was a cleaner, for God's sake. Everybody looked down on us, and so I wanted to come right back here and show them. Prove that I could move up in the world. I didn't want them remembering me as the girl who had nothing.'

Fiona took a careful sip of her hot coffee, but Leo could see a layer of pain beneath the composure. Fiona was holding her head high, but was gently stroking one arm with her other hand, as if offering herself comfort.

'It's a shame you felt like that,' Leo said. 'I'm sure that Ellie never thought of you as anything but her friend—and being a cleaner is a good, honest job. Where would we be without them? I don't think you had anything to prove at all.'

Fiona put her coffee cup back in its saucer with infinite care, avoiding Leo's eyes.

'It's easy for you to say, Leo, but I left Little Melham under a cloud of suspicion with a young heart that was broken in pieces. I wanted to come back in style.'

Leo leaned forward towards Fiona.

'I'm sorry. I didn't want to upset you.'

'You haven't, but you have a way of wheedling things out of people, Leo, and it's not a very attractive trait.'

A raw nerve had been struck, but Leo had more sense than to try to probe any further. She tried to remember what Ellie had said to her on Saturday night—that there were things about Fiona that she couldn't divulge. And although Leo remembered that Fiona had left the village, it was only yesterday that it was suggested that this was under something of a cloud. But as a topic, it was clearly closed.

'What I'd really like,' Fiona said, 'is another cup of coffee, and a change of subject.'

Leo turned round to look for the waitress.

'Huh? I don't bloody believe it,' Fiona muttered, as a shadow was cast over their table.

Leo turned back.

'Hello, ladies. Mind if I join you for coffee?'

'Yes, I do,' said Fiona. 'What are you doing here? Are you checking up on me?'

As always, Charles seemed impervious to Fiona's rudeness, and Leo wasn't sure what to make of his sudden appearance. He pulled up a chair from one of the other tables and sat down.

'I happened to be passing, and remembered you saying you were meeting Leo. I thought it would be nice to buy you both a cup of coffee. What have you been chatting about?'

'Nothing that would interest you,' Fiona responded. 'That's why girls have lunch together, so that we don't have to discuss the bloody economy.'

'Ah, all clothes and makeup is it. Well, carry on. Don't mind me.'

Fiona cast him an irritated glance, and Leo knew that Charles had effectively brought an end to their conversation. But the more she thought about the nuggets of information that Fiona had revealed, the more convinced she was that whatever Charles was up to, he wasn't the only one with something to hide.

29

Ellie was covering a shift for one of the other nurses that afternoon, and the ICU was busy when she arrived at the hospital. An accident on the motorway had resulted in the admission of a couple of other patients, but none of their injuries were quite so bad as Abbie's, and Ellie was pleased to be told that she would be nursing the young girl again today. As she walked through the unit she could see Kath Campbell in her usual spot, her chair drawn as close to Abbie as she could get, with one hand gently stroking her daughter's arm. But today she seemed to have lost all control and tears were flowing freely down her cheeks.

'Kath?' Ellie said quietly. She crouched down by the side of Kath's chair. 'What is it? I've checked with the other nurses, and they say Abbie's no worse—what's upsetting you so much?' She took Kath's other hand between her two.

'It's my fault she's like this. It's all my fault,' Kath sobbed. She was clearly finding it difficult to speak, and Ellie stroked her hand.

'Of course it's not. Listen, I'm going to get you a glass of water, then you can tell me all about it. Okay?'

Asking the nurse on the next bed to keep an eye open for Abbie, Ellie made her way towards the nurses' station. She could understand why Abbie's mum felt the way she did; she knew that if anything happened to the twins, she would inevitably feel that it was all her fault—whether it was or not.

As she was getting a plastic cup of water from the cooler, one of the student nurses grabbed her.

'Come with me, Ellie. I've got something to show you.'

Ellie looked at her wide grin and couldn't help reciprocating as she was dragged into the office.

'Ta da!' she exclaimed, pointing her hand theatrically to a huge arrangement of flowers on the desk. 'Look what's just arrived. Aren't they gorgeous?'

Every single flower was a rose, in every shade of yellow and apricot imaginable.

Ellie felt the blood draining from her face, but the student nurse was chattering on.

'The note is so thoughtful—do you want me to tell you what it says?'

Totally missing the point that Ellie hadn't said a word, she began to read.

'"For Abbie. Wishing her a speedy recovery and offering special and sincere love to those wonderful nurses who care for her". It doesn't say who it's from, but how nice is that?' she said, turning her beaming face to Ellie. 'I know we can't have them on the ward, but you should take them home with you. They're completely fabulous, aren't they?'

Ellie forced herself to smile. The student was so enraptured by the truly magnificent flowers that she failed to notice Ellie's shock.

'Do you know what?' Ellie said. 'I think we should give them to Kath to take home. Take the card off, and say they came for Abbie. Thanks for showing me, but I need to get back.'

She knew that her less than enthusiastic response had been noted, but she didn't care. She had to pull herself together and get on with her work. *What was he thinking?*

By the time she returned to the bedside, Kath was calmer. Ellie handed her the water and sat down in the spare chair, mentally telling herself to focus, focus, focus.

'Okay, Kath, tell me what's happened since I was here last. Something's obviously made you feel worse, so talk to me. Maybe I can help.'

'I've been a fool. I gave in to pressure, even though I wasn't happy about it. I only let her use Facebook because everybody else was doing it. If I'd said no, she'd have been the only one in her class, and she was enough of a loner as it was—not that it was her fault, poor lamb. And now the police believe that it was Facebook that caused the problem.'

Ellie didn't interrupt. Kath had to tell this in her own time.

'She made a new friend on Facebook. Chloe, she's called. It was a few months ago now. Chloe contacted her completely out of the blue—and Abbie was so chuffed. She'd tried asking the girls in her class to be Facebook friends, you see, and a lot of them had just ignored her. Why is it that some teenage girls can be so horrible to each other? She'd only got about half a dozen friends, and then this girl Chloe contacted her. She said her family were hoping to move to Little Melham over the summer, and if they did, she'd be starting school here. Her dad was being relocated, and she was looking forward to getting to know other girls from the school. Abbie checked her out, and she had quite a few friends in Durham where she lived. She and Abbie chatted all the time, and Abbie was so happy that she was going to be the first one in her class to know this girl. She said she'd told Chloe things about herself that she'd never been able to tell any other girls at school, and I was so pleased for her. She talked about Chloe all the time, and we almost felt as if we knew her ourselves.'

Ellie squeezed Kath's hand reassuringly, wondering what this could possibly have to do with Abbie getting knocked over.

Kath swallowed a sob. 'The police can't find Abbie's phone, but they've pieced together what happened via Facebook.' Kath pulled a sheet of paper from her handbag, and passed it to Ellie. 'This is the last of the messages between Abbie and Chloe on Friday night. Chloe and her mum were arranging to pick Abbie up from the back of the burger place.'

Ellie quickly scanned the messages, which seemed reassuringly normal.

'That's good isn't it? At least now you know where she went and why. What do Chloe and her mother have to say?'

'Nothing. They have nothing at all to say. That's the whole point. There *is* no Chloe. She doesn't exist.'

Ellie hadn't been able to get anything coherent out of Kath after that last dreadful sentence, so she had decided to break all the rules and for once make her a cup of tea.

By the time she returned to the bedside, Kath had calmed down and her mood had changed. Her lips were clamped together in a tight line, and her body was taut with tension. Ellie placed the hot tea on the bedside cabinet to cool down a little.

'I'm sorry,' Kath said. 'I shouldn't be burdening you with all this. It was such a shock, though.'

'You're not burdening me at all. But you said Chloe had friends in her home town. Wouldn't they have known that she didn't exist?'

'You'd think so, wouldn't you? Except the friends don't exist either,' Kath answered. The anger simmered right below the surface. 'It was a charade—don't you see? The whole thing. Pretending to move to the area, making up friends—all so that Chloe seemed real to Abbie—so that she could get to know everything about her.' Kath looked at Ellie with eyes round with horror. The next words sound as if they were being wrenched from deep within her. 'She was abducted, Ellie. My baby girl was abducted.'

Abducted? How could something like this happen around here?

Ellie felt as if cold water was running down her spine. But if it was too much for Ellie to deal with, how must it be for Kath? No wonder she was angry. Ellie would want to murder anybody that hurt her children with her bare hands.

But she was still puzzled. Chloe didn't exist, but whoever had abducted Abbie must know the area, because they knew where the burger bar was. Did this mean they were local? Oh God, what if it was somebody that she knew? Ellie shuddered.

Kath was talking as if to herself, not worrying whether anybody was listening or not.

'It's unbelievable. That somebody could plan this—somebody would harm a child. Just unbelievable.'

Kath reached out a shaky hand for her tea and nudged the cup, splashing some of the hot liquid onto Abbie's arm.

'Oh God, and now I'm trying to burn the poor child. What a useless mother I am.'

Kath put the cup down and started to mop Abbie's arm. But Ellie wasn't paying attention. She was watching Abbie, positive that when the hot tea hit her, her arm moved away just a fraction. Ellie jumped up and moved to Abbie's feet.

'Did you see that?' Ellie asked. Kath's face was suddenly bright with expectation as she watched Ellie run her usual tests. They weren't actually due, but if Kath believed that her accident with the hot tea had brought Abbie out of her coma, that was absolutely fine by Ellie.

And there was no doubt about it. The coma was definitely lightening

'This is great news. She's starting to respond to pain. We've got a long way to go, but it's the first positive sign we've had since Abbie was brought in. I know the doctor has explained to you that coming round from a coma isn't like it is on the TV. She's not suddenly going to sit up and start talking—but this is a very good sign. Do you want to go and call Brian and tell him? I'll sit here with her, don't worry.'

Kath was clearly torn between staying with Abbie and phoning her husband, but she couldn't bear the thought of him not knowing.

'I'll be two minutes—that's all. I promise.'

Grabbing her mobile phone from her handbag, she dashed for the door.

Ellie sat down by the bed, and started stroking Abbie's head—just as she had done the day before. She had checked out some of the words to Abbie's favourite song as well, and memorised the chorus. She started to sing very softly, close to Abbie's ear. This was all that mattered now. Abbie recovering.

But even the words of the song couldn't drive out the knowledge that somebody—somebody not too far away from here—had ruthlessly planned and executed the abduction of a teenage girl.

30

The route to Penny and Gary's house was imprinted on Leo's brain, as they lived right next door to Ellie and Max's previous home. She remembered that they had two young girls and as it was the school holidays, there was every chance they would be at home. She hoped she would get a chance to chat to Penny alone, though. With any luck on this bright, sunny day the girls would have found something better to do with themselves than sit around watching TV, chatting on their computers, or playing online games, although any recent experience Leo had had with kids of this age didn't give her much hope.

Leo had decided to call on Penny to see if she'd had any more thoughts about the life-coaching session, because in her view if anybody needed it, Penny did. As she approached the house, she looked at it with interest. The garden was beyond immaculate, far too much order and uniformity for her taste. Somebody had gone berserk with the bedding plants, and the garden was full of colour; but each plant was equidistant from the next and in a regular pattern—one red, one blue, one white. She wasn't sure if it was patriotism or a desire for high impact that had dictated the colour scheme, but either way it was a bit extreme. The front lawn was a neat square with crisply trimmed edges, and at each corner stood an identical pyramid-shaped shrub. Leo thought they were probably conifers, but since the only plant she could identify with any reliability was a rose, this was just her best guess.

Out of the corner of her eye, she caught movement at one of the windows. But when she turned her head to look properly, she couldn't see anybody. She had always thought it strange that a man who had aspirations to be an architect had chosen to live in a house like this. There was nothing wrong with it, but it was a flat-fronted 1970s detached house with nothing to differentiate it from its neighbours—apart from the fact that most of them, including Ellie and Max's old house, were semi-detached. The curtains at the windows looked unnecessarily fussy to Leo, and she could see that they were tied back with care so that the windows upstairs and down looked identical. She could just make out some flouncy pelmet on the inside as she walked up the drive. There were no more signs of life, though.

Leo rang the bell and waited. Nothing. Not a sound from inside the house. But there was somebody there, she was sure of it. She rang again, but still nothing. How weird. Maybe Penny hadn't seen her approaching the house, and had gone out into the back garden. Leo decided to walk round the side of the house and see if Penny was there. Lifting the latch on the gate to the back garden, Leo called out softly, not wanting to startle Penny if she hadn't heard the doorbell.

'Penny, it's Leo. Are you there?'

She made her way through the gate from the drive to the rear of the house. But the back garden was empty. This area was neatly and precisely arranged too, but fortunately not with symmetrical rows of annuals. Here there were beds of perfectly pruned roses interspersed with lavender. In one corner stood a small stone statue of a lady, emptying water onto some white pebbles. The perfect water feature, Leo thought with a smile. Against the fence was a large wooden-slatted kennel, with its own two patches of neat and tidy grass, edged with a low hedge. Even the dog, it would appear, needed pristine surroundings.

Leo didn't want to appear nosey by peering through the window, but as she approached the sliding patio doors which led through to the lounge, she was shocked to see Penny crouching behind a sofa, trying to hide from whoever had arrived at the front door. *How awful.* Penny clearly didn't want visitors, and Leo had no desire to force herself on anybody. She needed to get away before Penny saw her.

The decision was taken out of her hands as Penny and Gary's elderly and partially deaf Jack Russell became aware of her presence and trotted across the lawn starting to yap—a shrill, piercing noise which had driven Max to issue threats to strangle the dog on more than one occasion. Leo bent down, facing away from the window.

'Hello, Smudge. How're you doing, old man?' She knew Penny would have heard, but by focusing on Smudge Leo was giving her time to get up from behind the sofa and they could at least pretend that this was all perfectly normal.

The patio door slid open, and Leo could hear Penny's timid voice but couldn't see her.

'Leo—what a surprise. Give me a moment and I'll be with you.'

Leo waited patiently outside, scratching Smudge on his fat tummy as he lay on the floor with all four legs in the air.

'Not too old for a tickle then, are you, Smudge?' she said with a smile. She heard Penny's feet thudding up the stairs through the open doorway, and wondered what was going on. Sadly she wasn't surprised when Penny reappeared wearing a cardigan that she hadn't had on before, and sporting a pair of large sunglasses. But not quite large enough.

'Sorry to keep you, Leo. I thought as it's such a nice day we could sit outside. Would you like some coffee or tea?'

Leo didn't want either, but she needed to help Penny get past this difficult moment.

'I'd love a cup of tea, Penny. Thanks. I'll come and talk to you while you make it, shall I?'

'No need,' Penny answered in a breezy voice.

'It's no problem—Smudge has had my undivided attention for five minutes, so I'll come in with you.'

Penny had managed to avoid looking directly at Leo, keeping her head down to look at Smudge, and now in the kitchen she had her back turned as she prepared the tea. But the sunglasses had stayed on, even in the dark kitchen. Leo felt anger well up inside her, but knew that it wouldn't be appropriate to voice her feelings.

'Are the girls not at home today?'

Penny gave a jerky shake of the head.

'Gary took them to his mother's and he's left them there for a week. We were all supposed to be going on holiday, but Gary was concerned about a big project that's coming up. Even though he's off work on annual leave, he wants to be available. He says it's not something that will wait.'

Leo's face remained blank. Gary had never struck her as so diligent in his job that he would cancel a holiday, but it probably wasn't a good idea to say so. She wondered whether he had made that decision before or after his wife had taken to wearing sunglasses in the house. What a bastard. She had to put Penny at ease, though.

'The gardens are looking impeccable. Who's the gardener, then? You?' Leo asked.

Although she laughed, Penny's voice was shaky.

'Me? No, I'm afraid not. Gary likes it to be perfect, and I don't get my lines right. The house is my domain. I seem to do better at keeping the curtains straight than I do the lawn edging. And I like making curtains and cushions—especially if they're a bit complicated and I have to think about it.'

Leo looked through the wide opening from the kitchen to the dining end of the long through lounge, and could see exactly what Penny meant. Every peach and cream curtain and cushion had some sort of frill attached.

'Well. I'm glad I managed to catch you on your own. You mentioned on Saturday that you might be interested in finding out a bit more about life coaching, so if you've got time for a chat now I can tell you all about it and you can decide if you'd like a session.'

The tin of tea bags clattered onto the worktop and Penny cast a nervous glance at Leo.

'I'm sorry, Leo, but that won't be necessary. I think it was the wine talking on Saturday. Gary was ever so cross. He said I'd given everybody the impression that there must be something wrong with my life—and of course there isn't.'

Leo wasn't at all surprised by this. 'Where is Gary today? If he was here, I'd be happy to tell you both about it and put his mind at rest. It's not about anything being wrong—it's about what you could do to make life even better.'

'He's gone to take the Porsche back. I think it was supposed to go back yesterday—the three days were up. But he couldn't bear to part with it. He's very fond of nice things, is Gary.'

Penny splashed the milk into the saucer of her cup as she poured it.

'Oh dear. I didn't mean that to sound judgemental. He works so hard, he deserves the best of everything.'

Penny attempted an apologetic laugh as she cleaned up the spilt milk, but Leo could hear the quiver in her voice. The two women picked up their cups of tea and made their way out onto the terrace to sit at a small wooden table. It was a real sun trap, and perspiration gathered quickly on Penny's top lip and forehead.

'You know,' Leo continued, 'I get it that Gary doesn't want you to talk to me, but it doesn't need to be a proper session. We can just chat. And it's not about finding fault with relationships. It's about identifying where you want your life to go, and making sure that you're both heading in the same direction. It's really not about tearing things down. It's more about building them up.'

Penny hadn't lifted her head, and Leo wasn't surprised to see a tear trickling down her face. Reaching into her handbag, she grabbed a clean tissue from the pack she always kept handy, and passed one across the table.

'There you go, use that. And Penny,' she said very gently, 'you can take your glasses off. I know you've got a black eye—I can see the bruising below. It's okay.'

Penny started to weep in earnest, knowing that her secret was out. But still she tried to deny what Leo knew was the truth.

'I fell. It was a silly accident, and I caught my eye.'

Leo had been through this with other women so many times, and it never failed to infuriate her that somehow the victims were always the ones who felt impelled to lie. She would love to be able to give Penny a hug now, but she didn't know how. Her own upbringing had seen to that.

These situations usually followed the same pattern, though. The hardest thing of all was admitting that something was actually wrong; that you were *allowing* yourself—because that's how it felt—to be mistreated. Once the floodgates were opened and the irrational sense of guilt and shame removed, she knew that Penny wouldn't be able to stop and she hoped that Gary didn't get home too soon.

The first thing that Leo had to do was to help Penny to admit the truth. It was a bit like lancing a boil—make the first incision and watch all the nasty stuff come oozing out.

'Penny, I know that Gary hurts you. I know it—I'm not just guessing.'

Penny looked up with an angry stare, tears pouring down her battered face.

'No he doesn't. You're wrong. He would never hurt me on purpose. He loves me.'

'I'm sure he does, but I also know that he hurts you. Listen, on the night of Ellie's dinner party, I was sitting opposite you—do you remember? Well, right behind you was a huge mirror. When you were talking to Tom, Gary put his arm round you. Everybody would have thought it was an act of affection—but I *saw*, Penny. He lifted the sleeve of your dress and put his hand inside. Then he pinched you. Hard. And you weren't surprised. It made you jump and spill your wine, but only with pain, not with shock. So it wasn't the first time. And anyway, I could see other bruises on your arm. That's why I wanted to get you out of there.'

Penny's face was flushed with more than the tears. It was a flush of deep embarrassment.

'I'm so ashamed,' Penny whispered.

'I know that's how you feel. But you shouldn't. You've done nothing wrong. Nothing at all. For some reason, it seems to be human nature to take responsibility for other people's actions. But Gary's the one who should be ashamed, not you.'

Bullies were often arrogant bastards, though, and Leo could bet money on Gary managing to believe that none of this was his fault. She prided herself on her cool detachment with clients, but today it was letting her down as she looked at this broken woman, who was still trying to defend her useless husband.

Penny shook her head with some force.

'No, Leo. You don't understand. He doesn't mean to do it. It's only when something has happened that's disappointed him. He struggles to control himself at those times. But we can go weeks with him being happy. He can be quite affectionate then.'

Leo could picture the scenes in this house. She sensed that Penny would be practically delirious with joy and gratitude if Gary hadn't hurt her for a week or two. But it would be a type of manic euphoria, as part of Penny's unconscious mind waited for the inevitability of the next time he would turn on her.

'What do the girls think, Penny? Doesn't it upset them?' Leo asked.

'They don't know. It's not usually his fists, you see. But when I said I was going to talk to you about my hopes for the future, he lost it completely.' Penny blew her nose, and Leo felt a stab of guilt that she had caused this to happen.

Penny continued. 'But there's something else bothering him, I know that. His reaction was too strong for a simple suggestion that I talk to you. He went absolutely berserk—there's no other word for it. That's why he had to take the girls away—because there was no hiding *this*.' Penny pointed to her eye. 'I had to say I was ill, and the girls weren't allowed to see me in case I was contagious. We couldn't let them catch a glimpse of my face.'

As well as the tears on Penny's cheeks, beads of sweat were standing out on her face and neck.

'You know, you could take your cardigan off,' Leo said softly. 'I know about your arms, and there's nobody else here. You'll pass out in this heat.'

She slowly did as Leo suggested, and from her painful movements Leo guessed that it wasn't only her eye that had suffered a punching from Gary's fists. But she studiously avoided looking at Penny's arms, and focused on stirring the cup of tea that she didn't want to drink. Once Penny had managed to remove the cardigan, she sat clasping both arms as if to hide the bruises, but when it became obvious that Leo wasn't looking and wasn't about to comment, she seemed to relax slightly.

Leo didn't let her eyes stray. She looked either at her cup of tea, or at Penny's face. In her peripheral vision, though, she could see that most of the bruises were to the soft flesh on the underside of the arms—the part that would undoubtedly be the most painful.

'When did it start, Penny? Is this a recent thing?'

Letting her arms fall to her sides, Penny looked up to the sky, as if that would stop the tears from falling.

'We hadn't been married long. We got married when Gary was at university. He was doing his architect training—you've probably heard about that. He says I was the reason he failed his exams, but it's not true. He was obsessed with me. I hadn't wanted to get married so young, but he was insistent. He didn't want anybody else to have me. And then I got pregnant. I didn't want to tell Gary because I didn't want to distract him from his finals. I decided to tell him on the night of his results—a double reason to celebrate, I thought.'

Penny gulped back the tears and wiped her eyes. She lowered her head and looked at Leo.

'But he failed. He was so desperately disappointed, but I couldn't believe it when he blamed me. He said it was my fault that he'd failed—he was spending too much time looking after me, and not enough time on his studies. He started to hit me. And then he got me on the floor and he kicked me. He didn't know I was pregnant, though. It wasn't his fault.'

Leo could feel this poor woman's pain.

'Penny,' Leo said gently, 'it's not about whose fault it is. It's not about blame. It's about stopping it happening again. One of the first steps is admitting that it *is* happening, and you've done that now. Does Ellie know?'

'No. Nobody knows. As I said, he rarely hits me. He likes to pinch me—not only on my arms. His favourite place is . . .' Penny paused and mopped her streaming eyes with the now soggy tissue. Leo fished in her bag for another one and passed it over without a word.

'He likes to pinch the underside of my breasts. And it hurts, Leo. It really, really hurts. I'd rather he hit me, if I'm honest. But nobody sees, and I have spent the last few years of my life learning not to cry out when he does it. But it only happens when something has upset him. It's just that in the last few weeks, especially this last week, he seems more upset that usual. That's why. It's not always so bad.'

Leo didn't know how she was going to get Penny to stop excusing Gary's behaviour, and she knew better than to ask about the child that Penny had been carrying. If this had been when Gary finished his training, both their girls were far too young, so she could only assume that Penny had lost the baby. Leo felt a strong desire to inflict some bodily pain on Gary herself, and she knew exactly where she would like to hit him.

'Do you have any idea why Gary's more upset this week? Has he told you?'

Penny's head dropped to her chest, but there was the slightest nod. Leo waited.

'It's another woman.'

Leo felt a heaviness in her chest. Could this get any worse?

'Has he *told* you that he's got another woman?'

Penny didn't react for some time, but she was clearly trying to find the words—words that would somehow make the situation seem better than it was.

'There have been times over the years that Gary has needed another interest. He gets bored easily, and sometimes that interest has been another woman. I've always known, and he hasn't tried to hide it. I can't explain, Leo. It's too difficult.'

Leo stood up and made her way into the kitchen. She was going to fetch Penny a glass of water, and give her a bit of space. If she'd never admitted any of this in the past, the pain must be ripping her in two.

By the time she returned, Penny had wiped her eyes and put her sunglasses back on. Leo placed the glass on the table, and sat down.

'You don't have to tell me, Penny. I know this must be almost impossible for you. But I think you have to tell somebody. If you don't want it to be me, I'll find you somebody who can help. That's a promise.'

Penny gave a half laugh and blew her nose.

'I can't do this again. Now that I've started, it would be easier to tell you, if you don't mind.'

Resting her hands in her lap and sitting up straighter, as if to give herself strength, Penny unleashed a torrent of words, spoken quickly as if that way she could get it over with as fast as possible.

'The trouble with Gary is that he likes the chase. He loves to woo women, and he loves them to be bowled over by him. He'd got me, and not only was I his, but he was able to treat me any way he wanted, and I never complained. How sad does that make me? But in the early days, each time he was horrible, I withdrew a bit from him, and he had to woo me back to being in love with him. And then it would all start again; I would withdraw some more, and he would court me. It was a cycle, but when he was trying to coax me back to loving him, he was amazing. In the early days, each time he turned nasty I would start to think of leaving, and then he would lay on the charm. He brought me flowers, jewellery, took me out, cooked for me—you name it, he did it. He became a gentle and considerate lover, instead of demanding what *he* wanted all the time. And then when I was his again, he would gradually start to have the odd mean moment. It was as if he wanted to see how far he could push me.'

Penny stopped and took a sip of water. Leo didn't move. She wanted nothing to distract Penny. It was almost as if by telling this tale, she was seeing Gary for the first time. She put the glass down.

'Eventually, it stopped working. I neither withdrew, nor could I be wooed. It was always just more of the same, and I was no fun anymore. But by then, we had children. I've never worked. Not really. If I left Gary, I have no idea what I would do. I'm not a strong person who's organised enough to find somewhere to live, pack up everything for the girls and move out. And he doesn't do it all the time—usually he stops when he has a distraction. That's where the other women come in. He woos them until he wins them. He chooses the most difficult people because then it will take time for him to succeed. You know how good-looking he is. And he can be so charming. Those flowers that we brought to Ellie's on Saturday night—you should have seen the care he took in selecting them from the garden. They were all our flowers, not bought ones. He said he wanted every bloom in the bouquet to be absolutely flawless—we had to impress our rich friends. So he spent ages selecting each one. That's how he used to be with me—always making sure that everything he did for me was perfect.'

'What makes you think he's got a new woman now, if he's still being aggressive with you?' Leo asked.

'Because I don't think this relationship is going to plan. I don't think she's falling under his spell. She's resisting, and he's taking it out on me.'

'But how do you know this if he hasn't told you?' Leo asked, with a sick feeling in the pit of her stomach.

'I told you the other night that I don't take a sleeping pill if Gary's out. He doesn't know, though. I always pretend to be fast asleep, and I know he thinks I'm dead to the world. On Friday, he was out until very late. It was after one o'clock when he got in, and he was in a foul mood. I pretended to be asleep, but he stomped around the bedroom and banged the bathroom door with such force that I thought it was going to come off its hinges. I knew he'd been with a woman. Nothing else would make him so mad.'

31

The hospital canteen was busy, but fortunately there was nobody there that Ellie knew well, so she was able to grab a corner table and sit by herself to have her break. The progress that day with Abbie had pushed all other thoughts to the back of her mind until now. She was so pleased that the girl was showing signs of recovery and the doctor was talking about taking her off the ventilator the next day, if all went well.

The story of how Abbie had been abducted was infinitely more disturbing, though. The village had always seemed such a safe place to live. Apart from what had happened to Fiona, of course—but that was different. Ellie had lived in Little Melham all her life, and knew practically everybody. Suspicion would be rife everywhere, and she could only imagine the havoc it was wreaking in some households as doubt was cast on the integrity of friends and neighbours.

So had this person abducted Abbie and then knocked her over? Perhaps they thought that an accident might hide the abduction. She had no idea, but she hoped and prayed that this wasn't anybody she knew.

She wanted, more than anything, to be able to talk to Max about it. He knew kids of that age so much better than she did, and he might understand how it could all have happened. But she wasn't sure she wanted to talk to Max at all. The thick, heavy sensation of sorrow settled at the back of her throat again.

Max. She had never wanted anybody else. Even when he was away at university, she had waited patiently until he was ready to make a commitment. Max had thought that it would be better if they were free to see other people, but even though she'd tried, nobody had lived up to him. As a student nurse she'd had a great social life, but it was common knowledge that she was only interested in Max Saunders. And he had been worth the wait. At least, until now.

Ellie couldn't help feeling that she had already been abandoned by one man she'd loved and she couldn't bear to be abandoned by a second. Much as she held out hope that her father's disappearance was a foolish mistake that he'd regretted ever since, or that her mother had driven him away, the pain of realising all those years ago that he wasn't coming back had been so acute, she was certain she couldn't cope with that again. And this would be so much worse.

If she confronted Max, what would that gain? If he denied it, would she believe him? If it really *wasn't* true, it would expose a weakness—a lack of trust—that might forever drive a wedge between them. And if it *was* true, she would give him the very opening he needed to say he was leaving.

No. She was going to fight, and her best weapon was silence.

The problem with Max was that subterfuge was never his thing. She always knew exactly what he was going to buy her for every birthday and Christmas. He seemed to think that if people couldn't see him, they couldn't hear him either, and he always overlooked the fact that they both used the same computer, so browser history was often an unintentional giveaway. She couldn't help a small smile when she thought of some of the 'secrets' that he had failed to keep. The smile faded, though, as the thought occurred to her that perhaps she would have preferred it if he *had* been able to keep a secret this time.

If it hadn't been for that bloody Mimi, she would never have suspected anything. She'd even had a go on Saturday night, for God's sake. It was as if she hated to see them happy, and wanted to disturb the balance of their lives.

She couldn't ignore the fact that Max had been withdrawn lately. Not all the time; he could still clown around and be his usual silly self, but she sometimes glanced at his face and saw him gazing into the distance, as if he were present in body but not in mind.

Her thoughts drifted to the last few weeks, and the distance between them in bed. He often pretended to be asleep when she got into bed now, and that was so unlike him. And one night, after she had persisted, they had made love—but Max had eventually stopped.

'It's not working, Ellie. I'm sorry,' he'd said. 'I guess I must have drunk too much wine with dinner.'

She'd cuddled him, and told him it didn't matter. But they both knew that he hadn't drunk very much, and they both knew it was nothing to do with alcohol. He hadn't wanted to talk about it, so she had tried to be extra affectionate. But it had been like cuddling a plank of wood. Perhaps the problem *was* her. Maybe he didn't find her attractive anymore.

Ultimately though, it was when Mimi told her about the conversation she'd overheard in the pub between Max and Alannah that the damage was really done. It was exactly as she had told Leo that morning.

'You'd be surprised what barmaids hear, you know. People treat us as if we're invisible most of the time, until they want a bloody drink, that is. But you'd better be careful,' Mimi had said. 'I don't know what Max and that PE teacher were whispering about, but I did hear Max say, "I can't tell Ellie. We need to wait until everything is in place—when it's too late for her to stop it". I didn't know what to make of it, but I thought I should tell you.'

Ellie had tried to make a joke of it, saying Max was probably getting Alannah to help him with a housewarming present or something. And she might have believed it herself, if it hadn't been for the following day.

It was the day before they were due to move in, just a few short weeks ago. Max had promised to meet her at the house at lunchtime, but he had cried off at the last minute with an excuse. An excuse that wasn't true. He'd lied to her, and she'd found him out. All of which meant that maybe Mimi was right. There *was* something going on.

The agony of realising that Max had found somebody else had been so acute, she would have done anything to dull the pain. She had lain down on the floor in the empty sitting room and curled into the tightest ball she could manage in a vain attempt to ease the aching inside.

And then . . . Ellie didn't want to think about what had happened next. Her distress was so profound that she had made a terrible mistake; one that she regretted more than she could say. But she wasn't being allowed to forget it.

The vibration of her phone in her handbag brought her back to the present. The ring of the phone or a buzz of a text had always been a good moment; maybe it would be Max or Leo phoning for a chat, or a friend with an invitation to dinner. But now, every time her phone made a sound she was filled with dread. Each time she walked to her car she was scared of who she might find there, and even opening the front door was torture.

She'd not had time to think of the awful text she had received yesterday and what it could mean. But she was fairly certain it was *him*. Nobody else knew what had happened between them, or that they had met on Friday night. So it was just a trick to make everything seem even more unstable than it already did—if that were possible.

Ellie ignored her phone and put her head down on folded arms. She wanted to cry, but no tears would come. All she could do was think of the utter hopelessness of it all.

32

Throughout her life, or at least since the age of ten, Leo had believed that men were bastards and not to be trusted. Her own father had appeared to be a charming man on the surface, although underneath he was anything but, and since the day she had found out how shamefully he had treated her trusting mother, she had sworn that she would never have faith in any man—come hell or high water. As she had grown older, one or two men had stood out to her as possible exceptions to this rule, and one of those had been Max. But this very morning her sister had told her that she thought Max was having an affair. She struggled to believe that Ellie was right, but if it were true, if Max genuinely had been unfaithful, it would appear that her earlier assessment of the male population was fairly accurate.

But then, what about Ellie? She had still not explained her late-night car journey, and it was so out of character. She couldn't ignore the fact that according to Penny, Gary had been out that night too, but surely there was no connection? That had to be wrong. *Gary*? It was more likely that, given the revelations this morning, Ellie had actually been spying on Max. But then that wouldn't explain the late-night phone call.

Leo mentally shook her head. She was just speculating, and it was a waste of time. She needed to speak to her sister, to tell her what she knew and suspected. But not tonight. As she was walking back from Penny's, Max had called to say that he was preparing a special meal for Ellie as a surprise and he wondered if she would mind having something simple in the sitting room in front of the television.

'I know it's very rude of me, Leo, and I wouldn't normally ask. But you've seen Ellie these last few days. She seems so stressed, and I want to do something for her. Something that shows that I'm thinking about her, and how much I care. We don't seem to have had a moment together for weeks, with the move and everything. Would it be a huge problem for you?' he had asked in a very sheepish voice.

She felt sorry for Max. Apart from being very drunk on Friday night, he seemed to have been trying his best in every way possible—and this meal was just another example of his thoughtfulness. But if Ellie was right and he *was* having an affair, this could also be an act of guilt, or a way of softening Ellie up before the inevitable devastation that would accompany the revelation of his infidelity.

As she approached the village, Leo decided that she should be making tracks back to her own apartment, because she was confident she wasn't helping the situation at all. The trouble was, if she said she was leaving now, they would both think they had driven her out and feel guilty about it. She needed an accomplice—somebody who could call her and say that she was needed back in Manchester because a client desperately wanted to see her. And she knew just the person to ask.

Tom.

She had a feeling that he would understand her dilemma and help her out. She wasn't too keen on going back to Willow Farm yet, so perhaps she could drop in on him as she passed and ask for his help. But first she would call in at the shops and pick up some supplies so that she didn't arrive at Tom's empty-handed.

Pushing open the door of the off-licence, Leo was surprised to find it stocked with some excellent wines. She had become so used to the chains around Manchester that all carried the same range, and it was a delight to go into an independently owned shop like this one. It had the peculiar smell of good wine shops that was difficult to define. There was a background of fermented grape—as one might expect—but there was something warm and comforting in the smell too. Something vaguely woody—but it was hard to place.

The other great thing about this shop was that there was no pressure to rush. The man behind the counter merely looked over his half-frame glasses and smiled, then went back to his crossword.

Leo made her way around the shelves. She knew that Tom had a huge stock of wine, but that didn't mean that she couldn't take him a bottle, and she was about to select a Tin Pot Hut sauvignon when the door of the shop opened. A slightly out of breath Mrs Talbot hurried in.

'Oh, Leo. I thought I saw you coming in here. I wonder if I could have a word?'

Leo put the bottle of wine she had been holding on the counter, and turned towards Mrs Talbot.

'I wondered if you'd heard the latest about Abbie Campbell? I thought maybe Ellie might have said something to you?'

'Ellie's at work, Mrs Talbot. I haven't spoken to her since this morning.'

'Call me Doreen, dear. I'd much prefer it.'

'Okay, Doreen—but I'm sorry. I don't know anything about Abbie.'

'It's truly terrible. It was on the news—not half an hour since. They're saying that before she was knocked down, that little girl was *abducted*! I've been in the butcher's and the greengrocer's and nobody knows anything, but they're all saying that it had to be somebody from the village. Is there nowhere safe in this world anymore?'

This was indeed news to Leo, and dreadful news at that. But she couldn't cast any light on the subject at all. Poor kid. She could understand why the villagers would be in shock. It was bad enough thinking that the hit-and-run driver was possibly a neighbour, but if she had been *taken* by somebody from here too, that was even worse.

'I wish I could help,' Leo said. 'I can understand how you must all be feeling, but this is news to me.'

'Nothing like this has ever happened in these parts, you know. Well, there was just the once with that friend of yours, but that wasn't as bad as *this*.'

What on earth was this woman talking about? What friend of mine? Leo thought.

'You don't know, do you?' Leo could see that Mrs Talbot—Doreen—was slightly bewildered by Leo's apparent lack of knowledge. 'This business with Abbie reminds us of what happened to your friend—Fiona. She was a pretty little thing when she was at school, but then it happened, and she just upped and left without a word.'

'Families do that sometimes,' Leo answered.

'Ah—well, that's the thing, you see. It was *only* Fiona that left. Her family didn't go. They stayed—her parents and her brother—but they wouldn't say a single thing about it.'

Leo shook her head. Now she knew what Fiona meant about a cloud of suspicion.

'I only remember Fiona vaguely from then, I'm afraid. I do know that she left, but I'm sure there was nothing strange about it.'

Mrs Talbot seemed indignant, but Leo had had enough. She knew what villages were like for gossip, but there was a kind of salacious pleasure in it sometimes that Leo hated. She turned back to the shelves, grabbed a bottle of red wine pretty much at random, and fished out her purse to pay.

'Well, it *was* strange,' Mrs Talbot continued. 'Mind you, it must be fifteen years or more since it happened, but she was pregnant for sure. Nobody knew who the father was. Maybe *she* was abducted and escaped too. She's never said a word about it since she's been back. And now that snooty husband of hers has been arrested.'

Thinking that 'arrested' was a massive exaggeration of the facts, Leo finished paying for her purchases, smiled her thanks to the shopkeeper, and turned to Mrs Talbot with her best effort at a friendly smile.

'I sincerely doubt that it's anything at all sinister. I'm sorry, Doreen, but I've got to rush.'

Leo said her goodbyes and made her way out of the door, leaving a floundering Mrs Talbot in her wake.

It appeared that there was more to Fiona's story than she had realised, and she would dearly love to know Charles's part in all this. But there was no way that she was doing an information swap with Doreen Talbot. She'd have to ask Ellie to fill in some blanks.

Clearly something had happened to Fiona all those years ago, but it couldn't possibly have any relevance to what had happened to Abbie.

The spicy aromas in the kitchen were drifting towards Tom, and he had to admit was looking forward to dinner. But he wouldn't be ready to eat for hours yet. He'd decided to have an Indian cooking spree to fill his empty day; he would eat some of it tonight, and stuff the rest in the freezer.

Making his way from the kitchen into the adjoining living room, he picked up the book he'd been reading. Or trying to read. He had thought a detective novel would be perfect, but he got irritated by the inaccuracies and the obsession with painting all fictional policeman as anything from slightly unbalanced to seriously disturbed. His thoughts kept leaping back to the news that Abbie Campbell had been abducted. He was missing his job far more than he had ever imagined, and was struggling to stop himself from interfering in this investigation. As it was, he made several trips a day to the village shops, just to see what information he could pick up. The answer was—not much. Of course, everybody knew that he was a policeman, and perhaps they guarded their tongues when he was around.

There was one bit of good news, though. He'd heard from Greater Manchester Police that morning, and there was definitely going to be a vacancy in the Serious Crime Division. It was the same rank—chief inspector—but he was happy with that. He didn't want to become desk bound, and he hated anything to do with force politics. He was more than a little interested in the job, and was going in next week for a chat. He would be reporting to a woman who had once been one of his team, but she'd had a meteoric rise to power since he left and in his view her promotion was perfectly justified. He'd probably get the piss taken out of him for a while, but he could live with that.

He glanced out of the window and was surprised, but pleased, to see Leo walking up the path with a carrier bag that looked suspiciously as if it contained bottles. She was dressed in her customary black and white, but this time she was wearing white linen trousers that clung to her hips but moved gently around her legs as she walked. A short-sleeved black silk top with huge buttons hung loosely on her slender form, and her hair was swinging in the light breeze.

Nice, he thought. In fact, *very* nice. There was something about the splash of bright red lipstick that transformed Leo from smart to sexy. There was no doubt that she could be quite acerbic, but after their conversation over lunch yesterday he could understand where that was coming from.

He moved towards the side door and popped his head out.

'Hi, Leo—come round this way. It's easier,' he shouted.

With little more than a nod in Tom's direction, Leo made her way to the side of the house, holding the carrier bag in front of her as she approached Tom as if to ward off any advances, had he been thinking of making any.

'I've brought you a present, because I need to ask you a favour,' said Leo, as ever getting right to the point.

'Come in—and you don't need to bribe me to do something for you, you know. I'll either do it or I won't, depending what it is that you want,' Tom said, smiling to take the edge off his words.

They walked into the kitchen, and immediately Leo stopped, dumping the carrier bag on the nearest chair.

'What a *delicious* smell. Don't tell me you've found a good Indian round here and I don't know about it?' Leo asked, her eyes opening wide as she saw the dishes in the kitchen.

'I hate to disappoint you, but it would be a cold day in hell before I bought Indian from a takeaway. This is all my own hard work. You like Indian food then?'

'God, I love it,' Leo said, walking over to the stove and lifting the lid of a creamy chicken curry. She looked as if she were about to dip her finger in, then thought better of it.

She turned towards him and opened her eyes wide in a lascivious leer, although he was in no doubt at all that unfortunately the source of the arousal was the curry. She moved to the next dish and gave him a questioning look.

'It will be a prawn jalfrezi when I get round to adding the prawns.'

'Mmm mmm.' She lowered her face towards the pan and inhaled slowly. Lifting her head, she turned to Tom. 'Have you actually *made* all this?' she asked, her voice sounding slightly in awe of Tom's obvious culinary skills. 'Good grief, you're as bad as Ellie. You'll make fine neighbours—forever trying to outdo each other with elaborate dinner parties. Anyway—I'm disturbing you. I'll tell you what I came for, and let you get back to your cooking. It looks like you're expecting guests, so I'm sorry for intruding.'

Tom pulled out a kitchen stool and sat down, indicating the other one to Leo.

'You're not disturbing me, and I'm not cooking for guests. I'm cooking for me. I like to cook occasionally, principally because I love to eat. Let's face it, I've not got much else to do at the moment. So what can I do for you?'

Leo looked totally nonplussed at the idea of all this work for one person, but she sat down and rested her arms on the worktop and decided to get straight to the point.

'I need to go back to Manchester, and as soon as possible. Ellie and Max are not in a good place right now, for reasons I don't want to go into. But if I just up and go, Ellie will think they've driven me away, and she'll blame Max. He's already told me he wants to do a romantic dinner for Ellie tonight—although I can predict exactly what he'll cook. I thought if you could phone, posing as one of my clients who's in dire need of a face-to-face consultation, I would have the perfect excuse to escape and let them get on with it.'

Tom was sorry to hear that Ellie and Max were having problems. He'd immediately liked them both, but as he knew only too well, other people's marriages were always a mystery.

'First of all, it's no problem making the phone call if that's what you want. But why don't you stay here and eat with me tonight? As you can see, there's no shortage of food. And then you can see how things are in the morning. If they're not great, Ellie might actually appreciate having her sister around, you know.'

Leo's face lit up at the mention of dinner, and Tom could see she was tempted. Not by his company, of course, but it looked like the lure of the food was proving to be irresistible.

'Go on, Leo. I'd enjoy your company, and you'd be out of the way so Max and Ellie could have some space. If you hide somewhere in the house, Ellie will feel obliged to ask you to join them. Call them and say you're eating with me.'

Leo clearly didn't need asking twice, and she pulled out her phone.

'Shit—the battery's flat. Can I borrow yours to send Ellie and Max a message, please?'

Tom slid his phone across the worktop, and Leo picked it up and sent a quick text message to both of them. She knew her sister would still be at work, and Max would undoubtedly have his phone switched off, as he nearly always did. But they would find it eventually.

'Let me get you a drink, as you're staying. What would you like?'

'Well—my tipple of choice is vodka, ice cold. But if you've not got that, wine is fine.'

'Vodka coming up. It's in the freezer, so I guess that will be cold enough for you.'

Tom grabbed a couple of glasses and poured Leo her vodka shot and a glass of red for himself. He laughed as she downed it in one, but rejected a second, pointing at the red wine instead.

'I only ever have one shot. And only occasionally. It would be a very bad habit to get into, much as I love it. Anyway, I want to savour this food of yours, so one shot, one glass of red, and that will do, thanks.'

Putting her dead phone back in her bag, Leo turned to Tom.

'Why are all men such bastards, Tom?' she asked.

'Well, that's charming,' he said, laughing. 'I invite you to dinner, lend you my phone, and you tell me all men are bastards. Nice.'

Leo laughed.

'Okay, not quite all then. But so many of them are, aren't they? I've been talking to somebody today, who shall remain nameless, but her husband is a brute. The things that poor woman has gone through, and the fact that she consistently lies to cover up for him is so sad.' Leo rested her chin on her clasped hands, elbows on the worktop.

'That'll be Penny then, at a guess,' Tom said, pulling his mouth into a grimace of distaste. Not for Penny, of course.

'What makes you think that?' Leo asked.

'Oh come on, Leo. I saw the way he treated her. Gary's one of those guys who states his opinion as if it's a fact, and one that we should all agree with. Especially Penny.'

Leo looked at Tom with raised eyebrows, her head on one side.

'Well, well. That's very astute for a man, if you don't mind me saying so.'

'Does your insolence know no bounds, woman? I'm going to feed you, don't forget—so how about deciding that I don't fit into your stereotypical man mould and show me some respect?' Tom gave her a stern look, and Leo grinned at him.

'Okay—maybe not *all* men are toe rags. I'll allow you to be an exception. Mind you, I allowed Max to be an exception, and now I'm not quite so sure,' she said. Tom noticed the frown was back, and decided to be serious for a moment.

'What's up, Leo? What are you so worried about?'

Leo took a gulp of her wine.

'I'm worried about Ellie. There's stuff going on with Max at the moment that I don't think I should tell you about, mainly because I think—or sincerely hope—that Ellie is talking rubbish. But she's got a few things on her mind, and I thought I could help her with one of them, but it seems not.'

Tom said nothing and just moved around the kitchen getting some spicy nuts out to nibble with their drinks.

'I told you something about my father the other day, but there's a bit more to it. When I was about fourteen, he disappeared as he always did—but this time he didn't come back. Ellie was distraught, although I've always struggled to understand why. But then Ellie always did see the best in everybody.'

Leo grabbed a handful of nuts and munched them for a moment.

'The thing is, we've no idea what happened to him. Ellie's mother said she'd had him declared dead seven years after he left, but we've never seen a death certificate. Unfortunately, Ellie isn't convinced. She was always the sort of girl who believed in fairies, and she has it in her head that our father will, as if by magic, reappear now his hideous wife is dead.'

Tom looked at Leo's serious face.

'I take it you don't believe in fairies, or in reincarnated fathers either?' he asked gently.

'Do you know, Tom, I don't actually care if he's alive or dead. He didn't really give a damn about either of us, but there's no telling Ellie that. I've tried to check it out, but I haven't got enough information. To do a search, it seems I need at least an approximate date and place of death, and I have neither. I've got the date our stepmother provided, but that's yielded nothing. One of the reasons Ellie's moved back to Willow Farm is in case he miraculously decides to seek her out. I think Max has been supportive, but against his better judgement, and if I could only prove one way or the other what happened to our father, it might help Ellie.'

Tom sat quietly and thought about Leo's problem.

'Would you like me to see if I can help? I can't use any official channels, of course, but I've got a few tricks up my sleeve after years of tracking people down.'

'That would be brilliant, Tom. Thank you.'

Leo seemed to sag with relief, as if one burden had been lightened. Tom couldn't help feeling good about that. She shared the limited facts she had with him, and promised to e-mail her thin file of information over as soon as she got back tonight.

'There's another strange thing. We were all out on Sunday, although not for very long, but Ellie's convinced somebody had been in the house. We told her she was imagining things, but I'm not so sure.'

Leo explained about her laptop and the files.

'Did you call the police?' Tom asked,

'No. There were no signs of a break-in and nothing was missing. Maybe I should have spoken up at the time, but Ellie was blaming Max for leaving the back door open, he was swearing he didn't, and I just thought my evidence was too flimsy and I would be stirring things up unnecessarily if I voiced any doubts. What should we do, do you think?'

'If Max really is adamant that he didn't leave the door open, as a minimum I think you should have the locks changed and you should report it.'

'Not much chance of that, I'm afraid. Max thought Ellie was dreaming. With hindsight, I should have backed her up.'

'If you want, you can call the police now,' Tom said, 'and I'll come over too to make sure they take you seriously. But as it was a couple of days ago, it makes it a bit more difficult. Get Max to change the locks, and if it's making Ellie nervous, get some CCTV set up.'

Leo pulled a face.

'At the moment, everything seems to be making Ellie nervous. Let's hope that Max's romantic dinner calms her down a bit. He's been trying really hard to please her, but it doesn't seem to be working. Ever since I arrived, things seem to have been going crazy round here. I had to fend off one of the village gossips earlier who wanted to talk about Abbie Campbell. I couldn't believe it when I heard that she had been abducted. That poor child.'

Mindful of Steve's request to pick up any chitchat, Tom was keen to know what was being said, but wasn't quite sure how to get the most out of Leo. At the first sign of interrogation, she would back off. He was sure of that. He had to help her to volunteer the information.

'In a small, quiet village where everybody seems to know everybody else, it must come as a shock when something like this happens,' he said without looking at Leo, concentrating on topping up her wine glass.

'They've had Charles down at the station. Did you know about that?'

'I'm not a policeman anymore, Leo,' he answered, avoiding a direct answer.

'Did you know that Charles has decided to stay in Cheshire this week? From what I can gather, that's very out of character at short notice.'

Tom gave a noncommittal grunt, which appeared to satisfy Leo as she carried on talking with barely a break.

'They said that Pat was questioned too. Well, I presume it was Pat because they said a deputy head. He's not the only deputy, I don't suppose, but he was apparently out and about for some of the night. The weird thing about it is that nobody has been able to speak to Pat since Sunday. Max has tried to call him and failed—and according to Ellie, those two rarely pass a day without speaking. She says they're like a couple of old women. But he hasn't called Max either.'

'Perhaps it's because of the new love in his life. Maybe she's taking up his every waking moment.'

Leo pulled a face. 'I don't get that relationship either. You should have met his wife, Tom. I think you'd have liked her. I do feel sorry for Mimi, though. Everybody seems to blame her for it all. Anyway, there are more important things to think about. You're supposed to be the man in the know, so what have your police friends told you about progress on the Abbie investigation? Are they any closer to finding the abductor or the driver—or do they think they're one and the same?'

Tom moved over to the hob. He took the lid off the curry and gave it a stir. It didn't need it, but he didn't want Leo to see his face. Steve had told him about some of the people they'd interviewed, but it wasn't something he could discuss.

'Enquiries are on-going. I'm sure they'll catch whoever it was, but these things take time. They need to build a case.'

He didn't tell her that, according to Steve, they had no suspects at all—for either the abduction or the accident.

33

As Ellie opened the front door, she sniffed lightly. She recognised that smell. Max had been cooking, and she knew it was spaghetti Bolognese. He called it his speciality, but the truth was that it was the only thing he knew how to cook. She had really hoped to grab a cheese sandwich and disappear to bed, but she couldn't tell Max that. She didn't even know if they would be speaking, but at least Leo would be there to keep things on an even keel.

Dumping her bag in the hall, she made her way through to the kitchen, and paused on the threshold. The kitchen lights were dimmed, with only the light over the Aga shining brightly, and out through the glass doors to the terrace she could see a beautifully laid table, with candles burning in glass hurricane lamps. A brightly coloured jug stuffed full of flowers from the garden took pride of place in the centre.

Max was standing just inside the door, hovering anxiously. Given the mood she'd been in when she'd left, she knew that he wasn't sure how she was going to respond to his efforts.

'Where's Leo?' was about all she could muster.

'Leo's gone out—round to Tom's. The twins are in bed and asleep—so it's just you and me. Here, have a glass of wine and come and sit down.'

Max hastily grabbed a bottle of red wine from the worktop and poured two glasses. He picked up the iPod remote and Ellie was amazed to hear the soft tones of Snow Patrol coming through the speakers.

'"Chasing Cars"? Are you okay, Max? You hate this sort of music,' Ellie said, accepting the glass of wine that Max was holding out.

'Tonight's not about me. It's about you. So it's cheesy music all the way, I'm afraid. Come on, let's go and sit outside for a moment while the water boils for the pasta. I'm sorry it's nothing more exciting, but you know my limitations.'

Only a couple of short months ago, Ellie would have been overwhelmed by Max's show of consideration for her, but she was struggling to decide if he was motivated by a guilty conscience or if this was a genuine act of love.

As soon as she stepped outside, Ellie could see how much effort he'd made and she felt a hot rush of tears at the back of her eyes. But she needed a bit of space before she could put on the performance that would be expected of her.

'This looks incredible, Max. Really it does. Do you think, though, that you could put the pasta on hold for ten minutes? I'd love to have a shower before we sit down, and pop in to give the kids a kiss. Is that okay?'

She saw a brief flash of disappointment in Max's eyes. He clearly believed he had thought of everything, and she vowed to make it up to him when she came down. She was going to push everything else to the back of her mind, and focus on her husband. Maybe she could still save them from catastrophe.

She leaned over to brush her lips gently against his cheek, and made her way towards the stairs, picking up her bag from where she'd left it. As she walked upstairs, she sensed rather than heard her phone vibrating, and fished around amongst the debris of her handbag until she found it. She had two text messages. One from a number she didn't recognise, and one from a blocked number. When had the pleasure of receiving a message turned into alarm?

Throwing her bag on the bed, she sat down and stared at her phone. A wave of panic swept through her. Opening the one with the unknown number first, she breathed a sigh of relief when she saw it was from Leo, confirming that she would be staying at Tom's for dinner. Feeling a bit more relaxed, she hoped the second message was going to be just as harmless.

It wasn't.

> IT SEEMS SOME THINGS RUN IN FAMILIES, ELLIE. I THOUGHT YOU WERE BAD, BUT YOUR FATHER? THAT MADE ME LAUGH. THE PERFECT FAMILY, HIDING SO MANY SECRETS. DON'T FORGET THAT I'M GOING TO NEED SOMETHING FROM YOU. IT WON'T BE LONG NOW. AND DON'T FORGET WHAT I SAID, ELLIE—ONE WORD OF THIS TO ANYBODY, AND THE CAT WILL BE OUT OF THE BAG.

Ellie stared at the phone as if mesmerised by the words. The glow of the screen danced before her eyes. It had to be *him*. What was he playing at, blocking his number and sending her threatening texts? She knew he was trying to frighten her, but why? Was it because she wouldn't agree to see him, or to leave Max for him? Was he just trying to break down all of her flimsy defences? Of all the nasty, mean things to do. She would never have expected him to stoop so low as to use tactics like this. And why bring her father into it? The older people in the village were bound to remember Leo's background—where she came from and the welcome she'd had when she had arrived. He must have heard the gossip. It *must* be him.

Ellie punched the button to delete the message, and switched her phone off. The backs of her eyes were hot and stinging, but she fought back the tears. She couldn't cry—Max would know. And she had to appear normal for him.

Determinedly stripping off her clothes, she flung them on a chair and went into the bathroom. At least her body could be clean even though her mind was clogged with the remnants of bad memories and foolish mistakes.

She knew she had been a long time in the shower, but the Bolognese would keep, and at least she looked as if she had made an effort. She was surprised to catch Max slightly unaware, and as she saw him sitting dejectedly at the kitchen table, staring into space and idly tapping his fingers on the table, she wanted nothing more than to go to him and cradle his head against her. The room was quiet. He had no doubt turned off his least favourite music as soon as she went upstairs.

The second he saw her, though, he leapt up eagerly from the chair and moved towards her. Taking gentle hold of her face between his hands, he kissed her lightly on the lips.

'Feel better, sweetheart?' he said with an understanding smile. 'Come on— let's carry on where we left off.'

He steered Ellie towards the table outside, picked up her glass from where she'd abandoned it, and handed it to her.

'The shower was a good idea. You look more relaxed, and it's dark now— so even more romantic. You take it easy, and I'll sort out the pasta.'

With a final stroke of her still-wet hair, Max returned to the kitchen, flicking the iPod back on as he went. This time it was Keane singing 'Bedshaped'. He had certainly pulled out all the stops.

Ellie tried to focus on the relaxing notes of the music, and not on everything else that was happening. She forced thoughts of Abbie from her mind too, and turned her head to look back into the house, where she could see Max jumping around waving his hand in the air. He'd probably spilled some of the boiling pasta water on himself; for such an athletic and co-ordinated guy he could be incredibly clumsy, Ellie thought affectionately.

The music continued to soothe her, as track after track of all her 'soppy' music was played. She wished she could talk to him. *Really* talk to him. But she was too afraid.

The spell was broken as Max brought out two bowls heaped high with spaghetti and sauce, and they settled down to eat. The atmosphere between them had relaxed considerably since this morning, but both knew there were things left unsaid. Neither wanted to break the fragile peace, and they talked quietly about everything but the big issues.

Just as they finished their pasta, the music changed once again—this time to Aerosmith. Max stood up.

'Come here, beautiful,' he said. 'Remember this?'

Ellie knew what he was going to do—something they used to do regularly, but didn't seem to have done for such a long time.

He held out his hand and guided her away from the table. Then he wrapped one arm around her waist, and with the other he grabbed her hand and pulled it close to his chest. He rested his cheek against her head, and her lips lay gently against his collarbone. Slowly they started to dance. Ellie finally felt herself begin to relax.

> *'Don't want to close my eyes*
>
> *I don't want to fall asleep*
>
> *Cause I'd miss you babe*
>
> *And I don't want to miss a thing'*

Max gently sang the chorus softly in her ear, and she felt as if he believed every word of it. She couldn't keep this up any longer. They had to share the truth, and they had to do it now.

'Max,' she whispered.

'Bugger,' Max said, as the phone began to ring in the kitchen. 'Somebody's got impeccable timing! I'm sorry, sweetheart.' Max let go of her, and gently brushed the outer edge of her left breast with the fingers of his right hand, leaning in to kiss the corner of her mouth.

'Wait right there. I'm not finished with you by a long way.'

Ellie plonked herself disconsolately back at the table as Max made his way into the kitchen, switching the iPod off as he went.

Silence returned to the garden, but it was an uncomfortable silence and Ellie felt a strange sensation—as if dark eyes were piercing the back of her neck. She shivered, and turned quickly to scan the bushes.

What was that? She could just make out a small bright light somewhere near the fishpond. As Max answered the phone and said 'hello', the light went out.

And then she knew. The light was from the screen of a mobile phone. Somebody was in her garden. The nerve endings all over her body pinged with the rush of adrenaline.

She heard Max repeating 'hello, hello,' several times, but Ellie knew the phone would be dead.

Then she heard it. A whispering voice began to sing the opening lines of the same song.

> *'I could stay awake just to hear you breathing*
>
> *Watch you smile while you are sleeping*
>
> *While you're far away and dreaming'*

A shadowy figure stepped forward as the quiet singing continued, and Ellie was about to scream when she heard Max replace the phone, muttering under his breath.

'Nobody there, Ellie. Bloody typical.'

The shadow melted into the darkness.

Max came back through the open doorway, and held his hand out.

'Now where were we, sweetheart?'

But Ellie had started to gather the plates together noisily.

'Let's go back inside, Max. It's getting a bit chilly out here.'

She wanted to kiss away the hurt that she saw on Max's face, but she knew she mustn't touch him. She couldn't risk the shadow drawing closer.

34

Day Six: Wednesday

Another night without sleep. Why did life always seem so much worse at five o'clock in the morning? Was it because everybody else was happily snoring in their comfortable beds, while you alone were awake and living through your own personal hell?

The radio played quietly in the corner. But that was no help. Moody and sombre night-time music was introduced by voices speaking at a low pitch, smooth and silky, as if to coax you back to sleep. But the interruption by regular local news bulletins jerked you back from the brink.

All they wanted to talk about was Abbie Campbell. They spoke of the 'delight' of the family that she was showing signs of recovery, and how friends and the local community had rallied round.

And they were saying she'd been abducted—but that wasn't true. It was supposed to have been a *surprise*. They'd become such good friends on Facebook; Abbie should have been pleased when she learned the truth.

I just wanted to touch you, Abbie—to kiss you, to hold you. I've been watching you and waiting for a long time. But you didn't want me, did you? I'm not good enough, am I?

And now Abbie would tell, and nobody would understand. It would be exactly like the last time. Nobody had understood then either.

You rejected me, Abbie. You'll never know how much that hurt. How could you do that to me? I didn't mean for you to die—but if you live, that's the end of everything for me.

As soon as Abbie could speak, every carefully constructed edifice of this life would be destroyed, and that couldn't be allowed to happen. That's if the driver didn't speak first.

Time was running out. It was time for somebody to die.

And Ellie was going to have to help. But was she frightened enough yet to do as she was told? Without Ellie the plan would never work. She provided the vital missing piece—the lure.

Something else needed to happen—something that would *really* shake Ellie. She had limits, but she could be manipulated—especially if it was anything to do with her children.

I need to make her scared—scared to death of the alternative. Scared of what I might do to her children. Then she'll do as I ask.

There was a sort of inevitability about it all now—a sense of hurtling at breakneck speed towards a conclusion without any way of slowing things down. It would all be over soon. Life could return to normal, as if none of this had ever happened.

And now it was all down to Ellie.

Although Leo wasn't a religious person, she had always believed in forces for good and forces for evil. She had never been capable of seeing an aura, but she didn't doubt that people had them. Two individuals sitting perfectly still with expressionless faces could give off entirely different types of energy which could positively crackle around a room. So when she walked into the kitchen on Wednesday morning, despite only having sight of Ellie's back, she knew that—had she been capable of seeing it—Ellie's aura would have been the mud colour of tension.

What now?

After making herself scarce the previous evening she had been hoping that this morning life would be back to normal.

Everybody else had eaten breakfast and Ellie was clearing the dishes away. Max was on his way out of the door with the twins and on the face of it, everything seemed to be fine. He said he'd packed Jake's and Ruby's bikes into the boot of his car and was taking them off to a grassy place. Ruby wanted to ride without her stabilisers, apparently, and Ellie said she couldn't bring herself to watch. She'd excused herself on the grounds that she would make Ruby nervous. Jake, on the other hand, said he would see how many times Ruby fell off before he decided whether his were coming off or staying on.

Max left with a cheery wave, but Leo felt that it was a bit half-hearted. Obviously things hadn't worked out quite as well as he'd hoped last night.

She wished she knew what was *really* wrong. It wasn't like her sister to behave like a jealous harpy. She sat down at the kitchen table.

'What's going on, Ellie? I know you have this idea that there's something between Max and that PE teacher, but that's not the only thing, is it? You're so jumpy every time the phone rings, and you seem scared of your own shadow. Is it something to do with Friday night, because you still haven't told me why you went out?'

Ellie banged the dishes down on the worktop and the cutlery tumbled onto the floor. She muttered an expletive, but didn't turn round to face Leo as she spoke.

'Forget Friday night, Leo. I've told you—it was nothing.'

'So why is it so important that Max doesn't know, then?' Leo asked.

Ellie spun round.

'Don't you *dare* mention it to Max. It's got nothing to do with you. *Leave* it.'

She bent to pick up the knives and spoons and thrust them into the dishwasher basket.

Leo wasn't about to let this go.

'What's wrong with you two? This is so unlike the pair of you. You seem fixated on this Alannah woman, but what does Max have to say about it? Do you want me to have a word with him?'

Ellie gripped the edge of the sink, and even from where Leo was sitting she could see her knuckles were white. Ellie's back was rigid, and her voice, when she finally spoke, was tight—as if she were barely opening her mouth.

'My marriage and my children are the most important things in my life, and nothing is going to ruin that. *Nothing.* I'm not going to end up like my mother. I'm not going to drive Max away like she drove our dad away. Whatever's happening will pass. It *has* to. So speaking to Max is the very last thing that *either* of us should do. Do you understand, Leo?'

Ellie still hadn't turned round, but Leo knew, for now at least, that she needed to steer the conversation away from Max.

'Okay, okay—but don't you think that perhaps you might be a bit less stressed if you gave up these delusions about our father, and focused on what really matters?'

'Dad, Leo. He's our dad—why can you never call him that?' Ellie responded.

'He stopped being my dad when I was ten years old. Father is a biological fact. The title "Dad" is a term of affection and it has to be earned.'

'God, you sound priggish sometimes—do you know that?' Ellie switched on the tap, and started to run water into the bowl as if to drown Leo's voice.

Okay, Leo thought. This was probably a bad idea, but she'd started now.

'When are you going to stop pretending that he's going to come back? It's not healthy, you know. Not only is it impossible for me to understand why you believe it, I can't even think why you would *want* it.'

Ellie turned round and leant against the sink with her arms folded.

'I want to know what *happened* to him. Is that so strange? One minute he was here, next he was gone. And never a word of explanation, nor a word of goodbye. If he's alive, at least he'll know where to find me.'

'If he'd wanted to find you, it wouldn't have been difficult—even before your mother died. Accept it, Ellie, for your own sanity. He's gone.' Leo was keeping her voice level. A shouting match would achieve nothing.

'And you're not the slightest bit upset about the fact, are you?' Ellie asked, her mouth set in a tight line.

'No.' It was an honest answer.

'Why do you always pretend to be so fucking calm and reasonable? Do you know how irritating it is? Never let it be said that *you* could show any emotion.' She turned back to the sink and began slamming pots about again. It wasn't like Ellie to swear. Leo knew she should have left it. But then she'd been doing that all week.

'Look, I know how much he hurt you. I was there, remember? I promise you, I'm going to try to find out what happened to him, but I'm not sure it's such a good idea. I think it's time to let it go. Get on with your life and sort out whatever else it is that's bothering you at the moment.'

She looked at her sister. It was amazing how much somebody's posture could tell you about their thoughts. Ellie finally turned round, and the anger in her eyes shocked Leo.

'Stop telling me what to think, will you? It may surprise you to know that just at this moment our father, as you prefer to call him, is the last thing on my mind. I've got far bigger and better things to worry about.' Ellie's laugh was devoid of humour. 'And I know you've always thought that wanting answers is a complete aberration on my part—but actually, what's that phrase—"Physician, heal thyself"? I may have some issues and I may seem irrational to you, but what about you? You can't even stand to be *touched*.'

Leo felt a stinging behind her eyes. *Shit*. She couldn't cry. She never cried.

Ellie gave a small gasp, and bit her bottom lip. Her shoulders sagged, all anger spent.

'Oh Leo, I'm so sorry. That was a dreadful thing to say. I know it's not your fault and I'm truly sorry. There's nothing I'd like to do more than come over there and give you a big hug now, but I know it's not what you want.'

Just this once, Leo thought, I think I might like that. But she couldn't say so, because then she really would cry.

They had talked about her apparent lack of emotion so many times, even when they were children. *Especially* when they were children, but never like this. Mainly Ellie understood. But sometimes she wanted, and no doubt needed, more. Leo wished she could offer it and right now she wished she could accept it too.

Slipping back behind the safe mask of rationality, Leo steered the conversation back to Ellie.

'Ellie, come and sit down. I'll make us both a cup of coffee, and you need to *talk* to me. I mean properly. Not just a fleeting remark as you walk out of the door. I promise you I won't say a word to Max, but I can tell there's something very much the matter, because I've never seen you like this.'

Leo placed both hands on the table and pushed herself up from her seat. She walked across to the coffee machine, but Ellie had turned back to the sink, and was standing with hunched shoulders. She didn't utter a word. On her way to the fridge for the milk, Leo stood behind her sister. She lifted her hands towards Ellie, and then let them drop to her sides. She paused for a moment, and then lifted them again and gently touched Ellie's upper arms, giving them both a brief rub.

'Come on, Ellie. Whatever it is, we can talk it through.'

Leo let her arms drop and carried on towards the fridge. Ellie glanced over her shoulder, looking at Leo in surprise. But before she could say anything, the peal of the doorbell interrupted any opportunity they had to talk.

'Who the bloody hell is that at nine in the morning? Do you think you could go please, Leo? I need a moment.'

She made her way to the front door, and was surprised to see Tom standing there. She quickly tried to pull herself together and shake off the lingering pain of Ellie's words.

'Good morning,' she said. 'What brings you out so early? I was going to call round later and thank you for dinner. The food was seriously good, Tom. But now you've beaten me to it.'

Leo pulled the door open wider to let him in. She had enjoyed herself the previous evening. Tom was good company, and he'd kept her entertained with exaggerated accounts of some of his more bizarre experiences as a policeman.

He stepped in through the open front door.

'I was thinking about our conversation last night,' Tom said. 'I thought it might be a good idea to have a word with Max and Ellie about the security here. I'm a bit worried that somebody was able to come and go so easily—even if they didn't take anything. Are they in?'

Feeling a trace of untypical disappointment that Tom wasn't here to see her, Leo showed him through to the kitchen.

'Max is out with the twins at the moment, but Ellie's here. Can I make you a cup of coffee? We were about to have some.'

'That sounds good, as long as I'm not in the way,' Tom said as they walked through to the kitchen. 'Hi, Ellie. I hope you don't mind me dropping round like this, but I wanted to have a chat with you about your belief that somebody was in your house on Sunday.'

Ellie looked at Leo, and frowned.

'Everybody thinks it was my imagination, Tom. Max believes I'm getting a bit neurotic, and Leo didn't seem too worried.'

Tom gave Leo a questioning look.

'Ah,' she said. 'Sorry, Ellie, but I did wonder if you might be right. I didn't want to make a huge fuss because I thought it would spook you as it was probably a one-off. You've got enough to worry about. It seems as if somebody had been looking at files on my laptop, and Max said it wasn't him.'

Ellie's former fury had returned, and Leo could have kicked herself. Fortunately, Ellie contained her anger in front of Tom, and Leo thought this might be a good time to escape.

'Look, if you don't need me I'll make the coffee and then make myself scarce, if that's okay. I've got a few things I need to do this morning. I'll take that cardigan back to Mimi too, while I'm out.'

Leo offered a weak smile to her sister, poured the milk into the coffees, and made the swiftest exit possible.

Ellie didn't want to have this conversation. She'd already worked out who must have been in the house, and she wanted the subject dropped. She wished she'd never mentioned it.

None of that was Tom's fault, of course. He was genuinely trying to help. He asked her for more details about Sunday, but her replies were practically monosyllabic, and in the end he obviously decided that he wasn't going to make much progress with her.

It was with some relief that Tom finally changed the subject.

'Are you still nursing Abbie Campbell?' he asked.

'Yes, and there's been a change for the better. Did you know? They're taking her off the ventilator—possibly even today. She responded to some external stimulus tests yesterday, so I'm hoping that we'll see more improvement soon. Poor mite.' Ellie looked pensive. 'There was something that I wanted to ask you, Tom. I wouldn't mention it to anybody else but as you are, or rather were, a policeman, I thought it might be okay.'

'I might not be working at the moment, but it doesn't make any difference to my discretion. What's worrying you?'

Ellie pushed her empty coffee cup away. There was something about Tom that seemed solid and reliable, but she felt there was more to him than that. Even on Saturday when he was relaxed and chatting, she had noticed a hint of sadness in those eyes and she wondered what had put it there.

'Abbie's legs and feet when she came in. They were covered in nettle stings, and her feet were cut to shreds. Nobody has mentioned how it happened, but surely it must be relevant? I don't know why nothing has been said. And I was looking at her X-rays the other day, and both her arms have been broken at some stage. I asked the doctor about it, and he said they were very old injuries, and it was nothing for me to worry about. What do you think?'

'I knew about the nettle stings and the cut feet. The police have been keeping that to themselves until they work out what happened. The most likely theory is that Abbie escaped from wherever she was being held. We know that she came from the woods—we've found some traces—and there are plenty of nettles there. But her T-shirt had been rubbed in cow dung, so she must have come from the fields across the road. I've been speaking to my mate, Steve, who is working on the case. He said the trouble is that there are so many properties that back onto the fields, and they have no idea which direction she would have come from, or how far she ran. Anyway, announcements are going out on the news today—I think they've already started—to see if anybody can help at all with the enquiry.'

Ellie was relieved that this wasn't being ignored. *But the woods!*

She had all but forgotten the memories that had plagued her on Sunday. Should she tell Tom what happened there all those years ago? She had promised Fiona she would never tell a living soul, and surely it could have no relevance today? It was all so very long ago. Too many secrets and lies, she thought dejectedly. Fortunately, Tom hadn't noticed that her attention had wandered.

'As far as the broken bones go,' Tom said, 'they may or may not have any bearing on this case. The police will have looked into it, you know, so if you're wondering about the parents, they'll have checked when the bones were broken and what was said at the time.'

Ellie was appalled.

'God, no! I'm sorry, I wasn't suggesting anything about the parents. Kath and Brian are amazing and it's clear how much they love Abbie. I knew I shouldn't have mentioned it.'

'Don't worry, Ellie. It's right to ask questions—but it will have been covered, I can assure you.'

At that moment, one smiley and one not so smiley face appeared at the glass doors to the garden. Max followed behind, pushing one bike with, and one bike without stabilisers. Ruby was grinning from ear to ear, while Jake looked defiant. She didn't need to ask what had happened. Her cautious son had obviously decided he wasn't yet ready to take the risk.

Dumping the bikes on the lawn, Max opened the door and shooed the children inside. They ran over to their mum, both clamouring for her attention. She listened with wide-open eyes as they each told their version of the morning's events—adding the occasional 'wow' and 'how brave' or 'how sensible' as the occasion warranted. She grabbed them both, one in each arm, and gave them a huge hug. They were the best.

'Right, you two,' Max said. 'You can watch half an hour of a DVD, and then we're doing something else. Ruby—you get to watch for being brave, and Jake you get to watch for being honest. Ah-ah—NOT in my media room, thank you very much. In the playroom. Scoot!'

Max pulled out a chair and sat down.

'Tom—how are you? Do you fancy another coffee, because I desperately need one—mainly on the basis that it's a bit early for a beer.'

Ellie could see Tom looking at her to assess his welcome. She didn't think she could cope with half an hour alone with Max just now, so she tried her best to give Tom an encouraging smile, and he took the hint.

'Thanks, Max. That would be great, if I'm not taking up too much of your time.'

'I have a half hour reprieve, mate—and I plan to enjoy it. The joys of school holidays. Normally we plan loads of family trips, but with Ellie working this week I've drawn the short straw.' It was clear from Max's grin that this wasn't an issue for him. 'What are you two nattering about, anyway?'

'Abbie Campbell,' Ellie said.

'God, yes—that's terrible about the Facebook stuff, isn't it? Ellie told me. It sounds like she was *stalked*.'

'Sadly, it looks as if you're right—Abbie was targeted for some reason,' Tom said.

'Why did this person have all the fake friends, though?' Ellie asked.

'Anybody with no friends would be a bit suspicious, so they make up a number of phoney identities, and all friend each other. He'll probably have approached other girls—real ones—too. Whoever this abductor is, he'll most likely have targeted people of a similar age with a low number of friends—the ones that might be desperate.'

Max was shaking his head as he brought over the cups of coffee and sat down at the table.

'So somebody has cold-bloodedly planned this—to befriend Abbie. But why? It doesn't make any sense. Were any of the other kids in the network targeted, do you know? The real ones, I mean.'

'I don't know,' Tom said. 'It looks as if it was focused on Abbie—but she may just have been the first target. People reveal so much stuff about themselves nowadays—everywhere they've been, or worse still, where they're going. It's a gift to criminals. Imagine a young girl who's missed the last bus? She posts something about it as she sets off to walk home—forgetting that she's previously posted where she was going that evening—even down to the specific location. Sorry to say it, but even if she hasn't been daft enough to mention the bus number, she's easy pickings for anybody who's been watching her.'

'Is it really that dangerous?' Ellie asked. She wasn't much of a social networker herself, but lots of her friends were.

'It can be if you're not careful,' Tom answered. 'A woman was murdered because she changed her status on Facebook from married to single. It appears her husband wasn't too impressed. But even if you're careful yourself, a real stalker will contact your friends and get to know them, and get them to reveal private stuff about you.'

'Why can't they catch them, then? Surely things can be tracked back through the Internet?'

'In theory, but there are techniques people can use to make it difficult as far as this sort of crime is concerned. There are ways of rerouting communications round the world several times to make it very hard to trace back. Hopefully this guy isn't so savvy and might have given something away.'

'You keep saying "he"—and I know that makes sense. But surely she wouldn't have got in the car with a man, would she?' Ellie asked.

'Well, she was expecting Chloe's mum. If a man had turned up and said "Are you Abbie? I'm Chloe's dad—her mum was in the bath and we didn't want you to have to hang around", would she have believed him? I suspect she would, you know.'

'So this is cyberstalking, is it?' Max asked.

'Strictly speaking, cyberstalkers only stalk you online and not in the flesh. Digitally enhanced stalking is a different issue. That's when people use online information or a mobile phone or whatever to stalk you for real.'

'Mobile phones?' Ellie said. 'What on earth can they do with a mobile phone?'

Tom laughed.

'Ellie—you have no idea. There are apps you can buy online to put on somebody's phone that let you track all sorts of activity. Don't get me onto that or I could be here all day.'

'I'm not sure I want to know,' Max said.

'Actually, Max, all this talk of people knowing where you are and what you're doing reminds me. I was talking to Ellie earlier about this visitor you appear to have had on Sunday. What's your take on it?' Tom asked.

Ellie looked nervously at Max. His response to Tom's question was to look at Ellie and give her a smile, which to her mind had a hint of irritating condescension.

'I think that Ellie perhaps *thought* somebody had been in, but maybe the kids had messed things up a bit. I'm positive I locked the door, and there were no signs of a break-in, so I don't see how. Sorry, Ellie. I don't want to doubt you, but . . .'

Ellie was quick to agree with Max. She was positive she knew who it was, and she wanted this conversation to stop before Max worked it out.

'It's nothing, Tom. Like Max says, I probably imagined it.'

'What about keys? Could anybody have had keys to the house?'

Although she was sure it was irrelevant, Ellie suddenly realised that there was one thing that might put everybody off the trail.

'Sean brought round the spare set of keys that he had—do you remember, Max? I asked you about them on Sunday morning, and you said you didn't know what you'd done with them. Maybe somebody took them?'

Max turned to face Ellie with a look of total incredulity.

'Who, for God's sake? Those people are all our friends. Who on earth was going to take a set of keys so that they could come in and root around in your knicker drawer? Come on, Ellie. That's a bit far-fetched, don't you think?'

Ellie knew that Max was right—but it was the best story that she could come up with.

As soon as she possibly could without appearing rude, Ellie escaped to the bedroom, leaving Max to show their guest out. She had intentionally left her phone switched off since the previous night, and although she was anxious about what she would find when she turned it on, she couldn't put it off forever. And anyway, there was something that she was going to have to say. Once more she went into the bathroom. Ridiculous as it was, there was little choice if she wanted to avoid being interrupted. Leaning her back against the closed door, she switched the phone on.

As expected, the minute it sprang to life the phone beeped to signal that there were messages and missed calls. Five text messages last night, and two missed calls, plus more this morning. All from the same person. What did he think he was doing?

The messages were all along the same lines.

WHAT WAS THAT ABOUT, ELLIE? WHY WERE YOU BEHAVING LIKE THAT WITH MAX? I DIDN'T LIKE IT. REMEMBER THAT I'M WATCHING YOU. YOU MAY NOT BE ABLE TO SEE ME, BUT I'M ALWAYS HERE. ALWAYS WATCHING.

She knew he was telling the truth. She permanently felt as if hot eyes were boring into the back of her neck, and was constantly looking over her shoulder.

There were other messages, demanding that she call him. She truly didn't know what to do. Dropping her hands to her sides, she leant her head against the soft comfort of her dressing gown, hanging on the back of the door. Thinking there was nothing that she would like better than to wrap herself in its warmth and curl up on the bed, she thought about her options.

'Sod it,' she muttered, bringing the phone back to her ear and pressing the screen once. He answered immediately, as she'd known he would.

'About time,' he said. His voice sounded harsh, and Ellie felt a hard knot of fear. She had always thought that she could control the situation, but suddenly she wasn't so sure.

'What's going on, Ellie? I thought we were just waiting for the right time for you to tell Max that you're leaving him—and then you behave like *that*. Dancing with him, holding your body against him. What am I supposed to think?'

She took a deep breath, and tried to speak with a calm she wasn't feeling.

'I have never said that I'm leaving Max. Not once, and you know that. If he leaves me, that's his choice. But I'm not going to leave him—for you, or anybody else. I don't know what I have to do to convince you, but I want you to leave me alone.'

She heard a deep sigh of frustration from the other end of the phone.

'I know you're trying. I know you think you can make your marriage work. But you know that it's me you want. You *proved* it.'

'I proved *nothing*! I was stupid, hurt, angry—all of those things.' Ellie realised that she was shouting, and dropped her voice lower. 'How many times do I have to tell you?'

'Listen,' he said. 'I realised yesterday what the problem is. You don't know how to tell him, do you? Well, don't worry about it. I'll tell him. I'm not scared of Max. I'll tell him that you and I belong together, and then it will be easy for you.'

Not Max. Please don't tell Max.

But she couldn't say the words. That would only inflame him more. She had to keep him calm until she could work out what to do.

'I don't *want* it to be easy. If Max ever needs to know about this, I'll be the one to tell him. But there's something else. You've been in my house, haven't you? When we were out on Sunday, you came in the house didn't you? You went into my bedroom and my bathroom. Why? *Why?* I don't understand why you would do such a thing.'

'Is that what you think of me? Is it? Seriously?' There was a pause, and Ellie didn't fill it. 'What you and I have is special, darling. I would never do anything that would damage your trust in me. I promise you, I haven't been in your house. If you remember, on Sunday I was close to you. *Very* close. I couldn't have been in your house. The other day you were accusing me of knocking over a child and leaving her to die, and now you're accusing me of breaking and entering. I know your trust in men has been shaken, but for God's sake, Ellie!'

'I don't know what to think about anything anymore, but please, I beg you, don't say anything to Max, don't go to the police about Friday night. I know you want to see me. I *will* see you, but can you just give me some time. Please?'

She knew she was stalling. She had no desire to see him at all, but maybe if he thought she was coming round to his way of thinking, she would have a chance to calm things down.

'A couple of days, then. I can't promise longer than that. But remember that I'm always here. Always watching. Always keeping you safe. Just remember. And my patience is running out.'

With that, he hung up.

35

The weather had turned cloudy, and there was more of a cool breeze today, but Leo welcomed it as she made her way into the village. She didn't like hot, sticky weather. She hoped she had made the right decision leaving Ellie with Tom earlier, but she had needed to get away. She hadn't bothered mentioning the fact that one of the files opened on her computer was the information about their father. It felt like it would be adding fuel to the fire and it wasn't that important. Tom's arrival hadn't been brilliant timing, but now she was grateful to have a few hours alone.

The funny thing about Tom was that his outward persona didn't quite fit with the idea of him being a detective in the serious crime division. He was so relaxed and easy—not her idea of how a high-ranking policeman would be at all. But then last night she'd asked him in one of their rare serious moments how he dealt with some of the lowlifes that he must come across regularly, and she saw something. Nothing happened that she could put her finger on—he didn't tighten his lips or narrow his eyes. But his face changed in the subtlest of ways—it was as if his cheekbones had become more prominent, and his eyes turned cold. It was enough for her to know for sure that she would never want to be questioned by this man for a crime—whether she was guilty or innocent. It also made him more intriguing.

As a result of her self-enforced eviction Leo wasn't quite sure what to do with herself, until she remembered that the wine bar opened early to serve breakfast. Maybe she could set up her office there for an hour or so. She had calls to make and meetings to set up for next week. A few of her clients were going on family holidays this week, and she had a dreadful suspicion that on their return they might be in need of urgent appointments. Unhappy relationships and holidays were not often a good match.

Ordering an almond croissant and the ubiquitous cappuccino, she settled down in the corner away from other customers so that she wouldn't disturb them by speaking on the telephone. Not that it seemed to bother anybody else, as at least fifty per cent of people were doing something with their mobiles; texting, checking e-mails, or tweeting no doubt.

This week hadn't turned out in any way as Leo might have expected. Ellie was working too many hours and they'd had precious little time together, but when they *were* together, Ellie was prickly and distracted. Even without this morning's scene, it had been an uncomfortable few days. And then there was the accident. Just the thought that the driver could be someone from the village had been enough to upset everyone, but now that they knew that Abbie had been abducted, there was a whole new layer of suspicion added. It felt somehow like the hours before an electric storm; the air around them was heavy and crackling with tension.

Leo was worried about the fact that in her conversations with Tom she had failed to mention what she'd discovered about Gary—that he had been out late on Friday and then lied about it. But she couldn't say anything until she had spoken to Ellie about where she'd been that night, and God knows how she could raise that subject again. She didn't believe that there could be any link, but what if there was? If she mentioned Gary, would it make everything collapse around her family like a house of cards? And she had the feeling that Penny had said something that should have meant more than it did. But she couldn't catch the thought. It was like trying to remember a word or a name—it was literally there, in her head for a fleeting second, and then disappeared before it solidified.

She rested her chin on cupped hands. This was getting her nowhere. She was starting to miss the solitary silence of her own home. She loved her apartment, but it had taken so much hard work to be able to afford to live there. Even with an established practice as a life coach she'd had to spend a couple of years working in a bar at night to cover the mortgage. Situated in a renovated old warehouse, it was wonderfully spacious with high ceilings and bare brickwork. She had lived there for months with nothing much more than a mattress on the floor and a hanging rail for her clothes. But it had been worth it.

Much as she wanted to go home, though, she was starting to feel a compulsion to stay until those around her were at peace again. Whether she would be able to help with the process or not, she didn't think she could just walk away.

The scene with Ellie this morning had left her feeling drained. Since when had her sister become a glass-half-empty person? That had always been Leo's role.

She reached into her bag and pulled out her notebook and pen. Maybe some cathartic writing would help her to make sense of it.

A Single Step: the blog of Leo Harris

Listening to a different tune

Many years ago I saw a short film sequence of a little girl. She was wearing a pretty dress as she skipped down a narrow cobbled lane. The people around smiled fondly as she passed. The grainy, black-and-white image did nothing to detract from the happy scene, and the light, summery music gave a feeling of well-being. The audience's attention was focused entirely on the child.

Then the identical film was shown again, but this time with sinister music playing. There was a gasp from the audience. For the first time, every person in the room noticed an unsmiling man standing at the mouth of a dark alley, smoking a cigarette and watching the girl.

In spite of already knowing the ending, there was a sigh of relief when the child was reunited with her mother.

Same film. Different music.

For some people, life is like that. They filter out the positive and focus on the negative. They make assumptions about what somebody else is thinking, and believe only in the worst possible outcome.

They are listening to a sinister tune.

Is this you? If so, change the music, and focus on the positive. Listen to a happy tune, and see if the man skulking in the doorway disappears from view.

"Human beings, by changing the inner attitudes of their minds, can change the outer aspects of their lives." William James

Leo put her pen down. She would re-read it before she typed it into her blog, but she was pleased with what she'd written. Perhaps she would show it to Ellie. Then again, perhaps not.

Realising that she had already eaten two almond croissants and would feel forced to eat a third if she continued to sit here, Leo packed up her temporary office and reluctantly made her way out of the wine bar.

Thoughts of her years of working long nights serving drinks to largely ungrateful customers had brought one person to mind. Mimi. Somebody needed to drop off her cardigan, and Pat had been conspicuous by his absence this week, so it provided Leo with the perfect excuse to call round. The fact was that she felt a bit sorry for Mimi. It didn't seem quite right that everybody was oh-so sympathetic to Patrick, and treated her like a pariah. Pat was the one who was married and who had cheated on his wife. He was responsible for his own marriage, and Mimi shouldn't be shouldering all the burden of guilt. Perhaps if she took her some flowers to congratulate her on the pregnancy, she could offer the girl a sympathetic ear. She had precious little hope that Mimi would be interested in a life-coaching session, but at least the cardigan provided a reasonable excuse for her visit.

Clutching her newly acquired bunch of summer flowers, Leo made her way through the labyrinth of short streets that made up the recently developed estate on the far side of the village. She realised that she didn't know Mimi and Pat's address, but Pat had mentioned a cut-through path from the village that came out opposite their house, and she knew that it was the farthest street from the main road. It was obvious that the planners had tried to make the roads interesting, because instead of straight lines that were easy to navigate, the roads twisted and turned. Leo was glad she wasn't driving. She would never have found it.

She was unsure of the reception she would get. There was no doubt that Mimi was a difficult character, and she clung to Pat like chewing gum on the sole of a shoe. Unfortunately it felt as if Pat was constantly trying to scrape her off—which couldn't in all fairness do much for the girl's self-esteem. Her comment on Saturday night about everybody treating her as if she were a mistake was spot on.

When Leo finally found what she assumed was Mimi's street, she could see that the brand-new houses were compact—probably starter homes, and possibly only had one double bedroom and a bathroom upstairs. They were arranged into small terraces of six properties, with a side access at the end of each block to a rear passageway.

Each house had an identical white front door—a popular design that Leo had never understood, almost as if a very narrow front door had been built into a larger frame. As she stared at the doors wondering where to begin she noticed some movement in the parking bay across the road. It was Mimi, unloading her shopping. Leo's timing had been perfect. She walked across the road.

'Mimi—hi,' Leo shouted. 'Here, let me help you with those bags. They look heavy. Grab these—they're for you,' she added, handing Mimi the flowers and picking up the largest of the carrier bags.

'I was just coming round to see you—to see how you are and how you're getting on, and I've brought your cardigan back.'

Mimi looked surprised by Leo's appearance and for some strange reason, slightly nervous. Leo knew she could appear cold and aloof, but she hoped she hadn't frightened the woman.

'I hope you don't mind me popping round on the off chance. I know what it's like to be relatively new to an area, and I wondered if you fancied a bit of company for half an hour.'

Mimi pulled the flowers towards her face and sniffed. She shot Leo a wary glance.

'These are very nice. Thank you.'

'My pleasure. Which way with the bags?'

Mimi indicated the second house from the left, then walked ahead of Leo to unlock the front door, which led straight into a small sitting room, with an open-tread wooden staircase going up one side. A large beige Dralon sofa was squeezed hard into one corner and up against the back wall, and a wildly patterned carpet in shades of orange and brown covered the floor. A television sat on a table covered with a cream-coloured cloth in another corner, and under the stairs was an old style computer desk, with separate monitor and keyboard areas and space to hold the processor. A laptop was trying its best to find a comfortable spot there.

The house had a musty smell, as if no windows were ever opened. There was a vague hint of tinned tomato soup or baked beans, overlaid with stale air.

It appeared that the central area of the room had to be kept fairly clear, as this was the route through to the kitchen at the back of the house, and Leo dodged round a wooden rocking chair to follow Mimi. She couldn't help noticing that there were no pictures on the walls but ceramic figurines adorned every possible surface.

Leo realised that if Mimi was a barmaid it was quite an achievement to be able to afford this place. She remembered well the pittance that she'd been paid, and some of the hovels that she had put up with. Considerably worse than this, even if it did need a bit of TLC.

The kitchen ran along the back of the house—a long, thin room with a small space at one end to squeeze in a table and two chairs.

Mimi dumped the flowers on the worktop. She couldn't quite meet Leo's eyes.

'I know it's not much, but it will do until Patrick's divorce comes through. It's only a rental—so there's not much we can do to improve things.'

'Mimi, you don't have to make excuses to me you know. I lived in a squat for a while when I first left home.'

Mimi looked at her, as if to decide whether this was bull or it was real.

'Do you want coffee?' she finally asked.

'Actually, do you have any tea? I've drunk so much coffee this morning already that I'll get the jitters if I have any more.'

There was silence while Mimi made the tea. Leo pretended to look with great interest at the view out of the back window, which revealed a tiny square of slightly overgrown lawn leading to the passageway that ran behind the row of houses, and a flat and uninteresting field beyond. Mimi was obviously not going to break the silence, and Leo wondered if she was shy.

'Great to have a house that isn't overlooked from the back,' Leo remarked, trying to start a conversation.

'It's okay. We don't use the garden much. Do you want to sit down? We could go in the lounge if you like, or stay here?'

'Here's fine. I'm a kitchen person—well, not in the sense of being able to cook, but I like *being* in kitchens.'

Leo sat down and smiled encouragingly at Mimi, who still seemed a bit unsure of herself. She sat down opposite Leo, clutching the mug of tea between her two hands.

'What have you done with Patrick today, then? I often wonder how teachers amuse themselves in the long holidays. Max is kept busy with the twins, of course—but what about Pat?'

'He's had to go to a meeting at school.'

'In the holidays? That's a bit mean, isn't it?' Leo suddenly had a thought. 'I bet it's to do with Abbie Campbell—you know, the girl who was knocked over on Friday night. I presume you've heard that they're now saying she was abducted?'

'I don't know anything about it. Patrick's not said much, and I don't watch the news. It's too depressing. I expect it's all become a bit exaggerated, though, as things seem to in this village.'

'I'm not sure you'd feel like that if she was your daughter,' Leo said. 'Her parents must be going through hell, although Ellie does say that there are some signs of recovery. It takes time, though, and it could be weeks before she's able to tell the police what happened.'

Mimi appeared to have nothing to add to this conversation thread. It was like pulling teeth. She wasn't exactly hostile, but she was obviously not comfortable. There was a level of anxiety there, and Leo didn't seem to be able to break down the barrier.

'How did you end up in Little Melham, Mimi? Not an obvious place to choose, I wouldn't have thought. You're not from round here, are you?'

'I'm from the south coast.'

'Ooh, nice. I've been to Brighton, and Poole. There are some lovely spots down there.'

'Yeah, well—it all depends on where you live and how much money you've got, I suppose.'

Leo looked keenly at Mimi, who was absent-mindedly chewing her thumbnail.

'Are you okay? You seem a bit edgy today.'

Mimi pulled the nail away from her mouth and sat up straighter.

'Blame it on the hormones. I'm okay. I'm fine. I don't want to be rude, Leo, but is this a social call or did you have something on your mind? Only I need to go out again soon.'

Leo felt a twinge of guilt, although she wasn't sure why. She had come here with the best of intentions.

'There was no agenda at all, I promise you. Ellie asked me to bring your cardigan back. She's been trying to reach Pat, but he hasn't been answering his phone. And I just thought I'd see how you're doing, and repeat my offer of the free life-coaching session, if you're interested. With the baby coming and everything it would be a great time to think about how you'd like your life to pan out.'

Leo knew immediately it was the wrong thing to say. Mimi's eyes glinted like ice, but at that moment her mobile buzzed and she looked away, too soon to know whether it was the glint of tears or anger.

Mimi pressed a button on her phone, and her brow wrinkled in annoyance at whatever was on the screen.

'If you need to answer that, it's okay with me,' Leo said.

'I don't.'

Leo wanted to try to recover the situation. In one of the few normal conversations she'd had with Ellie in the last couple of days, her sister had told her that Pat was spending a lot of time with Georgia—trying to make things right. Maybe Mimi knew, and that would account for her stress, particularly now that she was pregnant.

'It's funny, but I once thought the whole idea of life coaching was ridiculous. Like you, I worked in a bar. More of a nightclub I suppose, and it was in central London. The hours were long, the pay crap. You know how it is. But I was a stroppy cow, and got very lippy with the customers. One night, I chose the wrong guy—the brother of the boss. He somehow got the idea that I'd like his grubby hands sliding over my backside, and I informed him otherwise.' Leo laughed at the memory. Mimi's face was expressionless. 'My boss was a woman, and a bit more sympathetic than a man might have been—but she told me I had "issues" that had to be sorted if I wanted to keep my job. There was apparently a better way of defusing difficult situations than a mouthful of verbal abuse. I was forced to go to a couple of counselling sessions which I thought were a joke, because all we did was examine the things that had made me the person that I am. But then I went to see a life coach and it changed everything. It doesn't stop me being who I am, warts and all, but it helps me to deal with it and make my little foibles work *for* me rather than against me.'

Leo could see that her speech had fallen on deaf ears. Mimi had folded her arms, and her hands were clenched. Her mobile buzzed again, and she whisked it off the table, transfixed by the screen.

Mimi stood up abruptly, her phone clutched tightly in her hand.

'Will you excuse me, Leo? I need the toilet.'

Without another glance at Leo, Mimi made her way out of the room and Leo heard her clattering up the wooden staircase.

This had not turned out the way she'd hoped at all.

She picked up the mugs from the table and stepped over the shopping bags to reach the sink. Her thoughts were miles away, wondering how difficult life might be for Mimi at the moment. Lost in thought, she turned to make her way back to the table.

'Bugger,' she muttered, as she kicked one of the shopping bags and the contents fell out all over the slate tile–effect lino. She bent down and started to pick up onions and potatoes from where they had rolled across the floor. As she started to stuff the groceries back in the bag, she noticed something unexpected at the bottom. But before she had time to give it any thought, she heard clattering coming down the stairs again and hastily started to stuff everything back into the bag.

She looked up as Mimi walked in the room. The two women regarded each other without a word.

Leo broke the silence.

'I think I'd better go.'

Nothing else was said. But then, nothing else was needed.

Leo had been right about one thing on Tuesday evening. There was a hell of a lot of tension in the Saunders household at the moment. Tom had felt it like a waft of cold air the minute Leo had opened the door. Leo had been pleasant enough, but there was nothing relaxed in her manner. Even when she was stroppy and sarcastic, she had an easy grace about her. But her movements had been jumpier, her voice less modulated.

And Ellie was worse. She hadn't even wanted to talk about their intruder, which was strange as Leo said that Ellie was the one who was most concerned about it. She was hiding something, but Tom couldn't think of any reason why she would.

Well, whatever was going on, all he could do was help when he was asked. Which reminded him—that's exactly what Leo had done the previous evening. She was desperate to finally know the truth about her father's disappearance, and Tom had a few routes to intelligence, although it was strictly forbidden to use police computers to track information for personal purposes. But he had done similar research before and had a good idea where to start. Local knowledge.

Sitting at his desk in the study, he grabbed the phone. Steve had called the day before and fortunately he had stored the number. There was one thing that his old sergeant might be able to help him with. The phone was answered almost immediately, but it was a noisy line and not very clear.

'Steve? Tom Douglas. Sorry to bother you—do you have a minute to chat, or are you in the middle of something?'

'Morning, Tom. Good to hear from you. I'm in the car on hands-free, and about ten minutes out from my destination. So shoot. I should warn you to keep it clean, because I've got my sergeant with me, and he's of a delicate disposition.'

Tom laughed as he imagined the accompanying wink from Steve. He heard an echo of his laughter from the noisy car. The sergeant, no doubt.

'I wanted to ask if you have any old-timers around the office who might be able to provide a bit of local information from about fifteen to twenty years ago. About a resident of Little Melham at that time, by the name of Harris. Edward Harris. Lived at Willow Farm.'

'We've got a couple of guys who are coming up to twenty-five years, so they might be able to help. What do you want to know?'

'His daughters have become friends of mine.' Tom was interrupted by laughter and a few remarks about the fact that he had used the plural term. He let them finish before continuing.

'His daughters, one of whom is happily married to my next door neighbour—just so that we're clear—don't know what happened to him. He disappeared, possibly in the summer of 1995, and they don't know where he went or if he's still alive. I know you can't help with that bit, but any background, gossip, local knowledge might help.'

'Okay—Edward Harris, you said? I'll ask my sergeant here to get hold of anybody who we think might be able to help, and see if there's anything we can find out for you. Do you know any more about him?'

'Only that he was a bigamist, but was apparently never done for it. One wife died, and the remaining one had him declared dead in 2002 allegedly, although his daughter can't find any trace of a death certificate in the relevant period.'

'Quite a little mystery, then. Perhaps the surviving wife topped him and buried him in the garden.' Steve laughed.

'Don't think that hadn't occurred to me,' Tom said, not entirely joking. From what Leo had said about her stepmother it didn't actually sound like an implausible scenario.

'Okay—we're on it. Somebody will get back to you as soon as. If there's anybody on duty now who might be able to help, I'll get them to give you a call. Otherwise it might be tomorrow. Let me know how it goes.'

'Thanks, Steve. How are things going with the Abbie Campbell case?' Tom asked.

'Crap. We keep hitting brick walls. Have you heard any gossip since we last spoke?'

'Nothing useful, I'm afraid. The villagers are breathless with excitement about the fact that you've been interviewing teachers and the like, but apart from that nobody seems to have a clue. I'll keep my ear to the ground.'

'Okay—that would be great. Speak soon.'

They said their goodbyes, and Tom continued to sit at his desk, turning a pen over idly in his fingers as he thought about Leo and whether helping her would be a good idea or bad. He had a feeling that, when the time came, he might have to implore Leo not to shoot the messenger.

❖

By the time Tom had made and eaten a bacon sandwich for his lunch and returned to his desk to start his online research, Steve and his sergeant had obviously done their stuff because the phone rang and Tom heard a voice he didn't recognise.

'Good morning, sir. My name's Ernie Collier. Detective Inspector Corby asked me to call you with regard to Ted Harris—is that right?'

This policeman didn't need to call him 'sir', but Tom knew that he would be uncomfortable with anything else if he was one of the old guard, so he let it pass. More interestingly, he called Edward Harris 'Ted', which indicated that he knew who he was.

'If Ted is Edward Harris, formerly of Willow Farm, Little Melham, then anything you can tell me about him would be useful. I'm trying to track him down for his daughters.'

'Not sure you'll be wanting to do that, sir, if I may say so as shouldn't,' Ernie said. That was a phrase Tom hadn't heard in a while.

He sighed. This wasn't going to have a happy ending, but then, given what he already knew about the man, it had always been unlikely.

'Why do you say that, Ernie?' he asked.

'I was a beat bobby in Little Melham for five years. I got to know the locals pretty well, and I knew about his other daughter coming to live there. She'd been there a couple of years by the time I arrived, but it was still news as far as the villagers were concerned. There wasn't much went on, so a good story could last a fair few years. They all knew the girl had a different mother and that Ted had a long-term relationship somewhere else.'

Tom decided not to mention the word bigamy, as this had never been pursued at the time.

'The girls know all about that, of course, but I'm wondering why you think it would be a bad idea to find out what happened to him, or to discover if he's alive.'

'He had a bit of a reputation—not something his daughters would be proud of. Liked to put it about a bit—you know—spread his favours, as it were. Not just in the village, but round the area in general. There were lots of angry men, and a few were baying for his blood from time to time. But as I understand it, he'd disappear for a while until things calmed down, then turn up again.'

'So do you think that one of these women's husbands might have got to him in the end, then?' Tom asked.

'Not husbands, sir. Fathers. He liked 'em young, did Ted. Legal—but barely.'

Christ, Tom thought. How the hell was he going to tell Leo any of this? Easy answer—he wasn't. This was rumour and conjecture. He would tell her the truth about her father as and when he found it.

'Was there anything solid, Ernie? Anything that might indicate what happened to him and why finally he went and didn't come back?'

'I've been pondering that one since DI Corby called, but nothing's coming to me. I'll think on—and if it does, I'll let you know. I don't know that any of this is fact—it's just village chitchat. Nobody reported him to us, so as far as we know officially, he didn't commit any crime. But on balance, I would say a smooth-talking slimeball, if you get my drift.'

Tom did. He thanked Ernie and hung up, wishing he'd never asked. It seemed to him that this opened up a plethora of possible outcomes to Leo's search for her dad—and none of them sounded promising.

36

After the events of the morning Ellie had to get out of the house, and so she had grabbed four bags-for-life from the cupboard and set off for the supermarket. Shopping for food and the thought of what she might invent for dinner once this phase of endless shifts was over had cheered her up a little, and by the time she got home she was sorry to see that the house appeared deserted.

As she drew her car to a stop by the front door, she looked at her watch. Max must have taken the kids somewhere again. She had expected to see at least his car, and probably Leo's too. So where was everybody?

Walking round to the kitchen door with the first of the shopping bags, she was surprised to find it very slightly ajar. She must have been wrong. Somebody must be home.

But the kitchen was deserted, and the house seemed silent.

She quietly lowered the bags onto the floor and stood still to listen. Nothing. Max must have gone out and left the bloody door open again—how many times did she have to remind him?

But what if he hadn't? What if it was *him*—sneaking into her house while they were all out? *Again.*

Ellie didn't know what to do. Should she face him and have it out with him now? What would he do to her? If they were alone in the house, she knew what he would want—far more than she was prepared to give. She never thought she would be scared of him, but after their conversation this morning she was no longer certain.

Perhaps she should go back and sit in the car until somebody came home.

No. That wouldn't do. She *had* to know. She didn't want to see him, or for him to know that she was here. But she needed to be sure. If anybody knew how to get into their house undetected, it was him.

Kicking off her shoes she silently made her way from the kitchen through the atrium to the hallway. She stood there quietly for a moment, but there wasn't a sound.

There was nobody there. She hadn't realised that she was holding her breath, but with a huge sigh of relief she turned to go back to the kitchen.

Clunk. Behind her, but above. Something dropped or closed. And she definitely wasn't imagining it.

There was somebody in her house.

She shouldn't be terrified, but she was. Why was he doing this to her? She really didn't want to be on her own with him in an empty house.

Clunk. There it was again. Before she could force herself to move, she heard the unmistakable sound of the creaking step at the top of the staircase, and she knew that he was about to appear. She couldn't make it back to the kitchen without being seen.

She had no choice—she would have to hide in the sitting room.

She silently eased open the door and crept inside, pushing the door as far as she dared so that it was almost closed, but not so far that it made a sound. Flattening herself against the wall, she held her breath for a long moment.

Oh God—please don't let him find me in here.

He was at the bottom of the stairs. She could hear him breathing, and she heard a soft laugh. One that she recognised only too well. He knew she was here. How, she didn't know.

The sitting room door slowly began to open inwards, and Ellie groped behind her for a weapon—her hands making contact with a pewter candlestick.

In the glass cover of a painting hanging above the fireplace she could see the silhouette of a man, backlit from the window in the hallway. She could make out no features, but those wide shoulders were a giveaway.

Then she heard the laugh again. He had found her.

Whipping the door open, she swung her body round to face him, her fear replaced by fury. She advanced towards him, and he backed away into the hall, holding his hands high in mock surrender.

'You *bastard*. What the *hell* are you doing in my house? You've gone too far this time—this is too much. I *knew* it was you all along—sneaking in and creeping through my things. You *shit*. What do you think Max would say if he found you here?' she screamed at him.

He smiled, and moved towards her, grabbing her arms and pushing her back inside the sitting room. He easily gripped both of her wrists in one of his large, strong hands and held them above her head, running his other hand down her body from her neck to her hip.

She was about to scream when she heard the last voice she was expecting, coming from the landing above.

'Ellie? What the hell are you shouting at Sean for?'

Max.

Oh Christ—what had she done? What had she said?

For a moment, Ellie was incapable of responding. Had she given herself away? Sean just smiled and let go of her wrists, guiding her out into the hallway.

She looked up to where Max was leaning over the banister, looking both mystified and annoyed. She was speechless. But Sean was still smirking.

'It's okay, Max. I think I frightened the life out of Miss Scarlet here. At least she didn't hit me with the candlestick that she's brandishing. She must have thought I was a burglar.'

Max didn't look entirely convinced.

'A *burglar*. For God's sake, Ellie. I asked Sean to come round and look at changing the locks. I thought that would make you happy. While he was here, he was just helping me to carry that new toy box upstairs.'

Ellie couldn't stop herself from shooting a glance of fury over her shoulder. I bet he thought *that* was a joke. As if Sean changing the locks would solve the problems. He'd just have spares cut, and they would be back to square one.

Pulling herself together quickly, Ellie managed to muster up a weak smile from somewhere.

'There are no cars here, though—I thought nobody was home.'

'We left the cars round the side—because that's where you keep telling me to park. Leo's gone out, and the twins have been given the special honour of thirty minutes watching the "ginormous" television in the media room to keep them out of the way. I'll be down in a second. Maybe you could offer Sean a drink or something by way of apology for nearly ripping his head off.'

Max disappeared from view, and Ellie closed her eyes and felt herself crumple with the relief, almost forgetting that she wasn't alone.

'I won't stay for a drink, Ellie. Don't look so worried.' The smile slipped from Sean's face. 'The truth is, I can't stand to see you two together. Not like last night. I didn't like that.'

He reached out and grabbed her wrist, gripping it tightly. 'I mean it, Ellie. I didn't like it.' He let go of her, and she rubbed her arm fiercely with the other hand as if to erase all trace of him from her skin. 'I'll be off—but you know where I am—always.'

He turned towards the door, then stopped. 'And by the way, while Max wasn't paying attention I used the opportunity to move a few things around. I like the thought of something I bought you being in your bathroom, watching you undress, take a bath, take a shower. That's why I bought it. Don't move it again, Ellie.'

I can hear things now. And I can feel things. I feel sore. My feet hurt—was that from kicking the door? No—that was THEN. That was a long time ago. I'm getting confused.

I was going to see Chloe. That's right! I'd forgotten. She was coming with her mum to get me.

But that's not what happened.

It didn't matter that Chloe wasn't in the car—I understood that there had been a change of plan. I didn't think that anything was wrong—I was so excited. I thought it was strange that I had to wear a blindfold, but it was supposed to be part of the surprise. I don't think so now. I think it was so that I wouldn't know where I was. I'd never be able to find my way back.

We went in the house, and we waited for Chloe. I kept asking—'Where's Chloe? When's she coming?'

'Soon—but it's nice for us to get to know each other while we wait, isn't it?'

Well, I suppose so—but I really wanted to see Chloe.

I don't know when I realised that Chloe wasn't coming, but I was worried. It wasn't right. It felt totally weird. So I asked if I could go home. I asked for the address so I could call my mum and dad to come and get me.

That was a bad move. My phone was whipped out of my hand and flung against the wall on the other side of the room. It's broken now.

'You're not going anywhere until I say so.' First there was anger, but then a shaky hand reached out to stroke my hair. That was worse.

'Don't touch me,' I squealed.

'Don't be silly, baby. It's okay if I touch you. I was meant to touch you. See, like this. It doesn't hurt, does it? Let me kiss you.'

Those lips came down and touched my cheek. They felt dry and cracked as they scraped my face and planted kiss after kiss on me. I felt sick. An arm went round me to pull me into a hug. There was a wet patch on the T-shirt and the smell of fresh sweat. It was horrible, but I couldn't move. I was too scared.

'I want to tell you a story, Abbie. It will be our secret.'

So I listened. And then I understood. In the end, it wasn't the words. It was the voice that I remembered.

I panicked, and started to scream. I knew I was in trouble. But I stopped when I saw what looked like a belt from a dressing gown. I knew what was going to happen as it was dangled in front of my eyes.

'Why are you behaving like this, Abbie—as if you hate me? I thought we could be friends. I would have let you go, once you'd promised to keep our secret.'

'We can be friends,' I cried.

There was a laugh. A nasty laugh—another reminder.

'You're lying to me—don't you think I know when you're lying?'

I begged and begged not to be tied up. I promised not to move. I kicked off my shoes to show that I couldn't go anywhere. I couldn't escape.

But it was the parcel tape I was most scared of. That's how people die. I was too scared to speak. I just kept thinking that I know how to be quiet. Shh. Be still. Be quiet. Not a sound. I remember, see! I know how to be quiet.

I don't know what happened then. There was a beep from a phone. Not my phone. But for the first time the intense, wild stare of those eyes was off me. I would only get one chance, because now I knew. I knew too much, and I couldn't be allowed to go free.

I was close to the back door. I prayed that it would be unlocked. I picked up the glass of Coke that I'd been given when I got there—when we were being friendly. I hadn't drunk any—I was waiting for Chloe. I threw myself out of the chair and grabbed for the door handle, turning round to hurl the contents of the glass at the horrified face behind me. Enough to make it impossible to see for a second. It worked. I was out of the door and running.

Ellie had been glad to get away from the house after the scene earlier with Sean. She'd managed to make it through lunch, but shuddered as she thought about how close she'd been to inadvertently revealing everything to Max. He, of course, had made light of it and laughed about Miss Scarlet in the library with the candlestick, but she had found it hard to join in. And she knew he was still puzzled by her reaction. Worse still, she didn't know what Sean was going to do next, but she knew that it wasn't finished. Not by a long way.

This week was supposed to have been an easy one for Ellie, with three short shifts and the rest of the time free to spend with Max and the twins. But it had turned into something of a marathon, working every day. In many ways, it was probably for the best. She couldn't resent little Abbie, and it got her out of the house. Max had tried so hard last night, and she had come close to telling him everything. But then she'd seen Sean emerge from the depths of the garden and terror had overtaken her. And now she was wondering about Max. If he really *was* seeing Alannah and planning something with her, why would he have behaved like that last night? None of it made any sense at all.

She gave a sigh of frustration as she shouldered her way through the doors into the ICU. She had no time to think about it now. Grateful that her request to continue to care for Abbie had been heeded, she would focus on the girl and put her needs first. Glancing towards the bed, she wasn't surprised to see that Kath was there as always. But she also noticed one piece of equipment missing from the side of Abbie's bed, and that could only be a good thing. The nurse she was replacing saw her arrive and made her way across to the nurses' station.

'Great news, Ellie. Abbie's off the ventilator and she's much more responsive. She hasn't opened her eyes yet, but her reaction to pain is good, and she's breathing by herself now. Kath and Brian haven't left her side—it's always one or the other. But I'm quite worried about Kath. She doesn't eat when she's here, and she's constantly talking about how they've let Abbie down. We had a couple of emergencies this morning, so I've not had much time to talk to her, but see what you can do, will you? She shouldn't be getting herself into such a state.'

When Ellie arrived at the bedside, the first thing she noticed was that Kath's hand was shaking as she played with a handkerchief on her lap. Not so much from nerves, Ellie thought, but more from exhaustion. Ellie squeezed Kath's shoulder and smiled at her by way of greeting.

'I'm pleased to see the ventilator's gone. You must be delighted. But you know, you might want to get a bit more sleep and make sure you eat,' Ellie suggested quietly. 'When Abbie comes round, she's going to want you to be strong and able to look after her. All the signs are good now, so do take care of yourself too.'

'I don't suppose that Abbie will ever want to speak to me again, when she wakes up,' Kath said.

'Kath, you have to know that's complete nonsense,' Ellie said. 'Of *course* she'll want to speak to you. You're her mum, so what makes you think that?'

'I let her down, didn't I? I promised we'd always keep her safe, and we didn't. After what happened to Jessica, we swore to Abbie that we wouldn't let anything happen to her. And look at her now. She doesn't deserve this, you know.'

Ellie was quiet for a moment. She didn't know who Jessica was, and wasn't sure she should ask. Kath glanced up at her.

'Jessica was Abbie's sister. It's not something we share with many people. It's Abbie's tale to tell, as and when she's ready. But right now, I need somebody to talk to, and I know you won't say anything.'

'You can trust me, Kath. That's a promise,' she said.

Kath was looking down at her hands, clasping and unclasping them on her lap. She spoke without looking up.

'Jessica was only two, and Abbie was four when it happened. Do you know, Jessica's middle name was Chloe? That makes it even worse. I'm sure Abbie felt a connection. But nobody else could have known that, could they? It was all so long ago. Everybody must have forgotten about it by now.'

Ellie reached for Kath's hand.

'Are you sure you want to talk about this? I know it must have been years ago, but whatever happened, I'm sure it's still painful. I didn't know you had another daughter.'

Kath gave Ellie a puzzled frown, followed by a glimmer of a smile through her tears.

'Oh, no. Jessica wasn't our child. Abbie's adopted, I thought you knew that. I assumed it would be in her records.'

'I had no idea. She seems like your child in every way. No parents could care more than you do.'

'We've had her for a long time, so it feels as if she's ours. I couldn't have children so we went for adoption and we were lucky enough to get Abbie. Poor thing—she was a complete mess, and was terrified of the dark. She still is. We never told anybody that she wasn't ours, and Abbie never said. None of her friends knew, but you know that Chloe? Well, she said that she was adopted too, and that was another link they had. She was the first person that our Abbie admitted it to. That's how close they got on that bloody website. Abbie still misses Jessica.'

Kath pulled a small photo album from her bag.

'This is Jessica,' she said. 'I brought these with me in case Abbie came round and couldn't remember anything. I wasn't sure about including pictures of Jess, but she still talks about her to us so I thought it might help. It's the only photo of her that exists, as far as we know.'

Ellie looked at the old photo of two little girls, and was shocked. The girls were pencil thin with downturned mouths and grubby clothes. She guessed that the older one would be Abbie, but as she had never seen Abbie without bruises all over one side of her face, she couldn't see any likeness. The younger one was wearing a patterned summer dress that was far too big and had a rip down one side. It hung from her tiny frame, revealing one bony shoulder. The older girl was wearing shorts and a T-shirt that looked a bit better, although not much. But it was clear to Ellie that one of her arms wasn't hanging properly and she could see bruising around both girls' wrists.

Kath was watching Ellie's reaction.

'These were taken by a neighbour. She was concerned about the girls, but by the time she got the pictures printed to show to the authorities, it was too late. Jessica was dead and Abbie had been taken into care.'

'Poor little mites,' Ellie said, her voice cracking as she looked at the damaged children. 'What happened?'

'Their mother was a prostitute. They lived in a one-roomed bedsit, and I suppose the children were bad for business. So when she had clients, the girls were locked in a cupboard, bound and gagged.'

Ellie's eyes were stinging as she looked back at the photo. Those poor, poor babies.

'Jessica died,' Kath said. 'A neighbour—the same one who took the photo—managed to get to Abbie just in time. She dragged her out of the flat and held onto her while she phoned the police. Abbie's mum got away, but they caught her soon enough. She was sent to prison for manslaughter and child cruelty, but they don't get long, you know. Kill a child and get eight to ten years. And she'd have been out under licence in half of that. She could be married again with a couple more kids by now. I would have strangled her with my own hands if I'd got hold of her. She referred to the girls as her "little mistakes" in the dock.'

Ellie had no words, but then none were expected. Anything she said would seem trivial in the face of this cruelty. She thought that her upbringing had been difficult, not to mention Leo's. Even Fiona had endured her fair share of indifferent parenting. But their problems seemed insignificant in the light of these revelations. And after an early childhood like that, Abbie was now suffering these terrible injuries.

Ellie sat and looked at the picture of two waifs. She glanced at Abbie again, but could see no resemblance to either child in the photo. Strangely, it was Jessica's face that kept drawing her back. Perhaps because she was the one who died, but there was something in that expression that rang a distant bell. Or maybe not. She couldn't place it anyway, so she was probably being fanciful.

37

Gary Bateman didn't know whether he wished they'd gone on holiday or not. He supposed it would have been fairer on the kids, but Penny was driving him insane with her whining. And the kids were turning out to be a bit too much like their mother for his taste. He was sure a house full of boys would have been better.

He was still waiting for Sean Summers to show his hand, and he was impatient to find out who the big investor was. Might be a bit of an earner there, if he played his cards right. He'd been promised the money today, but it was getting late and Sean hadn't called to say where they could meet.

There was one thing he could do while he was waiting.

He opened the sliding patio door and made his way out into the garden. He had bought a bench for the back corner, where he could talk on the phone to his heart's content and watch the house to make sure nobody sneaked up on him. Not that he gave a flying fuck what Penny thought. Maybe if she realised he was playing away she would make some effort to be nice to him. But even she was being odd today. Since he'd got back from dropping off the Porsche yesterday, she'd been different. And he was damned sure she was lying to him about something.

Nursing his mobile phone in his hand he looked back towards the house. At least there was only Penny there, and she would keep out of his way while he made this call.

Searching his contacts for the right number, Gary pressed the screen to connect. It was early days yet, and he hadn't bothered to commit the number to memory in case it proved a waste of time.

'Hello.' *Shit*. It was the husband. He should have called the mobile, but he'd called the house phone by mistake. He hung up. Fortunately, he had his phone set permanently to block its number—so there would be no caller ID.

Now what was he going to do? He'd been hanging around too long for this one, and he was getting impatient. It didn't usually take this long to get them gagging for it. He'd been put off on Saturday night and told that it was all about seduction, but you can't bloody seduce somebody if you don't see them.

His phone buzzed in his hand. It was her.

'Hello—I hoped you'd realise it was me and call back. How are you?' he said in his smoothest tones.

'Angry. That's how I am. I told you yesterday that this week would be difficult—so why are you calling me?'

'Come on—you know you don't mean that. You miss me—you know you do.' Gary smiled, even though he didn't feel like it. He had been told that you could hear a smile down a phone, so he pulled his face into a rictus of a grin.

'No. I don't miss you. Things have changed here and I'm no longer interested in what you have to offer. I think we should leave it at that.'

Gary was incensed. He had never failed before. 'Well, I don't. You wanted to be wooed, so that's what I did. You said we were nearly there. I played by your rules, for once in my life. Perhaps I should just have had my way with you—forced your hand. Perhaps you'd appreciate a bit of rough treatment. Lots of women do.'

'I can assure you that I cannot be counted among their number. Now, let's get some rules straight here. We're inevitably going to meet again at various functions. I will be polite. And *you* will be polite. But I don't want to see you alone again. Is that understood?'

'You don't know what you're missing. I thought you might be quite fun, under that frosty exterior. But I was wrong. And don't tell me it's because you've belatedly got the hots for that turd of a husband of yours, because I don't fucking believe it. You've wasted my time, lady. And I think that's something you may well regret.'

'Is that a *threat*, Gary? How splendid. I shall wait with bated breath until you enact your revenge. Goodbye.'

The phone went dead.

Snooty, toffee-nosed bitch. Who did she think she was?

His phone buzzed again. Perhaps it was her, begging his forgiveness.

He looked at the screen. Sean. He'd better not be fobbing him off with some cock-and-bull story about the money not being through. Because if he was, there would be trouble. Big trouble. He was in just the right mood.

❖

At the end of her shift, Ellie couldn't bear the thought of going home. After Kath's revelations that afternoon and the horror of Abbie's early life, she couldn't face more tension. She was perilously close to her breaking point.

She didn't know how she was supposed to react to last night's surprise dinner, and she didn't know how she was going to stop herself from blurting out the truth about what she'd done. She approached the car park in trepidation, though, wondering if Sean would be waiting there for her again, particularly after what had happened earlier. But there was nobody there, and no yellow rose.

Ellie breathed a huge sigh of relief, and got into the car. What now? An idea struck her. One thing that she hadn't dealt with this week was the problem with Georgia, which she had yet to understand. She should have followed it up sooner, but with everything that had been happening, including the extra shifts and Leo staying with them, it had been driven so low down in the list of priorities that she had practically forgotten. And that wasn't good enough. Georgia was her best friend, and the one person that she might be able to tell about all this *mess*.

Heading out of the car park, she turned left towards Georgia's house, hoping that her friend would be back from work. By the time she got home, Ellie knew the twins would be in bed, and perhaps Leo would be there so no awkward questions would be asked. She would miss kissing the children goodnight, but they'd got Max—for now, at least.

Using the flashy new hands-free device in her car, she said the magic words 'call Max' and the car was filled with the sound of a ringing phone. Of course he didn't answer. He never did. She left a message and hung up. Then tried to 'call home' instead. Nothing. He would probably be out in the garden, barbecuing something for the twins and no doubt making too much noise to hear the phone.

Georgia and Pat's house was one of Ellie's all-time favourites. If she hadn't felt compelled to renovate Willow Farm, she would have chosen something like this, and it had such a wonderful corner plot backing onto open countryside. She pulled her car up the drive, and was pleased to see that Georgia's car was already there. She was almost surprised that Pat's car wasn't, because she knew that since moving in with Mimi he regularly stopped off to see how his wife was getting along, or to pick up his post. Any old excuse. But he'd been very quiet since Saturday, and try as he might, Max had been unable to get hold of him on his mobile.

Ellie swung her legs out of the car, and walked the short distance to the front door, which was opening as she reached for the bell. Georgia's unsmiling face appeared, and without a word she pulled the door wide and turned and walked towards the back of the house, leaving Ellie to find her own way in. She followed Georgia as she disappeared down the hall, and didn't speak. She wasn't going to talk to her friend's back. She wanted to see her reaction. They ended up in the kitchen, as Ellie expected, and Georgia reached for the kettle.

'You're driving, so I suspect you'll want a cup of tea. Would that be right?' Georgia asked.

'That would be fine, thanks.' Ellie sat down at one of the high stools that ran the length of a wide worktop. She had spent many an evening in here, talking to Georgia as she prepared a simple supper for them both on her 'nights off' as Max always called them. Pat would go round to their house so that Max could babysit, and she would be free to go out with Georgia. But in practice, they always ended up staying in and talking non-stop about anything and everything until it came time for her to order a taxi home. It was usually a taxi on those nights.

Georgia had an amazing sense of style and she always looked elegant and professional. Like Fiona, Georgia had expensive taste in clothes, but unlike Fiona, she steered clear of the more vibrant colours and went for classic, well-cut styles and muted shades. She always said she was an Armani girl, and tonight was no exception. She had obviously only just returned from work, and was wearing a black knee-length straight skirt and a dusky blue fitted jacket over a simple white top. Not for the first time, Ellie felt frumpy in her black trousers and cotton top. She was going to have to spend some money on clothes, whether she managed to lose weight or not. Not that Armani and nursing went well together.

Ellie waited quietly until Georgia sat down facing her before she spoke.

'I'm sorry that it's taken me a while to get round to see you, but I've had to work a lot of extra shifts this week. The hospital is short-staffed because of the holidays, and there was the hit-and-run that you probably heard about. Otherwise, I would have been round here sooner. What's going on, Georgia? Why the sarky message?' Ellie spoke gently. She knew that Georgia had been seriously hurt by Pat, and could understand if she acted out of character from time to time.

Georgia gave her what could only be described as a sneer.

'*My* message? What about yours? "Mimi's a little treasure" was it? "We've got her all wrong". That was very nice, Ellie. Exactly the sort of text I wanted

when I knew that Pat was round at yours with his trollop and all our friends.
You have no idea how marvellous that made me feel.'

Ellie banged her mug down on the worktop.

'*What?* What are you talking about? You know I don't think that—not in a
million years. I think Mimi's a little cow. I don't actually think anybody has
given her a chance to be anything else, because we all feel so sorry for Pat
and that must make her feel like shit. But I don't *like* her. Good God,
Georgia—I wouldn't even think it, let alone send it to you in a text.'

Georgia reached for her handbag and grabbed her Blackberry. She flicked
through a few screens, and then held the message up for Ellie to see.

'Your phone. Your message. Saturday night. What more can I say?'
Georgia's mouth was set in a firm line, and her head tilted slightly to one
side. Raising her eyebrows at Ellie with a look of defiance, she was the
picture of fury. But Ellie knew this fury was covering a deep hurt. She got up
from her stool and went round to Georgia's side of the counter. Wrapping
her arms round her friend from behind, and resting her cheek against
Georgia's stiffly held head, she spoke quietly.

'Georgia, you're my best friend. I love you. I promise you that I would
never do or say anything to intentionally hurt you, and even if I thought
Mimi was God's gift to the world, which by the way I don't, I would still hate
her because she's not you. I can't stand seeing Pat without you. It's like
listening to the backing track of your favourite song without hearing the
words and the melody. It doesn't make any sense in isolation. Please believe
me, I didn't send that text.'

Ellie felt Georgia's spine relax, and she leaned back slightly.

'Sorry,' she whispered.

'No, *I'm* sorry,' Ellie said. 'I should have been round before now, but I did
try to call and you didn't answer, and the last couple of days have been . . .
difficult. But that's another story.' She made her way back to her seat, glad
that she had calmed the situation but kicking herself for not doing it before.

'What do you think happened with the text, then, if you didn't send it?'
Georgia asked.

Ellie raised her shoulders in a baffled shrug.

'I've no idea. I *was* going to send you a text. I remember that. Something
had happened that had upset me and I was going to ask you what I should
do. But I don't think I ever sent it. I can't remember. Did you get any other
texts from me that night?'

Georgia shook her head.

'No—but I got several from Pat. I'll get back to his weird behaviour in a minute. What was it you were going to tell me? What had upset you?'

Ellie made a quick decision. She couldn't tell Georgia about Sean. That would make her seem as bad as Pat, and she couldn't bear to see the disgust and disillusionment in her friend's eyes. She did remember something about the text, although not the exact words. She knew that it was about her stupid mistake, and having to go out after midnight to meet Sean—although she was convinced she hadn't mentioned his name—but that night had been such a living hell that she could barely remember what she'd even cooked. Thank God she'd never sent it.

'It was nothing much—just something to do with Max, and it's all sorted now.' From nowhere a memory of that evening and the blood-stained kitchen roll leapt into her mind. 'Bloody hell—I know what happened. I was in the middle of texting you and Mimi came in the kitchen. I left her there and went back into the dining room. She must have sent it herself. The little . . .' Ellie couldn't think of a suitable word that wasn't unpleasant. She didn't like the word 'bitch', but if the cap fits . . .

Georgia was shaking her head slowly from side to side.

'She really is something else, isn't she? I know every woman must think this when her husband walks out, but what does he see in her, Ellie? Please tell me, because I am lost here.' Georgia looked close to tears, but Ellie knew she would hate that. She liked to feel that she was in control even when she wasn't.

'He didn't walk out, Georgia. He made a foolish mistake, and you *threw* him out. He would never have gone out of choice, you know. I'm so very cross that Max and I were away that weekend, because I'm sure he would have come to us and not gone to her. We'd have sorted him out. Do you think you would have forgiven him?'

Georgia held very strong views on infidelity, as Ellie knew only too well. They'd spent many an hour talking about the famous and wealthy whose wives appeared to put up with all sorts of public 'indiscretions' without leaving their husbands, and wondering whether it was for love of their man, or love of their lifestyle. Maybe in retrospect they had been a bit judgemental. But her friend's insight now might help Ellie when Max's truth came to light.

'I know it sounds totally out of character, Ellie, but I think—I hope—I would have forgiven him. In a way, you know, it wasn't entirely his fault. I didn't listen to him. I didn't take anything he wanted into account. Pat's always been the one to give in to me on everything, but he was determined to win the battle of the children. I was equally determined that he wouldn't. I was being stubborn, and stupid if I'm honest. The daft thing is, I *would* like to have children. But Pat's version—that he would give up work and I could carry on—didn't fit with my ideas. I want to have kids and stay at home to look after them myself. I want to be a mum. But I couldn't bring myself to admit that.'

Ellie was staggered. This was completely the opposite of everything that Georgia had ever said.

'Why didn't you tell him, Georgia? Why didn't you just talk to him?'

A tear escaped from the corner of Georgia's eye, and she brushed it away angrily.

'I was in line for being made a partner. I wanted to achieve that first. I would have felt then that I'd made it, and so afterwards the rest wouldn't matter. But it's a sadder story than that. I've been very honest with myself recently, and I know that I simply had to win. It's as if we were in court, and I was the prosecution while Pat was the defence. It's always been like that. I think I've squashed him over the years. I've made him bow to my will over everything, and now I struggle to respect him. I know it's my fault, but since this business with Mimi I'm split between loving him for being the kind, sensitive, and—to me at least—sexy man that he is, and despising him for being such a bloody wimp. But in answer to your original question, yes. I would have taken him back. It would have been very hard, and I would probably have made him suffer for it—unfairly, I'm sure—but I would have tried.'

A great wave of sadness washed over Ellie. A year ago, the four of them were the happiest two couples you could ever wish to meet. Or at least, that's how they had seemed. But things are rarely as they appear, and hidden beneath the surface, out of sight, something had been eating slowly away at the fabric of this marriage.

'And what about now, Georgia? I know he keeps coming to see you, and Max was pretty sure that he kept going out between courses on Saturday to phone you or text you. Are you going to have him back?'

Georgia gave a mirthless laugh.

'Hah! Hardly likely now that madam is pregnant. I did think there was a chance, but he didn't seem to realise that it required some effort from *him*. He somehow believed that it would be okay for him to carry on living with Mimi until I was ready to welcome him back with open arms. But that wasn't the point. He had to decide to leave her *first*, to show that he didn't want to be with her *regardless* of whether I had him back. He had to stop hedging his bets. But that was a step too far for Patrick. In the last week or so, though, he's started behaving in a really bizarre way. For the first few weeks, he was always calling, popping round, sending me messages. But then he went all weird on me. He stopped taking my calls, sent me an awful message to say that Mimi was pregnant, and now seems to send me random texts all the time about how well things are going, or even what a bitch I've been and how miserable I've made him. I don't understand his game at all. If he'd just moved out of her house we could have started some sort of dialogue—with a view to sorting things out and getting back together. But I'm not having emotional conversations with him only for him to go home and cry on her shoulder—or worse, screw her senseless.'

'Why the hell didn't you tell me or Max how you were feeling? If Pat knew you would have had him back if he'd moved out of her house, he'd have left like a shot. You know that. Why didn't you *say* anything?'

Georgia leaned her elbows on the counter and rested her chin on clenched hands.

'Because he had to make the decision himself, Ellie. For God's sake, it shouldn't have taken much imagination on his part to realise that I wouldn't be happy with him sharing somebody else's bed while he was begging me to let him come home. All he had to do was to move into yours, or even into a B and B. But I wasn't going to tell him that. I may have made him submissive, but I wanted to see if he had a spark of initiative left, and it seems he hasn't.'

Georgia pressed both hands on the counter, and stood up.

'I know you're driving, Ellie, but can you manage a glass of wine? I don't like drinking alone, and I've been doing a bit too much of it lately.'

'Go on then—but only half a glass. I imagine the police are out in force in the village at the moment.'

Georgia spoke over her shoulder as she opened the cupboard for some glasses.

'Oh God, yes. That poor girl. Pat was very upset about her. He came here on Sunday after he'd been to see the parents. That must have been awful. I wanted to comfort him, you know, because he genuinely cares about those kids.' Georgia looked close to tears again, but she brushed the back of her hand irritably across her eyes. 'But then we had a row and I didn't have time to ask how they were before frigging Mimi tracked him down and he had to rush home with his tail between his legs, as always. Sod the pair of them. Much more importantly—how's the girl?'

As Georgia poured wine into both glasses, Ellie brought her friend up to speed with Abbie's progress. 'She's not out of the woods yet, but each time I look at her I wonder what happened and how she got herself into what must have been a terrifying situation.' Ellie didn't add that this wasn't the only terrifying experience this child had lived through.

Georgia was quiet for a moment.

'I probably shouldn't tell you this, but Pat was out and about that night,' Georgia said. 'I don't know what he was doing, but he left the rugby club early and came here. I told him to bugger off, and he left. But I know he didn't go straight home. He says he parked up somewhere and just contemplated life—the pillock—but from what I can gather, he's got a gap of at least three hours between leaving me and getting home. His car was picked up on CCTV at the garage. He told the police he'd been with me all evening, so they came to question me.'

'Oh no. What did you tell them?' she asked.

'I told them the truth. Perhaps that's why he's behaving the way he is, but I'm a lawyer. I can't lie to the bloody *police*. I think the only reason he didn't tell them was that they would think he was a bit wet, sitting in his car in a lay-by because he'd had a row with his wife and didn't want to go home to his mistress.' Georgia was unable to hide the sour note of contempt in her voice. 'Anyway, he's had to go back to the station and try to account for his time, but he can't. Of course, they're looking within a wider timescale now that they know Abbie was abducted. The last time we had any sort of a conversation was when he came round on Monday and asked if I would give him an alibi. I said no, but I had no time to explain because sodding Mimi called him again. So he left, snarling that she would give him an alibi, no doubt. The weird thing was, Pat told me he was sure he'd seen Charles Atkinson's car drive past in the early hours of Saturday morning when he was sulking in some lay-by or other. There aren't that many Aston Martins around. But he wasn't sure enough to accuse him of anything. And now he says that Charles actually mentioned on Saturday night that he only got back from London that day, so I guess he was wrong, unless Fiona drives his car.'

'I don't think she'd dare,' Ellie said, swirling her wine around but avoiding drinking any. 'The police came to our house too. Max got a lift home with Alannah, but her car was picked up somewhere, and Max had to give her an alibi.'

Georgia giggled. The wine was doing its work.

'Was he sober enough to give *anybody* an alibi? Don't forget, I picked the pair of them up after last year's party, and Max was singing rugby songs—he said he sort of had to, because they were in a rugby club. He was in very high spirits, but I doubt he remembered a thing the next day.'

'Well, maybe he was sober when he was with Alannah—I don't know.' Ellie couldn't see anything to smile about.

'Ellie?' Georgia said, giving her friend a puzzled look. 'What's up?'

She had to tell somebody—she really did. At least Georgia would understand, given that she had been in the same situation. Recognising that she was applying dual standards here—it was okay to talk to her friend about Max's guilt but not her own—she couldn't keep this bottled up for another moment.

'I think there's something going on between Max and Alannah. I think he's going to leave me.'

Georgia let out a hoot of laughter.

'Ellie, don't be so bloody ridiculous. Of *course* Max isn't going to leave you. Nor is he going to even consider having an affair. What in God's name has given you that ludicrous idea?' She laughed again.

'I don't know why you're laughing. I would never have said Pat would have done it to you—never in a million years.' She saw the look of sorrow flit across Georgia's face. 'Sorry, Georgia, I didn't mean to hurt you, but it's true.'

Georgia leaned forward.

'Listen, Ellie, you're wrong. Wrong with a capital W. Pat and Max are chalk and cheese. Max is strong. Even if he was tempted, he would resist—and I don't honestly think that he would even be tempted. If there's something between them, I would bet my life on the fact that it's got nothing at all to do with sex. Ask him, Ellie. Just bloody *ask* him.'

'And if he says he's in love with her? Isn't it better to pretend I don't know until it all blows over?'

'He is *not* in love with her. He is absolutely *not*. You know, I think this accident this week has made people start to see things that don't exist. Everybody's looking at everybody else and wondering what *they* were doing at the time of the accident, and now they know the girl was abducted first, everybody is suspicious and wondering whether it's somebody they know. So much has come to light because of it. You found out that Max was in the car with Alannah. Would you have known otherwise? Pat's going to have to explain what he was doing out in the car for all that time—not only to the police, but to Mimi too, no doubt. I'm one hundred per cent certain that Pat couldn't knock a child over and leave her to die on the side of the road. But will Mimi know that? Will she start suspecting him? And these are only the people that we know. All these thoughts and questions will be going on now in homes all over the village. One accident, but so many potential revelations; and the realisation that those we trust may not be worthy of it.'

38

In spite of the temptation, Ellie was glad that she'd only drunk half her glass of wine. She didn't know whether the police would be stopping cars to ask if they knew anything about the previous Friday—she had no idea if they did that sort of thing. But it wasn't worth the risk.

She had tried ringing Pat on her way home. Somebody had to talk some sense into him, even though there was a baby on the way. He needed to start treating Georgia fairly at least. But each time she called, the call was cut off. It didn't even go to voicemail. It was as if he was intentionally cancelling the call when he saw her name.

A distracted Ellie pulled into the drive and was surprised to see the lights still on in the twins' bedroom—well, technically Ruby's bedroom. When they had moved here they had given the twins a room each, but they hadn't liked that idea at all and had insisted on being in the same room. Jake didn't appear to have a problem with the pink girly wallpaper, so they had decided to let them get on with it. But they should have been asleep by now. She hoped neither of them was ill.

She pulled the car over to one side of the drive, grabbed her bag, and raced through the front door, shouting for Max. He appeared at the top of the stairs, looking slightly harassed, but still smiling. It couldn't be a catastrophe then.

'What's up? Why aren't the twins asleep?' Ellie asked, half running towards the stairs.

'Calm down, Ellie. It's something and nothing. Everybody's alive and well, and Leo's even cooking the dinner,' Max said, with a mock grimace.

'Oh Christ. That should be interesting,' Ellie answered. 'So what's going on?'

'It's Ruby. She's lost Muffin, and she says she can't go to sleep without him. I've tried her with Madge and Holly Dolly, but she wants Muffin.

We've turned this house upside down, but that scruffy little dog cannot be found. I even checked to see if you'd chucked him in the washing machine in disgust, but no. So he's around somewhere, and just as dirty and smelly as ever.'

'Did you take him out with you today? Has she dropped him somewhere?' Ellie asked, knowing that Ruby was going to be difficult, and they would have to find this floppy animal.

'No. We never take him out.'

Max was right. Ruby wouldn't let him out of the house. Each morning she put Muffin to 'sleep' in her own bed, so that he would be waiting for her at bedtime.

'Jake, before you ask, is adamant that he hasn't hidden Muffin, and I believe him,' Max said.

Jake was far too sensitive to be able to sit through the wailing and bawling that was going on.

'Do you want to see if you can help, Ellie? I'll go and bail Leo out. I'd rather cook than try to deal with Ruby when she's like this, so that gives you an idea of how bad it is!'

Dumping her bag on the hall chair, Ellie made for the stairs, passing Max halfway up. He leaned towards her and gave her a quick hug.

'Good to have you home, sweetheart. We all missed you today.'

Ellie paused, but said nothing and carried on towards Ruby's room.

'Hey, sweet pea, Daddy says we can't find Muffin,' Ellie said quietly, sitting down on the edge of Ruby's bed and stroking her daughter's damp curls off her forehead. Her little face was red with tears, and she was huddled in a tight ball with one fist pressed into her mouth.

'Where's he gone, Mummy?' Ruby cried. 'I left him in bed this morning, so that he could get some sleep. He needs to be awake at night so he can watch over us. I always let him sleep in the daytime.'

Ellie could remember when they had devised this story for Ruby. She was about three, and was going through a phase of believing there was a dragon living in the wardrobe. So they had made Muffin into a guard dog. Ever since then, she hadn't been able to sleep without him. Ellie knew that Max would have hunted everywhere for him, and it made no sense that he was missing. But she was going to have to calm her daughter down somehow. She looked around the room, and stood up.

'I tell you what, Rubes, why don't we put Spiffy in charge tonight? He's a tiger, and tigers are much, much more scary than dogs.'

'Spiffy's not scary—he's a gentle tiger.'

'Well, we might know that, but nobody else would. Shall I put him at the end of the bed, or standing over near the door?'

On her daughter's precise instructions, she placed Spiffy in the exact spot where he could best keep guard, and Ellie was pleased to see that Ruby's body had uncurled a bit. 'Budge over, baby. I'm going to have a little lie down with you. I'll watch Spiffy, and check if he's doing a good job.'

Ellie lay down with her lips next to her daughter's head and cuddled her close. She gave her a kiss and stroked her hair. She could feel that Ruby's warm body—tired from all the trauma—was gradually relaxing. She lay there until Ruby's breathing became regular, then slowly uncurled herself from the bed. After the horrors of everything that had been revealed about Abbie Campbell in the last couple of days, she thanked God that Ruby was safe. She kissed her soft cheek, bent over Jake to stroke his hair, and made her way quietly out of the door.

As she passed the top of the stairs on the way to their bedroom, she heard Max talking in the hall. He wasn't exactly whispering, but he was keeping his voice low.

'I agree. We do need a deadline, and I'm doing my best. Everything's pretty much sorted from this end. I told you that I'd transferred the money, so it should be in the bank now. Everything's in place.'

There was a pause.

'Okay, let's make the deadline Saturday. We can't back out then, so that's when I'll tell Ellie—when there's no going back.'

Another pause.

'Okay. We'll talk tomorrow when she's at work. It's best not to use the house phone again. I'll ring you from my mobile, or you call me. I'll try to remember to keep it switched on. I've got to go—speak tomorrow. Bye.'

Max replaced the receiver quietly, and sauntered back down the hall towards the kitchen, whistling as if he hadn't a care in the world. But Ellie knew better. When Max whistled like this, with his tongue behind his top teeth instead of through pursed lips, it was always a sign of stress.

Saturday, Ellie thought. No matter what Georgia had said, Saturday was going to be the day—the day when all would be revealed. And today was Wednesday. Just two more days of pretending they were a happy couple. She wanted to fly downstairs and ask him—beg him to stay. Her chest felt tight with despair, but she knew she had to stick to her plan if she was to keep him.

And what was this about money? She had given him total control of their finances and she never checked because there was so much it was accumulating more than they were spending.

She crept downstairs, but could hear that Max had put his favourite Elbow CD on and wouldn't be able to hear her. She made her way into the study. The computer was switched on, so all she had to do was log into their various accounts. The hunt didn't take long. There it was. Max had transferred three hundred thousand pounds out of their account, and paid it to a company called Cheshire Fields Developments. Holding her breath, she did a quick search on the name, but it came up with nothing—at least, nothing useful. She didn't have time to do more now, or Max would come looking for her.

She quickly closed the window on the bank file and her Google search, and made her way softly back upstairs. It was only when she had reached the top, away from the chance of being discovered, that the enormity of it all hit her. Three hundred thousand pounds—paid to a development company of some description. What was Max doing?

From nowhere, a dreadful thought leapt into her head. Max had bought another house. One for him and Alannah.

In a daze, she walked into their bathroom and shut the door. Sitting on the side of the bath, she dropped her chin and started to cry quietly. There was no rage or anger in her, just a deep, deep hurt. How had it happened? The pain was so fierce that she slowly slid from the side of the bath to the floor, pulling her knees as close to her chest as she could. She grabbed a towel to stem her tears.

From beyond the bathroom door, she heard a sound in their bedroom.

'Ellie?' It was Leo. 'Are you coming down for something to eat? You'll be amazed at my culinary skills—I can promise you that.'

Ellie tried to control her voice.

'Ten minutes,' she called.

'Are you okay?'

'Fine,' she responded, praying that her voice didn't shake. One thing about Leo, though—if Ellie wanted to pretend she was okay, Leo would respect her privacy. Perhaps this was the one good side of a sister who struggled with emotional attachments.

Ellie switched the shower on and stripped off her clothes. Maybe she should vamp herself up a bit? Go to some effort to look good for him? Don't be ridiculous, she thought. It's a bit late for that. She had tonight and then two whole days. A bit of lipstick wasn't going to make any difference now. She had to be who she was.

And so it was ten minutes later that she made her way downstairs in her stripy pyjama bottoms and a dark red vest top. As she reached the bottom of the stairs, she heard the message signal on her phone coming from the handbag that she had dumped as she ran up to deal with the children. She'd forgotten that she'd switched it back on to call Pat. Thank God Max hadn't heard it first, because he wouldn't hesitate to read her texts on the basis that hers were always more interesting than his. She could hear Leo laughing at Max in the kitchen, and wanted nothing more than to be there with them, happy and giggling at Max's silliness. She grabbed her phone.

Convinced that it was *him* she hardly glanced at the screen. Only as she pressed to accept the message did she register that the number was blocked. And she knew what that meant.

> HOW HAS YOUR DAY BEEN, ELLIE? HOW'S YOUR LITTLE GIRL TONIGHT? LOST ANYTHING, HAS SHE? NEXT TIME, MAYBE IT WON'T BE HER TOY DOG THAT I TAKE . . . BUT DON'T THINK OF TELLING ANYBODY. YOU DON'T KNOW WHO I AM, AND YOU WON'T CATCH ME. ALL YOU HAVE TO DO IS ONE THING. JUST ONE SMALL TASK. AND THEN IT WILL ALL BE OVER—AS IF IT HAD NEVER HAPPENED. I'LL KEEP YOUR DIRTY LITTLE SECRETS, AND YOUR KIDS WILL BE SAFE.

A cold fear gripped her. This couldn't be happening. Somebody had been in the house again, and Ruby hadn't lost Muffin. He had been taken. She'd never doubted that it was Sean, blocking his number and toying with her—making everything so unbalanced that she would simply give in. But it didn't quite add up. However much Sean might want her, she was certain he would never hurt a child. Despite his recent behaviour, he was a gentle giant of a man; she'd seen him with his stepdaughter and his little boy. He would never threaten her children, would he?

As if it had never happened—the text said. That couldn't be Sean either. That wasn't what he wanted.

The hairs on Ellie's arms were standing on end. She was still staring at the screen when she noticed something else—the time the text was sent. She remembered checking her watch as she got home with the shopping. This text was sent while Sean was in the house—with her and Max.

I've got it all wrong—it can't be Sean. It's someone else—somebody I don't know.

Ellie sat down abruptly on the stairs as her legs gave way beneath her. *It wasn't Sean.* The thought and all its implications were spinning round and round in her head.

It meant only one thing. She was being blackmailed—and it was *real*. Not some game dreamt up by a thwarted lover. And it was dangerous. This person had been in their *house*—not just once, but at least twice. And Ellie had no idea *how* they had got in. So they could do it again, whenever they liked.

Perhaps they were here now! It was a big house—they could be hiding anywhere.

Ellie jumped up from the bottom step. Her head spun from side to side, and back up to the dark void at the stop of the stairs, not knowing what she was expecting to see. She walked quietly towards the closed door of the library and slowly turned the handle, pushing the door quickly so that it slammed against the bookshelves behind. She saw a white face, eyes black with fear, staring back at her.

It took no more than a second for her to realise that the unrecognisable features were her own, reflected back from the mirror over the fireplace. Her face was drained of all colour, and her pupils dilated in wide eyes. She glanced around the room.

Nothing. What was she expecting? Nobody would hide here.

She sat down hard on one of the wingback chairs and leant forward, resting her forearms on her thighs, clutching the phone in her damp, trembling hands. Max would come looking for her soon, and she had to calm down. For now, the children were safe. There were three adults here, and she would find some excuse for checking all the rooms before they went to bed. But now, she needed time to think. Sean and his games suddenly seemed trivial. All she could think of was how to keep her children safe.

39

How Ellie had made it through supper, which was actually a very passable frittata and salad, she didn't know. Both Leo and Max had noticed how quiet she was, but she had managed to fob them off by saying she was upset about Abbie and worried about Georgia. At least everything seemed to be okay with Leo again. Never one to bear grudges, she had behaved as if nothing had happened that morning.

Ellie's head was all over the place. Max's phone call and the money transfer were bad enough, but the text had terrified her.

She had been certain that Sean was the one letting himself into the house. Max had asked him to change the locks at the weekend, and she had thought it was a joke. Now she knew it was essential. Much as she didn't like Sean having access to a set of keys, he was the lesser of two evils. She couldn't think of a single good reason to ask Max to find somebody else.

But if she admitted to Max that she was being blackmailed, she would have to tell him everything else too, although if she genuinely believed the children were in danger there was no other option. Maybe she should wait. The blackmailer had said that she only had to do one thing, and her children would be safe. Maybe the sensible thing would be to find out what she was going to be asked to do.

Her mind was spinning out of control. Max and Alannah, the weird texts, Abbie, *Sean*.

And she felt totally helpless.

For now she had settled on telling Leo and Max that, whether they thought she was paranoid or not, they mustn't let the twins out of their sight for a second in the house. They were not to be left alone in the kitchen, their bedrooms, or even watching a DVD. They must have recognised that she was seriously stressed, because they didn't argue. They knew of her suspicions that somebody had been in the house on Sunday, but neither Max nor Leo seemed to suspect that today there had been another visitor.

As she lay in bed waiting for Max to come from the bathroom, she couldn't help thinking about his behaviour. He had been chirpy all evening, but she wasn't fooled. It was all bravado. Could he really behave like that when he was about to leave her? But there was no getting around the missing money and everything she had overheard. She didn't care about the money; only what it represented.

The bathroom door opened, and Max walked naked towards the bed. Ellie couldn't help wondering if this was the last time she would see him like this. Perhaps if they made love, it would change things. She wasn't going to let him go without a fight, even if her weapon was silence.

He slid under the sheets, and lifted his arm so that she could snuggle down against him. Lying on her side, she moved her right hand so that it was gently stroking the fine dark hairs on his smooth, flat stomach. Max kissed the top of her head. Gradually, Ellie started to increase the range of her stroking, and she made her way downwards very slowly, knowing that this usually drove Max crazy. She kissed him on his chest, and started to give him tiny painless bites as her hand moved lower, and the hairs became coarser and thicker.

Gently, Max covered her hand with his own. Thinking he was probably imploring her to speed up, she gave a low chuckle. But she was wrong. He lifted her hand and moved it back to his chest.

'Sorry, Ellie. I think you're backing a bit of a loser there tonight. Nothing personal, sweetheart—it's just been one of those days. What do you say that we carry on where we left off tomorrow night?'

He brought his other hand up to wrap her in a tight hug, then freed the arm that was behind her and turned over.

'Love you,' he muttered. His breathing soon sounded regular, but Ellie knew he wasn't asleep.

A cloudy start to the day had deteriorated into a still, heavy night with dark, overcast skies, and there wasn't a glimmer of moonlight. There were no streetlights down this country lane, but the lack of a light source meant there were no shadows.

Dressed from head to toe in black, with only the eyes showing through slits in the balaclava, the figure waited patiently. It would only take a matter of moments for the eyes to adjust.

The front door provided the easiest access—the fastest route to the target—but the window to the master bedroom was standing open right above the doorway and the slightest sound could alert one of the occupants. The side door was out of the question too, because crossing the wide gravel parking area would create too much noise. So it would have to be the kitchen door. Once inside, that would mean navigating the kitchen and dining room and then the long hallway to reach the bottom of the stairs, but there was no choice.

The figure crept silently along the side of the house, using the grass to muffle any footsteps. Very familiar with the layout of this house after the forays of the last few days, the intruder knew that tonight's success would depend on Ellie's predictability.

The three keys were easy to differentiate. How stupid to leave them lying around like that for anybody to take. Inserting the largest into the lock, it turned without a sound. The door opened on silent hinges.

The intruder stood just inside the doorway. There were weird glimmers of light in the room; the small green lamp on the freezer door, the brightly displayed temperature on the fridge, and the luminous digital clocks on the control panels of the two matching ovens combined to throw faint shadows around the room.

Although there wasn't a breath of air, the door was gently closed—a rogue gust of wind could slam it and alert the whole house. Everywhere was silent. Strangely, though, there was no sense that the house was sleeping. It felt awake, aware—as if it were watching the intruder's every move on high alert.

Keeping to the centre of the room to avoid furniture, the ghostly shape crept towards the atrium. Unless there was a break in the clouds, there would be no light there at all, and all movement would have to be based on memory. The darkness was dense and solid, yet offered no resistance.

Every inch of this house had been explored in the last few days. More often than Ellie knew. It was important to learn one's way about, find out which stairs creaked, which doors could be opened soundlessly. It offered added pleasure that this was Ellie's house—the woman everybody believed to be perfect. If only they all knew. And they would do soon.

Sweat was making the balaclava stick to clammy skin, and breathing was becoming difficult. It was so much easier to sneak in when the house was empty—but for this task, Ellie had to be at home.

The hallway was easier. A gentle glow came from the landing—no doubt from a night-light left on for the twins. How very convenient. The goal was in sight as the black figure approached the bottom of the stairs.

40

Day Seven: Thursday

Leo was surprised to find Max sitting alone in the kitchen. She had kept out of the way for as long as possible this morning, but the house seemed quiet, so she'd decided to finally emerge from her bedroom. She was definitely going home today.

'Morning, Max. Where are Jake and Rubes?'

Max was playing with, rather than eating, a bowl of cornflakes. If he'd seen the twins doing that, she knew what he would have said to them.

'I'm at a bit of a loose end today,' he said. 'It's a friends' birthday, so about ten of them have gone off to Chester Zoo this morning, and then to the soft play place this afternoon. Whatever happened to a two-hour party with jelly and cake?'

'Not to mention the potted beef sandwiches,' Leo replied with a grin. 'My mum gave the very best parties when I was little. She made everything from scratch, and we had prizes for all the games. It took effort to hold a party then. Now it seems it's about who has the most money.'

'Tell me about it,' Max said. 'Even when they have parties at home, they have to have some sort of entertainer along. Well, when the twins have their sixth birthday they can have an entertainer. Me. And Ellie will make buns. It will be a novelty for them all.'

'Just thank your lucky stars you're not having to arrange a stag do in this day and age. If you don't go to Prague or Las Vegas for a minimum of three days, it's not much of a party, as far as I can see.'

'Bloody waste of money. Anything you've got should be spent on the wedding and honeymoon, in my book. It's not about getting pissed with

your mates, it's about dedicating yourself to somebody else for the rest of
your life, as far as I'm concerned.'

Leo went quiet. Max had given her an opening here, and she wasn't sure
whether she should take it or not. She pointed, as usual, to the fancy coffee
machine.

'Want one?'

'Please—but make it a large espresso. I need the caffeine. I didn't sleep too
well.'

Leo put the cup under the nozzle and pressed the button twice for a
double espresso. As the beans ground, she got some milk out of the fridge for
her cappuccino, and thought about how she was going to raise a tricky
subject. By the time she had made both drinks, she was pretty clear what she
was going to say.

She put Max's coffee in front of him, and sat down opposite.

'Max—I need to talk to you,' she said.

'No. You don't, Leo. I need to talk to *you*.' He held his hands up, as if to
prevent her from interrupting. 'I've done something crazy, and I don't know
what to do about it. I've been a complete idiot, and I don't know how Ellie's
going to forgive me. Every morning for the past two months, I have woken
up thinking, "This has to stop", but by the end of the day, I'm back to where I
started. Being a total wanker.'

Max put his head down, and rested his forehead on the heels of his hands.

Leo felt her heart sink.

'So it's true then. Ellie was right.'

Max dropped his hands, and the look of horror on his face didn't need any
interpretation.

'You mean she knows? Christ, how did she find out? How long has she
known? She's not been happy lately, but I thought that was my fault for
being such an arse. And last night . . . Well, never mind last night. Why
didn't she *say* something, if she knew?'

Leo felt an intense bubble of irritation rise up and explode.

'Why the hell do you *think* she didn't say something? Because she thought
that while it was all hidden, nothing would happen. But as soon as it's all out
in the open, she thinks that you'll leave her. She thinks the only thing
stopping you is the fact that it would be too difficult for you to tell her you
were going. Jesus, I thought you were different, Max. I really did. But you're
every bit as selfish, blind, and stupid as . . .'

Max's head shot forward, interrupting Leo in mid flow.

'*Leave* her? Leave *Ellie*? Why in God's name would I want to do *that*? She's my whole life—well, her and the twins. What can possibly have given her that crazy idea? It had better not be you, Leo. I know you have no time for men, but I thought you knew me better than that. I thought I might have given you a tiny bit of faith in the male species.'

'Piss off, Max. Of course it wasn't me,' Leo said, with righteous indignation. 'If you must know, I stuck up for you, although for the life of me I can't understand why I did now. That comment was out of order.'

To do him credit, Max looked mortified, as if he knew he had leapt to the wrong conclusion.

'Sorry, Leo. That was uncalled for, you're right. But I can't think of a single reason why Ellie would think that I was going to leave her. I've been an idiot, and she might decide to leave *me*, but not the other way round. Never.'

'So you expect her total forgiveness, do you?'

Max pulled a face.

'I know she's going to be mad as hell, and quite rightly. But you know Ellie. She'll get over it.'

'You arrogant, conceited, cheating bastard. How can you just dismiss it like that? You have an affair for months, and then you say she'll be "mad as hell". Do you have even the remotest idea what you have done to her? To my sister?'

Max looked totally bewildered.

'What the hell are you talking about, Leo? What bloody affair? You've lost me completely.'

'You and that PE teacher. Alannah she's called, isn't she? You and her. All hush-hush and making plans in private.'

Max looked as if a light had been switched on, and that it had illuminated a house of horrors.

'Oh God. You're not telling me that's what she thinks, are you? I know she thinks I fancy Alannah. That's why I try to avoid mentioning her. I don't fancy her, though. Not even slightly.'

Max was going to have to be a lot more convincing than that.

'So you think forgetting to mention that you've been to the pub with Alannah so Ellie has to hear it from somebody else is a good idea, do you? Or how about the fact that you've recently started telling Ellie she needs to do more exercise, as if she needs to look more like Alannah? Or getting a lift home from the staff party and going halfway to bloody Stoke on Trent and back, so you and Alannah could be alone—and then lying about it. Well done, Max.'

Max looked as if he was about to interrupt, but Leo hadn't finished. 'Oh, and what about making plans that you're not ready to tell Ellie about yet because she needs to be kept in the dark until it's too late for her to stop it—whatever "it" is. How do you think it made her feel to learn about *that* particular conversation? Jesus.'

Max's face had drained of colour.

'Shit. It sounds terrible when you say it like that. Look, I know I'm a brainless bugger but I'm not crazy enough to have an affair. I know perfectly well what that would do to Ellie. I know that her trust issues aren't on a par with yours, but she doesn't have the confidence that somebody so beautiful should have, you know.'

'Don't bring me into this. I'm not the one who's lied to her—even if only by omission.'

'You're right, and I'm sorry for the jibe. It was unnecessary.' Max looked straight at Leo, as if to demonstrate that he was speaking the truth. 'There is nothing going on with Alannah. I was simply helping a friend.'

'Then why all the sodding secrecy, Max? If it's no big deal, why didn't you tell Ellie?'

'Because Alannah asked me not to, and actually—it *is* a pretty big deal.' Max looked down. As well he might, Leo thought.

'Don't even think of not telling me, because my sister's welfare comes way above keeping a promise to somebody else. Get real, Max. Sort out your bloody priorities.'

Max looked as if she'd slapped his face.

'Leo, don't ask me to say anything more. I could lose my job over this.'

'And you could lose your *wife* if you don't speak up. For Christ's sake, you should know you can trust me. How bad is it?'

'Terrible for Alannah. Pretty bad for me. *Promise* me you won't tell Ellie, Leo. I will honestly tell her myself, but it has to come from me.'

Leo gave a curt nod of her head and watched while Max turned a teaspoon over and over in his fingers.

'Alannah came to me a couple of months ago with a problem. Apart from being a PE teacher, she's also a marathon runner, and a damn good one at that. But for one reason and another she'd been feeling a bit below par and lacking in stamina, so she started to get a little help.'

Max checked out Leo for reaction, and she had to wonder why. She knew exactly what he meant. Was he expecting her to be shocked?

'What was she taking?' she asked.

'EPO to start with. I don't know if you know anything about it, but basically it keeps you going for longer. I'm sure you're not interested in the science. It's not supposed to be addictive, and she took it to get her over a low patch.'

Max stood up from the table and walked over to the glass doors to the garden, as if Alannah's shame was strangely his own. Leo kept quiet and waited.

'She overdid it, and eventually she ended up injuring herself. But she had a big race coming up, so she had to block out the pain. She moved on from EPO, and bought some other drugs—Oxy, OC, whatever you want to call it. Whatever name you come up with, it's Oxycodone, illegal to buy on the streets, and highly addictive.'

'So? Why can't you tell Ellie that?'

'First of all, I kept it from her because the fewer people that know the better. Alannah would be sacked, but more than that I should have reported her, and I didn't. I wanted her to get treatment for it before it all has to come out.'

'And second of all . . . ?' Leo asked. Max glanced round at her, and could no doubt tell from her determined expression that Leo wasn't about to give up. He locked his hands behind his head and looked up at the sky through the window.

'She stole some money—from school. I was one of the organisers of the school play, and she helped. She took some of the ticket money. She'd planned to put it back, but she was maxed out on her credit cards and overdraft. I put the money back when I found out.'

Max dropped his hands to his side and turned round to face Leo.

'I'd lose my job too if any of this came out, Leo. I couldn't tell Ellie. She would be understandably furious that I should put myself at risk like this. But money doesn't seem to be such a big issue in this house anymore, and I thought it would help.' Max gave a humourless laugh. 'It didn't. On Friday night the reason we went via Stoke on Trent as you put it—although that's a bit of an exaggeration—is that she wanted to ask me to give her some more money. To help her out again. I was too pissed to give a sensible response on Friday—so she phoned here on Sunday. I told her never to do that again. Imagine if Ellie had answered? Anyway, I refused to give her any more. I said it wouldn't help, and she had the six-week holiday to get herself sorted. I don't know if she thinks she can blackmail me, but she can do her worst. I'm not giving her any more.'

'Well, I have enormous sympathy with her problem. But nowhere near as much as I have with my sister, who—thanks to the two of you—has been going through absolute hell for the past few weeks. She's distraught, Max. Frantic with worry. She's waiting for you to drop the bombshell that you're leaving.'

Max stared at Leo as if the world was collapsing around him.

'If I'd realised she thought that, I would have told her everything about Alannah. I promise you. It seemed like the least of my problems, frankly.'

Leo made herself take a long, calming breath. She was mad at Max, but it was nowhere near as catastrophic as she had thought. If this wasn't the problem that was haunting him and breaking her sister's marriage into pieces, she was determined to find out what was.

'So if you've not been having an affair, what have you been doing that you don't want Ellie to find out until it's too late for her to stop it?'

Max couldn't meet Leo's eyes as he told her of his idiotic plans that made a few pounds from the school play seem beyond trivial.

41

For once, it was a relief to be doing an early shift. Ellie wasn't sure she could have faced Max over the breakfast table. She had barely slept, and she knew that Max hadn't either. So many times during the night she had wanted to put her arm around him and ask 'why?' but she was still deluding herself that if she kept quiet, it might all go away.

And to cap it all, she couldn't for the life of her find her security pass. Somebody had let her into the ward, but she would have to report it. She always took it off and put it in her bag—but perhaps last night she had dropped it at Georgia's or something. She'd report it later, during her break or at the end of the shift. For now, she needed to focus on her job.

'You look like shit, Ellie. Are you okay?'

Ellie turned round. It was Sam Bradshaw, and he was just finishing his rounds. She gave him a weak smile.

'Thanks, Sam. It's kind of you to say so. I didn't sleep well last night, but I'm fine.'

'Is there something bothering you? Anything I can help with?'

Sam was a great guy, and Ellie was sorely tempted to drag him off for a cup of coffee so she could talk to an impartial listener. Since he had started shaving his head about three months previously in an attempt to hide the fact that he was going prematurely bald, Sam had become more confident around women, and despite a rather long and lugubrious face, his gentle nature seemed to be winning the hearts of several of the young nurses. But she knew he didn't have the time to sit listening to her problems. Glancing across at Abbie's bed she realised that she needed to relieve Maria, who was due to finish her shift.

'You're a gem, Sam. But I'd better go and see Abbie. How's she doing? Any change since I was last here, which incidentally was only about twelve hours ago?'

Sam laughed. 'After this week I'm told we'll be back to full strength and you can take it easy. But Abbie's actually doing great. She's been opening her eyes for a few minutes at a time, and she's trying to speak. Not having much success, but she's trying. Her conscious levels are improving and she's responding to pain. So it's good news. And Ellie . . .'

Ellie turned back towards him.

'. . . you know where I am if you need me. Any time. Okay?'

Ellie reached out and gave Sam's arm a squeeze in thanks. She didn't think she could speak without crying. Why was it that kindness was more likely to bring on the tears than harsh words?

As she approached the bed, she noticed that Kath was looking a bit more relaxed today. Maria was talking gently to Abbie, and Ellie could see that Abbie was showing some response although it would be a while until they could tell if there had been any permanent damage to her brain.

Kath and Maria glanced at Ellie, and Maria did a double take. *I really must look like shit* Ellie thought. *Sam wasn't exaggerating.*

'Hi, Ellie,' Maria said in a rather excessively cheerful voice. 'Good to see you.'

The two nurses had a brief handover chat about Abbie's care.

'Is there anything I can do for you before I go?' Maria asked, looking keenly at Ellie.

'No, you get off home. I'll take it from here. I've had a word with Dr Bradshaw and he's brought me up to date.' Ellie gave Maria a grateful smile and turned to Abbie's mum. 'Good morning, Kath. You must be pleased with the improvement?'

'We're thrilled,' Kath replied. 'Brian's actually gone back to work today. Abbie seems to be making improvements all the time now.'

'Any news from the police? Have they got any better idea of what might have happened?' Ellie asked.

Kath bit her top lip and gave a gentle shake of the head.

'No. They're trying everything, but they know nothing more than yesterday. They don't know if she was picked up by a man or a woman, they can't find any trace of this Chloe, who seems to know very well how to cover her tracks, and they've admitted that they have nothing on the driver in the hit-and-run. All they can hope now is that somebody will have the guts to turn in anybody that they knew was out at that time of night. It's the only chance they've got.'

Ellie felt an acute stab of guilt. She had done nothing about the fact that she was out—and she wasn't the only one. This was so very wrong. There was every chance that she might have seen something and thought nothing of it; and if she hadn't, Sean might have done. They were staying silent to save their own hides, but that was terrible. How was she going to feel if it came out that she could have been helping the police all along, while appearing to be sympathising with Kath and worrying about Abbie? As if she wasn't confused enough, she now felt nothing but self-disgust.

Ellie stayed quietly by the bed, and listened to Kath murmuring from time to time to Abbie. But she was miles away. She was remembering that night. The night of the accident.

She had left the house at about ten past midnight. She knew Max wouldn't have been on his way home by then. He was always the last to leave any party.

She had tried to keep the chances of being seen to a minimum by going the long way round, and she had approached the back road from the top end. The designated meeting place was a small road that ran to a disused barn about half a mile from where the accident had happened. The scene leapt into her memory, with all the pain and fear that accompanied it.

The minute she'd stopped the car, the passenger door had been wrenched open and Sean had jumped in. She'd started by taking an aggressive stance, but it hadn't taken long for her to realise that it wasn't going to work.

'You shouldn't have called me tonight. It's not fair to keep putting me under this pressure. You frightened the life out of me when I was in the kitchen. What are you playing at? It's got to stop.'

Sean had tried to put his arm round her.

'Get *off* me. I don't want you to touch me. Don't you get it? I made a mistake. I let things go too far, but you've got to put an end to this stupidity. What is it you don't understand?'

He had looked hurt. So hurt, in fact, that she thought he might cry. And that would have been terrible, because it was her fault.

'I'm sorry,' she'd said. 'I do know that I'm to blame. I knew how you felt about me, but you were in the wrong place at the wrong time. Can't we just forget it ever happened?'

Sean had twisted his body round so that he was facing her, and she couldn't bear to look at the expression in his eyes.

'Are you trying to tell me it's over, Ellie? Because I don't think I can accept that.' His voice was soft, but there was a level of menace that made her uncomfortable.

'It's not over. It never started. And you *have* to accept it. It's not optional.'

He had continued to stare at her, and she wouldn't meet his gaze. She didn't know what she would see, but she could feel that the emphasis had shifted from pain to anger.

'I'll tell you what's going to happen, shall I?' he'd said. 'I can't live without you now, and I don't want to. No. Correction. I *won't* live without you. Max has his little interest, as you well know. So you can either wait for him to leave you, or you can leave him. Either way, I can bide my time until the decision is made. But it *will* be made. And it will be soon. Until then, Ellie, wherever you go, I'll be there. Whatever you do, I'll be watching. And if I don't like what I am seeing, my patience will be gone.'

Ellie had turned to look at him, and seeing the sheer determination in his eyes she was scared. Really scared. She didn't think he would hurt her, but she knew without him saying so that he was threatening her. Not physically, perhaps. But it was a threat that was infinitely more terrifying.

'Please don't do this. I don't know what to say to you, but please, *please* can't we forget it ever happened?'

'Listen to me very carefully, Ellie. You are all I've ever wanted. I'm prepared to give up *everything* for you. Do you understand? *Everything*. Even if Max decides he wants you and not the lovely Alannah, he won't when he knows what happened. How you seduced me. How you've been lusting after me for months. How often we've spent time together. You know he won't.'

She'd stared at him in disbelief.

'But that's not true! I *didn't* seduce you. I succumbed to you once—and even then, I was able to stop. It is nothing *like* as bad as you're saying. It's bad enough, but it wasn't like that at all, and you know it.'

He smiled nastily.

'Who is Max going to believe, do you think? Can you afford the risk? I want you to think about this, and think hard. And until you've decided, I'll be around. You might not see me, but I'll be there.'

Ellie burst into tears.

'Please, can we stop this? What do I need to do to persuade you? Don't hurt Max. I'll beg, if you want me to.' She choked back the sobs and looked at him.

He put his arms round her and pulled her to him. For a moment, just a second, it felt good to be comforted.

'Kiss me, Ellie. For now, a kiss will do. Come here, darling. It'll be okay, I promise.'

She could remember feeling appalled at herself, but she didn't know what would happen if she didn't give in to him. She found a tissue in her pocket and blew her nose. He pulled her closer. She had let him kiss her, and as his tongue gently explored her mouth, his other hand had moved to her breast and stroked it tenderly.

This was going too far. His tongue was making her want to gag, and she thrust him away forcefully.

'A kiss, you said. Just a kiss. I'm not going to do this. I'm *not*. Get out of my car. Get *out*.' She put her head back down on the steering wheel, choking on her grief. The tears wouldn't stop coming, and she could hardly hear when he spoke softly, right against her ear.

'This isn't over. Don't kid yourself. This isn't over by a very long way.' Muffled as his voice was, she could hear the pent-up fury. She heard the door open and sensed rather than heard him getting out of the car. There was no mistaking the slam of the door, though, or the sound of tyres skidding on gravel as he sped off down the unlit dirt track.

She barely remembered putting the car into gear, or driving slowly back the way she had come. Almost blinded by the hot tears that spilled relentlessly down her cheeks, she had turned up the back road, away from the village. She at least had the sense to drive back the long way round, where she was less likely to pass anybody.

Ellie was jolted out of her reverie by a shocked recollection. There had been a car. She had completely forgotten about it, because her mind had been exploding with the torment of it all. There were no streetlights, of course, and the car had its headlights on full beam. She had been blinded for a few seconds, and saw nothing of the car—only an impression of something blue, or black maybe. A large saloon car, she was fairly sure. But the driver would have seen her. And her dark red Mercedes was one of a kind in the village. Why had nobody mentioned her? Surely an innocent person would have reported her distinctive car to the police?

But that hadn't happened. Nobody had come forward.

Was that because the driver was the person who knocked Abbie over, or even the one who had abducted her? A cold feeling of remorse settled deep inside her. If the driver was also the person that knocked Abbie over, Ellie could have been withholding vital information for days.

'Ellie? Ellie? Are you okay?' Kath was talking to her. 'You were miles away. Is something the matter?'

Ellie gave herself a mental shake. She was going to go to the police, as soon as her shift finished. Enough was enough. She would just have to live with the consequences.

'Sorry, Kath. I was just thinking about a couple of things that I was meant to do at home, and I'd forgotten all about. Nothing important. I'm sorry, did you need me for something?'

'No, it's nothing. I was going to go and get something to eat, if that's okay. I might get a bit of fresh air as well. Let you get on with your job.'

Ellie smiled as she watched Kath reach over and kiss Abbie's forehead.

'Back soon, sweetie,' she whispered.

Left alone with Abbie, Ellie went through some of her usual patient routine, washed her, and changed her dressings. She was pleased to see that the child's legs were looking much better, and the cuts on her feet were healing well. It was time for her break, so she had a quick chat with the nurse looking after the patient in the next bed. It was an agency nurse that Ellie hadn't met before, but she would keep an eye on Abbie.

Ellie didn't normally take her full break, but today she needed it. She had to work out what she was going to tell the police. Much as she was dreading it, this was something that she *had* to do. She could imagine the look of contempt in Kath's eyes if she ever found out that Ellie might have been able to lead the police to the driver of the car, which may possibly have shed some light on the abduction. Ellie had asked if she could be Abbie's named nurse, to look after her on every shift, and if her silence were discovered it might suggest a level of sinister intent that simply didn't exist.

She couldn't begin to describe how she felt about herself at this moment, but disgust wasn't a strong enough word. She was actually finding it difficult to swallow, and her head was pounding.

Following Brenda, the senior charge nurse, back through the door to the ICU she made her way to the water cooler next to the ward office. She'd just had a cup of coffee, but her throat was tight and dry with anxiety. Brenda had beaten her to it, and was picking up a couple of plastic cups of water. She looked keenly at Ellie.

Oh not you too, Ellie thought. The expression on her face must have said it all, because Brenda simply made a comment about the rubbish summer they were having.

Ellie gave a faint smile, turned towards the ward and stopped.

That was odd. Sam hadn't said anything about wanting to examine Abbie again today.

With a small frown she spun round to Brenda.

'Do you know what Sam's doing with Abbie?' she asked, indicating the closed curtains around Abbie's bed. Brenda flicked her head sideways, and Ellie looked in the direction she was signalling. She could just see Sam's bald head over the filing cabinets in the office, and he appeared to be talking on the phone.

'Did Abbie's mum come back?' Ellie asked.

'Not that I've seen.'

Ellie felt as if her back were crawling with spiders. She glanced at Brenda, and no words were necessary. Brenda kicked open the door to the office and said two words. 'Sam! Now!'

But Ellie had already gone. This wasn't right, and she knew it.

She reached the bed next to Abbie's in seconds and spoke sharply to the agency nurse as she ran past.

'Who's with Abbie?' she barked, knowing it wasn't this girl's fault.

The startled nurse looked up from where she was taking her patient's pulse.

'A doctor. Came a few minutes ago. Why? Is there a problem?'

Ellie didn't know. Perhaps she was overreacting. But seconds later she knew she wasn't. Sam and Brenda rushed to her side.

'I've got this,' Sam said, firmly pulling back the curtain.

But he was too late. The curtain on the far side of the bed was flapping, and Ellie could see a figure dressed in scrubs racing to the nearby emergency exit.

'Ellie—get in here,' Sam shouted.

Trying not to disturb the other patients, Brenda mouthed, 'I'll call security,' just as the alarm on the emergency door destroyed any chance of discretion.

Ellie didn't care about security. All she cared about now was checking if Abbie was okay. She pulled back the curtain to follow Sam, and found Abbie tossing her head and her upper body from side to side. She was trying to speak. Her eyes were wide open, as if with shock, and Sam was frantically trying to hold her still.

'Calm her, Ellie. I need to check her over. Make sure that whoever that was hasn't done anything to harm her.'

Ellie crouched down at the side of the bed, and tried to stroke Abbie's hair back from her head. But it made her worse. Abbie jerked her head away from the hand, as if Ellie's fingers were burning her poor skin.

'Shh,' Ellie whispered. 'Be still. Be quiet.'

Abbie's body went rigid, and she arched off the bed, at the same time moaning with such distress that Ellie's whole body was instantly covered in goose bumps.

'What the hell's happening to her?' Sam asked.

'I've no idea, Sam. I'm just talking to her. Soothing her.'

A slightly out of breath Brenda reappeared at the open curtain.

'Security are on their way,' she said as she turned to pull the curtain back around them. 'Christ, what's up with her?' she asked as she saw the state that Abbie was in.

'Brenda, get me one milligram of Midazolam please. We need to calm her down.'

Ellie had moved her hand away from Abbie's head, and was now stroking the back of her arm. That seemed to be causing less distress. She stopped speaking, and started to sing softly.

'Ellie,' Sam said quietly. With his head he nodded towards the edge of the curtains surrounding the bed. On the floor was one of Abbie's pillows.

Ellie knew that the shock on Sam's face would be reflected on her own. No words were necessary. Sam grabbed a pair of surgical gloves from his pocket and put them on, picking the pillow up by its corner as Brenda reappeared with the sedative for Abbie. She looked from one to the other of them, her brow furrowed with silent questions.

'Get security to cover the doors, Brenda,' Sam said. 'And you need to call the police.'

Ellie tried to quash her panic in case she conveyed her feelings to Abbie. She tried to sing again, but her voice was shaking too much.

Abbie continued to toss her head from side to side, but not quite so frantically. It was as if she wanted to tell them something. She was moaning, but they couldn't make out what she was trying to say. She sounded in such pain, but they didn't know where it was coming from. Finally, the sedative started to do its work, but just before she surrendered to the drugs, she said one word.

And this time, Ellie heard it clearly.

There was a sense of urgency and suppressed tension in the ward, and away from the patients the squawking of police radios was a constant backdrop that added to the general unease.

Ellie, Sam, Brenda, and the agency nurse had all been interviewed, but there was nothing decisive; nothing that told them who the hell had been on the ward, or whether they had actually tried to kill Abbie. CCTV was being checked, but the footage from the camera by the door was inconclusive, so they were trying to backtrack and trace the intruder's route through the hospital.

As far as they could tell, Abbie had come to no harm—particularly if suffocation had been the intention. They had taken all precautions, though, and changed the contents of everything on and around Abbie's bed—from the water jug to the drip.

Ellie knew that the other staff members would each be feeling as culpable as she did, but then they didn't have the extra burden of guilt that she was carrying.

When Kath Campbell finally made it back to the ward, Ellie could see that she had been shopping. She came in looking much more cheerful, and proceeded to fish some pretty new pyjamas for Abbie out of one of her bags, obviously pleased to see that her daughter was sleeping quietly.

Ellie looked towards the nurses' station, and saw Sam beckoning her.

'Kath, Doctor Bradshaw would like a word, if that's okay.'

Kath looked startled and was about to start quizzing Ellie, but Ellie gently took her arm and guided her away from the bed and towards the office.

Kath's face drained of all colour as Sam explained to her what had happened, and why the place appeared to be crawling with police.

'I noticed them at the door when I was waiting to be buzzed in,' she said. 'I thought there must have been a smash on the motorway or something, and they were waiting to interview somebody. I never thought it would be my Abbie. Why, though? Why?'

There was no sensible answer that either Ellie or Sam could provide. That was a question for the police, although it was fairly clear to Ellie that it either had something to do with Abbie's abduction or her accident.

'How did they get in? We have to be buzzed in, and the staff have security passes,' Kath said, not unreasonably.

'I've heard back from security,' Sam said. 'Everybody that came in swiped a card, or was buzzed in and has since been verified. No cards have been reported missing, so we're going through the CCTV to see if we can spot them, and find out whose card it was.'

Ellie felt sick. Her vision became distorted as if she were looking through shattered glass, with all the parts fragmenting. Sam's face was splintered into a thousand pieces, and his voice seemed to be coming from a long way off.

Now was not the time to admit that this was her fault. That could only add to Kath's distress—but she had to get out of there and talk to security.

Thankfully after a few moments her vision cleared, and the feeling of dizziness started to pass. Nobody had noticed. Sam was focusing entirely on Kath's horrified face as he outlined what they knew.

'All we have at the moment is the evidence from the nurse who was keeping an eye on Abbie. A doctor walked towards Abbie's bed and pulled the curtains round. He or she was wearing a surgical hat, and scrubs, which can be bulked up to make somebody look a different shape. Their height has been assessed as around five-eight or five-nine, and it looked like a masculine walk, but that means nothing.'

Kath was struggling to take all of this in, on top of the horrors of the last few days.

'The important thing is,' Sam was saying, 'she's fine.'

He was leaning forward in his seat, his hands clasped between his knees, looking at Kath with concern.

'In fact, more than fine. She was moving—*really* moving—on the bed, and making sounds. She's continuing to be more intermittently responsive.'

Kath looked up hopefully at Sam, and Ellie leaned towards her and took one of her hands, putting her own worries aside for the moment.

'She spoke, Kath. I could tell she was trying to speak, but it was just as she fell asleep that I was able to make out what she was trying to say. She was asking for you, Kath. She said "Mother". I heard it distinctly.'

Ellie smiled at Kath, but was dismayed to see the colour drain from her face again. Kath sat down heavily in a chair.

'After all this time, all that love, and she still wants her mother.'

Ellie crouched down next to Kath and grasped her hands.

'No—you're her mother. It's you she wanted. Why would you think anything else?'

'Ellie, Abbie has never once in her life called me Mother. She has never referred to me as that, and it's a word she never uses. It's what she called her birth mother. I've always been Mum, but now, when she's in trouble, she wants that awful woman. After everything she did to Abbie and Jessica.'

Ellie didn't know what to say. She'd been convinced that Kath would be delighted, but she looked as if the exhaustion of the last few days had caught up with her as she leaned back on the chair and closed her eyes.

42

Tom stared at his computer screen. This wasn't good. He didn't know what he'd been expecting when he'd started the search for Leo's father, but it wasn't this. Ernie Collier from the Cheshire police had been doing a bit of asking around, and had called back to say that there had been talk that Ted Harris had 'buggered off to East Anglia'. That piece of information had proved enormously helpful, and Tom had been working through all his sources by phone and e-mail to see what he could dig up.

An appropriate term, he thought.

He'd made a brief trip into the village to see if he could pick up any gossip. The newsagent's had been his first stop, and the only one that had revealed anything—although that wasn't much.

'Good morning, Mrs Talbot,' he'd said, picking up his daily newspaper and placing it on the counter. 'Haven't you got any of the local newspapers left?'

'They've all gone, I'm afraid, Mr Douglas. A lot of interest, this week. Was there something particular that you were looking for, because I've got my own copy in the back if you'd like to borrow it? I need it back, though, because I do like to keep a copy for a week or so.'

'That's very kind—but I wanted to read more about the accident. You know, Abbie Campbell?' He didn't want to do any such thing, but he'd needed an opening.

As expected, Mrs Talbot had voiced a number of theories, all of which Tom had heard before and all of which he knew to be nonsense.

'It must be a terrible shock for a village like this. I suppose it's rare that anything happens to disrupt the peace,' he said.

'Well, you'd think so wouldn't you. And on the whole you'd be right. But we've had our moments.'

Tom had noticed before that there was some kind of perverse pride in communities that have housed villains. It was the same with neighbours and acquaintances of the most evil criminals. Behind the expressions of shock and horror, there was always a gleam of suppressed excitement, as if somehow their familiarity with a monster made them, and their lives, infinitely more interesting.

'Surely not recently?' he responded, fishing in his pocket for change to pay for his paper.

'No. That's true. It's been quiet for a good few years now.' Mrs Talbot sounded vaguely disappointed. 'But we've had our share of scoundrels. It's interesting that all this seems to have happened to young Abbie in those woods, you know. It's not the first time people have wondered what's gone on there.'

Tom handed over his cash, and gave Mrs Talbot an encouraging smile.

'It's years ago now, but it was summer. I remember that, because it was hot and everybody had their windows open all the time. There weren't so many houses on that side of the village then, but more than one person swore that one night they heard a terrible scream coming from the woods.'

'Really? What happened?' Tom asked.

'We never knew. The people that heard it said they listened to see if it came again, but it was quiet after that. They convinced themselves that it was a fox or something. It was only when they all started talking to each other that they got a bit worried. Perhaps it *was* a scream. Somebody out there might be hurt. So some of the men went to the woods to see if they could find anything, but there was nothing that they could see.'

'Did they call the police?'

Doreen Talbot had the grace to look shamefaced.

'It was too late. There was nothing there, nobody was reported missing or anything, so least said, soonest mended we all thought.'

Tom had kept his thoughts to himself. A group of villagers out looking for evidence of a crime was not his idea of the perfect game plan.

'When was this? Do you remember?'

'Not properly. It has to be more than twelve years ago, because it happened before I went into hospital. But less than eighteen, because it was definitely after my Bert died.'

That had been it. The sum total of the gossip provided nothing that would help Tom with his enquiries, and the other shops yielded less. So it was back to his computer. He had double checked Leo's research to make sure that the information provided by her stepmother was definitely a lie. And it was.

There was no trace of his death certificate in the period she had stated. But thanks to Ernie Collier he now had other routes to research, and step by step the facts were revealed to him. He was able to use his status as an ex-copper to ask a few favours at local newspapers, and he spoke to the local force. Finally, he put all the pieces together. He knew all there was to know.

He was going to have to go and find Leo. And he wasn't looking forward to it one little bit.

43

It was mid-afternoon by the time Ellie finished her shift, and it had been a hard few hours. After the panic of the intruder on the ward, everybody had finally calmed down but she couldn't help remembering Abbie's rigid body as she'd touched her. She was showing good signs of recovery, but Kath was tormented by the fact that Abbie had said the word 'mother' and Ellie could think of no way of reassuring her.

She had admitted to both Sam and Security that her pass was missing, and had been since her shift had started. Sam had been so good about it, saying it could happen to anybody. Security were less tolerant. And rightly so.

Ellie drove home as if she were on autopilot, and she noticed nothing of the journey—stopping automatically when she had to, but otherwise oblivious to her surroundings. She was surprised but strangely relieved to see there were no cars on the drive as she pulled in. She was determined to go to the police, whatever the consequences, and it would be far easier to do if she didn't have to tell Max about it first. She had no idea where he'd gone, but she could hazard a guess. He'd be with *her*, but for now she didn't want to think about it. And Leo could be anywhere. What a dreadful time for her to have come!

Ellie opened the front door and headed straight for the stairs. She wasn't hungry and all she wanted was a bath and a bit of thinking time. She needed to prepare her story for the police. She tramped wearily up the stairs, feeling more like sixty-four than thirty-four. Throwing her bag onto a chair, she kicked off her shoes and lay back on the bed. She just needed a few minutes, then she would get ready and go and give her confession. She rested her head on the soft pillows, and her exhausted mind shut itself off, as if somebody had pulled down a blackout blind. She fell into a dreamless sleep.

She was shocked to find that it was after five when she finally woke up. Max would be picking the children up at six, although she knew he would stay and chat with the other parents for a while—but he would be home by six thirty at the latest. She needed to be out of here by then. She raced into the bathroom and had to forego the bath she had been anticipating, ducking under the shower for about two minutes instead. At least it woke her up.

She'd thought of wearing her best clothes in order to look smart for her visit to the police, but realised this was a ridiculous idea. With what she had to tell them, she didn't suppose how she was dressed would make the least difference. She grabbed a clean pair of dark blue jeans and a royal blue and white striped top and got ready quickly. She pulled a brush through her hair and contemplated putting some makeup on to hide her pallor. In the end, though, she thought that her tired face might indicate how much her conscience had been pricking her.

It was still only quarter to six, so she had time to get a quick drink of juice—although a large gin would have gone down a treat right now. As she walked into the kitchen, she saw a note propped up on the worktop.

ELLIE, it said on the front. It was from Max, probably explaining or making up some excuse for where he'd gone that afternoon. But she wasn't prepared at all for what the note said.

Ellie, sweetheart—we need to talk. I'm sorry not to be there now, but there is something that I have to sort out before I can talk to you. When I get back, I'll put the children to bed and ask Leo to make herself scarce. I don't know what time I'll be home, but I need to track Sean down and sort things out with him before I can talk to you. See you later. Love, Max.

She gave a brief cry of anguish and crumpled the letter in her hand, letting it fall to the floor. Wrapping her arms tightly round her body as if to hold in the pain, she could barely breathe.

Why had he gone to see *him*?

There could only be one reason. Sean must have decided that he wasn't waiting any longer, and he must have called Max. Ellie had known that going to the police was dangerous and there was a chance that Max might find out, but she had hoped they would handle the situation with discretion. But now she didn't have to rely on the police's tact. By the time she got home tonight, Max was going to know everything. And he was obviously planning to bring his big announcement forward by a couple of days.

Looking down at her hands, Ellie realised that she was shaking. Grabbing a glass from the draining board, she filled it with cold water and gulped it down. Georgia had been right yesterday. It was as if Abbie Campbell's accident had acted like a catalyst, and the still waters around them were erupting in seething turbulence, with a geyser about to shoot through the apparent calm surface of all of their lives.

Knowing that she was being a coward, Ellie had driven very slowly to the police headquarters, and it was quarter to seven by the time she arrived. Max would be home by now and wondering where she was. The truth was that in spite of arriving at her destination half an hour ago, she was still sitting outside, trying to pluck up the courage to go in.

She wasn't sure what she was going to say. She'd had it all so well planned, but it sounded hollow even to her own ears. One option was not to mention anybody but herself. She could say she had been going to pick her husband up from the rugby club, but had remembered before she got there that he was getting a lift. But that was pretty pathetic. Or she could tell them that there was a man who had been bothering her. She had gone out to meet him to tell him to get lost.

At midnight. Down a dark lane. A likely story.

Or the truth. That she had started a relationship with a man other than her husband, and he had wanted to meet her. The fact that she was going to see him to tell him to get out of her life would be irrelevant to the police. And they would be justifiably furious with her for not coming forward sooner. Particularly as she now remembered that she had passed the other car. Not that she could identify it, but she was sure that it was a dark colour.

She was just opening the car door when her phone rang. Max. She cut him off. But it unnerved her again, and she gave herself a minute or two to calm down. The phone rang again.

She was about to cut it off when she saw that it said 'blocked'. That couldn't be Max. He wouldn't have a clue how to block his number—but then, he'd never needed to before. Perhaps it was something else he had learned.

'Hello,' she said tentatively.

'Helllloooo Elllieee.' The voice sounded deep and slow, like a recording played at the wrong speed. It was impossible to tell whether it was a man or a woman—because it sounded like neither. It didn't sound human. Ellie felt a shiver run up her back.

'It's paaaayback time.' There was a brief and eerie laugh from the other end of the phone.

Ellie closed her eyes and bit her top lip. Should she hang up?

But she couldn't. She needed to know what this person wanted from her.

The deep, slow, echoing voice continued.

'I've saved this task for you, Ellie, because it's something that you—and only you—can do for me.'

'Why should I do *anything* for you?'

'Don't interrupt.' A momentary lapse in the smooth tones betrayed a quick anger, and Ellie recognised instantly that this person wasn't entirely balanced.

'You *will* do as I say, won't you Ellie? Imagine how you'll feel if your husband finds out what you've been doing, and your perfect little family is broken into pieces? If you want your secrets to be safe, you only have to do one very simple thing. If not, you'll have to face the consequences.'

The voice hardened. 'Or perhaps next time, it won't just be your security pass or a scruffy soft dog that goes missing.'

Ellie felt a wave of hot fury.

'Don't you come near my children. Don't you *dare*. I'll hunt you down and kill you if you so much as touch a hair on their heads.'

There was a sly laugh from the other end of the phone. Even through the distortion it tugged at Ellie's memory, but she couldn't place it. Who was it? Somebody who'd had a reason to take her security pass. Somebody who had wanted to hurt Abbie Campbell. But why? And if they could hurt Abbie, what might they do to Ruby and Jake?

Whoever it was, they seemed to be able to come and go in Willow Farm without detection, because she was sure that her pass had been taken last night, while they were sleeping. The thought made her shudder with horror at what else could have happened.

She didn't know what this person wanted from her, but if it was within her power, she would do whatever they asked to take the threat away from the children. That wasn't enough, though. If it was the last thing she did, she would track this bastard down and remove any lingering threat from her family.

The caller had assumed that Ellie's silence implied complicity, and the distorted voice continued with no further sense of familiarity or clues to gender.

'Just do what I ask. It's sooooo simple. You can protect your precious marriage and your children. After all, we don't want any more tragedies in the village, do we?'

Ellie didn't respond.

'Why are you so quiet, Ellie? It's not a big decision. I'm going to tell you what I need you to do, and don't even think of taking a chance that I don't mean what I say.'

Ellie listened. And finally she understood why she had been targeted. Why she was the one that had to be blackmailed.

44

'Can I take you out to dinner tonight, to thank you for Tuesday?' were Leo's first words when Tom opened the front door.

'Been chucked out again, have you?' Tom asked, unable to suppress a grin. He was going to miss Leo when she went back to Manchester. She'd certainly brightened up a couple of days for him, and made him realise how isolated he'd become recently. He had consciously avoided getting too close to any woman for the last couple of years, but it had left a big hole in his life. He enjoyed the banter, the subtle flirting, and the thought of a soft, naked body in his bed. It was time for his self-imposed monastic life to come to an end.

'Yes, and no. I was going to go back to Manchester, but Max has asked me not to. Not yet. Even so, I can't be around tonight. Those two have things to sort out. So here I am,' Leo said, with a childlike beam that Tom guessed was an attempt to cover her discomfort.

'You know, it would be nice to know that you'd come round because you wanted to see me rather than because you needed a port in a storm, but I suppose beggars can't be choosers. Come in. I'll get the vodka.'

Leo followed him down the hall, and he spoke to her over his shoulder.

'What have you been up to all day?'

'I was at home until about three, but Ellie was due back and I couldn't face her. I'll get to that in a minute. So I took myself into Altrincham and decided to have a pedicure and a few other bits and pieces at the beautician's.'

Tom had been around women for long enough to know not to ask about the 'bits and pieces' but assumed that they had probably been painful.

'Well, now you're all beautified again, have a drink and tell me if you definitely want to go out, or would you prefer to eat in? Nothing complicated, I promise. I've got some fillet steak and we could slap it on the barbecue and have it with some salad if that would do? I'll even make some homemade oven chips if you like, although you don't look much like a chip girl to me,' he said, glancing at her slim body.

'Well, looks can be very deceptive. And if there's one thing that I know how to do, it's peel a potato.'

He handed Leo a vodka shot, and took a bottle of Corona out of the fridge.

'Loads of time for that. We can eat at about eight, if that's okay. Let's go and sit in comfort. I've been shifting rubbish all day and could do with putting my feet up for an hour or so. I must have been to the tip about six times.'

'Ah ha—that explains the old Jeep outside. I thought you'd have some flashy number.'

'I keep the posh car in the garage, but unless I've got Lucy with me, I'd rather drive the Jeep. Suits the new laid-back image better, I think. Lucy loves the Lexus, though. Like you, I went for a coupé, and she thinks it's great when we have the roof down.' Tom grinned indulgently as he thought of his daughter.

He guided Leo into the sitting room and indicated that she should take a seat. It was time to be serious for a moment.

'I was going to come round tomorrow anyway. I've got something I need to talk to you about,' he said.

As they sat down, Leo looked at Tom warily.

'It's about your father. It's not great news, I'm afraid. I'd have told you as soon as I knew, but when I called round earlier the only car at Willow Farm was Ellie's and I wanted to catch you on your own. It's up to you how you decide to share it.'

Leo leant back in the chair.

'It's okay, Tom. You know I didn't have much of an opinion of him. Just tell me.' She downed her shot, as if Dutch courage was a prerequisite.

'Do you want another of those, or shall I get you a glass of wine?' Tom asked.

'Neither, thanks. I'm fine. Just get on with it, please.'

Tom was very aware that Leo liked her personal space to be kept completely clear, and although he respected that, on this occasion he felt she might need some sense of human touch. He moved across to the pouffe that was by Leo's chair and reached out for her hand, half expecting her to pull it away.

'Christ, it must be bad if you feel you have to hold my hand,' she said in a tone that would have driven most men to back off.

'Shut up, Leo. You're only human, and despite not thinking much of your dad, sometimes a bit of the old touchy-feely is quite comforting. Give it a try, eh?'

Tom wondered for a moment how many men must have been forced out by Leo's inability to accept closeness on any level. He looked straight into Leo's eyes as he spoke.

'I'm so sorry, Leo, but your father really *is* dead. He died about three years after he left home. Your stepmother never had him declared dead at all. She'd known all along.'

Leo's expression didn't waver, but nevertheless Tom gently stroked the back of her hand with his thumb. She had probably been expecting the news that her father was dead, but it was the rest he was worried about.

'How?' was all she said.

'I'll get to that in a minute. Are you okay?'

'Of course I'm okay. I'm not sure Ellie will be, though. It shows that her mother was a lying bitch. Why in God's name didn't she tell Ellie? Why on earth would she lie about it? Why not just say that he *was* dead? Ellie's spent years believing that he's still out there somewhere, because as far as she knew there was no evidence otherwise. She's been tortured by the fact that he didn't want to see her. She could have been saved *all* of that. It's Ellie I'm worried about. Not me. I've told you, I don't care.'

Of course you don't, Tom thought. *I can see that all over your face.*

'It's possible that she didn't tell you for a good reason, even though you might find that hard to believe.'

'What good reason? There's no good reason for not telling a child that her father is dead.'

Tom wasn't sure if she was referring to herself, or to Ellie, but he let it pass.

'Once I knew he was dead and when he died, I was able to spread the net a bit wider and legitimately ask a few questions. The sources are good. I'm confident that they're correct, and with the details I'm about to give you, you'll be able to check for yourself with the authorities.'

'If you say the information is correct, I believe you. You don't need to give me the provenance.' The prickly Leo was surfacing again.

'The thing is, he was in prison when he died.' Tom paused. 'This is going to be hard for you to accept, Leo. I'm afraid he hanged himself.'

Leo maintained the same facial expression, but he could feel her grip on his hand tighten and her skin had lost all colour.

'What had he done?' she asked in a level voice.

'He was on remand at the time of his death, awaiting trial.'

'You're avoiding the question—what had he been charged with?'

'There's no easy way to tell anybody this about their father.' Tom paused and saw a flash of apprehension in Leo's eyes. 'It was rape, I'm afraid.'

Tom saw the look of shock that flashed over her face before she managed to control her features, and he wished she would let herself go. He gently took her other hand.

'Is there more?' she asked, her voice harsher than before and tinged with a fake indifference.

'I know that you'll try to get hold of the details, so I'll tell you myself that he when he died, he left a note. He admitted to a series of other rapes, going back a few years.'

Leo's eyes were enormous in her narrow face. Her bright red lipstick looked lurid against her bloodless skin.

'And was it *true*? *Had* he done it before? How many times, for God's sake?'

'He didn't provide names—maybe he didn't know them. He did give dates and places, but Leo, none of them happened while your mother was alive.'

Leo gave a shrill laugh. 'Oh, well that's something, I suppose. Thank heavens for small mercies. If my mother had known what he was—even what he potentially was—she'd have castrated him personally. Christ, I hope she can't see any of this from the grave. Thank God I don't believe in ghosts, spirits, and reincarnation. Where did these rapes take place?'

'You don't need to know that—it doesn't matter,' Tom said quietly.

'Of course it bloody matters. *Where*, Tom? There must be a reason you're not telling me.'

'And I wouldn't tell you now, but as you have the basic details you could find out. In the three years after he left here, they happened in several places in East Anglia, which is where he was living.'

'And before that?'

'I understand that a few of them were local. According to his note, one was actually in the village.' Tom had known that she would want the details, but he had dreaded telling her this part.

'*What*? Who in God's name did he rape in the village?'

'As I said, there were no names given. Only approximate dates, and the area of the country. Some of them had been reported, and so the police were able to tie up a few loose ends. But nobody ever reported a rape in the village. I checked.'

'Just because it wasn't reported doesn't mean it didn't happen, though, does it? What percentage of rapes *are* reported, Tom? You should know. You're the bloody policeman.'

Tom didn't answer. He didn't need to. If her father said he raped somebody in Little Melham, he had no doubt that it was true. Some poor girl had probably been too ashamed to tell, at the risk of not being believed.

He looked at Leo. Her whole face tightened, and she looked very much as if she would like to cry but was fighting it hard. He wanted to pull her to him and wrap his arms round her, but he knew that would be one step too far.

Ellie was frantic. She had to act. She was right outside the police station. She could go in and report the whole story, but there were so many pieces missing. She could admit to the fact that she was out on Friday night and what she had seen, but she would also have to tell them now about the break-ins and the lost security pass. It would take *forever*.

The only consideration now was the safety of the children. She grabbed her phone and stabbed in the short code to get Max. *Please* let him be home, she prayed. The twins should be in bed by now, so they should all be there. But if this person was still able to get into their house, he might be there now—he might be with her children.

The phone was answered—but she barely gave Max time to speak.

'Listen, Max, I can't explain this to you now—but are you and the twins okay?'

'Of course we're okay. But Ellie, I need to talk to you.'

With a sinking heart she knew that Sean must have told him everything.

'I know you do, but for now please just listen. I need you to keep all the doors locked and bolted until I get home. Do you understand, Max? *Bolted*. And I want you to check on the twins all the time. And I *mean* all the time. Max—I was right about somebody getting into the house. I know it now, for sure. Please just do as I'm asking. I'm going to find out who this bastard is, and I'm going to find out now.'

'Ellie—what are you talking about? You sound demented.'

'I have been, but I'm not now. I've got to go, but Maxy—I love you.' She hung up the phone before he could answer.

She was about to turn her phone off when it beeped.

Sean.

She didn't want to read it, but she knew she had to. To find out what he'd said to Max.

I PROMISED I WOULD WAIT, BUT IT'S TWO DAYS NOW, AND STILL NO WORD. I'VE BEEN FAIR. I'VE GIVEN YOU TIME. MAX CAME TO SEE ME TODAY—I SAW HIS CAR WHEN I GOT HOME SO I STAYED AWAY, OUT OF SIGHT, UNTIL HE LEFT. I COULD HAVE SPOKEN TO HIM. BUT I RESPECTED YOUR WISHES. NOW IT'S TIME FOR YOU TO RESPECT MINE. I WANT YOU, ELLIE. AND THIS SECRECY HAS TO END. MEET ME TONIGHT, OR I'M COMING TO GET YOU.

Ellie's mind was assaulted with mixed emotions. Relief that Max still didn't know, fear of what Sean was going to do, and anger that, because of Sean, she hadn't taken the threat to her children seriously.

She flung her phone on the passenger seat and screamed. Nobody could hear her inside the car, and all the pent-up frustration and anger shot through her to find an escape. She banged her head backwards on the headrest. Once, twice, three times.

She leaned across and picked up her phone, and with shaking fingers, typed a response.

MEET ME AT THE OLD HASLETT'S FARM AT EIGHT. DON'T BE LATE.

She pressed send, put the car into gear, and turned around to head to the rendezvous.

45

The narrow sandy track that led to Haslett's Farm was deeply rutted and was slowly disappearing under the tenacious invasion of brambles and knotweed. Sean knew the farmhouse was derelict. It had been falling apart for years, but nobody would buy it to renovate because the ground underneath wasn't stable enough, as evidenced by the foot-wide cracks in the top storey. The whole place had been boarded up, and there didn't appear to be any way of getting inside. Old pieces of guttering were hanging off, and some kind of weed-like creeper was climbing up the stone walls and wrapping itself round drainpipes.

Ellie didn't seem to be here yet; at least, there was no sign of her car. Parking at the side of the track, Sean stepped out and looked around. There was almost total silence, although if he listened hard he could just make out the hum of traffic on the trunk road in the distance.

He made his way quietly round the back of the farmhouse, as if he were trying hard not to disturb a soul in this isolated spot. Fifty feet away from the main building stood an old barn with a rusted but largely intact corrugated iron roof. Perhaps Ellie would be waiting there.

He was eager to see her, and so pleased that she had agreed to meet him this evening. He knew they were going to have to break the news of their relationship very soon, but it would be good to be with her for a while before the storm came crashing over their heads.

Since the day he'd met her, he had thought Ellie was the perfect woman. Warm, friendly, beautiful, and a wonderful mother to her twins. He had found every excuse possible to touch her warm flesh—her arms, her cheek, even her leg once when he bent to pick up something from the floor. Just a brush with his fingers, when it didn't seem too obvious that he was practically salivating at the thought of caressing that same spot with his lips. A brief stroke of the arm as he leaned in for a polite peck on the cheek when greeting her, or a slight touch of hands when passing cups of tea. One day she had lifted her arms to take something from a shelf and he had seen a two-inch gap of flawless flesh between her T-shirt and jeans. He didn't know how he had prevented himself from reaching out and gently rubbing his thumb over her skin.

And then that day, three weeks ago now, when he saw the look in her eyes. The look that said she wanted him too.

But she wouldn't be his Ellie if she didn't have a conscience. She'd stopped him at the last moment. Not before he'd had the chance to kiss the velvet skin of her stomach, and stroke those beautiful naked breasts, though. He understood why she had stopped. They had to end their marriages before they would be free, but he couldn't wait any longer. Tonight they would make their plans, and difficult as it would be, finally they could be together.

As he made his way round to the barn, the dying sun caught a reflection of something metallic and he could barely make out the taillight of a car through a small gap. She must already be here. He felt his heart rate increase.

The huge vaulted barn had double doors at both ends, hanging limply from their old hinges. He could see piles of ancient, corroded farm equipment on the ground, and some half-chewed bales of hay were stacked roughly on one side. The summer sun hadn't yet set, but it was low in the sky, and the barn was full of shadowy depths where she could be waiting.

'Ellie? Are you there? It's me. Where are you, darling?'

There was no answer, but he thought he heard some scuffling from the hayloft, too big to be a mouse or a rat. He smiled to himself. Perhaps she'd brought a blanket. Perhaps she was up there waiting for him.

He made his way to the ladder, stepping over the detritus spread across the old, cracked concrete floor, and started to climb. It was darker up here. There were no windows, and the only light came from below, through the half-open doors.

He could see a figure at the other end of the barn, and he knew immediately it wasn't Ellie.

'Hello?' he said. 'What's going on?'

The person stepped farther back into the shadows, and Sean knew that for some reason he'd been set up. But he had no idea why.

'Where's Ellie? Who are you and what are you doing here?'

For a moment, there was silence. The voice, when it came, was little more than a hoarse whisper.

'Why has she sent *you?* I told her to send the other one—her lover. The piece of shit that dragged a child to the side of the road and left her for dead.' There was a trace of panic in the tone, but he still couldn't see the face.

'Her *lover?* What the hell are you talking about? Tell me what you've done with Ellie. Tell me where she is.'

Sean started to advance across the floor of the hayloft. This was a voice he'd heard before, but for a moment he couldn't place it. Whoever it was, he would strangle the truth out of the bastard if anything had happened to Ellie.

He kept his eyes fixed on the figure who was retreating towards the back of the barn, as if drawing him forward. A stray beam of sunlight pierced the dusty gloom and he saw there was another ladder at the far end, descending from the hayloft and providing an escape route. Nobody was leaving until he knew what had happened to Ellie. He had to get there first. He had to cut off the escape. He started to run across the hay-strewn floor.

His feet pounded on the thin board of the loft as the figure disappeared further into the shadows ahead of him. But he was gaining on the bastard who'd taken Ellie. His heart lurched as his right foot landed hard and met with no resistance. There was nothing beneath him. His leg disappeared into a void, and his momentum drove him forward. With arms flailing uselessly in the air, he couldn't stop himself as his left foot followed his right into nothingness. He lunged sideways to try to reach a solid piece of floor, but there was only hay-covered cardboard. He caught one final glimpse of sunlight illuminating the triumphant smile on a face that he recognised as his body crashed through the opening.

46

On her journey to the police station, Ellie had dawdled all the way and still got there quickly. Now she was trying every shortcut she knew to get back to the village, but time was racing by. Of course, her blackmailer would never be expecting her to turn up. It wasn't her they wanted. It was Sean.

The instructions had been clear. *Send 'lover boy' to me at the old Haslett's Farm at eight pm.* Ellie knew who they meant, but had to be sure.

'What do you mean? Who are you talking about?' she'd asked.

There had been a sneaky laugh from the other end of the phone.

'How many lovers have you got, Ellie? Little Miss Perfect? I want the one you were with on Friday night. The one you sneaked out to meet.' Another nasty giggle.

How could they know so much? Ellie was sure nobody had seen her with Sean, and she certainly hadn't told a soul about it. She nearly told Georgia when Sean turned up on Saturday night and left that bloody rose in the fridge—but she would never have named him. Of that she was one hundred per cent confident.

Whoever her blackmailer was, he was a clever sod. Ellie was the only person who could be relied upon to lure Sean to a secret assignation in a remote place. Initially, she hadn't been intending to involve him. She had planned on going herself to find out who was playing with her mind and threatening her children. But then Sean had sent that text, and this time his intentions were explicit. So she had done exactly what she had been asked to do—she'd sent 'lover boy'.

Ellie would be there too, though, and the blackmailer wouldn't be expecting that. But why Sean?

She looked at her watch. It was three minutes past eight, and she was still five minutes from Haslett's Farm. She was driving as if the devil were at her back.

Five minutes became ten as Ellie was stuck on the back road behind a herd of cows. She wanted to pip her horn and drive right through them, but she knew what the farmers round here were like, and this one in particular would be more likely to try to slow the cows down if she did that. She closed her eyes in frustration.

Finally, she was moving again. The turning was just up ahead, and she took the corner too fast, nearly ending up in the hedge. *Shit. That was close.*

Sean's car was there; she could see it parked at the front of the farmhouse. But there didn't seem to be anybody else. She slammed the brakes on right behind his car and got out.

Silence.

She walked towards the front of the farm, but it was clear that there was nobody inside. She would be glad when she found him—there was something ominous about the quiet. There wasn't a breath of air, and even the birds seemed to have stopped singing.

Suddenly the stillness was ripped apart. Ellie heard a brief shout of fear, followed by a terrible scream of agony. Then the silence returned as quickly as it had departed. It was almost as if she had dreamt it, but she knew she hadn't.

Ellie ran. Perhaps it was foolish, but she didn't stop to think. Seeing a huge building ahead of her and to the left, she sprinted towards it, skirting stones and debris from the ruined farmhouse and ploughing through the undergrowth.

As she dodged around the hanging door of the building, she caught a glimpse of movement at the edge of her vision, but she didn't even cast a stray glance in its direction as her whole being was focused on the sight in front of her. At the edge of the shadows that lay darkly beneath the hayloft she saw a foot. Her eyes followed the path from the foot up the leg, until the whole body was visible to her.

'*No!*' she screamed. '*Oh my God—no.*' She ran towards the mangled body. Sean was lying on what appeared to be a huge pile of old rusty metal—some sort of ancient farm equipment—and Ellie could see spikes sticking up through his chest and his neck. She knew before she reached him that he was dead. Blood would have been gushing from him if his heart had been beating. He had bled out in seconds. Nevertheless, Ellie leaned over him to see if there was a pulse—to see if she could do anything at all.

'I'm so sorry,' she cried, as she reached over Sean's blood-soaked body to feel his neck. Nothing. Even though she knew he couldn't hear her or feel her, she brought his hand to her lips and kissed it. Whatever had happened in the last few weeks and however badly he had behaved, she was every bit as guilty as he was.

At the back of her conscious mind, she heard a car start up and skid off down the dirt track, but she was too intent on trying to communicate her thoughts to Sean—without either hope or expectation.

She had done this. She had sent him to his death.

Sobbing and covered in his wet, sticky blood, she grabbed her phone from her pocket and called an ambulance. It was too late, of course, but she gave the details as calmly as she could then hung up and collapsed on the floor next to Sean's still-warm body.

'I'm sorry,' she sobbed. 'You didn't deserve this. You didn't. I'm sorry I couldn't love you—I know you can't hear me, but none of this was your fault.'

She had been cursing Sean for weeks now, trying to get him out of her life—but she would never have wished this on him. Why would *anybody* want to kill him?

Ellie held his hand while she waited for the ambulance, but as she lay by his side, she realised that there was much more to this. He had been lured to this spot. She knew she was to blame for that, but how could she explain?

Lying where she was, she pulled her phone towards her again. Scrolling through the list of texts, she found what she was looking for and pressed the call button.

Tom and Leo had been over everything that he had discovered for a second time as Leo tried to absorb the truth. She had remained composed, but he could see what an effort it had been, and he just wished she would cry. This was a hell of a legacy to live with.

Finally, Leo had thanked him very formally for his efforts, and finished by saying, 'Can we not talk about this anymore, please? I'd rather pretend that things are as they were until I've had time to think about this and deal with it properly.'

Since then they had been subdued, but oddly it hadn't felt at all uncomfortable. Tom was serving up the steaks and Leo was pinching chips out of the dish when the phone rang.

'Bloody typical,' said Tom. 'Sorry, Leo. I know that I could ignore it, but once a policeman . . .'

Leo gave him a scornful smirk and continued to pick at the chips. How she stayed so slim, Tom couldn't imagine. She had a hell of an appetite. He glanced at the phone, but didn't recognise the number.

'Tom Douglas,' he said. All he could hear at the other end of the phone was sobbing for a moment.

'Thank God. I was praying this was your number.'

'Ellie? Is that you, Ellie?' He heard a burst of static, then garbled crying and talking all at the same time.

Leo looked up sharply and was about to speak, but Tom held his hand up to quieten her. He could hardly make out what Ellie was saying.

'Slow down, Ellie—I can't understand you. Where are you?'

Tom heard two words clearly: 'Leo', and 'Haslett's'.

'Leo's here with me, Ellie. Do you want me to get Max?'

There was a shriek of 'NO!' down the phone.

'Okay, okay. Leo's here, but I don't know what Haslett's means. What are you trying to say to me?'

Leo started to speak and Tom raised his hand again. Leo grabbed it and pulled it down.

'Ask her if she means Haslett's Farm. Is that where she is?'

Tom nodded and followed Leo's instructions.

'Yes—and it's awful. It's truly terrible. Please come, Tom. Bring Leo too. Tom—he's *dead!* I've killed him.'

'We're on our way, Ellie. Sit tight. Don't touch anything. Are you in danger?'

'*No!* Just come.'

Tom was about to hand the phone to Leo so that she could talk to her sister as they drove, but Ellie had hung up.

'What? *What?*' Leo shouted at Tom.

'Ellie's in some kind of trouble. She's at Haslett's Farm. Do you know where it is?' She nodded. Tom decided that he wouldn't pass on the 'he's dead' comment to Leo until he knew some more. 'She specifically said that she doesn't want us to get Max, so let's go.'

Tom grabbed his car keys from the worktop and ran for the door, with Leo close behind. His old Jeep was facing towards the road, thank goodness. That would save them a couple of minutes.

They leapt in the car, and Tom had the engine running before Leo had managed to close her door.

'Out of the drive and turn left,' she said. 'The quickest way is down the back road.'

'Put your seat belt on, Leo.'

'What? For God's sake, Tom, it's only five minutes away.' Nevertheless, Leo wrestled with the archaic seat belt. 'I know you're a policeman, but bloody hell,' she muttered.

'There's no airbag on that side, Leo. Only on the driver's side. It's an old car—and I don't want to be worried about you flying through the windscreen every time I brake. Nothing to do with being a policeman.'

Tom could feel the tension rippling from Leo, but she had the sense not to keep asking him questions about his conversation with Ellie. She knew he would tell her whatever he thought he needed to. She was a smart girl. He reached his hand across and grasped one of hers.

'It'll be okay, Leo. Ellie's upset, but she didn't sound as if she was hurt.'

Leo grasped his hand tightly, and he managed the whole journey steering one-handed, glad that the old wreck he had bought for shifting garden rubbish and the like was an automatic.

They reached the farm in five minutes, and as they approached the farmhouse, Tom could see two parked cars.

'There's Ellie's car,' Leo said. 'But whose is the other one? I've seen it before somewhere—I recognise the cover over the spare wheel. It was parked down the lane on Friday night.'

'I think it's Sean's,' Tom said. 'It looks like the Discovery he arrived in on Saturday, and I saw it again on Sunday.'

He pulled up quickly.

'Stay in the car, Leo.'

'No,' she replied, opening the car door and jumping out. Tom had a quick flash of déjà vu. He remembered another crime scene where he'd asked a woman to stay in the car and she had refused. But he had no time to think about that now.

Leo was shouting at the top of her voice.

'Ellie? Ellie—where are you?'

A faint noise came from the direction of the barn, and Leo set off at a run with Tom right behind.

They both entered the barn at the same moment, and stopped. Leo was the first to react, and within a space of no more than two seconds she had raced across the barn and launched herself at Ellie, wrapping her arms round her blood-covered sister and rocking her backwards and forwards.

'Where are you hurt, Ellie? Where? Tell me what to do?'

Ellie was sobbing too much to answer.

'Leo,' Tom said calmly. 'I don't think Ellie's hurt. I think the blood is Sean's.' Tom nodded towards Sean's body. Leo must have seen it, but she'd been so intent on getting to her sister that she had shut it out of her mind. Tom saw the flash of horror in her eyes as she registered the blood-soaked body and the massive spikes that skewered Sean to the rusting machinery.

'Leo, you need to step away from Ellie and come back over here. This is a crime scene, and you are buggering it up something rotten. Come here.'

'Piss off, Tom. I'm staying with Ellie.'

Given that she had undoubtedly done the damage already, Tom told both of them to stay where they were, and not to move. He grabbed his mobile and made a call, turning his back on the girls in the hope that they wouldn't hear him. But he wasn't about to leave them alone in the barn either.

'Steve? I don't know if you're on duty, mate, but you're needed. Dead body. It's pretty bad, so I'd only bring people with strong stomachs. I'll stay until you get here. Haslett's Farm, if you know where that is. Okay. Twenty minutes.'

Tom turned his phone round and took some photos.

'What the fuck are you doing, Tom?' Leo shouted. 'I can't believe you just did that!'

'Shut up, Leo, and listen. Ellie's in a very compromising position. She's here on her own with somebody who is dead. She's covered in his blood. You have trampled all over the scene. I want to get you and Ellie away from that body, and I want to preserve what's left of any evidence—because I don't think this has anything to do with your sister, but I'm likely to be in the minority. Okay?' Tom was trying to be gentle, but he had to make Leo understand. The glare she gave him was one of outrage, but at least she had stopped arguing.

He took some more pictures, including upwards to where it was evident that Sean had fallen through a hole in the upstairs level of the barn. He could see sawdust on the floor to one side—the other side having been trampled by first Ellie and then Leo. Once he had finished with his photos, he spoke again.

'Leo, help Ellie to her feet. I can hear sirens, and at a guess she's called an ambulance. Is that right, Ellie?'

She nodded.

'Well, there's not much they can do for Sean, other than pronounce life extinct, but they might be able to help Ellie with something for the shock. Can you help her up, Leo, and take her outside?'

Leo nodded.

'Come on, Ellie. Lean on me.'

With her arm wrapped round her sister, Leo helped her to her feet, and then walked her towards the door as the ambulance pulled to a halt in the now busy forecourt of the farm. Tom went over and had a brief word with them, and Leo guided Ellie towards her car.

'Not in there,' Tom shouted, and came running over. 'She's got sawdust on her feet—she can't get in her car.'

'So? She needs to sit down—what does the state of her feet matter?'

'Jesus, Leo, can't you do as you're told for once?' Tom whipped off the denim shirt he was wearing over a T-shirt and placed it on a rough-looking hay bale. 'Here you go, Ellie. Sit yourself down here.'

Ellie sat, and Leo perched on the very edge, holding on tight to her sister. Tom crouched down to face Ellie.

'The police are going to be here in a few minutes. They're going to want to understand everything. Now would be a good time for you to tell me what you know so that I can do whatever possible to help you. Do you think you can talk?'

Leo gave Tom another of her fierce looks, which he studiously ignored.

'I'm trying to help, Ellie.'

Ellie buried her face in her hands, and her words were barely audible.

'It's my fault. I sent him here. I was being blackmailed—"do as I say, or I'll tell Max". So I told him to come. I was coming too—but I was late. God help us, Tom, I never thought for a minute that he'd be *killed*.'

'Who was blackmailing you, Ellie, and what would they tell Max?' Leo asked, a look of incredulity on her face.

'Leo—I like you, and I think you know that,' Tom said. 'But if you don't shut up, I am going to have to ask you to leave. Is that clear?'

Leo scowled, but resisted the temptation to respond. She hugged Ellie closer to her.

'Take your time, Ellie. Start at the beginning.'

Before she had a chance to speak, a young paramedic appeared, and offered Ellie a cup from a thermos full of some hot, steaming liquid.

'Have some tea—it's only what I bring when I'm on duty, so I don't have enough to go round—but it might help,' she said kindly.

Ellie tried to give a smile of thanks as she took the cup in shaky hands. She dropped her head again, staring sightlessly into the plastic beaker.

'It started about three weeks ago. It was the day before we moved into the house. The carpet fitters were coming to finish off downstairs. Max was supposed to be coming home, but he was with *her*—that Alannah from his school.'

Leo looked as if she were about to speak, but Tom threw her a warning glance. *Let her finish, Leo,* he thought, willing her to keep silent.

'I knew by then that Sean liked me—I mean *really* liked me—and he was there, you see. Just when I needed somebody.'

Without looking up, Ellie took a sip of her tea, and nobody spoke.

'Max had said he would meet me at lunchtime—so we could see our finished house. I thought he would be as excited as me. But he called at the last minute to say that he was going to have lunch with Pat—because Pat was devastated about the whole Georgia thing. I was a bit put out, but it was okay. Then in the early afternoon Georgia called me. She said Pat had been round for lunch, but they'd made no progress. So Max had been lying to me, and he'd only do that for one reason. He must have been with *her*. I knew things weren't right, but I would never have believed he was having an affair. And he's going to leave me. I heard him. He's going to tell me on Saturday, but I already know. He's not very discreet on the telephone, you know.'

Ellie gave a brief laugh, her fondness for Max showing through despite everything.

'I was so upset. I knew he didn't want me anymore. He tried, but . . . Well, things didn't always work out, and that had never been a problem for Max until the last month or two. So I knew, you see. He didn't want me. And I knew that Sean did. I'd known for months. He found me lying on the floor— on my beautiful new carpet—and I was crying. Sean had called to see if the fitters had done any damage and if any paintwork needed touching up, but he sat down next to me and pulled me into his arms. I told him everything.'

Ellie started to cry again. Leo looked at Tom as if begging him to stop, but he knew it was all going to have to come out. He waited in silence, just leaning forward to give Ellie's arm an encouraging squeeze.

'The landscapers were outside finishing off my yellow rose bed, so he guided me upstairs—away from prying eyes, he said. He sat me on our new king-sized bed and put his arm round me. Then I had this mad notion that if I was unfaithful too, it wouldn't seem so bad when Max came clean. I thought that I wouldn't have to leave him, because I was as bad. Does that make sense?' Ellie looked up for the first time. 'I'd always said that trust had to be the most important thing in my marriage, and if Max ever betrayed it, I would leave him. I didn't want to become an embittered old hag like my mother. But I *couldn't* leave him. I love him. I adore him. So what could I do? This way, I would be able to forgive him.'

Leo grabbed a tissue from the pocket of her jeans and passed it to Ellie.

'I didn't have sex with him, though. I couldn't. But you see, I let him get close—so what does that make me? When I was at school, we'd have called somebody like me a prick tease. But I didn't mean to. Sean was nice. But then he became a bit weird. I know that it was my fault. But after that day, he wouldn't leave me alone. Wherever I went, there he was. Whatever I did, he knew about it. It was the most dreadful feeling.'

'Ellie,' Leo said softly, 'I know Tom has told me not to interrupt, but there's something you need to know. Max has never had an affair. Not with Alannah, or with anybody else. I know what the problem was. It was just the money. He told me this morning. He felt he wasn't the man of the house anymore, and so he did something stupid—something very stupid—but I promise you, it had nothing to do with another woman.'

Leo gave Tom a defiant look.

'I know you told me to be quiet, but she needed to know that, Tom.'

He gave her a gentle smile, and a brief nod.

'We understand, Ellie. I can see how it happened, and it sounds as if Sean became obsessed, would that be right? Why was he here, though? The police will be here soon, so if you can it would help if you told me everything now. Then I can help you.'

And so Ellie began her tale. Of the blackmail, the stalking, the breaking into the house, and how Sean came to be at Haslett's Farm.

Ellie was so grateful to Tom and Leo for coming to her rescue, but she knew that somebody was going to have to tell Max what was happening. He'd been calling her endlessly, and she had finally switched off her phone. Leo had done the same. At least he was at home to keep a careful watch over the twins, although now that the blackmailer had what he wanted, maybe that threat would be over.

She had been so wrong about Max. In spite of the horrors of this evening, the fact that he wasn't having an affair had lifted a lead weight from around her heart. It was wrong to feel this way, because whatever Sean had done and no matter how he had frightened her, she was far from blameless, and this was something that she was going to have to face.

The police had arrived just as she finished explaining everything to Tom, and he had spoken to them. Nevertheless, she was an obvious suspect. They had found Sean's phone, with the message that she'd sent asking him to meet her here, at the farm, and she was covered in his blood. Tom had pointed out that the floor upstairs had been sawn through, and the hole covered in cardboard and straw so that it was invisible, but they hadn't found any tools of any description and she had no alibi. She hadn't seen a soul since she left work. She hadn't spoken to anybody, and she'd not been home when Max returned with the twins. In fact, she had been sitting outside the police station, but nobody would have seen her there.

Tom came towards her with the detective, a huge man, whom he'd called 'Steve'.

'Ellie, I'm sorry but you're going to have to go down to the station with Detective Inspector Corby here. I don't want you to worry too much, but they will have to arrest you. It's procedure, and under the circumstances they don't have much choice. But whatever you do, don't panic. Tell them the truth and we'll get it sorted, okay? I'll take Leo home, and she can get you some clean clothes. We'll bring them to you. We'll speak to Max too. What do you want us to tell him, Ellie?'

Before Ellie had a chance to answer, one of the other policemen came over and whispered in the inspector's ear. He nodded a couple of times, and turned to Tom.

'Apparently we have a very positive lead on the driver of the car in the Abbie Campbell accident. Have you got a moment, Tom?'

The detective inspector put his hand on Tom's elbow and guided him away from Ellie, but not before she had heard one name.

Charles Atkinson.

47

As Ellie was driven away in the back of a police car, Tom could feel Leo's rigid body beside him. He knew she was trying to deal with everything that the last few hours had thrown at her, but now she had one more thing to face. She had to talk to Max.

Tom put his arm firmly round her shoulders. She might try to shrug him off, but she needed to know that he was there and he was going to help.

'Come on, Leo. She's gone now, but it won't be for long. On the face of it, the evidence might be stacked against her, but she didn't do it. So it's only a matter of time.'

Surprisingly, Leo didn't move. She didn't exactly melt against him, but she didn't push him away either, so Tom let his arm rest there.

'What about a solicitor, Tom? Doesn't she need somebody?' Leo was looking straight ahead at the departing cars as they bumped over the ruts in the road.

'She said that the family solicitor wouldn't be up to the job, so I called somebody for her. I briefed him, and he won't let them keep her in any longer than necessary.'

As the last lights of the cars disappeared, Tom felt Leo sag against him, and he tightened his grip.

The crime scene guys were still busy in the barn, but Tom steered Leo towards his Jeep.

'Let's get you back to Willow Farm. We need to decide what we're going to say to Max.'

Leo stayed close by his side, but looked up at him.

'What about Ellie's car?' she asked, as if this were the most important thing in the world at the moment. She was in shock, and he knew it.

'The police will want both Ellie's and Sean's cars, so we'll have to leave them, I'm afraid. But it's good, Leo. They'll want to check if there's a saw in the boot, or traces of sawdust, and there won't be either—so it's good. Don't worry about it.'

Leo gave him a guilty glance at the mention of the sawdust, but he just squeezed her shoulder.

Even though it was a warm summer night, Tom felt her shudder under his arm, and he dropped a light kiss on her head, much as he would have done to Lucy. He dropped his arm from around her shoulders and opened the passenger door, guiding her gently into the Jeep.

By the time he had walked round the other side and got in, Leo had strapped herself in and was staring straight ahead.

'So what shall we do about Max? It doesn't seem like our place to tell him about Sean and what happened between him and Ellie. That should come from her, if she decides to tell him. What do you think?' Tom asked.

Leo turned towards Tom, and he could see that for once, she genuinely didn't have an answer.

'I don't know what to do. I honestly don't. And more to the point, I don't know what Ellie should do. Do you think she *should* tell him, or should she lie—tell him it was all in Sean's head?'

Tom took a deep breath, and blew it out soundlessly.

'I think there are two types of people who don't tell, and keep—or at least try to keep—the secret for life. There are those who have no sense of guilt whatsoever. They say nothing, then they think, "Phew, I got away with that!" and end up feeling pleased with themselves. Don't look at me like that, Leo. I know Ellie isn't that sort.'

Leo's expression relaxed, and Tom continued.

'There are others who think the guilt is theirs, and therefore they should be the ones to live with it for the rest of their lives, without damaging the person they love.'

Leo nodded, but looked sceptical.

'And the other way is to tell everything, right?' she asked.

'Yes. Some people believe that if you don't tell everything, you can never share the same intimacy, the same level of trust again. Others believe that by telling everything, you shatter that trust and it can never be rebuilt. Only the people concerned can make that judgement.'

'What would you do, Tom? Do you believe in total honesty, no matter what?'

Tom reached over and took Leo's hand in his. This was going to be difficult.

'I think lies are corrosive and if you're holding something back, you're holding back part of yourself. But . . . sometimes people have to keep secrets for other reasons. To protect things from their past, or people they've cared about.'

Leo hadn't removed her hand, but now she turned to look at him, her face expressionless. She was clearly waiting for him to explain.

'There are things in my past that I can never tell anybody. It's got nothing to do with infidelity or causing harm to another person. But I can never talk about it. It makes me wonder whether it will always be a barrier to a relationship in the future, but I have to live with it. It was my choice.'

Tom looked into Leo's sad and confused eyes, and had to turn away. He gently released his hand, switched on the ignition, and put the car into gear.

'This isn't about me, though. Perhaps that's a conversation for another time. This is about Ellie and Max, and we need to work out what we're going to say.'

He put his foot lightly on the accelerator and they moved down the rutted track, leaving the now brightly lit barn behind them.

The journey back to Max and Ellie's home only took a few minutes, and Leo had to force herself to concentrate on the task ahead of her. But it was hard, given what Tom had said. She would have thought that he was an open book, but something in his past was still with him and she couldn't help but wonder what it was. Tom was right to think that it might be a barrier to a relationship—most women hated secrets; or at least facts that were withheld from them.

Max, though. She had to focus on Max. What in God's name could they tell him? But the time for thinking had run out, because as they turned up the drive to Willow Farm, Max flung open the front door and came racing out towards them. Poor Max. He had absolutely no idea what was going on. She could see immediately how agitated he was.

As she wearily got out of the car, Leo saw Max's look of astonishment as he saw the blood on her clothes. There wasn't much, but Ellie had been soaked in it, and some had transferred to her white shirt.

'Ellie? Has something happened to Ellie? Why will nobody talk to me?' Max was almost crying.

It was Tom who spoke, his voice calm and reassuring.

'Ellie's fine, Max. She's not hurt, and this is not her blood. I promise you, she's fit and well. Can we talk inside, do you think? Leo needs to get changed and wash some of this blood off her, and then we can explain.'

Max's concern appeared to have hardly eased at all, but he stood back and indicated that they should go into the house.

Leo felt like going straight upstairs and having a long soak in the bath, but she needed to speak to Max first.

They walked silently down the hallway towards the kitchen, the hub of this house. Dumping her bag on the table, she leaned against the Aga for warmth as her body shuddered with ice-cold tremors of shock. Max's head was pivoting from side to side, looking first at Leo and then at Tom. Leo couldn't help it. She gave Tom a pleading look, which fortunately he interpreted correctly.

'Ellie found a body, Max. She found the body of Sean Summers. That's where the blood is from. Ellie tried to see if she could save him and got covered in his blood. Some of that transferred to Leo.'

Max sat down with a thump.

'Oh God, no. Poor Sean. Where did it happen? Was it a car crash? And where's Ellie now?'

'She's at the police station,' Tom responded. 'It looks as if there was foul play involved, but as Ellie was the only person there, she has to be questioned.'

Max looked dumbfounded, and hopelessly confused.

'Foul play? Do they suspect Ellie?'

Leo realised that, much as Tom was doing a decent job, she should be showing a bit of solidarity here. She walked across and crouched at Max's feet so her eyes were level with his.

'Sean was found at the old Haslett's Farm. It seems that somebody asked Ellie to set up a meeting with Sean. She probably thought they were thinking of renovating the farmhouse. When Sean got there, he fell through the floor of the barn onto some old farm equipment. I think the police said it was an ancient sickle bar mower or something, but the hole in the floor was pre-prepared. Ellie was thinking that the meeting all sounded a bit fishy, so went to check if everything was okay. That's when she found him.'

Max had gone white. He looked up at Tom, who was still standing with one hand leaning on the back of a dining chair.

'So they suspect Ellie?' It was more of a statement than a question. 'Why would Ellie want to kill Sean? Why would anybody? Except me, perhaps. I thought I would quite like to kill him earlier today.'

Tom pulled out the chair and sat down abruptly. Leaning forward and resting his forearms on his thighs, he looked at Max's pallid face.

'Look, mate, don't say that to anybody else. Okay? We know it wasn't Ellie, but there's nobody else in the frame at the moment, so don't put yourself there unless you did it. And I don't believe for a second you did, so don't say that. Okay?'

Could Max have found about Ellie and Sean? Leo didn't think so in the few hours since she'd spoken to him, but Tom wasn't to know that. She jumped in quickly, before Tom could inadvertently give anything away.

'Was it because of your deal, Max? Is that why you wanted to kill him?'

Leo looked at Tom as she spoke, hoping that he would interpret her 'shut up' signals. He gave an almost imperceptible nod.

'I wanted to pull out. I went to see him this afternoon, and I waited hours but he didn't come back.'

Tom was clearly trying to hide his confusion at this turn of events, and Leo thought he deserved some sort of explanation.

'Max had a business deal with Sean. They were going to develop some properties together. Max had invested quite a lot of money. That's what he's talking about.'

A bit of colour was returning to Max's face now, and Leo decided she should find him some brandy or whisky or something. She stood up from her crouched position, as Max started to talk.

'I've been a complete prat, Tom. I wanted to make some money—the whole "man the hunter" thing. You see, all of this,' he said, indicating the extravagant kitchen, but clearly meaning the whole property, 'was down to Ellie. And, plonker that I am, I wanted to equal her contribution to our life. I know, I know. Pathetic—but it seemed like such a great idea. Sean had some get-rich-quick scheme, which involved a site for which planning permission had proved difficult. But he'd been talking to Gary, and it appeared that things had changed, and something might be sorted. I provided the capital. Or rather, Ellie did. I was going to tell her all about it on Saturday—when everything was finalised and there was no going back.'

Finally, Max's overheard conversation in the pub made sense.

'Did you talk to Alannah about this, Max?'

He looked guilty just at the mention of her name.

'Another stupid mistake. When she asked me to keep her habit a secret, I told her I was already keeping one secret too many from Ellie, and I wasn't happy about it—but at least we were getting to the point where I would soon be able to tell her the truth.'

Knowing that Tom would be totally bewildered by this conversation, Leo gave him a slight smile that she hoped he would interpret as 'I'll tell you later'.

Max ran his fingers through his hair so that it stood up on end.

'I decided today that I wanted to pull out of the deal. It wasn't so much the building part—I thought that would be exciting. But I found out a couple of days ago exactly *what* had changed in terms of the planning. The laws hadn't changed at all, but Gary said that with a bit of a sweetener, he could push it all through. Ellie might have accepted my secret ambition to make some money with Sean, but *bribes*? She would flay me alive if she thought I'd been bribing anybody, and quite rightly so.'

Leo clinked the glasses as she grabbed three between the fingers of one hand.

'Be careful, Max. Don't forget Tom's a policeman,' she said, not entirely joking.

'Not tonight, I'm not. What happened?'

'I didn't know about the bribe until I'd already transferred the money. Sean had said that he thought planning regs had softened a bit, but it was only when the funds were in place that he mentioned Gary's role in all this, and I went ballistic. That's why I spent most of the afternoon hanging round outside his house. I couldn't go in—I didn't know what state Bella was in, and if she was drunk in charge of those kids, I didn't know whether I would have to report them to social services. That would have been the final straw, wouldn't it? I was going to go to see Gary too, but not until I'd spoken to Sean. What a sodding mess.'

Leo sloshed some whisky into three glasses, and pressed one into Max's hands. She couldn't imagine how he was feeling.

'Max, I know I said I wasn't a policeman tonight,' Tom said, 'but you're going to have to tell DI Corby about the deal between Sean and Gary. If Sean didn't pay Gary, or there was a third party involved that you don't know about—well, people have murdered for less.'

Max gave a defeated nod of the head.

'Fine. I'll speak to him. But what happens now, Tom? With Ellie, I mean.'

'Leo's going to sort her out some clean clothes. I think it's inevitable that she'll be arrested. They have the text she sent him to set up the meeting at the farm, and they have her there all covered in blood. But it'll be okay, Max. We'll find out who did it, I can promise you that. Ellie asked me to contact a solicitor for her, so we just need to offer as much support as we can.'

Leo put a glass down on the table in front of Tom, but much as he looked like he needed it, she wasn't surprised when he didn't touch it. No doubt he thought there would be some more driving ahead tonight. Clearly deciding that nobody would mind, Tom walked over to the kettle and switched it on.

48

Gary Bateman was seriously sick of his wife. She had no idea what his life was like, and how he had to cope with a crap job just so they could live in a half-decent house and not have to look like the riffraff of the village. Not that she would care. No aspirations—that was her problem. 'I just want to be happy' was her favourite moan. Stupid bitch.

He walked over to the curtains and released them from their absurd tiebacks. He didn't want the world to see what she had coming to her. Of all the brainless things to do. He couldn't believe it when she'd admitted she had told Leo Harris about the Porsche—what day he'd picked it up, and how long he'd had it. He always knew Penny would be the weak spot in the plan. The whole world thought he'd been driving a bright red Porsche since last Thursday, and then blob-gob Penny had to screw it up. It was okay her saying that Leo didn't notice or comment, but Leo was nobody's fool. He'd told Penny not to let her in the house. He knew Leo's type—they wheedled their way in until they found everybody's darkest secrets.

He was fairly confident that Ellie hadn't seen him that night—or at least not recognised his car. He would love to know what she'd been up to, but could never ask. He would have been in the clear. Nobody even knew he'd been out; well, at least nobody who was going to admit it. Fucking Penny.

He pulled the curtains together in anger, but just as they were closing he thought he saw some movement in the garden. He pulled one back again and peered out, but there was nothing there. *Must have been a cat*, he thought. Once he'd finished with Penny, he would go and chase the damn thing off. He didn't want a handful of cat crap next time he was weeding round the roses. Where the hell was that stupid Smudge when he was needed?

But he knew where he'd be. Lying by Penny's feet as she sobbed again. Christ, what a life.

Sean had improved things a bit with the wodge of cash that he'd handed over last night. He'd still not said who his private investor was, but Gary suspected it was that supercilious twat Charles. And wouldn't he like to stuff 'em both so that Charles lost his money. Nothing would give him greater pleasure. He had a good mind to delay the permission, just to put the wind up them both. Or maybe he would find some reason to refuse it altogether. Hah!

On second thoughts, he wouldn't want to get on the wrong side of Sean Summers. He appeared to be the gentle giant type, but Gary had seen his jaw set firm when somebody wound him up, and much as he could look after himself, he suspected that Sean might play dirty. He'd have to think about how best to deal with him—but for now, Penny needed teaching a lesson.

'Penny,' he yelled up the stairs. 'Get down these bloody stairs. Now. You don't want me to have to come and get you, do you?'

This last week had been shit. His cock tease of a would-be mistress had given him the brush-off too. She was talking bollocks, though. He was going to sort it after the weekend. Nobody treated Gary Bateman like crap.

'Penny! I'm not telling you again. Get down these fucking stairs.'

Penny appeared on the landing. Her face was blotchy with tears, but there was a stubborn set to her mouth that Gary didn't like at all.

'No,' she said. She put her hands on her hips, and stared down at him defiantly. 'I am not coming down to be brutalised by you. Leo says that I need to take the matter into my own hands and stand up for myself. I don't need to let you do this anymore.'

Gary charged up the stairs. She wasn't talking to him like this.

But Penny was too quick and raced for the bathroom door, locking it behind her. Smudge was attempting to stand guard, growling as fiercely as his little body would allow, his teeth bared as if ready to take a lump out of anyone who tried to get close to Penny. Gary was incensed.

'Stupid fucking dog,' he said, and lashed out with his right foot.

Smudge yelped in pain as Gary's foot connected with his fat little stomach, but as his body hit the wall he didn't make a sound. Nor did he move.

Penny screamed. 'What have you done to Smudge? Gary? What have you done?'

'Shit,' muttered Gary. Now look what she'd made him do. The girls would be devastated. He was going to have to say Smudge was knocked over. Penny wouldn't argue. She wouldn't bloody dare tell them what had really happened. *Shit.*

'I haven't finished with you by a long way, lady. Don't think that door is going to stand between us. I'm going to see to Smudge, but I'll be back.'

'What do you mean, see to him?' Penny was crying, but that was nothing new. He knew how she would be thinking now. She'd be cowering behind the door, wanting to come out to see to Smudge, but knowing what would happen to her if she did. Well, he had news for Penny. She could stay in there for now, but she was going to get what was due to her as soon as he'd dumped this shitty little dog in the middle of the road to be squashed by every passing car. See how she liked that.

The latch on the back gate was lifted, gently and silently. There was movement in the house—shouting, doors slamming.

He must be home.

The dark figure slipped through the opening and moved towards the shrubbery, where deep shadows would disguise the presence of an intruder. A copper beech tree stood proudly above the precisely trimmed bushes, its purple leaves rustling in the gentle breeze. Its low-hanging branches would provide a secure place to wait.

And waiting was the only option.

His car was in the drive. The keys were in the ignition. He didn't seem like a man so careless that he would leave them there all night. He would have to come out. And then it would be over. It had to end tonight.

He had to die, but it wasn't supposed to be like this. Another plan gone wrong. So many mistakes.

Why had Ellie sent Sean? She said she was upset about a stupid mistake with a man. He had forced her to go out and meet him after midnight on Friday, and he kept leaving her yellow roses to let her know he was thinking of her. It was all there—in her text.

But I saw who took her the rose. He cut it himself. It was Gary—the bastard who knocked Abbie over. The one man who can blow my life apart.

It didn't matter that Sean was dead. All that mattered was killing the right person now.

There was more shouting from inside the house, and a muffled cry of distress. A dark silhouette passed in front of an upstairs window, walking hurriedly. A light came on in the kitchen, but the blinds hid the identity of whoever was there.

The back door was abruptly flung open, so hard that it crashed against the kitchen units, sending glasses toppling. The sound of their shattering reached the black depths of the shrubbery along with a muttered expletive.

'Fuck.'

He was carrying what looked like a small dog, and there was no time to waste. This might be the only opportunity.

The intruder took a step forward, and the light from the open doorway glinted off the steel of the knife.

'Who's there?' Gary shouted. 'What do you want?'

The move had been made too soon. Gary was close to the door and could be back inside in seconds. But there was no turning back now.

The intruder stepped farther into the light.

'Shit,' Gary said. 'It's you. What the fuck are you doing hiding out here in the garden? You nearly gave me a sodding heart attack.' The relief was clear in his voice. No threat, then. Is that what he honestly thought?

The intruder moved closer, hiding the knife from view.

Gary was beginning to look wary. *As well he might.* His face changed as he took in the outfit—solid black from head to toe. No balaclava tonight—that wasn't necessary. It had never been the intention to stay invisible for long.

'What do you want?' Gary asked, a hint of nervousness entering his voice as he advanced towards the intruder.

Good. He was moving away from the door.

'I've come for *you.*'

Silence. Gary could never have believed that this was a casual visit, and confusion shone in his eyes.

'You've come for *me*?'

'I know what you did. I was watching. Didn't you see her? Or were you too drunk to see the road?'

Gary pulled the little dog closer to him, as if for comfort.

'I don't know what you're talking about, or what you think you know. But you've got it all wrong.'

'I've got *nothing* wrong. I was *there.* I watched you from the woods. I saw you hit her, and I saw you drag her by her ankles to the side of the road. But you saw me too, didn't you? You looked into the woods—straight at me. You've been keeping quiet to save your own skin.'

Gary's natural arrogance briefly resurfaced.

'What's it to you, anyway? And you weren't in the woods. That's a lie.' Gary took a step towards the dark figure.

Come on, Gary—get closer.

'We're not here to talk about me. But I don't trust you to keep your mouth shut. When they find you—and they will—you'll send them to me, and everybody will know who I really am. And once again, I'll be the focus of their unfair hatred.'

It was clear that Gary had the scent of danger, because he was stealthily walking forward, and the two of them began to slowly circle.

Perfect. You're a fool, Gary—you've let me get between you and the light.

With a sudden shout, Gary dropped the still body of the dog onto the grass and lunged towards the figure, his arms outstretched and reaching for the neck.

It was the last move he made. The knife was out in a flash, and driven hard into his stomach.

'She was *mine*. Mine. She would have come back—I could have convinced her. But you took away my only chance.'

The knife was withdrawn and plunged again, higher up between his ribs.

Gary crumpled to his knees and fell forward, driving the knife farther in.

A foot came out and flicked him over so the knife could be withdrawn, and the intruder calmly and purposefully wiped the blood from the knife on the grass.

Gary's attacker opened the back gate and started down the drive, keeping close to the wall to avoid being seen. The car was parked at the end of the cul-de-sac—far enough away not to be noticed.

In an explosion of sound on this quiet street, as if from nowhere two cars came speeding down the narrow road and screeched to a halt, parking diagonally and blocking any exit. A man and a woman alighted from the front car and two police officers got out of the second one, taking up a position by its bonnet with arms folded. Nobody was getting out of this road either on foot, or by car.

Shit.

There could be only one reason for this. They must have found out about Gary. Somehow, they must know that he was the driver of the hit-and-run vehicle. How they knew was a different matter, but there was only one way out of the close—by passing the two policemen standing by their car. Quickly turning back into the garden and stepping over Gary's supine body, the attacker looked around. There was no escape.

High fences bordered the garden, with no obvious way of getting over. Eyes that were by now accustomed to the dark flicked around the perimeter, looking for a gate. Nothing.

Fuck. I'm trapped.

But what was that? The light from the open back door was picking up the reflection of something metallic—some writing—and it was just possible to see the shape of an object up against the fence at the end of the garden.

The front doorbell pealed. It would only be a matter of moments until somebody came around the back and found Gary's body. Creeping as quickly but as silently as possible towards the shape and the metallic glint, the attacker was finally able to make out the lettering.

Smudge.

The cheap, glittery letters were stuck onto the front of a very smart kennel that seemed way too big for such a small dog.

Clutching the knife firmly in one hand, the dark figure clambered onto the top of the kennel, grasped the top of the fence, and with a grunt managed to roll over the top, crashing painfully into the adjoining garden. But the car was still there, trapped at the end of the cul-de-sac, and it wouldn't take the police long to work it out and come looking.

49

Leo had finally left Max and Tom to a serious conversation about police procedure, as Max tried to understand exactly what would be happening to Ellie. She knew she couldn't afford the luxury of a bath now. She needed to give support to Max and be available if Ellie needed her, so she quickly washed any visible blood off her body, and pulled on the first clothes she could find.

As she made her way back downstairs, hugging some jeans and a T-shirt for Ellie to her chest, the phone was ringing in the hall. Hoping that it would be Ellie to say that she could come home, Leo picked it up.

'Hello,' she said. 'Ellie?'

'Leo—thank goodness I've managed to get through. What's going on with all your phones? I haven't been able to phone Max for days, and he hasn't phoned me either.' It was Patrick.

'Sorry, Pat, I know nothing about that, but now's not a good time to talk to Max. I'm sorry. I can't explain right now, but I'm sure somebody will talk to you tomorrow and let you know what's going on.'

'Actually, I only want a phone number and you might be able to help. Do you have that policeman's number—you know, Max's new neighbour, Tom?'

'I can do better than that, Pat. He's here. But it's all a bit tricky just now. Will tomorrow do?'

'Sorry, Leo. It won't. I think I've found something important. It's about Abbie Campbell. But I'm not sure if I'm getting excited about nothing. Maybe I'm reading too much into stuff, which is why I thought I would speak to Tom first. I don't know how long my money will last in this bloody thing. Probably been vandalised in some way.'

There was a brief pause.

'Are you ringing from a phone box, Pat?'

'I can't explain, Leo. I'll tell Tom what I think, and see if he decides that I'm crazy. I need him to come to the house, though. Mimi's house. Can you ask him, please? I can't hang on now, but if he can come, it would be very helpful.'

The line went dead.

Leo tried speaking into the phone a couple of times, but got no response. She wasn't sure she could deal with anything else tonight, but wearily she made her way to the kitchen.

Tom looked up gratefully when Leo entered, and she felt terrible for leaving him alone to deal with Max's distress.

'That was Pat on the phone. I was hoping it was Ellie.'

'What did you tell him?' Max asked. 'I can't even think about calling him back now, and anyway every time I've tried to call him, the line's cut off straight away.'

'He was asking for Tom's number, actually. He wants some advice. But it was odd, because he was calling from a phone box. Weird, don't you think?'

Max looked indifferent.

'Well, odd or not, he would like you to go round to Mimi's, Tom.'

Tom's lip curled up at the corner in a 'you must be joking' kind of expression.

'What, *now*?' he said.

'It seems so, yes.' Leo repeated everything that Patrick had said, and Tom looked at Max.

'I don't want to leave you, Max. But if it really is about Abbie I think we need to work out who's best placed to do what.'

Max looked expectantly at Tom, and it was clear that his mind wasn't able to compute the options, so Tom continued.

'Somebody has to stay here with the twins, of course. I need to go to Pat's now, unfortunately, and somebody needs to take clothes to Ellie. I think on balance that you'd be better waiting here, Max. Ellie might come back—the solicitor will bring her home as soon as he can get her out of there. You've had a drink, and you don't want to roll up at the police station smelling of whisky, even if you *are* under the limit. Leo—can you take Ellie's clothes?'

Leo shook her head.

'You'll never find Mimi's house. It's a maze of streets and you've no sat nav in the Jeep. Why don't I come with you, and after you've seen Pat we'll take Ellie's clothes. Hopefully he won't need you for long—it sounded like he just needs your advice. What do you think?'

They both looked at Max, who just gave them a confused nod. Leo could feel his pain and shock. His face was devoid of shape and colour, as if the skin were moulded to the bone, and his eyes were huge and lost. She picked up her bag from the table and leant over Max, putting her arm around his shoulders in a tight squeeze.

'It's going to be okay, Max. I promise. We'll get everything sorted out.' It spoke volumes that Max didn't betray any surprise at Leo's gesture of affection.

'We'll be back as soon as we can, and we've got mobiles with us. I'll get Leo to text my number to you while we're driving. Okay?'

Max was staring at them without seeing, but he bobbed his head in acknowledgement.

'Sorry we've ended up in this heap of junk again,' Tom said as they clambered into the Jeep. 'I could go back for the car, but it would waste a bit of time. Are you okay with this?'

'It's not a date, Tom. I don't think we're out to impress each other.'

Despite the circumstances, Tom almost smiled. Leo reminded him of an arrow, straight and true. Not just because of her tall, slender body, but because she didn't mess around. She got straight to the point by the shortest possible means, and would cut through any junk that got in the way. Incapable of dissembling, it would seem. He liked it.

'I meant what I said, you know,' Tom said. 'We *will* fix this. Ellie will be okay.'

'I hope you're right. It doesn't help poor Sean, though. I just can't make sense of any of it.'

Leo rested her head against the back of the seat and closed her eyes, but Tom could see the furrows of tension that hardened her face. This, of course, wasn't the only thing she'd had to face in the last few hours.

'I'm so sorry that I had to break the news of your father today. With everything else, the timing was pretty crap, wasn't it?'

'Do you know, I'd almost forgotten about that,' Leo answered. 'All I can think about is Ellie.'

'Have you decided what you're going to tell her? It's going to be unbelievably hard for her to hear just at the moment.'

'I know. It's difficult. Her mother kept it from her and lied about it, so although she didn't have the highest opinion of her mother, that will hurt too.'

Tom glanced at Leo.

'You know, you might find this difficult to believe, but as I said before, it could be that she had yours and Ellie's best interests at heart. She might not have wanted to upset you.'

Leo said nothing, but leaned forward and peered out of the windscreen, looking towards the sky.

'What's up? What are you looking for?' Tom asked, trying to keep his eyes on the road, but flicking his gaze to Leo.

'There it is!' she said with mock glee, pointing upwards. 'Now I see it!'

Tom couldn't see anything.

'What? What are you talking about, Leo?'

'A flying pig,' she said with a sour expression, leaning back with a thump against the seat.

'Very funny,' Tom said. 'Okay, I'll stop trying to give credit where maybe it's not due, and perhaps knowing your dad's dead is one thing. But finding out how and where he died is going to be hard on her at the moment, even if we leave out the bit about *why* he was there.'

Leo's head was hard back against the headrest, and she was staring straight ahead.

'I know. I *am* going to have to tell her. But not now. I'll tell her that you've found out that he's dead and when, but I'll probably say that's all you could find out—and convince her that it's enough. When she's got her emotional strength back I'll tell her the rest. We mustn't have any more secrets. But she's too fragile at the moment, and she's going to have so much else to deal with. She's not as tough as me.'

Tom resisted the urge to comment. Leo had one of the toughest and most resistant exteriors he had ever come across. Which perhaps made the softness that was lurking beneath infinitely more interesting.

'You need to turn left here,' she said. 'We're nearly there, but this is the tricky bit.'

As Leo gave him brief but concise instructions, Tom turned his thoughts to Pat. What could he want that was so urgent? He didn't like the feel of this.

'When we get there, I want you to stay in the car,' he said to Leo.

'Why?'

'Because I don't know what's going on, and until I do it's better if you stay out of harm's way.'

Leo turned to look at him without saying a word, and he cast a quick glance in her direction.

'I know you think I'm mad but just do it, please. There was something about Pat that seemed a bit shifty at Ellie and Max's dinner party. I don't know what it was, but he didn't come across like a totally honest sort of man to me.'

Leo gave a derisive snort.

'I'm not surprised. Ellie said that at every break in the eating he was sneaking out to phone his wife, or text her. He might have physically left her, but he's still there mentally. No wonder he looked like he was up to something. He was. I almost feel sorry for Mimi. I know he's Max's friend, but he's not coming out of all this in a very good light, is he?'

'I'll reserve judgement. I don't know any of them. But nevertheless, if he has something to tell me or talk to me about it might be easier if you're not there.'

Tom knew without looking that Leo would be casting her eyes up in irritation, but she said nothing else and continued to give him instructions until they pulled up in one of the parking spots close to Mimi's house.

'Mimi must be out,' Leo said. 'Her car's not here.'

Pulling on the handbrake, Tom turned to Leo.

'Maybe that's a good thing. Listen, I'll be as quick as I can. Don't run away, will you?' he smiled and leaned across to give Leo a brief peck on the cheek. He didn't know why he did it but it felt like the most natural thing in the world, and she didn't pull away.

50

Pat was waiting by the open door, obviously anticipating Tom's arrival, but he was casting anxious glances around the neighbourhood.

'Everything okay, Pat?' Tom asked.

'Sorry—I was checking to see if Mimi was back yet. I need to talk to you before she gets here. You'd better come in.'

Tom walked into the small sitting room as Pat shut the door and walked over to the computer, where a screen saver was drawing vaguely nauseating patterns in blue and green.

'I'm sorry to drag you out tonight. I hope you weren't busy.'

Tom smiled to himself, but shook his head.

'I do have somewhere that I need to be shortly, but Leo said you sounded worried on the phone.'

'I wanted to show you this, to see what you think,' Pat said, pointing to the laptop on the computer desk. He walked across and sat down. Tom stood behind and watched over his shoulder.

Pat rolled the mouse and the screen burst into life, revealing what appeared to be a list of phone numbers, some of which had the word 'blacklist' next to them. The numbers didn't mean anything to Tom, although one looked vaguely familiar.

'These numbers are all on my phone,' Pat said. 'Those that are marked "blacklist" are Georgia, Max, and Ellie.'

It must have been Ellie's number that he recognised from when she'd called earlier.

There was a menu at the top of the screen that offered other options, such as SMS, e-mail, and GPS. Pat selected SMS.

'This is a list of all the texts that I've received and sent for the last week or so. There's even a section for texts that I *didn't* send, but have been sent as if from my phone. What does it mean, Tom?'

Tom knew immediately what it meant, although this was by far the most sophisticated of the software applications that he had seen.

'Where's your phone, Pat? I want to show you something.'

Pat fished his mobile from the pocket of his trousers and put it on the desk.

'This is why I didn't call Max's house from my mobile. I'm not sure I understand what's happening, but I'm sure that I don't like it.'

Tom leaned forward towards the desk.

'You did right. But can I have control of the mouse for a moment? Hold your phone up as if you are looking at it, but watch the computer screen.'

Pat lifted the phone until it was in front, but slightly to the side of his face so that it wasn't blocking sight of the monitor.

Tom rolled the mouse to the menu and clicked.

'Shit!' Pat stared at the computer screen, as a mirror image of his horrified face stared back. He looked at Tom. 'What did you do?'

'I switched your camera on remotely. Look at your phone.'

Pat glanced at his phone, and could see that the camera light was on.

'How did you do that?' he asked.

'Your phone has been tampered with and an app has been installed. I can switch on your camera wherever you are, and whatever the camera can see will be displayed on the screen. I can even switch on the speaker remotely so that I can hear every word you're saying.'

Tom looked at Pat with sympathy. Mimi had clearly not trusted him an inch, and from what Leo said she was probably right not to. But installing this sort of application on his phone was extreme. She would have known his every move, and would have been able to manipulate all his relationships by blocking calls, sending fake texts as if they were from him—the works.

'Bloody hell,' Pat said. 'What a mess. It feels as if she's invaded my body—knows my every thought and shares every moment I have with somebody else. No wonder she knew every time I went to Georgia's. She always phoned me on some pretext within moments of me arriving.'

'That would be from your GPS. It tracks where you are. She would have been able to log everything on here, but it would also have sent alerts to her own mobile every time you sent a text. How did you find this, Pat? Wasn't there a password?' Tom asked.

'Yeah, but this is an old computer from school. They all have password logger software on them. She didn't know it was there—why would she? So I called up the password for her user area. The daft thing was, I was only looking at the cricket scores, but when I saw how many times she'd been on this site, I decided to have a look. That's where the logs of all my mobile activity were.'

Pat closed the computer window and turned round in his chair.

'Sorry to drag you into this, Tom. I just wanted to know if I was going mad or not. It's an awful thing to say, and no reflection on the child, but I wish to God that Mimi wasn't pregnant. I can't live with somebody who has so little faith in me.'

Tom couldn't think of a single appropriate thing to say, so he changed the subject.

'Leo said you mentioned Abbie Campbell when you phoned, Pat. This is actually about you and Mimi, and I can't see where Abbie comes into it. Did Leo misunderstand?' He was trying hard to curb his irritation. He didn't need to sort out Pat's domestic issues at this moment.

'I'm sorry,' Pat said, turning back to the computer. 'I got a bit carried away with the mobile stuff, but it *is* relevant. When I was looking through Mimi's files to see what else she might be hiding, I decided to look in the trash folder. I found some photos. They're not of anybody I know, but they're all of young girls. And one of them is called Chloe.'

Leo wasn't happy sitting out here on her own. Too much thinking time. Tom had been inside the house for what felt like hours, when in actual fact it was probably more like ten minutes. It was ridiculous, making her wait in the car. She wasn't in any danger from Pat. The trouble was, with nothing to do and nobody to talk to, all she could do was think—and all this soul-searching wasn't doing her any good at all.

She had been so wrong about Ellie, believing that she'd been meeting *Gary* that night. Of all the ridiculous ideas. And Ellie had been wrong about Max too. How had they all got into such a mess?

But none of it answered the burning question—who killed Sean? And why, for God's sake?

Leo fought to dismiss the image of Sean's mangled body from her memory, but she only succeeded in replacing one grim thought with another. Try as she might, she couldn't eradicate from her mind the facts about her father that Tom had shared earlier, and now that she was alone they hovered at the edge of her consciousness like black vultures, ready to swoop.

She may not have thought much of him as a man, or at least any love she may have felt for him had been violently suppressed after she had been offloaded onto Ellie's mother. As she had grown older and begun to understand what he'd done to her own mum, the last remaining fragments of affection had turned to contempt. But who wanted to live with the knowledge that they had been fathered by a *monster*? How could she come to terms with the fact that the man her mother had loved had such a dark side? The thought made her feel physically sick, and she was terrified of what it would do to Ellie.

It was strange, but since Tom had told her about him she could now vividly recall details of her father that had eluded her only a couple of short days ago. He would have been just over fifty when he disappeared for the last time, but he dressed like a much younger man. Or at least, he tried to. She remembered smart suits on work days, and brightly coloured ties. But when he went out in the evening—which she seemed to think he did practically every night—his jeans were that bit too tight in an era where others were wearing looser clothes, and his leather bomber jacket always made her think that he was trying that bit too hard. But maybe all teenage girls feel like that about their fathers. She did remember some girls at school saying her dad was cool, but she wasn't impressed. She had felt vaguely embarrassed by him.

Now, she was ashamed, although shame had already played a huge part in her life so it was nothing new. Ever since arriving in this village, she had been viewed as something of a dirty secret, but she had learned to hold her head high and ignore what other people thought. If all of this ever came out, she would just have to do the same again.

The silence in the car was broken by the ringing of a phone. She knew it wasn't hers and realised that Tom must have left his in the side pocket of the Jeep. She leaned across, but couldn't reach it.

'Bugger.' She shuffled onto her knees, and managed to scuttle across the wide central console and squeeze down behind the steering wheel. After all that, when she picked the phone up it stopped ringing. Looking at the display to see if it was Max, she noticed that it said 'Steve'. Wasn't he the detective that Tom had been talking to? If it was important, no doubt he would phone back.

Deciding that she would stay on this side of the Jeep until Tom had finished with Pat, she switched the ignition on to get power, and started to fiddle with the radio. She needed something to drown out her thoughts. Her uninformed twiddling resulted in a burst of loud music, and she couldn't for the life of her find where to switch the volume down. She felt a brief draught on her neck from somewhere just as she found the right button and managed to take the level down to something tolerable.

And then she felt it. She knew, without looking, that somebody was in the car behind her. She could feel their breath changing the atmosphere, and every inch of her flesh tingled with fear. For a second, she didn't move. She felt a shifting of the air behind her as she groped blindly for the door handle.

Pat opened the folder, and Tom could see a number of image files.

'There's a whole folder of pictures of girls at around the same age here—but it was the name Chloe that made me think. Of course, it could be a coincidence, but I thought I should ask you before wasting anybody else's time.'

'Can I grab your chair for a moment, Pat?'

Sitting down quickly and leaning towards the computer, Tom checked out all the files that Pat had found and confirmed that he was right. They were all pictures of girls around fourteen or fifteen years old. All the photos were low resolution, so it was unlikely that they were original. Tom guessed that they had been grabbed from social network sites.

He checked the browser history, but couldn't find what he was looking for. That wasn't much of a surprise. If his guess was correct, there was a degree of expertise here. So why hadn't she emptied the trash and cleaned her computer?

Tom had an idea.

'What are you looking for?' Pat asked.

'I'm no expert,' he said, 'but I know a bit about computer security. My brother made an absolute fortune out of it before he died, and I did listen occasionally to some of the less technical stuff he told me about. Do you mind if I have a look round? There's a couple of things that I want to check.'

Tom clicked a few items on the screen and opened a few menus. It only took him three or four minutes.

'Bingo,' he said.

As Leo reached for the door handle, there was a rush of movement from behind her left shoulder.

'Don't even think about it,' said a voice that she instantly recognised. A voice that usually sounded so timid but which Leo had acknowledged yesterday was a clever act. Still, she would never have expected this.

A sharp, cold point was stuck into the side of her neck, and she could smell the hot, sweaty body that was crouched in the gap between the front seats. 'Make any move and this knife goes through your throat.'

Leo tried to keep calm.

'What do you want, Mimi? If it's money, take my bag. Take what you want, and go.'

'I need a car. The police will be here soon, so I need to get away, and you're going to take me.'

The knife pressed sharply against Leo's neck, and she could feel drops of warm blood running down to her collarbone.

'Why don't I just get out? Take the car. You can have it.'

She heard a snigger in her left ear, as if that was a ridiculous suggestion.

'Because I'm not thick. You'd run straight to your policeman, and this heap of a car would be picked up in no time. If Tom comes out and you're gone, he'll assume that you were in a strop and drove off without him, because you *are* a stroppy bitch, aren't you? Besides—you're my insurance. You can be my hostage. But I *will* get away, Leo—it's up to you whether you help me or you die right now.'

The mirthless laughter from behind made Leo's blood turn to ice.

Tom turned round on the computer chair and looked at Pat's dazed expression.

'It's all there. There's no doubt about it, I'm sorry to say. Mimi has been setting up false identities on Facebook. She's the Chloe that the police have been looking for. She knows her way around this stuff somehow, because she'd hidden her tracks pretty well for an amateur. She's disguised her IP address, and erased most of the files completely. I couldn't understand why some files were still there when she had been so careful about everything else. But she'd set her files to be wiped on restart, so it was either a mistake or she forgot to shut down.'

'That would be my fault, I guess.' Patrick admitted. 'She started the shutdown process as she was going out, but I interrupted it so I could log onto BBC Sport.'

Tom stood up.

'I need to make a call, I'm afraid.'

Pat ignored Tom. He looked totally baffled. 'Why would she do this? Why would she pretend to be somebody called Chloe so that she could be friends with Abbie Campbell? It doesn't make any sense. And why all those other fake names too?'

'She had to seem real to Abbie. What do you know about her past?'

Pat couldn't quite meet Tom's eyes.

'Not much. I wasn't that interested. I had a senseless fling with her that lasted about five minutes. I was feeling sorry for myself. Pathetic. But what could a woman like Mimi want with a young girl like Abbie? Do you think she was in cahoots with a man?'

'I don't know, Pat. It's very unusual for a woman to abduct a child, so she could have had an accomplice. And I imagine we're not going to know until we find her. I need to get the police here.'

Tom fished around in his pocket for his mobile while Pat continued to talk.

'I wish I'd never met her. If Georgia hadn't found out, everything would've been fine. But she got some anonymous text. Mimi swore it wasn't her, but now we know differently I suppose. I never asked Mimi much about herself. If she hadn't been pregnant, I was going to move out this week.'

Tom was getting slightly sick of Pat feeling sorry for himself. This wasn't about him and Georgia.

Where the hell was his mobile?

'Sorry, Pat, but I need to phone the police and I need to do it now. You've got to stop thinking about what might have been, and think about where Mimi might have gone. *And* where she came from,' Tom said.

Tom tried his other pocket, attempting to stem his irritation at Pat's feeble behaviour. In the end, he gave up the search.

'We have a problem. I must have left my phone in the car. We can't use yours because we mustn't alert Mimi. Do you have any idea at all where she is, because if she comes home we're going to have to keep her here until the police arrive.'

'She went out at about six, and I haven't seen her since. We weren't speaking. She was mad about something, and I just assumed it was something that I'd done. I didn't bother to ask.'

'Right, well, you wait there and I'll go and get my phone.'

'Drive, Leo, or I'll kill you now.'

'No you won't. If you didn't need me, you'd have killed me already.'

Leo could feel Mimi's sweaty body as she manoeuvred herself farther into the gap between the front seats. She felt hot breath, fetid with nerves, settling damply on the side of her face, and the knife was pressed harder against her throat. Leo knew she was going to die, but not yet if she could help it.

Mimi's voice had turned brittle with emotion.

'All you smug bastards did everything possible to break me and Patrick up, didn't you? He wasn't part of the plan, but he was a bonus—until I found out what he's really like. But if Gary hadn't wrecked everything, I could have made it work—all of it. Me and Patrick. Me and Abbie. I could have seen my Abbie in secret. She'd have liked that.'

Abbie? What could this possibly have to do with Abbie?

'You didn't know, did you? None of you guessed that she was mine. My little girl. I was going to make it up to her, all of it. She was my baby. I just wanted to see her—to show that her mother isn't a monster. It wasn't my fault Jessica died—none of it was my fault. I wanted her to understand.'

Mimi was Abbie's *mother?* Leo had no idea who Jessica was, but she knew that time was running out.

'Abbie liked me when I was Chloe. But the real me wasn't good enough, was it? Not good enough for Abbie, not good enough for Jessica, not good enough for Patrick. She said she hated me, do you know that? She *screamed* when I tried to touch her. I wish she hadn't done that.'

Leo could sense a blistering anger, tinged with the heartbreak of a woman who had no illusions left.

'Get moving, Leo, or I'll enjoy every moment of watching you die. You won't be the first person I've killed tonight.' The knife was prodded harder, and Leo felt a new stab of pain as the point penetrated farther into her flesh.

'I'm not driving anywhere with a knife pressed against my neck. If I go over a bump in the road, you'll slice through my carotid artery. Move the knife, and I'll drive you wherever you want to go.'

There was a pause.

'Hands on the wheel. The top. Hold it tight, and lean your head against your hands. *Now*, Leo.'

She felt a new stab of pain as the knife twisted in the open wound. She did as she was told. But she wanted to keep Mimi talking.

'Why Sean? Why did he have to die?' Leo asked, her voice muffled as it rested on her arms.

The knife never leaving her neck, she felt a shuffling, and realised that Mimi was climbing through the gap in the seats and into the front. If she could just time it right . . .

'Don't move a muscle—I know what you're thinking,' Mimi growled as the knife jabbed harder. Leo winced in pain, but Mimi was too busy talking.

'Sean was a case of mistaken identity. I was sure Ellie was screwing that cold-blooded, murdering bastard Gary, and only she could deliver him to me on a plate. It was *Gary* I wanted. He knew I was there. He knew I was the one that had taken Abbie.'

Mimi had only needed seconds to climb into the front seat, and the pressure on the knife never eased up all the time she was talking. Had Mimi slipped, Leo knew it would all have been over.

'Sit back. Seat belt on,' she said.

'Why?' Leo asked.

'I keep telling you, I'm not stupid. You can't leap out of the car at traffic lights if you've got your seat belt on. And I'll be watching. You're my insurance if we get stopped.'

The position of the knife was adjusted so that it hovered over Leo's hand as she fastened the seat belt.

'Where do you want me to drive to?' Leo asked.

'Put the car in gear, and leave your left hand on the gear stick. Just get off this crummy estate, and then I'll tell you.'

Leo put the car into reverse, and felt a piercing pain as the knife cut into the thin skin on the back of her hand. Steering one-handed and without looking to her left for fear of seeing the madness in those watching eyes, just inches from her own face, she backed out of the space using mirrors and a lot of hope. She knew beyond doubt that as soon as she had driven to whatever destination was chosen, she would be dead.

She had to think.

Then she remembered something that Tom had said to her when they left his house earlier this evening. She had one chance. It was going to hurt, but there was only one thing she could do.

She put the car into gear, and slammed her foot hard on the accelerator.

Tom had only taken two steps towards the door when they heard the sound of a car revving loudly and accelerating down the road. The noise lasted no more than five seconds before there was an explosion of sound as metal hit brick with considerable force.

He finally knew what it meant when somebody says their heart leapt into their throat, and he was out of the door and running in an instant. All he could see were the taillights of his Jeep, and smoke pouring from the bonnet, which was buckled to half its size against the brick wall that marked the entrance to this part of the estate.

"Leo!' he shouted, fear giving him speed he didn't know he still had.

'Pat, call an ambulance. Don't just stand there. Call a fucking ambulance,' he yelled over his shoulder as he ran. And yet he knew that Pat would be standing watching, open-mouthed.

Fortunately the noise had brought other people from their homes, and out of the corner of his eye he saw a more alert neighbour grab his phone as Tom covered the four hundred yards to the car. He raced towards the passenger door. That's where he'd left Leo. He gulped back of cry of dismay when he was still fifty yards away. He could see that she hadn't been wearing a seat belt, and with no airbag her head was protruding through a hole in the windscreen, her neck at an odd angle that in Tom's experience meant only one thing.

'Oh no,' he whispered. 'Oh God, *no*.'

He made it to the car and scrambled onto the twisted metal of the bonnet. He could see little but the upper half of a body, and blood. He was blocking out the light from the street lamp behind him, and he tried to pull himself round, sliding all the time on the hot surface. He needed to move so that the light shone on Leo's face, so he could get to her and check if she was alive. Then he saw it. The hair covering the face was blond and limp, not Leo's thick dark tresses. He knew instantly who this was, and a brief hope flared in his chest.

He slithered across the bonnet and dropped down at the driver's side, frantically pulling on the handle. The door wouldn't budge, but he could just make out Leo's crumpled form behind the steering wheel. She wasn't moving, and her head had lolled forward onto the now deflated airbag.

Tom tried the rear door. It only opened inches, but he yanked it as hard as he could, and slid in through the gap. He heard his shirt rip, and felt a sharp sting of pain as a piece of exposed metal tore into the flesh covering his ribs, but he barely noticed. Climbing onto his knees on the back seat, he leaned forward very gently so as not to disturb Leo's body or the seat in case her spine was injured.

He held onto the grab bar with his right hand to steady himself, and with his left hand felt for Leo's neck, and her pulse.

51

I'm awake. I can't speak, but I can hear sounds—people talking, and I can feel soft hands stroking my arm. I know I'm going to get better.

I still have dreams, though. I dream about Jessica and the day she died.

We're on our own in the room. The Mother has gone out and we're making a den. But Jessica is frightened.

'It's okay, Jess—it's just a den. It won't be like the cupboard, I promise. We've got to play quietly or we'll be reported.'

I don't know what that means, but I think it's bad.

Jess is crying. Her arm is sore. The Mother doesn't like it when we cry. She pushed me down the stairs the day before, and now my arm looks funny and really hurts. But it'll get better. It did last time. I won't cry again.

I hear her coming, and know that we have to be very, very good. I pull Jess close to me.

Then we're in the cupboard. We've been good, but it doesn't matter—we still have to hide away. Jess doesn't look right. There's something wrong. And suddenly I'm kicking, kicking, kicking.

Somebody is screaming. I'm being dragged across the floor by my ankles. The fat, greasy man is pulling the tape off Jess's mouth and sick is pouring out. Jessica isn't moving.

The man is getting dressed—and nobody's helping Jess. I try to shout, but he runs out of the door as if he's being chased by The Bogeyman. The Mother is wrapping Jessica in a dirty sheet. I try to scream, 'Help her, help her,' but I can't. My mouth is taped shut.

I can't run for help. My legs are tied together, but The Grunter's left the door open, so I roll towards it. The Mother sees me.

'Come here, you little bastard,' she shouts.

I can hear somebody on the stairs. The Mother drops Jessica, my little Jess, on the floor and runs towards me. She's got my feet, and she's pulling me away from the door. But she's too late. Somebody's got hold of me. Somebody's taking the tape off my mouth and hugging me close to their body. There is only one word that I can say.

'Jessica.'

I remember now. I remember it all. Each time I dream about Jess and what happened, Mum tells me I'm safe. I'll never hear that voice again.

But I did. Chloe's mum. It was her.

In the end, it was the voice that I recognised.

I thought I'd escaped, but then she was here—here in the hospital where I was safe. That voice—again, whispering in my ear, so close to my head.

'My little Abbie. I didn't want to hurt you—I wanted to be friends—our secret.'

I couldn't speak, but I wanted to scream and scream.

'I shouldn't have come for you on Friday. I got greedy. Chloe could have been your best friend, and as long as we never met, you would never have known it was me.'

A hand reached out and stroked the hair back from my face. Those dry lips brushed my forehead. I was trying to cry out, but I couldn't. I knew the sounds weren't coming out.

'And each day when you told me what you were doing, where you were going, I could have watched you. I've been watching you for months, but you never saw me.'

I tried to move my body, to turn away from those horrible hands. The voice turned harsh.

'You didn't want me, though, did you? You wouldn't let me explain. You were just like everybody else, judging me and finding me wanting. You're the reason I went to prison, but I forgave you for that. Now it'll be just like last time. You'll tell lies about me, won't you? You'll say that I abducted you—but that's not true. We were friends, you and me.'

I felt a pillow being yanked from under my head.

'You left me no choice, Abbie. You should have loved me. It wasn't much to ask.'

Suddenly there was a lot of noise, a breeze as the curtain was whisked back, and then she was gone.

Or that's what I thought.

I heard a voice saying, 'Be still. Be quiet.' A hand was stroking my head. I knew it wasn't the same voice, but for a moment I thought she was back. I thought The Mother was back.

52

Two weeks later

A Single Step: the blog of Leo Harris

Going all the way

Forgive me for my recent silence. An injury has prevented me from typing, but today I have a scribe—my beautiful sister, Ellie—and I feel compelled to write about truth, because 'truth' surpasses all other qualities in terms of its importance within a relationship.

How often have you excused a small omission, a white lie, or a twisted version of the truth on the grounds that 'what he doesn't know won't hurt him'?

This is not just about lies. It's about the absence of truth. Failing to be open and honest at any level is as damaging as a lie; secrets and deceit will ultimately undermine a relationship's stability, durability, and longevity.

Friedrich Nietzsche said, *'I'm not upset that you lied to me, I'm upset that from now on I can't believe you.'*

Honesty and trust go hand in hand. Once a lie has been told, deception practised, or truth omitted, trust is destroyed. Some say that love is giving someone the power to break your heart, but trusting them not to. So without trust, what happens to love?

Never hide the truth from someone you care about. It is an act of cowardice that serves only to weaken and damage.

"There are only two mistakes one can make along the road to truth; not going all the way, and not starting." Buddha

For the first time since the day of Sean's death and Leo's accident, Ellie felt the remnants of her optimistic nature fighting their way back to the surface. Perhaps it was because Leo was showing signs of returning to normal. This was the first time she'd displayed any interest in updating her blog since the accident, and her words were so appropriate that Ellie couldn't help wishing that Leo had written the post sooner—and insisted that they all read it.

Or perhaps the improvement in the weather was making her feel more cheerful. It had been vile—constant rain, and not what anybody could call summer. But today, for a change, the sun was shining. Ellie took two cups of cappuccino out into the garden, and put one down on the table close to Leo's right side. Her left arm was in a sling. As Mimi had catapulted forward through the windscreen, her knife had gone straight through Leo's hand and the damage still needed some further treatment.

'Did you manage to sleep any better last night?' Ellie asked her sister.

'Not really. I don't want to start taking sleeping tablets, though, because I'm sure I'd get hooked and we know what problems *that* can cause. I've never been the world's best sleeper, so while I can I'll doze on and off throughout the day. I'll be fine.'

'Does your hand hurt much now? I can probably get Sam to prescribe you something for the pain, if you like.'

'Yes, it hurts. But it does serve as a reminder that I actually killed somebody, and I think I need that.'

Ellie looked at her in astonishment.

'Leo, what you did was incredibly brave. Mimi would have killed you. You didn't have a choice. She'd already murdered Sean, and tried to kill Gary. And we mustn't forget that Mimi had already killed one daughter, and got pretty close to killing the other one.'

'Do you think she really would have killed Abbie? I know she managed to get as far as her hospital bed—but would she have gone through with it?'

'I guess that's something we'll never know. She had a lot to lose if her daughter lived, and apparently Abbie had made it abundantly clear that she was horrified at the thought of having Mimi back in her life.'

'At least Abbie's recovered,' Leo said. 'Do you think she's going to be okay?'

'She's traumatised, and not for the first time in her young life. Kath says she was terrified when she found out who 'Chloe's mum' really was. She'd been told she would never have to see her birth mother again after her tortuous early years. And if that wasn't enough, then that bastard Gary knocked her over.'

Ellie was glad that the whole episode had given Penny the strength to kick Gary out. She'd said that when she realised she was more concerned about Smudge's recovery than Gary's, she knew it was time to say goodbye. And Leo had provided Penny with a whole host of contacts to help her to deal with the inevitable aftermath of so many years of abuse.

'Tom's told me why they believe Mimi went after Gary,' Leo said. 'Gary says she was raving on about him seeing her in the woods, but he didn't see a thing. He thought he heard a noise, but when he turned to look, his headlights were shining straight into his eyes. I guess he wanted to get out of there pretty quickly too.'

Leo's lip curled in disgust, as it did every time she mentioned Gary's name. She picked up her coffee cup, and the sisters were quiet for a moment, each lost in her own thoughts.

'Does Tom know how Mimi tracked Abbie down?' Ellie asked.

'There's only so much he's prepared to tell me, but he did say that although Abbie's surname had changed, her birthday was the same. Just one Facebook app apparently, and the rest was easy, especially for somebody who had spent their years in prison studying IT. They think she'd never planned to meet Abbie, just be her friend in disguise. "Chloe" could have stayed in touch for years with nobody being any the wiser. She'd just intended to stalk her daughter—on- and offline. The opportunity on that Friday just fell into her lap. But Abbie rejected her. God knows what Mimi would have done if Abbie hadn't escaped.'

Ellie was stirring her coffee entirely unnecessarily, but there was something she wanted to ask Leo and she wasn't sure how she was going to take it.

'I was wondering, Leo, whether you were struggling to sleep because of the baby.'

Leo turned to Ellie with a puzzled look.

'What baby?'

'Mimi's baby. Oh, we know *now* that there wasn't a baby, but when you crashed the car you knew that you were probably going to kill a baby, and that must have been incredibly hard.'

To Ellie's amazement, Leo laughed.

'I knew there was no baby, Ellie. I'd known since the day before but hadn't got round to telling you. There was always so much else going on. Mimi had a giant pack of Tampax in her shopping bag. It was a Mimi-type con to keep Pat with her until it was too late for him to do anything else. I don't know what I would have done if she'd actually been pregnant, but I'd rather not think about it. I didn't intend to kill her either, you know. I thought I could knock her unconscious so that I could get away. But she would have killed me without hesitation.'

'I can't believe that Pat actually lived with her. Slept with her even.' Ellie shuddered. 'What the hell was he thinking? There's no way that Georgia's going to take him back now, even though she feels sorry for him. But sympathy doesn't seem such a good basis for a marriage.'

Ellie leant down and moved the small table away so she could shuffle along the bench to sit closer to Leo. She leaned slightly against her sister's good arm, and was pleased that Leo didn't move away. If anything, she moved nearer.

'Thanks for finding out about Dad, Leo. I know you've not told me everything, but that's fine. I don't want to hear it just now. I'll let you know when I'm ready to hear the rest. I trust you, and I know you won't hold anything back when the time is right. At least I can stop expecting him to make an appearance, and we can decide whether to carry on living here, or to move. I know you didn't think much of him, but he's the only dad we'll ever have. Don't you mourn him—not even a bit?'

Ellie knew immediately she shouldn't have asked that question. Leo's face appeared to be carved of stone.

'No. He was married to your mother, but in spite of that he came and swept my mum off her feet. Ellie, she was only seventeen when he got her pregnant with me. Seven*teen*. That's only three years older than Abbie. And he was thirty-six. Then he went through a mock marriage and lived a lie for all those years. I don't think my mum had a clue.'

Ellie nodded her head. She knew that Leo was going to take some persuading to see a good side in him.

'But he made a mistake, Leo. Look at Max and me recently. We've made mistakes, but you don't think that we're devils in disguise, do you?'

'Of course I don't. But there are mistakes and mistakes. I might have forgiven him that one, because my mum was so very special, but I couldn't forgive his neglect. He handed me over to your mother and then ignored me. He didn't care what happened to me. After my mum died, I was *distraught*. My world had ended. You tried to comfort me, but how many times did he try? Never. Not once. Too busy out doing whatever he was doing all the time.'

'What's that supposed to mean? Come on, sis. He was working.'

Leo didn't respond and Ellie was quiet for a moment.

'I suppose if he'd been more of a role model, I might have been less suspicious of Max. I instantly leapt to a conclusion—the wrong one. Poor Max.'

Ellie felt a slight increase in pressure from Leo in mute sympathy.

'Am I allowed to ask? What have you told him?' Leo said.

'It was a hard decision. I did wonder whether telling him everything would be just an effective way of giving me absolution, and whether I shouldn't live with the guilt. But Max and I had, until recently, been so close that we could practically see into each other's minds. My mind would have permanently had a shutter in place, and I knew he would be able to see it and not understand what was behind it. So I had to tell him. I told him everything while you were in hospital.'

'And . . . ?'

'And nothing. He's angry, but partly at himself. He'd put up quite a few shutters too with that sodding Alannah. And God knows what he thought he was doing, going into property development with Sean!'

The two women were quiet for a moment.

But they'd had enough tension in the last weeks, and Ellie needed to help Leo to lighten up a bit. She gave her a gentle nudge in the ribs.

'Anyway, how about you and your dashing policeman then? I hear he has a job offer in Manchester—is that right?'

Leo laughed.

'He's not *my* policeman, but yes. He has been offered a job, and I think he's going to take it. He doesn't want a promotion, he says, because he doesn't want to be too office bound, and he doesn't need the money. He'll keep the cottage for weekends, but it's a bit far for a daily commute so he's going to look for something else for during the week.'

'Leo, that man was a complete star in all this. What would we have done without him? Do you think that you and he might . . . ?'

Leo nudged her sister back.

'Enough, Ellie. We get on well, it has to be said, and he does have a few redeeming features.'

'What, you mean apart from his good looks and his calm demeanour?' Ellie asked with a grin.

'For the record he can be a stroppy bugger so don't let that Mr Nice Guy act fool you. But apart from that, he's not the kind of guy to just jump me, if you know what I mean.'

'Pity,' Ellie said with a grin. 'Anything else?'

'Well . . . he cooks a mean curry, and I don't think he's ever likely to call me "Babes". Two huge points in his favour.'

Ellie laughed and tucked herself in a bit near to her sister, making the most of the moment of closeness and wondering if it could last.

It was good to laugh after the previous two weeks, because there had been so much to cry about. The laughter was almost painful, as if it was something they'd forgotten how to do, and was forcing them to exercise muscles that were weak from lack of use.

Leo was relieved that they had changed the subject from her father. She had come so close to telling Ellie, but she knew that her sister was still very vulnerable. So despite her blog post, she was going to abide by Ellie's wishes. Not keep anything from her, but wait until her sister decided she was ready to hear it. For now, it was too much.

Leo felt sorry about Sean, though. Whatever his crimes and however much he had confused Ellie, he hadn't deserved to die. Ellie had told her all about the blackmail texts, and how she had ignored them because she believed they came from him. But Mimi had been getting into the house all the time, driven no doubt by her hatred of Ellie as Georgia's best friend and greatest ally, mixed with her belief that Ellie was having an affair with the person who had knocked Abbie over and ruined all her plans.

Nobody knew even now why Mimi had thought that Gary was Ellie's lover, and Leo had never admitted that she had believed the same thing.

They had found the keys to Willow Farm, which was a huge relief. Pat discovered them when he was clearing out Mimi's stuff. As Ellie first suspected, Max had put the keys down on the worktop, and Mimi had picked them up.

It was going to take time for them all to recover, but things were—at least on the face of it—gradually returning to normal. The twins were watching sport with their dad—only the best bits, they said—which for Ruby meant cycling as she was now so proficient without her stabilisers. So it was good to have a bit of time alone with Ellie, sitting in the sunshine.

No sooner had this thought passed through her head than she heard the hum of an expensive car coming up the drive. They caught a glimpse of Charles's Aston Martin as it pulled up at the front of the house.

'We're round the side,' shouted Ellie, as she heard the car door slam.

A very different looking Charles and Fiona approached across the lawn. Leo couldn't quite put her finger on the difference, but somehow Fiona looked more relaxed and at ease with herself, and for once was dressed in jeans and a T-shirt. A very smart one, but nevertheless, a T-shirt. The biggest surprise was that they were actually holding hands.

'Hello, you two,' said Ellie with a welcoming smile. 'It's good to see you. Pull up a couple of chairs. I'll make some coffee in a second.'

Charles scurried round organising the seating, seeming a bit flustered.

'We thought we'd see how you all are,' he said.

'We're fine, thanks,' Leo said. 'I'm on the mend.' She gave them her best smile. Nobody needed to know how she was feeling inside. As she remembered the suspicions she'd had about Charles, she cringed inwardly.

'We're nowhere near as bad as Bella and Penny,' Ellie added. 'They've had so much to come to terms with.'

Everybody was silent for a moment.

'If only the police had found out about Gary earlier and arrested him, most of this wouldn't have happened,' Ellie said. 'Sean wouldn't be dead, and Mimi wouldn't have been on the run. We still don't know how the police finally found out it was Gary. Tom knows, but he says he can't discuss police business.'

Charles was looking at his feet. Fiona reached for his hand.

'That's what we've come to tell you,' she said. 'It was Charles who finally told the police about Gary. He didn't see the accident, but he knew that Gary had driven down the back road that night.'

'But you were in London, Charles, weren't you?' Leo asked

Charles had still not looked up, and Fiona took a deep breath.

'I'm afraid it's my fault,' she said. 'Look, this is terribly embarrassing, but we feel that we owe you an explanation. It's only in the last few days that we've admitted everything to each other, but we felt we couldn't leave it any longer before we spoke to you.'

Leo and Ellie exchanged glances, but clearly neither had any idea what this was all about.

'Charles actually came back from London on Friday evening. He was going to surprise me, but when he got home, he saw Gary's car in the drive. He knew I'd been talking to him about the planning permission for the conservatory, but it was late—too late for a business visit. Or a social call, come to that. And anyway if I'd invited guests, I would have told Charles.'

She looked up at her husband, and he gave her a gentle smile.

'I couldn't bring myself to go in,' he said. 'I didn't know what I would discover, and on the whole I preferred not to know, if that makes sense. But I waited. I wanted to see what time he left—if he left at all.'

Fiona leaned forward.

'But he *did* leave. Nothing happened. Charles knows that now. He didn't come home after Gary left. He couldn't think of any plausible reason for arriving home at one in the morning, given that the last train got in four hours previously, so he went off to a hotel. He followed Gary as far as the top of the back road.'

'My car was picked up on the ANPR system, so I had to go and account for myself. I should have told them then. I know that. But they would have questioned Fiona, and I didn't want anybody to know about my suspicions. I wasn't even sure how I would deal with it all myself. It was only after we talked and it all came out that we both agreed I should tell the police, so I called them on Thursday evening and went down to the police station. It seems I was a few hours too late, though. I understand that by then Sean's body had already been found. I'm so sorry—both of you. I could have prevented so much of this.'

'No, Charles,' Fiona said, pulling his clasped hand closer and enclosing it in her other hand. 'You mustn't take all the blame. I knew which way Gary would probably have gone home, given the amount he'd been drinking. And I knew he was lying when he said on Saturday night that he'd had the Porsche for a few days. I honestly didn't put two and two together. Of course, he was driving his BMW on Friday night, but just in case he'd been seen he wanted to put people off the scent.'

Ellie frowned. 'Oh my God. It must have been Gary's car that I passed that night. He would have recognised me, and I couldn't think for the life of me why the person that passed me hadn't reported seeing my car, because it's so distinctive.'

'Didn't you recognise him?' Leo asked.

'No—that's the stupid thing. I'd forgotten that I'd passed anybody until Thursday, and then I only remembered it was a dark saloon car. If I'd realised it was a BMW, I might have figured it out—but then Gary turned up in a red Porsche saying that he'd had it for a couple of days, so I'd probably have ruled him out. A waste of effort on his part, because I completely forgot.'

'All irrelevant now. There was no evidence at the scene, but there were minute traces of Abbie's clothes caught on the grill of his BMW, so he can't talk his way out of that one. It doesn't alter the fact that I really should have done something sooner.' Charles was gazing down at the ground again, looking as if he wished it would open up and swallow him whole.

Leo was keen to move away from the blame game. They'd all made mistakes.

'Thanks for explaining it to us, Charles. It's one more mystery solved. I'll go and make us all some coffee, if you'd like a cup.'

Ellie started to get up.

'No, Ellie,' Leo said. 'I'll go. With that machine, even I can manage.'

Leo had to escape. If only she'd realised that Gary had been lying about his car, she might have put all the pieces together. She'd kept quiet about him being out on Friday night too, in a foolish attempt to protect Ellie since she believed Gary was the person Ellie had gone out to meet. So she was every bit as guilty as Charles.

53

Fiona and Charles hadn't seemed in the mood to leave, but after they had finished their coffee Ellie had excused herself, saying she wanted to bath the twins with Max. She didn't like them being out of her sight for more than five minutes at the moment, and was glad that they were going on holiday very soon. She could have all three of them to herself.

Leo had looked rather alarmed at the idea of being left with Fiona and Charles, and Ellie was relieved to see that they had gone when she returned to the kitchen.

She could see her sister through the window, sitting on the garden bench, and she was sorry to see how dejected she seemed. She heard a sound behind her, and realised that Max was looking too. He pulled Ellie's back tight against his chest and wrapped his arms round her, resting his head on her shoulder as they watched Leo.

'She'll be okay, Ellie. She had a terrifying experience, and she's struggling with what she did, but she's a tough cookie.'

'No she's not. You know that. She *talks* a good fight. I don't like leaving her, Max.'

'Then she can come with us,' Max said. Ellie smiled at his thoughtfulness. She knew that wasn't what he really wanted.

'She won't do that.'

'Why don't you pour the two of you a glass of wine each, and I'll join you in a while? I've got a job to do first.'

Ellie grabbed a cold bottle from the fridge and a couple of glasses and made her way into the garden just as Max appeared from the shed carrying a pump sprayer.

'What on earth is Max doing now?' Leo asked as Ellie joined her on the bench.

'He's spraying the roses. According to Gary—who actually does know quite a lot about plants if not much about people—our yellow roses are suffering from some kind of fungus. He cut one—one of my favourites, as it happens—on the night of the party and sneaked it into the dining room to show me that it was diseased. He said he didn't want to embarrass me in front of our guests.' Ellie gave a snort of derision. As if diseased flowers mattered in the overall scheme of things.

Leo smiled. 'I remember that now. He came looking for you in the kitchen.'

'It was all very peculiar. It's a mystery to me how a man who cares so passionately about the perfection of plants can be such a pig to his wife. I'd like Max to dig the whole bed up if I'm honest. They've always been my favourites, but Sean was forever leaving me yellow roses—even one in the fridge on the night of the party.'

'Bloody hell—was he in John Lewis on Sunday too?'

'Yep—that's why I was so freaked out. And he'd left one on the doorstep the night you arrived. It was so creepy.'

'Why didn't you tell me—I wouldn't have judged you,' Leo said, giving Ellie a sad smile.

Ellie was spared the necessity of answering as her glance strayed above Leo's head to the path that led to the front of the house. Another visitor.

'Hi. I thought I'd find you all out in the garden. Is it okay if I come in?'

'Hi, Tom,' Max called. 'Perfect timing. My excuse to stop this job and go and get another couple of glasses.'

'I don't want to interrupt—I just came to see how everybody was, and I wondered if I could persuade the walking wounded to have dinner with me,' he said, making his way towards the bench and resting his hand lightly on Leo's shoulder.

'Only if you're prepared to cut my food up for me,' was Leo's less than ecstatic response. But Tom had clearly got her measure.

'Of course. It will be like taking Lucy out when she was little, although I doubt if the standard of behaviour will be as high.' He grinned at Leo.

'Do I need to get changed? It's such a faff with this arm.'

'No—I can cope with you looking scruffy. Come on—we'll walk back to mine and we can travel in style, seeing as how I no longer have a beat-up wreck to take you out in.'

'Thank God for that,' said Leo. 'I'll get my bag, then.'

❖

Tom looked at Leo as she returned to the garden ten minutes later, and smiled his appreciation. Contrary to her previous remarks, it was clear that she had gone to some effort to look good, but he knew better than to comment. She gave him a typically Leo defiant glance.

He stood up and walked towards her, casually dropping his arm around her shoulders. He felt her tense for a moment, and then she surprised him by relaxing.

'I've been telling Tom about Fiona and Charles and their rediscovered *lurve*,' Ellie said. 'It's great that something good has come out of all this.'

Leo was less kindly disposed towards Fiona's newfound harmony.

'If you say so, although I'm not sure that they deserve it given that she was prepared to have a relationship with Penny's husband. I thought she was up to something because she got a phone call when we met for lunch, and she went all coy for a moment.' Leo paused. 'By the way, Ellie, I've been meaning to ask—what is Fiona's big secret? She told me she'd had her heart broken, and Mrs Talbot says she was pregnant. What's the big mystery?'

'Oh, bloody Doreen Talbot ought to learn the art of discretion,' Ellie said. 'I've kept this secret for so many years, but I'm sure it's not a problem telling you now, especially as Charles has finally been told the whole story. It happened when we were about seventeen. Fiona was always quite secretive, you know. Still is, it would appear. I knew she was seeing somebody, but I didn't know who and she wouldn't tell me. They used to meet in the woods, by the back road. All I knew was that he was older than her—and I suspected one of the teachers from school, but I may have been wrong. She was such a pretty girl. Do you remember?'

'Not really,' Leo answered. 'She was your friend and I saw her at school, but I never actually thought about how she looked.'

'A lot of men found her very attractive—and I say "men" for a reason. She had the sort of looks that appealed to grown men rather than teenage boys, and she had some of the teachers twisted round her little finger.'

'So she got pregnant and was sent away?'

Tom had a terrible feeling that he knew what was going to happen. The truth was racing towards them like a freight train, and he couldn't for the life of him think how to stop it.

'Oh no. She was never pregnant. That was just village speculation—and wrong. No, it was much worse than that.' Elle paused. 'It's best if you don't mention it to her, but actually she was raped.'

Tom felt every muscle in Leo's body tighten, and he gripped her shoulder, pulling her gently towards him and willing her to keep calm.

'Who, Ellie? Who raped her?' Tom could hear the strain in Leo's voice.

'She wouldn't say. Her parents didn't believe her and told her she'd brought it on herself with the clothes she wore and the way she flaunted her body—none of which was true. Or at least, no more true than the rest of us. She told me because I found her sobbing her young heart out in our garden, of all places.'

'Did she say what had happened?' Max said. It was clear that this was news to him too, and Tom kept a firm grip on Leo's taut shoulders.

'She was incoherent. I tried to get her into the house, but she wouldn't come. Probably afraid of The Old Witch, and who could blame her? So I took her home. All I could get out of her was that she'd thought he loved her. She'd gone to meet him in the woods as usual, and he just wouldn't stop. She wasn't ready, so she'd fought him and even screamed, but he'd laughed at her and told her to stop teasing him. In the end, he forced her and she was completely devastated. Anyway, I made her tell her parents, thinking they would support her and call the police, but they packed her off to her aunt's in London. That was it. She flatly refused to say who it was—not even to me—but I never went near those woods again. I didn't hear from her after that until she turned up in the village a few years ago. And she never told Charles anything about it until this week.'

Leo was silent. She turned tragic eyes towards Tom, and he knew she was willing him to get her out of there. His arm tightened even more.

'A sad story,' he said. 'But fortunately it seems things have turned out okay for them now.'

He leant towards Leo and brushed his lips against her hair, speaking softly.

'Come on. I think we'll have a night in. I've got a bottle of vodka in the freezer, and a huge biriani ready for the oven. Let's go, shall we?'

Knowing that Leo's stiffness would be interpreted as a typical reaction to such an overt display of affection, Tom raised his eyes to the sky and gave a slight shake of the head as if to signify how hopeless she was. Max and Ellie grinned at him as he raised his hand in farewell and guided Leo gently towards the garden gate.

As they made their way to the cobbled drive, Tom could hear Max and Ellie's laughter and was glad Leo had said nothing. They would have to learn the truth sooner or later, but for now they deserved to enjoy their holiday and make peace with all that had happened. It was bad enough that Leo had to bear it, but at least he'd been there for her.

Still with his arm around her, Tom felt the pressure of Leo's head lighten and he knew she was pulling away. Her moment of weakness gone, she would retreat behind her wall of indifference again. And he had no idea how to help her.

She stopped about half way down the drive and turned back to face the house, oblivious to the happy sounds from the garden, the hum of bees in the lavender, or the cool evening breeze that gently stirred her hair, lifting it from her shoulders. Tom remained silent as he watched her expressionless face. She seemed lost in a sea of memories. Then she took a deep breath, and the tension left her body. She looked at Tom with lips curved upwards in valiant attempt at a smile, but her eyes were as bleak as frozen rock pools.

'Come on. Let's go and eat,' she said.

Leo didn't wait for Tom's response. She turned abruptly away from him and walked down the drive towards the gate without a backward glance.

Links

When writing *The Back Road*, I discovered a very useful document that explains the dangers of digital stalking. Even if you have never been a victim, it clearly outlines some of the risks and suggests best practices for safe use of social media. The PDF can be found at http://www.digital-stalking.com/library/guidelines/digital-stalking-technology-risks-for-victim.html

Throughout the novel there are various references to music—particularly when Max plays Ellie's 'soppy' music. The Rachel Abbott website (**http://www.rachel-abbott.com**) includes links to YouTube videos of many of the songs. The website also includes a number of tried and tested recipes from the novel. Select BOOKS from the menu, and follow the links.

Acknowledgements

I owe a debt of gratitude to many people for their help in writing this book, and I sincerely appreciate the advice so willingly given by so many people.

As always I would like to thank John Wrintmore for his insights into the workings of the police, and for answering every question—no matter how trivial. Brenda Duncan and Becky Scrivener—with many years of experience between them of working in ICUs—were incredibly helpful with the details that hopefully make the hospital scenes realistic, and for explaining so much about coma patients. Any errors are entirely mine.

There were many people who offered nuggets of information—some of which didn't quite make it into the book—but Patrick, Daniel, Claudia— thanks for taking the time to inform me about everything from teen-speak on Facebook to the maximum cash an individual can draw out of the bank without raising a red flag.

My early readers have been fantastic, providing excellent feedback and suggestions. Thank you Annie, Kath, Trevis, Janna, Sarah, Kathryn, Steven, Kenni, and Lindsay—your comments were all so encouraging and positive. Particular thanks go to Judith for reading it not once, but twice.

Once again, Alan Carpenter has excelled in the design of the cover, despite being asked to go around the block more than once, ending up where we started and resisting the temptation to say 'I told you so'.

I've had two terrific editors—Clare and Charlotte. You have helped so much in pulling all the threads together and making this a much better book than it might otherwise have been.

My particular gratitude goes to my agent, Lizzy Kremer, who has been a constant source of support and guidance, as have the rest of the team at David Higham Associates—especially Laura and Harriet.

Finally, as always, my thanks to John for indulging me and allowing me to talk ceaselessly about the plots, the characters, and the next book. Your belief in me is a source of inspiration.

About the Author

Rachel Abbott was born and raised in Manchester, England, and trained as a systems analyst before launching her own interactive media company in the early 1980s. She sold her company in 2000, and in 2005 she moved to the Le Marche region of Italy. She now divides her time between the home she shares with her husband in Italy and their home in Alderney, one of the Channel Islands, where she is now writing her third novel.

Rachel Abbott's first book—*Only the Innocent*—became an international bestseller, reaching the number one position in the Amazon charts and staying there for over four weeks.

Connect with Rachel Abbott online:

Twitter: **https://twitter.com/Rachel__Abbott**
Facebook: **http://www.facebook.com/RachelAbbott1Writer**
Website: **http://www.rachel-abbott.com**
Blog: **http://rachelabbottwriter.wordpress.com**